Balloon

Balloon

TIM WYNVEEN

KEY PORTER BOOKS

Cataloguing in Publication Data

Wynveen, Tim
Balloon

ISBN 1-55263-096-X

Title.

PS8595.Y595B34 1999 C813′.54 C99-931327-4
PR9199.3.W96B34 1999

The publisher gratefully acknowledges the support of the Canada Council for the Arts and the Ontario Arts Council for its publishing program.

Canada

We acknowledge the financial support of the Government of Canada through the Book Publishing Industry Development Program (BPIDP) for our publishing activities.

Key Porter Books Limited
70 The Esplanade
Toronto, Ontario
Canada M5E 1R2

www.keyporter.com

Electronic formatting: Heidi Palfrey
Design: Peter Maher

Printed and bound in Canada

99 00 01 02 03 6 5 4 3 2 1

To Christine, Claire and Anna

Acknowledgments

Many thanks to my friends. During the nearly five years I worked on this book, I sent up many trial balloons, mostly in conversation with them. Their wit and intelligence are a constant pleasure and inspiration.

Most of all I am indebted to Barbara Berson, my editor at Key Porter. She has guided me through two novels now. She is also responsible for the fact that there have been two novels to edit, rescuing my first book, *Angel Falls,* from the limbo of unsolicited manuscripts. For that, I am forever grateful.

ONE

Day of the Dead

We all want something, or rather many things that somehow bind together—a tangled web of preference and affinity that maps the human heart. We want love and respect and kindness, of course, but beyond that the richer states of mind, the deeper meanings, the secrets of heaven and earth. We want favors, sexual and otherwise, the slack, the space, the wherewithal to be ourselves, develop fully our insane potential. We want smooth roads through rolling vistas. We want the fast lanes, the slow dances, the daily bread and yearly vacation, the patience of a saint, the wisdom to buy low and sell high, to choose the right school, the right career, the chef's best and, above all, to have the grace and good fortune to avoid those wrong turns and simple blunders that through some sly twist of fate can lead us to disaster.

We lie when we say we want only to be loved or respected or useful. Even at the extremes, with the purest of saints, the lowest of sinners, desire is never so uncomplicated. We want more than we let on, more even than we can express. Always.

The same holds true for those who inhabit the uncertain middle ground, people like Parker Martingale, an average guy filled with dread, his bottom resting on the waxy white paper sheet of an examining table. He is waiting for his doctor to arrive with test results. All other thoughts have been cast aside as unnecessary, allowing him to focus his energies, physical and spiritual, on a single shining hope. And if his doctor were to ask, Parker would lift his gaze from the pink bony pathos of his feet and say, quite predictably, that all he wanted, all he really wanted, was good news. As if it could ever be that simple.

The doctor, Norbert Singh, understood only too well how the push and pull of our desires can reduce a dream's rich weave to a knot of dissatisfaction. A small, balding, bird-like man with thick black glasses that he often wore perched on top of his head, Singh had come from Durban, South Africa, twenty-five years ago to practice medicine in Canada. He never seemed an especially happy man, even though he had a thriving practice, a fine home, a loving family. He once confided to Parker that he had never felt at ease in Toronto, never part of the society. He missed the Durban nights most of all, he said, the evenings when men would crowd the streets talking politics, the air humid and warm and full of life as though the city were wrapped inside a fragrant flower. In Canada, he said, he seldom went outdoors. The air, even at the waterfront, even in summer, smelled to him as stale and lifeless as a freezer.

Parker had been one of his first patients, hobbling into the University of Toronto student clinic one winter morning with a badly strained knee, the result of an ill-considered game of touch football. Since then, for almost two decades now, Parker had revealed to Singh all his weaknesses, doubts and fears—things he had shown to no one else, not even Mersea Harrow, with whom Parker had lived for most of his adult life. Despite that honesty, or maybe because of it, neither man felt wholly comfortable in the presence of the other.

When Singh finally entered the room, he was studying Parker's chart and frowning. Without a word of greeting, he peered over the top of his bifocals and said, "There is nothing else I can do, I'm afraid."

Parker, who had been anxiously shifting his cheeks on the paper sheet, suddenly became very still. "What about the pain?" he asked.

"Pain?"

He rubbed his side gingerly. "That twinge I feel."

"You first called it a sensation."

Parker sat up straighter, suddenly on the defensive. "I didn't know what else to call it. All my life there was nothing there. Silence. Now suddenly I close my eyes and feel something inside me. A swelling. A heaviness. A presence."

Singh removed his glasses and folded his arms, a weary man. "We've done physicals, X-rays, CAT scans, MRI—all at your insistence. And as I predicted, there is no swelling, aside from a bit of middle-age spread. No tumors, no enlargements, no abscesses, absolutely nothing out of the ordinary. It is the same always, Parker, as if I should somehow feel guilty for giving you a clean bill of health."

"But you're not one hundred percent certain."

"You're as healthy a man as I've seen for your age. Now get out of here and quit wasting my time. You're forty-five. You're allowed a few aches and pains now and again. It goes with the territory."

Parker reached for his clothing, a crisp mound of natural fabrics—black jeans, white shirt, leather vest, the expensive Norwegian loafers that were giving him a corn—and said, "Thanks for cheering me up, Singh. I feel a lot better now for a man my age . . ."

Singh slipped from the room then, without further comment, and Parker slowly dressed, watching his reflection in the full-length mirror. He never imagined himself this way—the sags, the folds, the constellation of small warts and cysts that marked the passage of the years. He normally pictured a younger man with smooth skin and a taut physique. But "ripeness" was the word he would use to describe his state now, that rosy corpulence of a peach before it falls to the ground with a splat, all its juices already beginning to ferment, its natural goodness just a little off, a little too far gone.

He smoothed his hair in place, tucked his shirt neatly into his jeans, and then strolled through the reception area, waving to Suzie, the cute young nurse fresh out of school. She had a tiny birdlike mouth that hinted at reduced appetites and nibbled food. She struck him as the kind of girl he had liked a lot in high school, the kind who could be your friend, who could laugh at your jokes without getting ideas.

Slowing his stride, he searched for some witty remark to light up her sweet face; but he wasn't as funny as he used to be, couldn't remember the last time he had made someone laugh. Instead he slumped outside and into his car, his mind already turning to the thousand-odd worries he had at work, to the party he and Mersea had been invited to that night, and most especially to the ordeal that awaited him next morning. He prodded his side with his index finger (he was almost certain he could feel something) and, his mood growing darker by the moment, he gazed distantly at the people drifting by on the street, everyone so hunched and unhealthy, so in need of medical care and grooming and maybe a good time.

The store windows up and down the street had been tricked up for Halloween, with most of the displays made even gaudier by campaign signs for the upcoming municipal election. The provincial government had decided to create a "megacity" of Toronto by forcing it to unite with several other districts. Local councils and school boards and services would be amalgamated in the name of efficiency and tax savings. Everywhere tempers were running high, the air full of harsh talk. And Parker, who should have been encouraged by these developments—he was a businessman, after all, who had made a career of cutting costs and seeking efficiencies—instead felt sick and sad and lonely, afraid of the future. Not that he had paid much attention to the issues. Nor did he have a feeling one way or the other about who might win. He simply felt uneasy. Forcing unequal parties into a grudging alliance hardly seemed the basis for sound government.

When Mersea came home and dropped her briefcase in the front hall, Parker lay curled on the bed in his paisley boxers. He didn't answer when she called his name. Instead he listened to her wander around downstairs, the floorboards singing out her every step, listened as she opened the fridge and closed it. She paused there in the kitchen, picking up clues, then began to climb the stairs, no longer calling now. She knew where he would be, already prepared for the sight of him.

"This a crisis," she asked coolly as she swept into the room, "or a bad back?" Right into the closet. Off with the shoes. Off with the jacket.

"Paralysis," Parker muttered.

He looked away as she stepped out of the closet and unbuttoned her blouse, but not because he found her unattractive. By almost every standard she was a beautiful woman who wore beautiful clothes. She had a heart-shaped face and dramatic cheekbones, the kind of look favored by Native carvers. Her hair was long and thick and chestnut-colored. It was just that he couldn't bear to watch her undress anymore. The imprint of brassiere and underpants and stockings. The blurred contours where once there had been high definition. The wrinkles, the sun damage. He would have given anything to spare her this vulnerability.

"So what's the problem?" she asked, her attention carefully focused on the closet again, ignoring his dramatics. "Corporate or personal?"

"Everything. I don't want to go to this party, I don't want to stay home by myself, I don't want to work—I don't want to do anything."

She wrapped herself in her silk robe and moved onto the bed, curling up behind him, the point of her long, straight Ivy League nose nuzzling the vertebrae of his neck, his secret spot. It never ceased to amaze him how swiftly she could shift focus, mood.

"Bad day?" she asked, her voice gentle and low.

"No, a good day. Not bad, at any rate. And I mean it's not work, or at least not much. It's—well you know what it is."

"I know. Poor baby." She kissed his shoulder blade and then got up on one elbow to kiss him lightly on the cheek.

"You have to come to this party, though. Darryl and Rudi would never forgive you. Everyone is going to be there."

"Oh, well, everyone . . ."

Parker no longer shared Mersea's enthusiasm for some of their friends. Increasingly of late he had found them a little annoying. Like artists refining a theme, they had all become over the years more purely like themselves, more eccentric, and therefore harder to take. Mersea naturally defended everyone. She saw this progression as a good thing, thought it meant they were becoming exceptional people when in fact they had merely grown edgy and selfish, no longer willing or able to make the sacrifices that could make them whole.

"I have to be up early in the morning," he continued. "You know that. As it is, the whole day tomorrow is going to be a nightmare."

Mersea rolled off the bed and returned to the closet to root around. "Tomorrow will be fine. Stop worrying. Besides, we'll be home before midnight. This is Darryl and Rudi we're talking about, remember, the original early birds."

Little by little her breezy responses were backing him into a darker mood. It was like she wasn't taking him seriously. He sat up and picked at the callus on the bottom of his foot. "It's not fatigue I'm worried about," he said, his voice pitched a little higher. "I'm just not in the party mood. I'll be heavy company."

Mersea finished choosing her wardrobe and placed her selections on the bed. All calm and understanding, she gently touched his cheek and said, "You've always been heavy company, Parker. No one will even notice, believe me." Then she snapped the elastic of his shorts and headed down the hall to the bathroom.

She showered, powdered herself and brushed her teeth. When she returned to the room he still hadn't budged, prompting her to heave her wet towel at his head. "Move it," she said. "As it is we're late."

Then she quickly dressed, fed up with him now. She rummaged around in his closet and threw him pants and a shirt. "Bring your cable-knit sweater," she reminded him as she headed downstairs. "And your leather jacket. It'll be freezing."

They took Mersea's Lexus, driving east of the city to a marina at the Scarborough Bluffs. All the way there Parker debated whether to mention his appointment with Singh, but in the end he said nothing. What could he say? Singh had declared him perfectly healthy. If Parker brought it up now, she would see it as an emotional problem, not a physical one, and that was the last thing he wanted.

Darryl was waiting for them topside in his heavy bomber jacket and watch cap, staring into the wind. Mersea pecked him on the cheek, showed him the bottles of champagne under her jacket and then skipped below, leaving Parker to help cast off.

Though Parker was not a sailor, he had always been comfortable around the water. He could tie a few knots, knew port from starboard, bow from stern, and the correct colored light for each. He knew how to fold down sails and put them up again, and more or less understood the basic premise of sailing. He was pleased that Darryl counted on him for these outings. It was a type of usefulness he was proud of, and he moved into position with only a nod of greeting. He untied the mooring ropes like a professional and stowed them the way he had been shown. Then he scooted to the bow and crouched there in the wind as they motored out of the marina and into open water, thankful already that Mersea had forced him to come along.

Darryl had inherited the boat—a thirty-five-foot C&C—from his parents. Forest green with teak trim, mint condition, it was more than just a boat for Darryl. It was where he had come from, his culture. He talked about it in the same terms that others might refer to their Irish roots or farm background. And every Halloween now for the past nine years Darryl had taken the sailboat and a few friends out to the middle of the lake for an end-of-season party.

Parker had been on that original crew nine years ago, and in all the years since had missed only one outing, last October, when his father had called, voice all weak and whispery, and said to expect the worst. Parker packed a few things and kissed Mersea good-bye. "Go to Darryl's party," he had told her. "There's no telling with these things. Could be weeks yet. We've already had so many false alarms." But his mother's passing was mercifully swift, without pain or struggle. And though Mersea cursed herself afterward for not being at the hospital to share in his grief, he was secretly glad she hadn't seen him come undone.

For a year now he had devoted himself almost entirely to work, feeling a little sober, a little sad, unable to really match the energy level of most gatherings. The same would be true of the cabin below deck, despite the fact that he had known these people for years. If he went down there he would feel distant, dopey, like someone with a slight cold.

A few months ago, Mersea had surprised him with tickets to New York, a little weekend getaway. They saw

Rent, went to a popular little Cuban restaurant and wandered through a listless afternoon at the Museum of Modern Art. And while he had an okay time, it was just okay. Nothing seemed to get him really excited these days, not even work.

The boat motored beyond the breakwall, and the wind picked up out of the east, the surface of the water working itself into a chop. Following Darryl's instructions, Parker helped raise the sails, watching with satisfaction as they caught the wind and propelled the boat forward. His job finished for now, he made his way to the stern.

"I'll be right back," he said to Darryl, making an elaborate hand gesture to indicate that he would return with refreshments. Then he descended to the cabin.

Rudi and Mersea sat shoulder to shoulder at the table, carving small pumpkins into jack-o'-lanterns. Beside them Lyle Beckwith, a researcher at *Maclean's* magazine, fumbled tunelessly with Darryl's cheap acoustic guitar. Lyle wore small wire-rimmed granny glasses, his coarse black hair twisted liberally with gray and tied in a ponytail that hung down to the middle of his back. Taken together with his black T-shirt, faded jeans and grimy Stan Smith tennis shoes, he presented the image of a man trapped in a picture of himself yet growing inexorably older.

On a low sofa Wendy Couture and her twin sister, Nadine, owners of a children's bookstore, huddled by the heater and commiserated with Brendan Masters, a disgruntled high-school teacher and professor manqué. The province was threatening to cut a billion dollars from the education budget in order to improve the schools, and that had left the twins limp with disbelief, the first time in memory that they had agreed with Brendan about anything. He talked increasingly these days about early retirement.

"Ah, that bracing sea air!" Parker said in a stage voice, though no one had made the slightest acknowledgment of his presence. His party smile fixed in place, his movements exaggerated, he bounded over to the small stove and hurriedly grabbed two cups of hot rum and cider. "Need to fortify our captain!" he proclaimed. Then he climbed back into the night, the cold bluster of autumn wind in his face.

He offered a mug to Darryl, who sat proudly at the tiller. Knowing Darryl's fondness for Tennessee Ernie Ford, Parker raised his mug in a toast and said, "Another year older and deeper in debt."

Darryl shrugged and took a drink. "There are worse things," he said at last, wiping his lips on the sleeve of his leather jacket. "It makes us human, debt. It's what we owe each other, I'd say, that takes our measure."

Behind them, the floodlights of the marina seemed surreal, casting the area in a sci-fi glow; beyond that, stretching along the shore, the hulking windswept bluffs. The horizon itself had disappeared completely, the sky and water an uncompromising shade of black save for the scattered flash of whitecaps as the wind hurled the sailboat toward the islands. Parker settled into the darkness and let his features relax. Darryl continued speaking.

"Anyone tells me they are debt-free, anyone who even aspires to such a condition—I am immediately suspicious. It shows a fear of commitment, don't you think? A kind of narcissism? Or cowardice. Yet that's what our politicians and business leaders hold up to us as the shining ideal. Get rid of The National Debt. Except it's totally cool to lend billions to a handful of boring, middle-aged white guys, captains of industry, so they can inflate their egos a bit more. But lend billions to the government and, hell, they would only use it to make life a little better for the poor, right? Wouldn't want that . . ."

He laughed at himself then and scooted over so Parker could sit on the bench beside him. Up close, Parker could see how happy Darryl was, despite the grousing, something beyond drunkenness or sentiment, something deep as primary color. Parker envied him that purity of feeling, saw his own life as a curiously mixed metaphor—both hopelessly confused and one step removed from the real thing.

Down below, Beckwith yammered about his investments. The guy imagined himself a kind of Warren Buffett. He subscribed to money newsletters and tip sheets—he haunted mutual fund seminars like a groupie. But everyone knew he had lost more money in the market than he had made. He was, from almost any perspective, a loser. From up on deck, Parker could hear him preaching, most likely to Rudi, who was always perplexed by money matters.

"You gotta do your homework," Beckwith said. "All that historical performance stuff—the P/E, the ROE—it's super-critical. But you gotta look around, too, look ahead. Is the economy expanding? Contracting? The mistake, and the big guys will tell you this, is paying any attention to the noise. Fact is, the market isn't a thermometer. It can't tell you anything useful about the present. More like it's a barometer. It's telling you what the economy will be doing six months from now, a year from now. So you gotta have blinkers on all the day-to-day shit."

Parker could imagine Mersea's face, the complicated smile that could be decoded in any number of ways: admiration, sarcasm, surprise, boredom. Aside from her beauty, it was the thing about her that attracted the attention of most men, her Mona Lisa mystique. In this instance she would know, as would everyone on board, that Beckwith's Wall Street routine, though directed at Rudi, was most assuredly for her benefit. She was the vice-president of marketing for a mutual fund company, the kind of job that Beckwith could only dream about. He had tried for years to talk shop with her, and she would nod and smile enigmatically. If he persisted, she simply laughed and told him to get a life.

"How's work?" Parker asked Darryl out of the blue. "The Council has been getting press lately. Last month, right? That pay-equity thing?"

Darryl grew suddenly serious and pointed off to starboard where the Toronto skyline had come into view, distant and eerie as a dreamscape. With a rueful chuckle in his voice, he said, "What does it matter? This province is doomed."

Parker gave him a disapproving look. "It's not like you to sound so bitter."

"Incredulous is more like it. In two years this government has gutted social programs that took decades to create. And if the polls are right, in a couple of weeks we'll have a clown as our new mayor—the fifth-largest municipal government in North America in the hands of a buffoon."

Parker knew little about politics and cared even less. Unlike Darryl, who had carried many a left-wing banner, Parker had always assumed that politicians, even social democrats, were liars and crooks and incompetents. He accepted that state of affairs as the way of the world and marveled when people took these matters seriously. With a casual shrug, he said, "Business seems to have the upper hand now, but the pendulum could swing back the other way, right? I mean, stranger things have happened."

Darryl scoffed. "It's over, Park, done. Not that you have too much to worry about—you're white, male, heterosexual. Even so, you better hope you're never sick or unemployed. They're rolling up the safety net and going home. And they're never coming back. Not in our lifetime, anyway."

Parker emptied his cup and closed his eyes, sinking into a more reflective mood. Darryl often did that to him, made him look beyond the edge of things. Tentatively, feeling his way, he said, "Maybe that, all of it, isn't so bad. Maybe, like they say, the rest of us will pick up the slack. You know, what we owe each other?" But then he laughed at his own naïveté and shook his head. He had seen the truth himself. Every week there were more people looking for handouts, sleeping on the streets, hitting the food banks. Ten times a day he was asked for spare change, and it wasn't making him more sympathetic, it was making him feel oppressed.

"Of course," Darryl added, "it's not provincial governments we really have to worry about. It's that circus in Ottawa . . ."

His words trailed off to nothing, as if he was just too tired to carry on. But he didn't need to spell it out any further. Parker knew what he meant. In the recent federal election Canada had been quartered, redrawn on regional lines, with four parties each taking a corner of the country and the once powerful Conservatives reduced to a memory. Everyone knew this would make for a difficult Parliament. As the parties became identified with specific regions, politics would become personal. Vision would be replaced by division.

Darryl let the boat swing around until the sails were luffing in the wind. "Anyway," he said, "this is one night I don't want to think about politics. How are things with you?"

"Fine, I guess. Can't complain. More in debt than last year, if that makes you feel any better."

Parker tipped his empty cup to his lips then and pretended to drink, pondering what else to say. No one outside of the office would understand the first thing about his work. And he didn't know Darryl well enough to discuss more private matters. Darryl was Mersea's friend, really, which was too bad. Parker liked him, and not for the first time wished they could connect more fully. Their only bond was a wry appreciation of the cheesy side of popular culture, most especially Las Vegas and all things Newtonian. Darryl and Rudi had just returned from their latest pilgrimage, in fact.

"So tell me about your trip," Parker said. "Did you see Wayne?"

"Only every night. *Conk-chi-conk. Conk-conk-chi-conk.* I've never seen Rudi so happy. You'll be there soon, won't you? You should take your old man along with you. He'd have a ball. There are some real players there."

Parker recoiled at the picture of going to Las Vegas with his father, and he and Darryl laughed again, more easily this time. In the silence that followed, they listened to the wind whistle in the rigging, and Parker sensed that it was the kind of rich moment he might remember all his life. He felt so wise.

That sensation lasted a few minutes longer. Then he helped Darryl bring down the sails and drop the anchor. When everything was secure topside, they went below.

Rudi immediately got up from the table and wrapped his arms around Darryl's waist. "Playing Hemingway again?" he scolded, pulling him over by the heater. "You're chilled right through." In reply, Darryl pecked the top of Rudi's head and smiled a little drunkenly.

They were both six feet tall, with sandy-colored hair and fair skin, both handsome and athletic and—to use a favorite phrase of Parker's father—"bent as a dog's hind leg." Where Darryl leaned to corduroys and button-down flannel shirts, Rudi, the owner of a vintage clothing store, and younger than the rest of them, dressed as a rule more exotically, in silks and linens. Never on Halloween, though. For sentimental reasons he always wore sandals, denim cutoffs and a T-shirt, never wandering far from the space heater. This evening he sported one of Darryl's old hand-me-down shirts with a picture on the front of the scales of justice, and below that image the words: The Ontario Council for the Status of Women.

While Darryl and Rudi whispered by the heater, Parker busied himself opening the Veuve Clicquot. "They're calling for possible frost tonight," he said to no one in particular. "We'd all be better off with hot cocoa." Then the cork went sailing, and he hurriedly spilled the straw-colored liquid into fluted crystal, barking at everyone to grab a glass.

Rudi stepped forward, champagne held high and said, "Okay, okay, we're a few days early, no surprise, right? But here's to love on the Day of the Dead. To Puerto Escondido."

They all drank, murmuring their congratulations. Then Darryl lifted his glass and waited until he had everyone's attention. "To Rudi," he said, "my golden surfer boy."

Wendy loved nothing so much as a story. In a voice naturally attuned to little children and Mother Goose, she said, "The par-ty's not oh-fish-ull unless the tale is toe-old!"

Everyone murmured encouragement, and Parker worked on opening a second bottle. He had heard the story on numerous occasions, and what amazed him was the openness with which Darryl and Rudi discussed the details of their emotional lives. Parker, who never talked to Mersea that way in the privacy of their own home, was always suspicious when people spoke so candidly about passion and desire. His own feelings were at best rather muddy, characterized by the kind of unfocused, intransitive longing he used to feel as a young boy, lying on a dew-slick lawn and staring up at the Milky Way. There had been pointed moments, of course, when strange women had looked at him, when dreams had colored the whole of a waking day with a sensual veneer; yet it was always just that—a dream, a distant view, something not entirely substantial.

Darryl continued to stare into his glass, conjuring visions in the pale liquid. Finally, without looking up, he said, "It was 1985 and I'd been in Mexico almost six months, most of that in Puerto Escondido. A couple of restaurants, a couple of hotels, piglets running up and down the red dirt road and snuffling the people on the beach. Once a day the bus would rumble into town in a cloud of black diesel fumes, fresh bullet holes courtesy of the *bandidos* south of Acapulco. And there I was, the lonely poet, stoned every night, of course, drunk every day, Malcolm Lowry doing Timothy Leary doing André Gide."

Perfect timing on the cork, ecstatic punctuation, Parker scrambled glass to glass while Darryl waited patiently.

"All Souls' Day," he continued when Parker was seated again. "November the second, Day of the Dead, the little village band starts tuning up for the parade, right outside my *posada*. Snare drum, tuba, saxophone, trumpet, every kind of makeshift percussion you could imagine. Brilliant, really, all those rhythms. First thing in the morning, though, after a night of mescal, I wasn't in the frame of mind to appreciate it fully, so I pulled on some clothes, grabbed my journal and stumbled over to the restaurant for a *líquado* and *torta*. The morning bus pulls up and off steps Rudi with his surfboard, Mr. California, wearing cutoffs, *huaraches* and a shark-tooth necklace."

Rudi sang the two-note melody from *Jaws*, and everyone laughed.

"It's true," Darryl said, finally looking up from his glass and sliding his arm around Rudi's waist. "Just like the movie. One glimpse of him and I was pulled right under. Haven't surfaced yet."

Lyle was divorced, with two children he neither liked nor wanted to support. Of all the group, he had the most jaundiced view of romance, a sarcastic response to most news. He put aside Darryl's guitar and said, "Twelve years and still haven't surfaced . . . sounds to me, Dare, like you're dead. You drowned and you just don't know it."

Parker laughed at that, louder than anyone else. And Rudi, his lips pursed to hold back a grin, wagged his finger and said, "Don't worry, Darryl and I are still thrashing around. Still plenty of life left."

This brought another roar of laughter. And Nadine, whose normal speaking voice was a chuckle, especially when she had had a bit to drink, said, "It's called motivation, right? You have to work harder at sex. Once that goes all you have left is what, friendship? Knickknacks? Judy Garland movies?"

"It's true," Darryl replied, his voice arch and dry,

"straights get all the breaks. One look at Beckwith here tells you how babies can revitalize a relationship. And then there's Parker and Mersea."

Parker cleared his throat. "What about Parker and Mersea?"

"Well," Rudi chimed in, "you guys are the original sexless duo, aren't you? The basic all-work-and-no-play-upwardly-mobile hetero couple?"

To Parker's relief, Mersea jumped in. "And how would you know what our sex life is like?"

"Simple math," Beckwith said, smelling blood in the water and moving in for the kill. "Couple of over-achievers, twelve-hour days, one of you out of town every other weekend. Mersea, there's no way you two are gettin' it at the national average."

She stood a little straighter, squaring her shoulders defiantly. "Maybe we manage our time better than the rest of you."

Everyone hooted, and Parker could see the color rising in Mersea's cheeks.

"And it may just be," she continued, her voice taking on a tone of impatience, "that for some of us it's a matter of priorities, what one wants out of life."

Satisfied, Beckwith laughed again, a low wet snuffle. "That's true," he said. "Priorities. And we all know what Rude and Dare want out of life."

Darryl thought about that for a moment and seemed on the verge of replying. Instead he grabbed the largest of the pumpkins and headed onto the deck. By the time everyone had joined him topside, he had the candle lit and was holding the jack-o'-lantern above his head, like Moses with the stone tablets.

"You've all heard me say it before," he said into the

wind, "but it's worth saying again: A life without desire is not worth living."

Whenever Darryl told this story, he ended with the same dramatic pronouncement. This time, however, it didn't have the same effect on his audience. Instead of an awkward respectful silence, he got Beckwith howling like a coyote. Others immediately joined in until they were all barking and laughing into the wind.

Darryl laughed, too. It was not as if he believed those words. He said them for sentimental reasons mostly, to conjure up an earlier, more poetic self. Then, as everyone watched, he leaned over and gently set the pumpkin adrift on the water, where it bobbed uncertainly a few moments and then capsized, sinking slowly beneath the waves.

TWO

The Shrine of Nancy

Mersea hated to wake up. When the alarm went off to herald the beginning of a vacation, she would bury her face in her pillow and moan that she didn't want to go, no matter where it was—the cottage, Bermuda, New York. Her reaction was immediate and unthinking, a primitive reflex; her one desire was to stretch out the dreamy half-sleep world that existed between the first chirp of the clock-radio and the touch of her bare feet on the chilly wooden floor.

It worried Parker, this bone-deep languor of hers. Years ago he had read an article about Stevie Wonder, how for days Stevie had remained unconscious after a car accident until one of his friends whispered in his ear the lyrics to "Higher Ground." Such an awakening could never happen with Mersea. If she ever fell into a coma, no amount of coaxing would bring her to the surface again.

Parker didn't leap out of bed, either; but he was convinced that was more a physical problem than an emotional one. He needed to sort his dreams, let his eyes moisten, work out the kinks of a heavy, drooling sleep. With Mersea, it was like she was being dragged to her execution.

That's why Parker was lying awake next morning, just waiting for her to punch the Snooze button for nine more minutes of fitful sleep. That's why he was primed for her to start grumbling. It was the first anniversary of his mother's death. He understood that Mersea wasn't coming to the cemetery with him—she had work to do, an important meeting—but he'd been worrying about this day for weeks, and the last thing he wanted to hear was her whining about lack of sleep. Or rather, that's exactly what he wanted to hear. He had a speech worked out, a beauty.

Instead, Mersea turned off the alarm, rose lightly from the bed and drifted out of the room like a ghost. The faint tinkle of her pee echoed down the hall, one of his favorite sounds, filling him with a feeling of homey tenderness. When she returned from the bathroom, she had a sad, wistful smile. "Time to wake up," she said, grabbing his foot through the duvet and rocking it back and forth. "You going to be all right?"

And Parker suddenly thought that maybe they should have a quickie before he left, tumbling and fumbling, all frantic and panting and then—*bang bang bang*—going off like skyrockets.

He knew why, and it had nothing to do with last night's talk on the sailboat, or at least not directly. Staring at the contours of her body in her white cotton nightgown, it had hit him that someday she, too, would die.

They were both in their mid-forties. And even with Singh's assurance that Parker was in good shape, who was surprised anymore when a fifty-year-old keeled over? They were approaching that sobering realm where death stops seeming a tragedy and becomes one's just reward for a misspent life. And on this grim anniversary, he wanted to love Mersea one more time, that was all. Nothing delicate, nothing to do with kindness or gentle healing. He wanted a white-water ride to remind them both that they were still alive, that unlike his parents they could have made love every night for the past year, could do it every morning and every night for the rest of their lives . . .

That idea faded quickly enough, however. Rudi and the rest had been right. Sex with Mersea was an infrequent pleasure, even though their lovemaking was perfect in its way. Highly stylized and choreographed, very Bob Fosse, their couplings took into consideration historic preferences, hidden strengths and weaknesses, and were generally animated by the kind of overwhelming hunger that only a withering abstinence can produce. Some other time, he would have required very little coaxing—they were already long overdue—but Parker couldn't stand the taste of his own mouth in the morning, and Mersea was extremely sensitive about her breath, so if he voluntarily put his lips to hers before breakfast, she would know he was being sentimental, know immediately what was wrong, on this of all days, and would feel touched, maybe under the circumstances a little sorry for him, and then he'd get irritable because she had read him so easily. When she did that, and she did it too often for his liking, she got a soft, distant look on her face, like she was watching an old Hollywood movie, something with Ronald Coleman or Paul Muni.

Rather than suffer that kind of scene, Parker shrugged into his bathrobe, stepped around the bed and hugged her from behind. "I'll be fine," he said. "It's Dad I'm worried about. He's been so moody lately. But I'll give him your regards."

She turned then, into his arms, her lips pressed against his ear. After several deep breaths, she pulled back slightly to look at him, and he saw it, her complicated Mona Lisa smile.

"What is it?" he asked, searching the blue of her eyes for some kind of clue.

And she shook her head softly, rubbing his arm the way you might smooth ruffled feathers. "It's nothing," she replied. Then the moment passed, her eyes danced away from his, and she blushed, suddenly embarrassed.

The sun wasn't up when Parker went outside to start his car, but his neighbor Art had already manned his post, removing gum wrappers and leaves that had blown onto his yard during the night. A dapper old guy with a silver mustache and an endless supply of pastel cardigan sweaters, Art kept his lawn and garden trimmed with a military precision. Many times he had offered Parker the use of his clippers and snips.

"Everything under control?" Art called out, the same greeting he had given for nearly a decade, as if Parker and Mersea lived in a state of constant upheaval.

Parker waved and said, "Everything's fine, Art. Beautiful morning for a drive. Going to Unionville to see my dad."

While the car warmed up, Parker inspected it, kneeling here, bending there, and Art sidled over to watch. Art was one of those men who never tired of looking at engines. If Parker lifted the hood, he knew Art would stand there for half an hour, reminiscing about cars he had owned. But Parker was already behind schedule, so he slid behind the wheel of his Saab and rolled down the window.

Art leaned over and said, "You tell that father of yours I said howdy." Then he rapped three times on the hood of the car and backed away as Parker reversed onto the street and raced through the early-morning quiet to the northbound freeway.

Mersea loved to tell everyone that Parker drove like a maniac, and it was true he loved speed. Nothing was fast enough for him. He fiddled with his computer to increase its performance. He videotaped hockey games so he could zip through commercials and intermissions, skipping the fights and boring bits to create his own little highlight package. But that didn't mean he was a demon on the road—nearly everyone drove faster than the speed limit. Yet, listening to Mersea, you might get the impression that Parker belonged in a daredevil show. Darryl and Rudi agreed with her, naturally. "Just being an aggressive male," they had told him on countless occasions.

At first he enjoyed their playful carping. He used to egg them on by flexing his muscles and swaggering around like a professional wrestler, clenching his teeth till the veins bulged in his neck. It was one of those routines that had made him feel alive, part of a rich urban culture. But after a while he started to resent their tag-team approach. Those words had been repeated so often that they had lost their brightness, their entertainment value. They had begun to sound a little too much like a weapon.

Occasionally, and only when he was by himself, Parker admitted there might be something childish in living a life like it were a video game. Mersea was right about that, and he knew it. Even as he zoomed about, cutting precious seconds off his life's performance time, he wondered what he was saving all that time for. They had no children or pets to make demands on their day. Neither of them had a hobby to speak of. And whenever he left work early, Mersea inevitably had to stay late. Rudi had been right enough about that, too—there was not a lot of face time in their relationship.

She was head of marketing for The Galaxy Group, a small but respected mutual fund company. She put in long hours, even went on the road one week every month with the sales guys, visiting brokers and dealers, making presentations, getting a feel for the clientele. Parker's job was equally demanding. As part owner of Texpan, a software developer, he often worked twelve-hour days at the office.

Despite their hectic schedules, however, Parker felt a great deal of tenderness for Mersea, a genuine fondness that showed itself whenever their busy lives gave way to silence and stillness: when he rolled over in bed and heard her mumbling in her sleep; when they went for walks in the snow or sat together with a bowl of popcorn and watched the news. And if it wasn't love they shared—and who, these days, could be certain of such things?—it was at least a comfort, a kindness, a beauty.

Mersea talked a lot about beauty, believed that life was an art, perfectible; and Parker more or less agreed. Certainly their first few years together were as graceful and clean as a Japanese watercolor. But the past while, everything had changed. When he looked at their life now he saw the kind of art he didn't understand, like he was staring at a Rothko or a de Kooning. And although a great deal of thought had gone into the patterns of this shared existence, it made him wonder if he even knew what he liked anymore.

At breakfast, for example, they usually started out with a glass of watery apple juice. Straight from the can the juice was too sweet, and orange was too acidic, so it had to be apple and it had to be weak and cold, and it had to be just one glassful. They drank coffee, of course, but not too much—one and a half cups of French roast each. They took multivitamins and echinacea. They had one slice of whole-wheat toast with a thin wash of organic apple butter and, occasionally, organic peanut butter. Whenever possible they also tried to fit in a small bowl of whole-grain cereal topped with half a banana and a few ounces of milk, their nod to the specter of osteoporosis.

They were careful about these details, knew from experience the physical complaints, the foul moods, that could follow should they stray even slightly from the program. And although it was a routine, it had seemed perfect. Or it had until Parker's mother died. Starting that day, everything began to change.

He had often heard people talk about death as something meaningless, but in Parker's experience death did not mince words. It told him a cold and terrible truth he had not been prepared for: All our good thoughts, good intentions, good habits and good deeds hold no weight in the end. We think by living properly we can invest in our own future, like one of Mersea's mutual funds. The Cancer Society, the Heart and Stroke Foundation—they suggest that you can hold death at bay. They fill the air with statistics, percentages. But it is only a comforting story, another kind of prayer. Like the fine print says: "Past performance is not necessarily indicative of future returns . . ."

As a result, Parker had begun to question his perfect, measured life. Until his mother died he could have pointed to any aspect of his routine and said quite honestly that it was exactly right. Now, he wasn't so sure. Lately he had found himself thinking about fried eggs and bacon, doughnuts and takeout coffee and, inevitably it seemed, the young woman who worked the early shift at Dunkin' Daddy's, just around the corner from his office.

Laurel was her name. Parker had never spoken to her, only watched her come and go, watched from the doorway as his partner Dana Caldwell joked with her at the counter. She had thick black hair in a perky Fifties cut. "Cleopatra with Cadillac fins" is how Dana had put it. Her face was pretty but common, her most distinguishing characteristics a gold stud on the left side of her tiny upturned nose, a handful of earrings strung along the curve of her ear. She had no figure to speak of, lithe and angular as a cat. He doubted she stood much more than five and a half feet tall, and would have been surprised if she weighed even a hundred pounds, showing through her uniform the lean frame of the long-distance runner. That she jogged he had found out from Dana, who had seen her trudging along the waterfront in gray sweats. Dana also said she sang in a pop group called Learning Curve.

From Parker's office window he could see Dunkin' Daddy's, and he often found himself daydreaming about Laurel—embarrassing stuff, really. Parker was not a big man, five-something-or-other, but enough under six feet that he never considered himself tall. And he was more pudgy than muscular, the one physical trait he had inherited from his father. But with Laurel he imagined himself a force of nature. He had this vision of making love to her standing up, slamming into walls and doors, knocking over small tables and chairs in their mad dance around whatever dingy little room she inhabited. It was sick. He knew that. He felt ashamed whenever his thoughts turned in that direction. Wanting to appear a brute was so obviously a sign of weakness.

Just north of the city, Parker listened to a call-in show from somewhere in the Midwest. The host was in the middle of a rant.

"You know what else rattles my cage is fitness clubs, every Tom, Dick and Harriet lugging around some stinky old gym bag and heading off for a workout. Used to be people played games at least. Teams, or *mano a mano*. Now everyone is too busy working on their abs and their pecs. You know what I'm talking about—the rock climbing, the stair stepping, the laps in the pool, the weight room. People call it self-improvement, but you ask me, it's preening. Where's the sportsmanship? Where's the camaraderie? And boy, don't they all just take it so seriously. Like these bogus challenges are real ones. Like I shave two seconds off my lap I'm a better person. Like I climb the big wall today I'll be fulfilled. Like I crawl to the North Pole on my hands and knees my life will somehow be worth something. Self-absorption, am I right? I'm telling you, today Florence Nightingale would be running marathons, Albert Schweitzer would be pumping irons . . ."

Few things in this world pleased Parker more than racing along a deserted highway in the middle of the night with the radio turned up loud and fading in and out of frequencies from beyond the horizon—Nashville, St. Louis, Boston. It reminded him of those all-night bus trips when his father played saxophone with the Duke Kenny Orchestra. Parker would curl up on a seat in the darkness, his little pocket transistor pressed to his ear; and while the musicians yukked it up, playing cards, swapping tales, he would pretend he was an astronaut trapped in a space capsule, whizzing through the galaxy, and those faint scratchy transmissions from earth were his only connection to his past.

Parker smiled sadly at the memory of those days, how sunny it had all been before truth and facts and sensibility had drained the color out of life. The truth had even gotten to his father in the end, Jack Martingale, the life of the party, bottle of Jameson's always, the rude talk and crazy songs. The past year the joker had gone out of him. He never sang, never horsed around, never even played the sax anymore—a man in mourning. And although Parker had long prayed for his father to grow up and assume his share of life's burdens, now that it had happened he actually felt sorry for him, wanted to protect him from the pain.

Traffic was light at that time of the morning, and Parker arrived at the cemetery before the sun had cleared the horizon. He had come early because he wanted a few hours alone, before he brought his father out. He had some thinking to do, of course, but he also wanted to make sure the site had been properly maintained. In the trunk of the car he had garden gloves, snips and a weed trimmer. He knew his father would be inconsolable if he arrived and saw things looking shabby.

The graveyard lay thick with autumn fog, the bare trees black and dripping. Parker could hear sparrows chattering in anticipation of the light and was thankful they weren't crows. He wasn't sure he'd be able to handle crows just then, such a depressing bird. And slouching low in his seat, the heat up full, the radio off, he tried to conjure happy memories, things he might be able to mention when his father got that look of desperation in his eyes.

He saw his mother's fine pink features and trim body. Nancy O'Donnell was her maiden name, the youngest of five children who grew up on a farm outside of Dublin, Ontario. She was the only one who left the farm, too, taking a job as a secretary in a law office in big bad Toronto. In her spare time she took classes in home economics, etiquette, conversation, hoping one day to become a refined young woman.

Parker could have used a lot of adjectives to describe his mother, but "classy" most often came to mind. She never wore a lot of makeup, but she wore it all the time, even when the three of them sat around the house watching television, or when she lay dying in a hospital bed. She dressed always in a pleated gray skirt and cotton blouse. She never raised her voice, even when she laughed, and she rarely drank and never used coarse language. Her idea of fun was an afternoon drive with Jack, her hair up in a silk scarf, the two of them listening to the CBC and nibbling cashews from a can. Her idea of spice was an onion or two in a boiled dinner.

Smoking was her one vice, but even that she undertook with a kind of sweetness. It had nothing to do with a young woman's rebellion or wickedness. It was Jack, the love of her life, who offered her the first cigarette, and she took it without a moment's hesitation, entered that halo of smoke to be there with him, to share another pleasure, another experience. In much the same way she would sit on the patio with him on a summer night, nursing an ounce of beer in a wineglass while he downed three or four bottles. Being pleasant company is what she would have called it.

Parker finally opened the trunk of his car and slipped into galoshes and overalls. He grabbed the trimmer and a rag and walked slowly along the gravel path, over the rise to Founders' Circle where his mother's stone was located. The mist was thinning out. The sky had taken on the spooky color of a peach. And he told himself, as he did whenever he managed to get up before dawn, that he should do this more often. It was the most encouraging part of the day. But when he came over the crest of the hill, he stopped in his tracks and rubbed his eyes.

Leaning against his mother's stone was a balloon made of space-age plastic, silver on one side, a picture of Lady Diana on the other, affixed to a hollow plastic wand, which in this case was broken off to a stub. Florists had sold hundreds of these items since Diana's death and funeral that summer. The balloons normally carried a message beneath her likeness, and this one was no exception, the single phrase—Reach Out!

As he stood there watching, a tiny gust of wind pushed the balloon bumping along the grass, where it paused at the next grave and the next. The sight of it there made Parker feel kind of spacey, almost as if he, too, were a balloon—one of those monstrous figures that float above the street in Macy's Christmas parade. His arms and legs behaved more or less realistically, transporting him after the balloon; but with every uncertain step he had the sense that his appendages might drift off in their own direction if he gave them any slack at all.

When he finally grabbed the balloon and carried it over to the trunk of the car, he took out a screwdriver and pierced it—not an easy task. Then, with a dreamy Quaalude calm, he returned to his labors.

First he wiped the stone of cobwebs and bugs,

polishing the pink granite as best he could. Then he knelt and began trimming and pulling weeds, a surprisingly pleasant task. Very therapeutic, he would say when Mersea asked. And it was true, he could feel the tension leaving his back. The sore elbow felt better than it had for months. The hollow sensation in his arms and legs was gradually replaced by the heavy tug of gravity.

Down near one corner of the stone, Parker found a dead mouse or a mole or something—it was hard to tell, it was so shriveled. All he knew for certain was that it had grayish-brown fur, long delicate claws curling in toward its legs, and two large front teeth the color of Cheez Doodles. He picked it up by its stiff stringy tail and carried it over to the gravel path, far enough away that his father would never see it.

There beside the path he discovered a freshly turned grave. Douglas Portland. Born 1923. Died 1997. Several bouquets of carnations and a large wreath from the Legion leaned against the headstone, and Parker grabbed a few flowers and laid them beside his mother's stone, ashamed of himself for neglecting such an obvious detail. Then he returned to the car, switched on the heater and tried to get warm.

Parker was twelve when he first learned his mother had cancer. It was a cool, rainy summer that had people talking about the Russians maybe fooling with the weather. His father had driven into the city that evening to play a benefit of some kind, so after supper his mother asked if Parker wanted to go for a walk. He agreed, but only on the condition she buy him a treat, and she laughed brightly at that and touched his arm. They both knew that she was the one with the sweet tooth.

They stopped for a while at the park and watched part of a softball game. She bought them each an ice-cream bar, and they sat at the top of the bleachers without talking much. Then after a couple of innings he noticed she wasn't watching the game, wasn't even watching the crowd, which she normally liked best. She just stared at nothing, chewing her lip.

When he asked what was wrong, she smiled sadly and took his hand, leading him away from the game. She laced her fingers with Parker's, and in her prim, soft voice, the one she used for all serious talk—the facts of life, report cards—she said, "I have to have an operation, honey."

That word, "operation," made Parker think right away of George Stack's grandmother. Emily Thompson was her name, and she had lived with the Stacks until she died. She wasn't much taller than a child, and her skin was nearly translucent. She had arthritis, too, her fingers twisted and clawlike. During the last year of her life, she seldom left her bedroom.

Parker met her only the one time. She was standing by herself in the Stacks' kitchen, and when he and George burst into the room, she asked them in her thick Scottish accent to take the pot off the stove and set it on the counter. It was a big enamel pot, like you might use for corn on the cob; and it was heavy. When she removed the lid, they all peered inside, the pot half filled with steaming melted wax. And without a moment's hesitation, Emily lowered her hands into the mixture. George gingerly touched the surface and showed Parker the thin white coating on his fingertip. Parker did likewise, wincing slightly at the heat, and giggling at the strangeness of it all.

Emily let them dip both hands before shooing them away. Then they went onto the back porch, and

George demonstrated how to peel the wax off in one piece. When Parker asked what Emily was up to, George said that she had to have an operation. The doctors planned to sever the tendons in her fingers.

Parker turned to his mother and looked for evidence of arthritis. That's when he noticed the tears in her eyes, and he knew instinctively that this was much more serious. She tried to smile, but made an awful face instead, all squinty and wincing, like she was prying a splinter from her flesh. She touched his face and said, "I haven't told your father yet. I was hoping you might help me. Maybe if you're there . . ."

Her voice trailed off, ending with a doubtful sniff, as though she knew Parker's presence would have no effect. She knew Jack well enough. He would come completely unglued. And in fact they all came undone. Over the next few weeks, hardly a day went by without tears, a meaningful look. She had a small tumor on her uterus and had agreed to have a hysterectomy.

In the days leading up to her operation she suggested that Parker stay out on the farm for a while with her brother, John, but that didn't go over so well. "Who'd take care of Dad?" he said, voice quavering. "Who'd take out the garbage, or buy the groceries?"

This was more than a lame attempt at humor, and they both knew it. Jack Martingale had never done anything in his whole life that didn't have to do with music and having fun. Without Parker around to keep things running smoothly, the house would soon be a dump.

When the big day arrived, they drove together to the hospital. It was that reckless time before seat belts, and Parker normally would have sprawled across the back seat. But that morning all three squeezed into the front for a change, dressed like they were going to church. They walked hand in hand up the front steps of the hospital, a light rain falling.

Up to that point Parker hadn't said a word lest it all come out in a torrent. In fact he didn't make a peep until they started wheeling her toward the operating room. Then, when she was halfway down the hall, he bleated something unintelligible and waved, too late for her to see. His father babbled enough for all of them, however, not his usual happy chatter but something distracted, compulsive. When he wasn't talking, he was pacing nervously and slapping the coins in his pockets. He reminded Parker of a mechanical toy that you quickly tire of and regret getting for Christmas.

Midmorning the doctor came out and said the operation had been a success, that she had an excellent chance for a full recovery. Although Parker felt too numb to react, the coiled spring inside his father released with a nearly audible snap, and he slapped the doctor on the back and whooped like a cowboy.

They stayed at the hospital all day, filling the room with every flower they could get their hands on. When his mother finally regained consciousness, she took one look around her and said, "Jack, honest to God . . ." Then she turned to Parker and said, "How could you let him do this?" And his father kissed her and hugged her and fussed over her until the nurse told them to leave and let the patient rest.

They stopped at the beer store on the way home and picked up a case. They ordered a pizza with the works. It was party time. After Parker's third beer, though (one granted, two furtive), and too many slices to count, he fell asleep on the floor in a drunken doze.

The next thing he knew he was lurching into the bathroom to be sick, a common enough occurrence back then. But this was different. Without his mother there to hold him, it was the lowest feeling in the world to be crouching by the toilet in the moonlight, cold and miserable and alone.

He washed his face and stumbled out to the living room, his head muzzy, his stomach threatening to revolt once again. That's when he heard music, distant as a dream. He drifted through the kitchen and den, but found no sign of his father. Then Parker looked out the front window and saw him. He stood barefoot in the middle of the road, hunched over his saxophone.

Parker stepped onto the porch then. He knew he should coax him into the house before someone called the cops, but he couldn't bring himself to do it. Something in the way his father stood there, something in the sound of his horn, told Parker that this was necessary. So he stood and listened and tried not to cry as his father played, again and again, "Nancy (with the Laughing Face)."

Parker arrived at his father's house at eight a.m. Although the temperature hovered just above freezing, his father sat on the front steps in his pajamas, a trench coat draped over his shoulders. He looked totally wrecked, his hair standing up in spikes. He needed a shave. He was eating a candy apple.

"Nutritious breakfast," Parker said as he sat beside him.

His father held the apple in front of him, inspecting it the way you would a glass of wine, turning it in the light. After a moment's reflection he sighed and said, "Not much of a turnout this year. You want a couple dozen?"

Parker looked up and down the street at the big old homes, some of which dated back to the original German settlers. Unionville, named in honor of the Act of Union of 1849, was for the most part an artful little town that worked hard to cultivate an air of bygone times. A frequent destination for city people on Sunday drives, the downtown area consisted of antique shops and tearooms and an abundance of wrought iron and old-English spellings. A half-mile in any direction, however, brought you to dreary modern suburbs.

Despite appearances, only a few artisans lived and worked in town. Most of the locals toiled in Toronto's big glass office towers then came home to mow the lawn or wash the car or shovel the snow. They had never known what to make of Jack Martingale. Some of them hated him. They hated that the house was by far the messiest one on the block—peeling paint, maple forest sprouting in the eavestrough, bumper crop of dandelions every summer—even though he was home all day, every day, just loafing around. They hated him for never working a normal job, too, for not playing the game, for the sense of anarchy he brought to their quiet, ordered lives. Those neighbors not given to hatred merely found him bewildering. Every five years or so they had watched him, not a wealthy man by any means, buy a nearly new Lincoln then not even wash it or wax it or take it in for tuneups. It was like a slap in the face.

As a boy, Parker was mostly disappointed that his father was so unlike everyone else. Some of his worst memories were of the times his father tagged along on school trips with some of the stay-at-home moms, wandering about petting zoos and pick-your-own orchards in his shades and natty suits, and smelling of smoke and cologne and hair of the dog.

His father had his own disappointments, of course, but they stood in direct contrast to Parker's. It bothered Jack that his son wanted so desperately to fit in, that he displayed no flair or imagination. Jack always encouraged Parker to try something unconventional for school projects and Halloween costumes. When he opted instead for the suggested topics, the prepackaged outfits from Woolworth's, Jack suffered it like some kind of personal failure.

Even at the time, Parker knew that this state of mutual dissatisfaction was not as onerous as it could have been. There were plenty of fathers and sons with worse relationships. That didn't make it any less aggravating, however. Parker was thrilled, therefore, when he finally left town for the cool anonymity of Toronto.

Still, as a place to grow up, Unionville had offered him everything he could want. Their street ended at the edge of a farmer's field, from there the countryside spreading northward for miles. And though in Parker's life those fields had never blossomed (the farmer obviously counting on suburban sprawl), they provided a pleasant landscape in which to unfold his boyish dreams. He had creeks to explore, trees to climb, old rusted implements he could pretend to drive. Now, though, housing stretched to the horizon.

Shivering from the dampness, Parker helped his father get to his feet, then led him inside and made him an instant coffee and a couple of fried eggs. Throughout the whole procedure his father sat on his kitchen stool, counting the candy apples that trick-or-treaters had left unclaimed.

"Here," Parker said, standing beside him and offering a dripping forkful of egg.

While chewing, his father said, "Fifty. Can you believe that? I bought fifty apples too many." He dabbed at the yolk on his chin. Thinking for a second, he added, "I could give them to the food bank, I guess. Even beggars like treats." Then he grabbed the plate from Parker and shoveled in the rest of the food himself.

Parker followed his father upstairs to help him dress, trotting out jackets for his approval. Each article of clothing seemed to trigger another memory.

"Oh, brother," he crowed when Parker showed him a blue double-breasted serge. "That suit, I bought that one with Bobby when we were in Detroit . . ."

Parker smiled patiently. Bobby Flint was the drummer for Duke Kenny, a real character. Parker had spent more time with him than with all of his aunts and uncles combined. There were a million stories about Bobby. And sure enough, his father had settled on the edge of the bed, remembering.

"Talk about a live wire," he said. "Where was it now, the Rushton Ballroom, I think. God, this was just before the bus died for good, and Bobby, the guy wasn't a day under sixty, right? But he acted like a kid always, twenty-four hours a day nonstop."

"Dad . . ."

"It was New Year's Eve, you know the one we had that godawful sleet storm? I was never so scared in my whole life. Duke was half-pissed before we even got to the gig, the bus sliding all over the road. It was fucking brutal. And Bobby, the guy is totally steamed because Duke had raked him over the coals about his drum solo the night before, so when we get to the gig, he gives me the eyeball and I follow him into Duke's dressing room."

Parker gave the jacket a shake. He'd heard this story a dozen times already.

"Now Duke, you know Duke, the guy is a complete mental case. Couldn't remember a lyric to save his life, ruined half our arrangements. But the man had an image. Knew how to dress. The hair, the shoes, he had it down to a science. And he never went anywhere without his pack of mints and a bottle of Listerine. So Bobby closes the door real sneakylike, whips out that enormous prick of his—you remember, the size of a goddamn billy club—and half fills Duke's Listerine bottle with piss. I mean, Jesus, was that Bobby or what?"

Parker was losing patience. There was a term he had heard his programmers use—a memory leak. He had no idea how it applied to computer code, but it always reminded him of his father. He held the jacket out to the side, like a matador, and said, "Can we move it, please?"

Something in his father's face closed down right then. He rose wearily to his feet and walked right past the jacket. Suddenly he was peeved.

"What are you doing here?" he said at the bathroom door. "You think I can't dress myself?"

"I know you can," Parker replied. "But will you?"

"Why should I? Why should I do anything?"

Parker paused a moment, choosing his words carefully. "For starters," he said when his father finally turned to look at him again, "because we made plans."

"No, you made plans. If you'll remember correctly, I didn't say a thing."

Parker nodded. "You don't want to go to the cemetery?"

"Not particularly."

"Okay, so we'll stay here. Only it seems kind of

odd, we go to the trouble of buying this beautiful stone, dedicate it for eternity to the memory of your wife, and then you refuse to go there."

His father squinted as if Parker had suddenly receded a great distance. "Why should I? It's just a piece of rock. She's not even buried there, for Christ's sake. You think it's some kind of shrine?"

"Could be."

"The Shrine of Nancy?"

"Sure, why not?"

THREE

Lake Tusco

The cemetery in full light was more forbidding. What in darkness had seemed a sanctuary, sealed off from the rest of the world, now stood revealed as a flat field of sodden grass with, here and there, a clump of dark decaying leaves. The wind was raw and damp, and carried the smell of grass and clay, and the thinner tang of diesel fumes from the highway. Litter from the fast-food strip nearby shivered against the black iron spikes of the fence. Trees made menacing gestures. A jack-o'-lantern lay smashed on the gravel path, the thoughtless prank of a teenager.

His father walked ahead, looking to Parker like a derelict, the shoulders of his tweed overcoat hunched up, his hands shoved into his pockets. Parker felt the cold, too. The damp had already stiffened his fingers, creeping into the bone; and as he trudged along behind, he thought grimly that this was what death was all about, this inescapable withering cold that entered the flesh and the bone and the spirit until nothing else existed: the cold wet Kleenex in the long grass, the one gray sock lying in the ditch beside the road, the black muck in the bottom of the eavestrough.

His father stopped to let him catch up, as if sensing the darkness of his thoughts. Hooking his arm over Parker's shoulder, his voice low and full of warmth, he said, "I know the stone and all was your idea, an actual place we can come to. And don't get me wrong, I'm not blaming you. Far from it. But this is the only place on earth I can't picture her face, son. I try and try and don't see a damn thing. I don't hear her voice. Fact is, the only thing I remember when I'm here is that she's gone. It's why I stopped coming."

Parker said nothing, head down. It was true, it had been his idea. After they had gone up north and scattered the ashes, a kind of desperation had swept over him that there wasn't a defined spot on earth where he could go to be with her, no focus for all the pain he felt. So he went right out and bought a stone with his own money, a plot in the cemetery.

He looked at his father and said, "I guess I have trouble picturing her, too, hearing her voice. What I do remember most of all is that she was such a good person and"—he clucked his tongue—"that she deserved better."

His father's face suddenly buckled. After a bristling moment he snorted and said, "Why do you feel you need to bring that up again?"

"I'm not bringing anything up. I'm telling you what I feel."

"That I didn't appreciate her."

"I didn't say that."

"No, but you meant it."

"You know very well what I meant, Dad. She was a wonderful, giving person who didn't have the easiest life, especially. I wish we could have made it better for her somehow. I wish I could have."

His father turned then and walked to the gravel path, as if he needed a more legitimate reason to raise his voice. "I know you, damn it. You bring me here to make me feel bad. One thing you saw, one thing thirty years ago. So how come I'm the only one who's supposed to feel guilty?"

Parker had grown accustomed to these sudden outbursts. All that year they had been uncomfortable in each other's company, as though she had been the only thing keeping the peace. He let his head fall forward in resignation and said, "You're putting words in my mouth."

"Yeah? Well I'm tired of putting words in your mouth. I'm tired of feeling like the bad guy always. I'll wait in the car."

After they brought her home from the hospital, they fluttered about, trying to make her comfortable—fluffing pillows, bringing hot drinks, offering to turn the pages of her magazines—until she finally had to shoo them away. But the weekend was approaching, and the band had a gig, Friday and Saturday night at the Laurentian on Lake Tusco eighty miles away. Parker desperately wanted to go. Swimming all day, hanging out with the musicians all night, it would be a blast. But his mother didn't like the idea of his mixing with that kind of crowd. She thought he'd be better off at home with her and Mrs. Dreidger.

At first his father didn't say much either way, but Parker knew he was thinking about it. That night they stood out on the driveway, leaning on the back of the car with their cups of tea, and his father mentioned how worried he was, how he wished he could just cancel the gig. Then he stopped and nodded his head as if he was agreeing with some invisible third party. "Okay," he said, staring into the distance. "Look, you come with me. She needs to get her strength back. But mum's the word on the way she looks, right? It's just you and me having a time." And Parker nodded soberly, suddenly feeling much older. He wondered how he could possibly feel so guilty and so happy in the same moment.

His mother didn't have much strength for arguing, but she did her best. "Jack," she said, "you don't exactly have the best track record. Remember Port Dalhousie?"

A garden party southwest of the city. Parker was ten years old, and Jack had taken him along to help carry equipment, fetch drinks. Parker got so drunk, sneaking sips of bourbon and scotch, that he threw up all the way home on the bus.

Jack patted his wife's hand reassuringly. "Don't give it another thought, Nan. He's a big boy now." Then he gave Parker the look, and Parker stepped forward and said, "Don't worry, Mom, I've learned my lesson. Honest."

Finally she relented, and pretty soon his father had them both laughing with his impersonations of the guys in the band. He had a talent that way, making people feel good about the things he had talked them into.

The night before they left for Lake Tusco, Ingrid Dreidger came to cook dinner for them and sleep in the spare room. Parker had mixed feelings about leaving his mother in Ingrid's clutches. She was a square-shouldered no-nonsense Mennonite woman whose family had emigrated from Russia in the Twenties. She had a full-moon face and gaps between her teeth, and always smelled of Vicks VapoRub. Many times she had come to baby-sit. Once Parker even spent a bruising weekend at her place. She had a hug like Bulldog Brower and a fondness for root vegetables, salads floating in brine, dark sour breads. All day long she sang sturdy German hymns; and at bedtimes she mauled him with a washcloth until his skin was raw. Unfortunately no one else was as capable as Mrs. Dreidger. She could, if necessary, heft his mother over a shoulder and carry her from a burning building.

Next morning he and his father got up bright and early, tiptoeing around the house but seeming to make more noise because of it. When they were ready to leave, Parker kissed his mother good-bye. She made him sit beside her on the bed.

"You mind your p's and q's now," she said, patting his hand. "I'm counting on you to take good care of that father of yours."

He promised he would, then lugged the suitcases and saxophones out to the porch and sat there waiting for the tour bus to arrive. Mostly he wanted to be out of the way when his parents went through their good-bye routine. Given the situation, he was certain that one of them would have tears.

When the bus arrived, Parker stowed their gear underneath and climbed aboard, waving to Mrs. Dreidger who stood frowning in the doorway. All the guys in the band made a special effort to welcome him, as if they hadn't seen him in years. They slapped him on the back, shadow-boxed, the whole deal. Any other time Parker would have been thrilled—he loved it when they paid attention—but that morning he felt self-conscious. All the effort on their part made everything seem out of balance. So he took a seat near the back, stared blankly out the window and didn't start breathing properly until they were out of town.

Throughout its long and colorful history, the lineup for the Duke Kenny Orchestra expanded and contracted to suit the gig—a mere combo for club dates, twenty men strong for engagements like the one on Lake Tusco. But the core members were Duke on vocals, Bobby Flint on drums, Chick Champlin on piano, Lenny Dukatch on bass, and on tenor saxophone, Jack Martingale—or Mink Martingale, as he was known to people in the business, the common refrain being: "Nobody plays as smooth as Mink." Stan Getz, Zoot Sims, these were the names mentioned when people heard Jack play for the first time. He was an impressive talent, so much so that everyone wondered why he had continued to play with Duke Kenny all those years when he could have been in New York, or Los Angeles even, playing with the big boys.

The most popular assumption, and it was easy to make, was that Jack had some serious character flaw, a hidden weakness, crippling doubts. Nancy shouldered her share of the blame, of course, as if she had tied him too close to the ground. More likely it was her love, and the stable kind of life she provided, that allowed him to be as brilliant as he was. Without her he would have been a free and floundering musician, blown off course by every ill wind.

Parker didn't think about any of that until years later. But one thing was certain: in that twilight Duke Kenny world where everyone smoked and drank and cursed, his dad was a star. People respected him, gave his words more consideration than they deserved, as if he spoke in some kind of religious code that pointed others to the promised land.

Like most boys his age, Parker normally tried to hide his feelings; but he always got a secret thrill when his father cozied up to the microphone to play. Even on the bus sometimes the guys in the band would stop what they were doing, cards in hand, bottles poised, eyes fixed on the scenery flashing by, and they would listen to him breathe into that horn, unfolding melodies like a flower, petal by petal—soft, silken, sensual.

The bus was an old Greyhound, silver on the sides, white on top, with green-tinted windows. Duke had taken out half the seats and put in a couple of bunks at the back, some tables, a well-stocked bar, what he liked to refer to as his "hospitality suite."

Parker loved the bus, but that morning as they cruised northward, he felt little of the usual excitement. He suspected he had taken advantage of his mother's illness in going to Lake Tusco. His father was quiet, too, not his lively old self, back-slapping and horsing around. Even the other musicians seemed more sedate now that they were on the highway. And with the mood threatening to get positively somber, Bobby Flint walked up the aisle and said, "Hey kid, wanna see one of my impressions?"

Even back then Parker knew about Bobby, how the man never did anything that wasn't a joke. But he had a streak of goodness in him, too, a notion of duty. He was, he once explained, The Keeper of the Vibe. So this was one of his functions: to read the mood of the band and start the gig off on the right foot.

He stood there in the aisle, legs spread for balance as they sped down the highway. Then he turned the pockets of his dress pants inside out, leaving them to hang at his side. "So," he said, flapping the white lining back and forth like elephant ears. "Dumbo. What do you think?"

Parker smiled sheepishly and leaned away from him. He knew intuitively that he was not the audience but part of the act, helpless as Bobby smacked his forehead and said, "Geez, kid, I forgot the best part." And with lightning speed he unzipped his pants and whipped out his enormous prick, waving it about and going "Haw haw haw." Then, to Parker's relief, Bobby did a crazy little Three Stooges shuffle to the front of the bus and said to Duke, who was driving at the time, "Hey, Duke, hold this for a minute, will you?" And that was all it took. Before you knew it, a card game was going, Jack had his horn out, Bobby was mixing himself a rye and water—they were on the road.

The Laurentian was a white clapboard lodge built in the Twenties. The main building stood three storeys high, and each storey had its own separate veranda facing the water. Off to the right of the main building, hidden in the trees, were a dozen or more small but very exclusive log cabins. When Jimmy Cagney came to Lake Tusco to make a film about a bush pilot, he lived for three weeks in one of the cabins and, according to Vince Belton, the man who owned the lodge, Cagney was the most gracious and well-mannered patron he had ever known.

In its heyday, the Laurentian was booked solid, sometimes up to a year in advance. Tommy Dorsey, Paul Whiteman, Guy Lombardo had all played in the big bandshell near the water. When Glenn Miller came to the Laurentian before the war, two thousand people paid to dance under the stars.

Things had changed, of course. The crowds had dwindled to a few hundred on a good night. The rooms weren't as plush, the kitchen not as respectable, the lawn not as green and manicured. But it was still a plum of a gig. The acoustics were God-given; the view breathtaking, especially when the moon was full, and even more so when Vince felt moved to turn on the colored lights along the waterline.

These days the cabins were more rustic than luxurious, and that's where the musicians stayed. Duke, of course, got the nicest one, the one Cagney had used; but Parker and his father got the cabin with the bottle of Chivas. Vince was a big fan of Jack's playing. And that afternoon he dropped by, and the two men drank and talked about Ben Webster, Johnny Hodges, Lester Young.

Parker listened to them for a while, then went outside to swim with a few other kids who were guests at the lodge. When he returned to the cabin several hours later, his father had disappeared, so he grabbed a book and went outside to wait for dinner. He lay on the grass with his head propped against a tree, too drowsy to read, too excited to sleep. The ride on the bus, the coziness of the cabin, the tomfoolery on the beach—Parker had expected to feel guilty for having fun and leaving his mother in Mrs. Dreidger's rough care. Instead he was convinced now that everything would be fine. To breathe such clean air, to run so hard along the sand, to feel his skin so taut and warm, his hunger so acutely, made it that much easier to believe that his mother was on the mend. In a world this glorious, how could she not be?

He gazed across the wide expanse of lawn where that night all the couples would be dancing. Butterflies had sole possession now, two small white beauties flying tight circles around each other, whispering, it seemed, telling secrets fast and furtive then wheeling away only to come circling back with second thoughts, rising higher from the ground as they danced, up and up until they were nearly level with the third storey of the main building, then spiraling down to the grass to begin again their mysterious ballet, the most lovely, the most perfect moment, complicated in ways beyond his knowing, so dense a beauty that tears flowed instantly down his cheeks and he knew, as surely as he knew anything, that those tears, that welling of emotion, had something to do with his mother—not her illness but her nature, their nature, a thing they shared, a soft center.

He quickly rubbed his eyes with the front of his T-shirt and forced his gaze out to the water, to the small dog barking on the dock, to the laughing couple in the canoe, to the cloud-dappled hillside of the far shore. He didn't want to think about what had just happened, but he sensed that it pointed beyond anything he had ever known or suspected about himself, something larger than the notion of himself as "Jack's boy." There on the grass at the Laurentian, in fact, he realized that "Jack's boy" did not exist, that increasingly "Jack's boy" was a fiction he could neither sustain nor endure.

When Parker turned back to the lodge, the butterflies had disappeared, and his attention was drawn by a movement closer at hand. In the shade of the big cypress tree that dwarfed the nearest cabin, his father stood talking with a woman. That in itself was nothing out of the ordinary; his father loved to talk and didn't much care who listened as long the person knew how to keep quiet. What was strange was the fact that neither one of them was laughing. In fact his father looked perfectly miserable.

Parker sat up and squinted to get a better look. The woman had short black hair and a startlingly white complexion. She wore Trotsky glasses and, on such a glorious summer afternoon, a dark turtleneck sweater and a long black skirt that came to mid-calf. On her feet she had heavy-looking sandals.

Parker sat there breathlessly, afraid to move. The woman spoke and was very animated, waving her hands; his father replied, his face serious and full of pain. More than once he reached out to touch her shoulder, but she brushed him off. Moving closer then, he took her face in his hands and placed his lips on her forehead.

They remained like that for the longest time, and Parker rose slowly to his feet. It seemed he was seeing so much more than a kiss, as if his father had discovered a way to speak directly to this woman's anxious mind. And for a moment it worked. She pulled away from him, blinking, taking deep breaths. But with the quickness of a cat she reared back and punched him once on the chest. She swung out again, halfheartedly this time, then marched up the hill and around the corner of the lodge, leaving his father there stoop-shouldered and hurt.

After a long moment of stunned helplessness, Jack roused himself and half-turned. He locked eyes with Parker across the lawn. And Parker, not knowing what else to do, turned and ran.

At dinner that evening they ate in the main dining room with Lenny Dukatch. If Bobby Flint was the custodian of The Vibe, Lenny was the glue that held the band together. Everybody liked him. More important on the road, no one disliked him. He had no edges or angles, no axes to grind. Soft-spoken, courteous and with something that approximated social graces, he was an obvious choice when looking for a dinner companion. He could talk when needed but knew how to listen, too.

And that night the need was evident. Jack was uncharacteristically silent, poking at his food like a teenager, so Lenny picked up the slack.

They mostly talked about science. Parker's mother had bought him a telescope a few years before, and he could go out on a clear night and name a few dozen stars. He had a microscope, too. Where other boys his age spent their allowance on candy and baseball cards, Parker bought prepared slides, maps of the solar system. He loved the idea of the two views, the unimaginably large and the infinitely small, and how in so many ways they were the same. He also told Lenny about the books he was reading—by George Gamow and Fred Hoyle—things that Parker didn't really understand but that amazed him all the more because of it. Throughout their conversation, Parker kept scanning the room for the mysterious woman, darting an occasional glance at his father, who seemed to be doing some heavy figuring.

In the first lull in the conversation, his father leaned over, suddenly all smiles, and said, "Hey, you guys are way over my head. Whaddaya say you come back down to earth for a second?"

Lenny chuckled at that and wiped his lips with his napkin. He was proud of his ability to get along with people. He subscribed to *Reader's Digest* and worked hard to increase his word power. He was a big one for frank discussions and meetings of the mind.

His father said, "Tell you what, maybe you guys could bunk together tonight, you got so much to yack about."

Parker glanced at Lenny, who seemed to be just as puzzled, then back to his father, who wore a mask of sincerity. Eventually Parker had to look away. That face ruined everything, casting its shadow everywhere. And he suddenly wished that he had never come to Lake Tusco, wished that he could plug his ears and not hear any more. But he could do nothing to prevent it. The words fell around him like cold rain.

His father said, "The thing is I got this meeting, right? A booking agent. You saw her, Parker, today. She wants to talk after the gig, and I thought maybe, Lenny, you could help me out here, whaddaya say, take the kid for the night."

In that moment Parker realized that his two views—the telescopic and the microscopic—could never have prepared him for this sort of experience, the bald lies of a father, the destruction of paradise. There had to be another, a third view, that made sense of the dark middle ground.

Parker got up from the table and, after wandering around blindly for a few minutes, headed for the bus, thinking he could spend the night there. But the minute he stepped on board, he saw Duke chasing a half-naked woman around the hospitality suite—the blonde from Reception, the one with the double chin and lipstick on her teeth—Duke himself without a stitch of clothing save for the pillbox hat he had perched on his head, part of the woman's hotel uniform.

Without even bothering to cover up, Duke rolled his eyes and said, "Hey, Parker, buddy, rotten timing, man. Get the fuck outta here."

And Parker turned quickly and ran outside, the sound of the woman's high horsey laughter following him down the road. He walked for a long time, hoping to get his thoughts straightened around. When he returned, still hopelessly confused, dark had fallen, the band was on stage, and he squatted on the grass and leaned against a big maple tree, hugging his knees.

The crowd was sparse, maybe two hundred people in all, half of them dancing, the other half seated at the wrought-iron tables and chairs that had been set up around the perimeter. There was something desperate about these people, he thought, something pathetic, trying so hard to make the evening special. They drank too much, laughed too hard, a nervous energy about them as if they had forgotten how to behave.

Up on the bandstand Bobby Flint pounded on his drums, his opaque animal gaze fixed somewhere over his right shoulder. Duke sucked on a throat lozenge ("Meloids for a Mellow Voice") and scanned the audience for another receptive female face. His father poured his soul into his Selmer, so hot, so cool, the only one on stage who didn't need to read charts, the only one with his little music lamp turned off, and therefore the only one not swatting insects.

The longer Parker sat there, the farther he seemed to drift away, and that reminded him of something he had read a few days before in his astronomy book, how the universe resembled a raisin pudding, where the dough corresponds to empty space and the raisins represent stars. As the universal dough expands, each raisin moves away from every other raisin, each star moves away from every other star. Everything grows distant. Everything moves outward and away. Everything.

That idea gave Parker an odd sense of comfort. His life simply mirrored the mechanics of the universe. Everything drifted apart. That idea was enough to keep him in the shadows as his father packed his horn, climbed into a taxi and slipped into the darkness. It allowed him to go to sleep in the same room as Lenny

Dukatch and, when his father came back about noon the next day, act as though the whole incident had been imagined. And to be honest, Parker wasn't exactly sure what he had seen. But he knew intuitively that everything had changed for the worse. Some invisible cord had been severed, and now they were all drifting outward.

Not long after that weekend he came down with a cold, slipping from one illness to another, from strep throat to tonsillitis to a quick tonsillectomy. His mother blamed herself, as though her letting him go to Lake Tusco had caused his poor health. But she kind of enjoyed having him around, too, there in the post-op ward. They spent whole afternoons on the couch together, playing Crazy Eights. They developed a taste for flat ginger ale, for arrowroot biscuits dunked in tea.

That's when Parker realized she was still smoking. Her doctor had ordered her to quit, but every now and again she would excuse herself from their card game and slip sheepishly onto the back porch for a few quick drags. She made Parker promise not to tell. It was only a couple a day. She would cut down gradually, she said. She just needed time. And whenever Jack poked his head into the room, she'd hide her smokes under a cushion and say, "Sorry, Mr. Martingale, I'm afraid I'll have to ask you to leave. The Invalids Club is very exclusive. Members only." Then she'd give Parker a sly wink.

As a result of his illness, Parker spent five weeks of that summer vacation indoors, coming out of isolation for the final week of August. His mother nudged him onto the front porch like she was teaching him to fly.

"Go on," she said. "A little fresh air won't kill you."

He sat on the steps awhile, a little shocked at how frail he felt. The summer breeze grated on his skin, the sun on his pale arm too intense to be natural. Next door, George Stack and his brother sculpted Dinky Toy subdivisions in their gravel driveway. Across the street Terry Wilson bounced a rubber ball off the roof, his Ernie Harwell routine better than his fielding. He called out all the Tiger greats—Al Kaline, Charley "Paw Paw" Maxwell, Stormin' Norman Cash—weaving them together in a golden, heroic narrative. But Parker didn't feel like playing. He sloped off to the right, across the empty lot and into the weed-choked field, heading toward the railroad tracks on the other side. The air was hot and humid. Somewhere far away he heard the harsh metallic drone of a cicada. And once again he felt that same sad sensation, that feeling of distance and failure as if his family, as if the universe, was spinning away.

Parker patted the top of his mother's stone and headed back to the car. When he got near, he saw his father sitting inside, eyes closed, lips moving as if in prayer.

He looked like a different person this past year—kinder, more thoughtful, more serious. He was mostly bald now, with fine red tufts at the side that he had trimmed every week. His skin, if pinched between thumb and forefinger, wouldn't snap back into shape but take its sweet time. And it hit Parker suddenly how old his father was, how old *he* was, Charles Parker Martingale. His life had a clear shape now. All the defining moments had come and gone. And the image that came to him, inspired no doubt by his experience that morning, was of a big multicolored balloon, fully inflated. The end was tied, pulled tight like a navel. A child's hand came out and batted the balloon lightly, sending it up to bump against the ceiling and then drift slowly down to the carpet, the dust, the forgetting.

He climbed behind the wheel of the Saab, but his father didn't open his eyes until the car started rolling. As they neared the cemetery gate, Jack said, "I was thinking maybe we could make a run to the cottage. Close it up for the year."

Parker turned to look at him. "I didn't know it was open."

"Yeah, I went a couple times." He shrugged. "The house, you know, it reminds me of your mom's illness. I fucking hate it. Up there at least I can remember when we were young. Whaddaya say?"

A long moment passed, and Parker let his tongue wander about his mouth as if looking for clues. He said, "Look, Dad, why don't you just call the Hendersons and ask them to close it up for you?"

"Because I want to do it. And I want you to do it, too."

"So we can fight some more?"

"No, so maybe we can stop fighting. I think we need to talk, clear the air. There's things I need to tell you."

Parker stared a moment in the rearview mirror, at the winding path that led back up the hill to Founders' Circle. Then with an imperceptible shrug, he pulled onto the highway and headed back to his father's house. They would do each other a favor. His father had come to the cemetery; Parker would go to the cottage. That seemed fair, a family thing to do.

FOUR

Considering Olivia

Parker called home and left a message that he'd be back late. Then, while his father banged around upstairs, Parker fixed him a coffee.

His father was fussy about his instant. You had to dissolve the crystals in the milk before you poured in the boiling water. He said it tasted better that way, but Parker figured that anyone who cared about the taste wouldn't drink instant at all. Nevertheless, he followed the instructions exactly, knowing he could be grilled about it later.

When his father finally came down to the kitchen doing his jazzy high-hat thing ("*CHH ch-ch CHH ch-ch CHH ch-ch CHH*") Parker knew right away that they were starting over. His father brought the coffee cup to his nose and sniffed suspiciously. Then he took a sip and gazed out the kitchen window. "Packed a few clothes," he said. "Thought maybe we could stay the night."

Parker was surprised to see how miserable his father looked just then. In his own stubborn way, he was pleading, and Parker didn't exactly know how to respond. He shifted his gaze to the floor and cleared his throat. "I left a message for Mersea that I'd be home tonight," he said, searching for a neutral tone. "I thought we were just closing up the cottage."

His father shrugged like a foreigner unfamiliar with the language, then stood there and let Parker take it all in, the bloodshot eyes and heavy, pallid flesh like some kind of prod. Not that Parker needed much coaxing. He truly felt sorry for his dad. And if he was this desperate for companionship, Parker figured he could take a day off to tend to him. Everyone at work was scrambling like crazy to get things ready for a trade show in Las Vegas, but Dana could cover for a few days. He owed Parker. And Parker figured he owed his dad.

He called home again and left another message. Twenty minutes later they locked up the house, and his father walked over to throw his suitcase in the back of his ten-year-old Lincoln.

"What's wrong with taking the Saab?" Parker asked. "We'll get there in half the time."

His father slapped him on the shoulder. "Nothing's wrong with your car, Parker. It's loveliness personified, but I want to bring back some of that dolomite for the garden here, and I didn't think you'd be too happy with that."

So they started driving, in the Lincoln—no shocks, spewing oil, a big, black cushy barge. Parker thought it was just like his dad to suddenly do some landscaping, at a time when he should be selling the house and moving into an apartment, a man who, for thirty years, refused to cut his lawn without a court order.

The road north was as familiar to Parker as his fondest memory, a two-lane lullaby full of comfort and promises. It cut through cattle country for the most part: hard, rocky pastures, homesteads that dated back to another century, desolate terrain even in summer. One bitter January weekend they had seen wolves tearing apart the carcass of a steer.

Some of the homes along the highway had been reborn, of course, with sandblasted brick, with the wide verandas and ornate trim and the hand pumps out front all painted in bright colors, the yards prettified with barrows of flowers and Muskoka chairs. These homes were owned by city people mostly, solid, earnest men and women who had traded the traffic and chaos for a simpler life of deerflies and sulfur-tasting water. Each trip to the cottage there were a few more of these interlopers, people with money, leisure, taste. Some locals thought that the arrival of these weekend farmers amounted to a kind of foreign invasion, but Parker felt the changes to the farms were mostly an improvement.

And what always made Parker smile was the notion of these people, well off the beaten path, knocking together an existence out of the most unlikely talents. It gave him a sense of how close to the edge everyone was, but also a feeling for people's resourcefulness, their talent for making things work out. In that regard he had really come to appreciate the people with the fancy yards. Where a lot of the old-timers got by with odd jobs—the permanent garage sale, small-engine repair, a bit of home baking—these new neighbors, these city people, came at the problem of employment from two extremes. They might raise organic rabbits and chickens, say, but also offer desktop-publishing services, or a fax machine and color copier. That's what Parker liked the best, that as different from the locals as these people were, with their high-tech gizmos, their style, they were very much the same.

His father pulled into Dot's Place for lunch, the same restaurant where they had always stopped. Parker chose a chef salad with no dressing and a large glass of tomato juice. His father ordered the hot beef sandwich with fries.

They sat in a booth, and that gave Parker ample opportunity to observe his father's hands—fat and stubby and covered with freckles and fine red hair, the nails gnawed and sore-looking, the baby finger of each hand graced by a nearly identical onyx ring. A tiny amethyst sparkled in the corner of one ring, a tiny diamond in the other.

Parker hated the look of those rings, on those hands. It bothered him just as much to watch his father use his cutlery: that is, properly, with his fork in his left hand, his knife in his right. Everything else about the man—his bull head, his thick-necked wrestler's body, his crude jokes and barrelhouse ways—would lead you to believe he would eat like a boor, handle his utensils in the meanest, most ham-handed fashion. Instead he wielded his knife and fork with the delicacy of a surgeon, his rings glinting in the light and cutting across expectations. Parker couldn't help feeling that secrets lay at the root of this mixed message. Worse, it reminded him that he didn't understand his father as well as he should.

For most of the meal, Parker kept his eyes averted. His father was in a low-key mood as well, not stirring his coffee for twenty minutes, not clearing his throat after every bite.

When they had both finished eating, Jack wiped

his lips and said, "I'm sorry, Parker, back at the cemetery—it's been a bad year. I sit home, you know, and I think I'll go crazy if I don't get out of there, so I go downtown for a coffee with Bev. He's about the only guy in town I can stomach anymore. We talk a bit, shoot a game of pool, and pretty soon I'm feeling just as lousy. I keep remembering things she said, things we did. Even here, this stupid little restaurant, God, how many times did we stop here, a thousand?" He swallowed heavily and scanned the room. "She's everywhere, Parker, and sometimes I just wish I could forget about her for a while and get on with things."

Parker looked down at his lap, where he folded and unfolded his napkin. He had always thought there was something wrong with people like his father, people who seemed immune to the years and the griefs and the losses. But the bags under his eyes now, the unmistakable gravity of his voice, the sudden poetic phrases of the past year—these were a welcome surprise. Grief suited his father. It knocked some of the jester out of him.

Gently, with respect for his father's feelings, Parker said, "That's what Mersea and I have been saying all along, Dad. You could have stayed with us this past while, or you could have rented one of those seniors' apartments down by the marina. And, who knows, maybe you need a hobby."

His father shook his head wearily. Putting his cup down without a sound, he said, "You're like a broken record. I don't want you to baby-sit me. I don't want one of those shitty little apartments where they expect you to play canasta and shuffleboard, where you sit around with old geezers all fucking day, gluing alphabet macaroni onto pieces of felt. You think a hobby's what I need? You think diddling around with a model railroad or playing bridge or golf—you think anything like that could make me feel better, make me forget even for a second that your mother is gone? I mean, fucking hell . . ."

Parker pushed up from the table as if to leave, then on second thought dropped into the seat again. Leaning forward, his voice reasonable and measured, he said, "What do you suggest, then? You going to stay unhappy for the rest of your life?"

His father looked out the window at the steady stream of trucks roaring past. Then thumbing a cavernous nostril, he said, "I suggest we buy a box of Dotty's tarts. Then we'll stop at Perron's for a couple of steaks and buy a case of beer."

Parker gave him the lidless, unflinching glare, sniffing once for effect. "I thought we were being serious. I thought we were going to talk."

His father waved for the check. Then stifling a burp, he said, "I am being serious. We will talk."

The car smelled of sweets, and it was giving Parker a stomachache. Worse than that, his father had switched from humming to outright crooning. Not that he was a poor singer. In fact, he sounded a bit like the seventy-year-old Sinatra, the Frankie who gave you more gruff talk than melody, now and then wavering out of key but pulling it off with attitude. In some ways, his father was a better singer than Duke Kenny ever was, so it wasn't the crooning itself that bothered Parker but what the tunes revealed—Mr. Rorschach.

Like the morning they took Parker's mother in for her first operation. She was in the shower, taking forever, and Parker sat at the kitchen table and toyed distractedly with his Ovaltine and cinnamon toast while his father stared out the back door. It was a cool wet morning, the rain pouring over the edge of the clogged eaves and spattering on the driveway. And Parker, who had never once been to church or Sunday school, wondered whether a little prayer might be in order under the circumstances. Then little by little his father's voice began to penetrate Parker's anxious gloom, the faint but unmistakable strains of "Mack the Knife." Parker wanted to shoot him for that. Till that point he had done a good job of blocking out the gruesome details of his mother's operation, and suddenly he could see a scalpel slicing into her flesh, carving out great gobs of tumor. Yet his father just stood there and hummed as mindless as a lark, never even wondering what she might think if she heard him.

And now he was at it again, in a northbound car filled with the smell of grease and sugar, crooning his wife's favorite song, "Say It Over and Over Again," and making Parker feel unbearably sad.

Desperate to put an end to that particular melody, Parker wondered if he should mention his latest trip to the doctor, the sensation he had of something swelling inside. But his father, who had never been sick a day in his life, had always been particularly sensitive to medical talk and was spooked by the mumbo-jumbo. Instead Parker said, "How about those idiots in Ottawa, arguing whether 'distinct' means more than 'unique.' They're going to tear this county apart through sheer incompetence."

His father stared blankly out the window as they rumbled past a seedy little gas station with a sign in the window that read: Dew Worms And Spawn. Finally, without taking his eyes from the road, he said, "When you think how damn near impossible it is for even two people to get along, I'd say it's practically a miracle that countries stay together at all. How do you satisfy all those desires?"

"You don't satisfy them all," Parker replied. "You compromise."

His father snorted at that. "Maybe in the States they do. The melting pot and all. Up here we try the impossible and fuck everything up royally. No wonder this country is falling apart. Everyone's pulling in a different direction."

That shut Parker up quickly. He should have known better than to talk politics. It always came down to the same response from his father, a rant on the spinelessness of Canadians. By that he meant English Canadians and how they had knuckled under to the French, given in to American culture, allowed "foreigners" to make a travesty of sacred Canadian institutions like the Mounties by tarting them up with turbans and face hair and all manner of ethnic gimcrackery. Dangerous ground, certainly, and terrain that Parker would just as soon not travel again.

He flipped on the radio instead. As if on cue, there was Roy Romanow, the premier of Saskatchewan, praising the unity plan he and the other premiers had knocked together that week. People had already started calling it The Calgary Declaration. "This is a huge step forward from where we were," Romanow said. "The sleepwalk is ended."

Over on the CBC, a panel was discussing the prospect of the new European Monetary Union, and which countries were likely to be allowed to join on the first round. "It all becomes official in 1999," said one of the commentators. "But before that can happen, the core European nations—specifically Germany and France—have a long way to go in order to harmonize their currency and interest-rate policy . . ."

With a groan of fatigue, Parker turned down the sound and slumped lower in his seat, his knees propped on the dashboard. For the next hour they rode in silence, gradually settling into the rhythm of the highway.

What he had always liked best about the drive to the cottage was the narrowing of the path, nature closing in. That morning he had left the city through a maze of interchanges and cloverleafs, the freeway at times sixteen lanes wide. From his father's place in Unionville, they had turned north on a highway that had four lanes for the first while, dwindling to two. At Baxter Station they left the highway and traveled along the Lake Road, a narrow bit of winding blacktop that was meant for two-way traffic but often required deft steering to prove it. At Big Moose Camp they took Miggs Road—treacherous, rolling, covered with loose stone and gouged everywhere into potholes. Finally they turned onto their driveway, a tortuous quarter-mile that cut through dense forest, that in winter could be traveled only on snowshoe or ski. At the end of the driveway a wide rocky ledge sloped down to Hidden Lake where a tree leaned precariously over the water, very Group of Seven.

His father climbed out of the car before the engine gave its final shudder. "I'm going down to say hello to the lake," he said. "You go ahead and build us a fire."

Parker paused on the porch and breathed deeply the smell of wet pine needles and rotting leaves. All along the fieldstone foundation on strands of cobweb, mayfly carcasses twisted gracefully in the slight breeze, their one day of anarchy now a distant memory. His mother would have swept all that away. She would have planted flowers in the garden, washed the "bird dirt" off the picnic table. This was clearly a man's domain now, a more primitive dwelling. And though Parker used to criticize her for trying too hard to civilize nature, he realized while standing there that the cottage was a poorer place without her constant puttering.

He pushed through the doorway and drew the blinds. His father never locked the cottage. There was nothing inside worth stealing, really. Much better to let intruders nose around than have them break down the doors and windows. Besides, his father believed a cottage should be available to people in an emergency. He had left a guest book on the coffee table should anyone care to leave a message. So far no one had, but then there really wasn't a lot of traffic on the road.

Parker started a fire, exactly the way his father had shown him many years ago. He plugged in the refrigerator and switched on the water pump. Then he walked into his bedroom and looked around for mouse droppings.

It was a tiny room—two single beds that he and Mersea had pushed together, an old dresser, cheap wood paneling and a varnished plywood floor—not much by any standards; yet every time Parker set foot in that room he felt connected to the center of something vital. Whenever he had trouble sleeping in Toronto, he pictured himself in that little room, the windows open, the lake whispering . . .

Satisfied that the mice had yet to find their way into the cottage for the winter, he went down the back steps and along the stone path to the water. His father had a stick in his hand, the same old piece of maple he'd used as a walking stick for as long as anyone could remember. Parker watched him poke the dock with it a few times, making an elaborate production of knocking pine needles into the waves.

Then his father knelt and scooped a handful of water and let it trickle through his fingers. He said, "I tried to make her quit, you know. I bribed her with money, threatened to leave her. But she just couldn't do it. Me it was easy. I just stopped cold-turkey, right after her first operation."

Parker sniffed sadly. For years, as a badge of honor, his father had kept a rumpled pack of Viceroys in his shirt pocket, with the same three tattered smokes. Her inability to show the same strength became a source of never-ending guilt for her, that she was letting everyone down.

Looking out across the lake, Parker said, "I've never understood how anyone could start in the first place."

"Yeah, well," his father muttered, "we know whose fault that is. I've gone over that night a thousand times in my head. If only I'd kept the damn things to myself."

"It was her choice, Dad."

"Well." He cleared his throat softly. "Like that's some consolation."

Parker turned, arms folded across his chest, and faced the far end of the lake. The wind was sharp and steady and blew the hair off his forehead. Then his father stood and said, "This means a lot to me, son, our coming up here. I was thinking maybe in the morning we could take the boat out to Sunken Island. I mean, if you want a memorial service, this is the place for it."

His father walked slowly back to the cottage then, and Parker stood there watching waves wash along the shore. He noticed the clamshells under the dock, courtesy of the mink who lived in the boathouse. He heard the screen door bang shut, the rattling around in the pantry. And despite the cold, he stayed there on the dock, ripped a strip of wood off the edge and tore it into little pieces that he dropped onto the surface of the water. A solitary minnow skipped close to investigate and departed just as quickly.

The appeal of a cemetery, he realized, lay in its passivity. When we go there to remember and show respect, the flow of ideas is entirely our own, the quiet and greenery merely a canvas on which we paint our recollections. But other places are not so tactful. The home, the office, the cottage have the power to call forth memories on their own—and not all of the memories are happy ones. For Parker, certainly, a memorial service at Hidden Lake would have its share of thorny reminders.

Not that he had ever disliked being at the cottage, but in the context of his mother's illness and death, a memorial service, even without a trip to Sunken Island, was bound to cast him in an unflattering light. And one of the more painful memories was the summer of 1968.

Duke had arranged a six-week tour, out to Vancouver and back, so Parker and his mother spent half of July and all of August alone at the cottage. It was three years after her first operation, and she had settled into a life of apprehension—not ill, but never able to put thoughts of illness far behind her, always assuming the worst when greeted by a new twinge or sniffle or fever, unable to look more than a few months down the road. For fifteen years she would pretty much keep on that way, every breath tentative, every step. Even at the time, Parker suspected she was wasting her reprieve; and now, in hindsight, he could feel the full weight of her mistake, especially when he considered the final decade of her life: the specialists, the operations, the clinics, the treatments, the counseling—modern science's bleak and wasting dénouement.

That summer at the cottage, however, Parker only knew that he had grown weary of her illness. He was a teenage boy, distant as the stars, and he gazed down at her with the cool disdain of a young god. When she spoke, it was to his back; when he spoke, it was with attitude, curled lip, pocketed hands. That he hurt her feelings was undeniable. He went out of his way to be callous and cruel. It was the one part of his life that he would now erase if he had the power.

All that summer, to her credit, she tried her best to get along. She offered to play catch but always got hurt. She dragged Parker along on walks and then never shut up, asking the dumbest questions, things she already knew. She made Jell-O salads and cornflakes chicken, food he had liked as a little kid but hated as a fifteen-year-old. Each day of that summer seemed worse than the one before.

Then one night after supper he was fishing from the dock, his line cast way out near the dropoff. He wasn't paying much attention, sitting cross-legged and staring out at Kennedy Point. It was the Fourth of July, and most of the cottagers on the point were Americans who chipped in every year on a fireworks display. It was never a big deal, but it was better than nothing.

After his mother finished the dishes, she carried out a lawn chair and sat beside him. She sensed that things had changed between them, and she was trying again to recover the connection they had once had.

"Is that star Androgena?" she said, pointing to the first bright object to appear in the twilight.

"*Andromeda*," he said sullenly, "is nowhere near us right now. Even if it was, you'd need a telescope to see it. That's Venus, not even a star."

They sat then, locked into their separate silences, waiting for the fireworks. His mother began to gently stroke his hair, putting every strand in place. He had always hated that, even as a little boy, and he jumped to his feet and started fiddling with his rod, tempted to say something sarcastic. But then he looked back at her and noticed the sadness in her eyes. He knew what that meant. Even with her illness she was seldom in a bad mood, a complete stranger to anger and depression. Her one weakness, if you could call it that, was sentiment, and that summer she had given in a lot.

Stiffening in anticipation of another trip down memory lane, he turned away, hoping the mood would pass. But she cleared her throat and said, "Before we built the cottage, your father and I used to come here camping. The land belonged to your Grampa Martingale, did you know that? We used to pitch our tent right over there."

She wiggled her fingers at the wide rock ledge on the other side of the boathouse, and Parker sniffed, the most appreciative sound he could muster. She said, "That's where you were conceived, Parker, sixteen years ago to the day. Two weeks later your father and I were married."

Parker winced, as if she had described the most gruesome medical procedure. And she laughed and said, "You needn't look so disgusted!" Then she looked down at her lap and laughed again.

Laughter was one of her great talents, a bright cascade of musical notes that she used unerringly to manipulate her loved ones. Parker knew well enough how effective this laugh of hers could be, and didn't want to give in to her, but he could feel his resistance slipping. With one last gasp of opposition, he knelt down and scooped a handful of water in her direction.

Immediately she scrambled out of her chair, transformed into a young woman again, someone who knew nothing of disease and death. Her face came alive with mischief, her eyes no longer sad but dancing with fire. Then, slowly but inexorably, the weight of her worries settled over her again, reclaiming her; and in that sudden glimpse of vitality he realized how vengeful his recent scorn had been. She had grown old before his eyes, and for that he could never forgive her. So he squatted on the dock again, turned away from her, and fixed his gaze on the slate-gray water. Hunched over that way, cross-legged, he didn't even have the strength to lift his face to the bright explosions that began to color the night sky . . .

Parker shook away that distant memory and looked out across the water to the ridge where they used to pick blueberries. His father was right, of course; this was the best place for a memorial service. But then, it was the best place for most things, the only spot in the world that he never wanted to leave. He and Mersea had traveled to Europe, Central America, the Caribbean; and as much as they had enjoyed those vacations, he had always been eager to return to Toronto. Their home in the city, too, was a place that he often thought about leaving behind, the way the disabled must dream of throwing off their shackles. But never the cottage, even with its dark memories.

Some of that, of course, had to do with a life devoted to pleasure and in step with nature. The cottage unified, the way no other experience could, bringing family together, knitting the years, even the decades, into a complicated pattern of quotidian pleasures: that sense of excitement each generation feels as it wheels into town for groceries; the age-old poetry, fresh even to this day, of waking early to wash underwear in the sink and hang it on the line under the birch trees; the unmistakable pride, that feeling of harmony that comes to young and old alike when they walk the road picking raspberries, or when they come in from the lake to clean the day's catch. Even weather made so much more sense there, an integral part of the grand design rather than an inconvenience.

Parker watched the sky darken, the surface of the water like mercury, dotted here and there with the last of the autumn leaves, the far shore a deepening patchwork of brown and beige and gray. And he was suddenly glad his father had dragged him along—a common enough feeling. He tended to deny himself the very things that would make him happy and was always thankful whenever someone forced him to overcome his nature.

Shoving his hands into the pockets of his jeans, he walked slowly up the path to the cottage where the clang and clamor of his father's kitchen routine had risen to a fever pitch. Of course, at home these days his father never cooked, at most heating up soup or a TV dinner. Often he would open a can of salmon and not even bother to make a sandwich, eating straight from the tin. But at the cottage, even when Nancy was alive, he did all the cooking, leaving her to read and sew and go for long walks with Betty Henderson from down the way. "Meat medley" was his favorite dish—beef, pork, chicken and sausage all fried together with onions and bacon. The last time Parker ate that particular meal he was constipated for a week.

He stepped into the kitchen, grabbed them each a beer and offered to help. His father, opening a can of potatoes to fry with the onions, nodded toward the fireplace and said, "Add a few coals to the wood, will ya?

Gotta be nice and hot for these steaks here. Vince gave us a couple of bee-yutes."

When Parker finished poking at the fire and his father had the potatoes sizzling, they sat in their favorite chairs—Parker in the rocker, his father in the plaid La-Z-Boy—and stared into the flames. After a minute or two his father said, "This is great. I'm real glad we did this. It's been a coon's age since we've done anything good together."

Parker nodded. It did feel good. There was no other place where the two of them could be so at ease, despite their differences, their disappointments. "Maybe the three of us could come skiing this winter," he offered.

Just like that the mood shifted. His father looked down the neck of his bottle and swirled the beer around. Fidgeting nervously, he said, "I wasn't going to get into it this weekend, but now you mention it, how do you think Mersea would feel if I asked another woman along? Would she mind?"

At first Parker nearly fell for the dodge, trying to imagine Mersea's reaction. Then he looked at his father with growing comprehension. "Wait a minute," he said, laughing awkwardly, "what about me? Don't you care how I'll feel?"

His father got up then and stirred the fire. He held his hand just above the coals, testing. In a distant voice he said, "Okay, so tell me—how will you feel?"

Parker laughed again uncomfortably. "I think I'll probably feel funny, won't you?"

His father made a face then, confessing his uncertainty in the matter. As he returned to his chair, he smiled sheepishly and said, "It's hard to know how long to wait. I'm not getting any younger, son. I'd just as soon be on the other side of this business. And the thing is"—he looked down, working the label on his beer bottle—"I guess you'd have to say I'm a bit beyond that already. I've asked someone to marry me."

Parker felt frightened suddenly, the kind of unreasonable terror you might feel on drugs. He not only heard the words, he could see them. They hung in the air and refused to go away.

His voice thin and unnatural-sounding, he said, "I guess I was wrong, I don't feel funny at all." Then he got slowly to his feet and walked to the window. The lake was pimpled with raindrops. Except for the bright green of the canoe, shades of gray and brown were all he could see. "Do I know the lucky lady?"

His father cleared his throat. "You've never actually met."

"Meaning . . ."

"You saw her once, I think, a long time ago."

Parker knew then as surely as he knew his own name. Lake Tusco. The black-haired woman. The woman who had pounded his father's chest. Only now it was Parker who wanted to do some damage.

He edged slowly across the room, never taking his eyes from his father's pained expression, knowing that this had all happened to him many times before, in dreams, that he had come to this place and found his father here, writing words in a ledger. And in every dream he had backed away because he'd been afraid of what those words might say, afraid of what he might find when he looked too closely.

His father turned off the potatoes and fetched a couple of glasses and the bottle of Jameson's Irish whiskey from the cupboard. He said, "It's not what you think, son." And what a great line, because nothing was what he had thought. His whole life he'd been looking for answers in the wrong places, taking directions from the wrong signs. The microscope, the telescope—what good were they for seeing the truth?

His father continued, his voice low and gritty. "Her name's Olivia, Olivia Collins. I've known her since forever, but the point is I never once touched her when I was married to your mother."

"I saw you, Dad. Lake Tusco, remember?" Parker was overcome suddenly with sickness and sorrow at the thought of his father and this woman prancing about in their own low-rent version of a hospitality suite.

His father ran his palm across the table. "You didn't see anything, son. You saw me trying to calm her down, and then you saw her punch me. And that's all there was to it."

"What about that night? Remember how you foisted me on Lenny so you could sneak off with her? You didn't come back until the next day."

"All we did was talk, son. I swear."

"Oh, and I'm supposed to believe that. Or was it the kind of talking Duke did with all those women at the back of the bus?"

His father pounded the table with his fist. "Don't you ever compare me to a pig like Duke Kenny. You don't know anything about it."

"Really? Well, I saw things, Dad. I saw lots."

"You saw fuck-all."

This time his father bolted to his feet and walked over to the window, but it was pitch dark now and all he could see was his own face and the rest of the cabin reflected in the glass. In a calmer voice he said, "Look, I'll explain all that later. Let me just—let me just talk for a second, okay? Let me talk."

Parker took a sip of whiskey and held it in his mouth, letting it burn. Finally he swallowed it and said, "Okay. Talk's cheap, but that's what you've always been good at. Go ahead."

His father remained at the window, staring into the night. In a hoarse whisper, he said, "I first met Olivia in 1950. I was twenty-eight years old and had just started with Duke Kenny. I had a nice car, money burning a hole in my pocket, the world on a string. I had just met your mother, too."

He laughed then, more like a sad little puff of air. "'Course, your mom was not the liveliest woman I had ever known. Didn't drink or smoke or dance, but man she scared me, you know? Those damn eyes of hers. Olivia, on the other hand, was the kind of woman I had chased all my life—sexy, smart, something to shoot for. Just twenty years old and a poet to boot. To support herself she worked the bar at a speakeasy on King Street where I jammed after-hours with the guys. She had a real sharp tongue, too, the only woman I've ever known who could button Bobby's lip. Once in a while she'd take me back to her apartment, make breakfast and we'd, you know, fool around. But mostly we just talked. Truth was she was only interested in my scrawny ass when it suited her, and by the end of 1950 that wasn't very often. Too busy being a writer, I guess.

"Not that I cared. I was gigging six nights a week. If Olivia didn't want me, that was her problem. And truth was, I was falling hard for your mother. We had so much more in common. Then that spring Duke rolled his Buick into a ditch and broke his collarbone. Put him out of commission for five weeks. The rest of the guys scooped up some other work right away, but me, I figured it was time to make a few decisions. And the more I thought about it, you know, the more there seemed to be only one question in my life: What would it be, Nancy or Olivia?"

Jack turned around then to see if Parker was still listening. With a hesitant step he returned to the table and took a sip of whiskey, rubbing the edge of the glass against his lower lip, his gaze all dreamy and distant. Then slouching lower in his seat, he said, "The choice was dead easy. They were both more beautiful than I deserved, but I figured I'd rather spend my life with a woman who worshipped me. Who wouldn't? Besides, as young as she was, Olivia had been around the block a time or two. I wasn't her first lover, and she had pretty much told me I wouldn't be her last. Your mother, on the other hand, was a sweet girl. It took me months to even get my hand inside her blouse."

Parker made a sour, disapproving face, and his father nodded an apology and said, "I decided to ask your mother to marry me, but only after I asked Olivia out one more time. That girl knew how to party, and I figured we would have one last blowout before going our separate ways."

Parker poured himself another inch of whiskey. It was happening again. He had no idea where the story was leading, but the easy charm and the sure delivery were winning him over. Of course he had always been a sucker for stories about his parents when they were young, spent innumerable Sunday afternoons on the living-room sofa poring over the old black-and-white photos of the young couple.

He sat sideways to the table, staring at the fire, hearing in his father's voice all the years of abuse.

"It was the May twenty-fourth weekend," Jack continued. "Victoria Day. It broke your mother's heart that I didn't ask her out. I'd told her about Duke, so she knew I wasn't playing that night. Man, I felt like such a heel. I knew how much she had her heart set on seeing the fireworks with me. And tell you the truth, when the big night rolled around, all I wanted was to hold her in my lap and sing to her the way she liked. But instead I took Olivia to The Cancan. We sat with Duke and Bobby Flint. We got totally blasted and, later, went onto the roof to watch the fireworks and smoke a few joints. Then we went to the speakeasy and played some music. We smoked a bit more, drank a whole lot more, and round about dawn I drove Olivia home, thinking I would drop her off, catch a few hours sleep and then go see your mother next day. But Olivia had other ideas. As I parked in the lane behind her apartment, she slipped out of her drawers and jumped in my lap."

Parker nearly choked on his spit. "Dad, for God's sake, spare me the grubby details."

But it was like his father didn't hear. The lines in his face had deepened, his color fading to ash. "I got out of the car," he said, "and tried to hustle her into the building. My night was over, I figured. All I'd wanted was a few drinks, a few laughs. But that Olivia is one stubborn cookie."

"Dad, I don't want to hear this . . ."

"You got to, son. There's no other way." And then, in a voice full of regret, he said, "It was all so damn fast. Before I knew what was happening, my pants were around my ankles and we were fucking like a couple of animals on the hood of my Nash Rambler."

When Parker clamped his hands over his ears and made another sound of disgust, his father rose to his feet and tossed a log on the fire. With his forearm resting on the mantel, he gazed down into the flames and said, "I spent the night at the Clinton Hotel. I felt like such a bum. I felt like I didn't deserve your mother. But I wanted her more than ever now, so I ran to her next day and proposed. The date was set for the end of July. I promised myself that, from that day on I would lead the life of a saint. And damn it, I did. I loved her so fucking much. But . . ."

His voice drifted away to nothing. Then he turned and gave Parker a smile that was sad and sweet and very old. He said, "Few weeks before the wedding, I got the shock of my life. Olivia shows up at one of the gigs, looking wild as ever. Lucky for me your mother had stayed home that night, and between sets I walked over to the bar. All I was gonna do was say hello and then ask her to leave me alone because I was engaged. But before I could say a word, she took a drag of her cigarette, washed it down with a sip of my whiskey and told me she was pregnant.

"I'll tell you, Parker, I got that stoned feeling, everything kind of sliding into slow motion, only my mind was going a mile a minute. I turned away from her and rested both hands on the bar. I asked if she knew who the father was, and she says, 'Cute, Jack. Think back a bit, it'll come to you.' And I couldn't believe it. I just couldn't believe I would be that unlucky. But it was true. It all happened on that Victoria Day."

At that point in the storytelling, his father got even antsier. He started pacing the room and touching things as if they helped keep him anchored in the real world. Then he cleared his throat and laughed ruefully.

"Olivia's plan was to have an abortion in Montreal. She was counting on me for the money. Only trouble was I didn't have that kind of dough just lying around—I even had to borrow from the in-laws to get set up in our new apartment. So I bummed the cash from Bobby and gave it to her a week later, making her promise that she would never call me or see me again.

"Naturally, I thought my troubles were over. The beginning of July, your mother and I came up to the lake here, camping. Two weeks later we were married. I had a new life."

His face brightened at the memory. "You should have seen the reception at the Pender Ballroom. It was nuts. Farmers rubbing shoulders with musicians, your mother's family dancing the fox-trot while my friends stood in the alley out back and smoked reefer. Me, I was scared to death that Bobby would whip out his dick and shake it at one of your mother's relatives. But I guess in the end I found it exciting, too. I figured I had the best of both worlds. And that feeling stuck with me for several months until Olivia started leaving messages for me at the club again. Suddenly I had trouble sleeping. My playing took a real nosedive.

"Went on like that for almost a month. Then one night just before Christmas Bobby showed up at the gig with an envelope from Olivia. Inside was a note that said: 'I'm going crazy, Jack. Give me a call.'

"My first reaction was to ignore it. The woman was nothing but grief. But I figured she was feeling guilty about the abortion and all. I figured I owed her a bit more than a handful of cash. So I wandered over there after the gig.

"Her apartment wasn't far from the club, but I ran the whole way, so I was out of breath when she opened the door. And the moment I saw her, I thought I had lost my mind. I hardly recognized her, Parker. Her face, her body, her legs—she looked like an inflatable doll that was ready to burst. And when I asked her what had happened in Montreal, she said, 'Oh, Montreal . . .' as if that whole fucking idea had only existed in some other lifetime. She told me then how she had decided to keep the baby, how she hadn't planned on telling me at all, her little secret. Of course she'd already spent the money I gave her. Olivia was never very good with dough. Somewhere along the line, she said, she had made up her mind that it was a husband that she objected to. Just her and a kid, writing poetry—that started sounding pretty cool to her. So she let it slide, got into the whole mothering thing. Only she was scared, now. She'd been reading maternity books and was convinced there was something wrong with the baby. She was just being hysterical, though. As usual. Everything was just fine."

Parker shook his head, refusing to believe what he had just heard. "So like what, you had another kid?"

His father nodded soberly and pointed to his amethyst-studded signet ring. "That February. Name's Ed. Part of the reason I was always short of cash."

"You gave them money. That's so weird. That is just so fucking weird. What were we all doing back then? I mean, did you ever live with them? Were you lying all those times when you said you were on the road?"

His father sucked in his breath. "I never once lied to you. And I never once cheated on your mother. You've gotta believe that. I sent them a bit of money when I could and that's it. It's only this last year that I've been seeing Olivia again."

Parker thought about that for a moment and said, "That's a lie right there. What about Lake Tusco?"

His father scrubbed his head and looked off into the distance. "Olivia was never cut out for mothering. She's a poet, for Christ's sake. If the kid came down with sniffles, she thought he was dying. That summer he had to have his appendix out, that's all. She wanted me to come to the hospital. She needed someone to lean on. I couldn't just turn my back on her."

Parker got to his feet and then sat back down again. A part of him wanted to laugh at the craziness of it; a part of him wanted to lash out. "So now you want to marry her?"

"I love her. And weird as it is, she seems to love me."

"But love? That seems a little sudden, Dad, don't you think? One minute you're the grieving husband, can barely function, and *presto-chango* you're talking about love? Mom's only been gone a year."

His father puffed out his cheeks, both nervous and annoyed. "You just finished telling me, back at the restaurant, that I should get on with my life. That's what I'm doing."

Parker closed his eyes and took a deep breath, holding in the stream of hurtful things he could say just now. When he had everything under control, he said, "So. I mean, what a surprise. A wedding, and a half brother. Of all things."

His father nodded sympathetically. "Only met Ed a little while ago. Seems a nice enough guy, considering."

"Considering what?"

His father clucked his tongue then and shook his head. "Considering Olivia."

FIVE

God's Bright Balloon

When Parker woke next morning, his father and the boat were gone. From the dock, with the binoculars, Parker could see him anchored above Sunken Island, a rock shelf in the middle of the lake that came to within five feet of the surface and sloped off in all directions to a depth of about thirty-five feet. It was their favorite spot for catching pickerel. On sunny days in the fall, Parker had seen muskies lolling about on the rocks below, like giants from Atlantis. More significantly, it was where they had scattered his mother's ashes.

His father wasn't fishing. He was slumped forward with his head resting on his arms, which were folded across his knees. Possibly he was sleeping, but whatever he was up to, the sight of him out there gave Parker a lump in his throat so big that he had to turn away.

After a quick breakfast, he started his part of the shutdown routine. He got out the ladder and cleaned the debris from the eavestrough. He chopped wood and filled the box with dry logs. He collected kindling and sharpened the ax. Then he went down to the dock with the binoculars again. His father had moved, but not much. He was stretched out on the bench seat now, his hat pulled down over his eyes. He was fishing, too, or at least he had a rod in his hand.

Taking that as a cue that they wouldn't be leaving anytime soon, Parker cleaned himself up a bit and went for a walk to the end of the road and back, two hours round-trip. He spooked a family of partridge from beneath a spruce tree, and had a good look at a white-tailed doe before she backed up slowly and then bounded away. And despite the fall flowers and the brilliant carpet of autumn leaves, despite the cleansing wind off the lake and the white-throated sparrow singing high in the treetops—*"O, Ca-na-da, Ca-na-da, Ca-na-da"*—he did not enjoy himself. He couldn't get his mind off his father's shocking revelation, and how the rest of their lives would never be the same.

When Parker returned to the cottage it was almost noon. His father sat at the table, eating a piece of fried pickerel, and without looking up from his plate, he said, "There's a couple pieces left if you want 'em. Otherwise I'll force 'em down."

For both of them the best meal of all was fresh pickerel, a slice of tomato and a piece of buttered bread. At the moment, however, Parker didn't feel all that hungry. "You didn't even ask if I wanted to come along," he complained halfheartedly.

His father shrugged, cheek bulging with food, and gave an apologetic smile. "I wasn't sure you were still talking to me," he said. He got slowly to his feet and rinsed his dirty dishes in the sink. "Are you?"

It was Parker's turn to shrug. Then he grabbed a fork, a slice of bread and the frying pan, and polished off the pickerel, nearly weeping it tasted so good.

They returned to Unionville in the brilliant sunshine, arriving around dinnertime. Neither of them had uttered a single word the entire trip, but as Parker got out of the car, he leaned his head in and said, "Look, Dad, I guess I'm still kind of in shock. Give me some time."

His father nodded at the steering wheel, an elaborate gesture that said he sympathized with Parker, and that he neither blamed him nor was surprised by such a response. Then Parker climbed into his Saab and drove off.

He knew better than to expect a roast in the oven or a fire in the grate when he arrived home, much as he would have appreciated the comfort after the weekend he had just spent. Left on her own, Mersea crawled out of their healthy habits and into a world of Dr. Pepper and taco chips. She had been known to take to her bed and devour an entire Sara Lee cake. At the very least, however, he had counted on her being there. He had so much to tell her.

He tossed his keys on the mantel, draped his coat over the arm of the sofa and checked the answering machine. The only new messages were his own. He checked his e-mail. Nothing. Finally he slumped down in his favorite chair and called Darryl and Rudi. There, too, an answering machine.

How was it, he wondered, that in this so-called age of cocooning, no one was ever home to answer a phone? Then he shuffled into the kitchen and grabbed a beer, some bread and cheese, and returned to the living room.

Thinking about the weekend now, he could forgive his father for keeping his secret. In fact Parker had helped keep it, and for very good reason: they had both been afraid to hurt the one they loved. He could even forgive his father his terrible mistake. After all, he'd been young, invincible, drunk and stoned, with a beautiful, headstrong woman pressing her case. Who could say how any man, single or not, would act under the circumstances?

No, what really bothered Parker was his father's willingness to try again. He couldn't understand this sudden reblooming of an old love affair, nor did he appreciate the timing. It seemed all wrong to Parker that his father should have this second chance. And the fact that he would even contemplate such a thing made Parker hate him a little. Why couldn't he just bite the bullet and accept his loneliness like a man? Why did he have to be so weak, so ready to abandon his past, so ready to inflict his secrets on others?

Parker drank another bottle of beer and settled slowly into a bad mood. Tired of waiting for Mersea to come home, he drifted up to his office and sat at the computer. She had obviously gone out of town—her small suitcase was gone, her closet less crowded. He'd send her an e-mail update.

> Surprise, surprise, you're not here. And I need to talk. Is my father all right? Just peachy. He dragged me to the cottage to help him close it. And then out of nowhere he tells me his deep dark secrets.
>
> He's getting married, Mersea. To some woman by the name of Olivia Collins. A poet, he says. And get this—they had a son together, a few months before I was born. Now Dad wants to marry her. Just like that I have a half brother. Maybe soon a wicked stepmother.

Parker looked away from the monitor and sighed, wishing Mersea was there. She had her shortcomings, but she was big on sympathy. She melted in the presence of pain, blanketing the afflicted with murmurs and caresses. Parker sometimes felt that he did not give her enough opportunity to express that side of herself. Like most men, he preferred to suffer in private—or at least he thought he did. Still, he had seen her in action many times and knew from experience her healing powers.

He turned back to the computer and continued typing:

> So, a new sibling. Ed's his name, and he and his mother sound like a real couple of wingnuts. Could be she's an interesting woman. Been all over, Dad says. And in the picture he showed me, she looks kind of pretty. But I can't believe he wants to marry her. Just picture it—the jazzer, the poet, the bastard son and the frazzled entrepreneur—one big happy family.

Parker had a long hot shower, another beer, and then sat in front of the television, flipping through the channels in robot mode. Ten minutes later he was ready for bed. When he slid under the duvet, he found a half sheet of computer paper lying on his pillow, her proper girlish penmanship.

> Hey, there, Babyface, out of town for a few days. Spur-of-the-moment decision. I'll explain later.
>
> —La Mer

He lay on his back beneath the duvet, his hands clasped

behind his head, remembering suddenly one of his last thoughts before leaving the previous day—a brief desire to share with Mersea a boisterous fuck—and he closed his eyes and thought about it again. Only now, in light of his father's startling revelations, and this curious little note, he felt not so energetic. He wanted not fireworks but comfort. He wanted to nuzzle and embrace, to lose himself in her gentle form.

"Mersea," he whispered, rolling onto his side and scrunching her pillow close to his body.

They first met in an empty room above a West Indian grocery store. It was late one winter evening, and the sounds of commerce and traffic had subsided. From the top of the stairway Parker could hear ducks and chickens squawking in their cages down on the street, a siren wailing somewhere in the distance. The smell of spices, overripe fruit and vegetables seeped into the air from down below and nearly masked the dusty taint of neglect.

He was twenty-two, and he and Derek Wilmer, ace reporters on the university paper, *The Vanguard,* had drunkenly decided to attend a special meeting of A Gauche, a Marxist group on campus that had heavy connections to activity in South Africa.

They entered the room and found seven men and a woman hunched over an old cafeteria table strewn with plastic coffee cups and loose papers. One by one the eight revolutionaries looked up without expression before returning to their discussion.

The leader of the group was Marek Svoboda, a tall, dark and sinuous man, a jungle vine. He wore wire-rimmed glasses and spoke with a high, rapid-fire delivery. He had everyone's undivided attention as he described the latest developments in Johannesburg, and the recent arrest of Robert Dobay, that country's latest but far from greatest Prester John.

Derek, who not only edited *The Vanguard* but was also the president of the Young Conservatives, greedily devoured the scene, contemplating his line of attack. Derek liked nothing better than trampling left-wing visionaries and bursting their balloons. Parker's own interest was captured by the tall, dark-haired woman beside Marek. She seemed the sort of woman Hollywood would cast for the role in a political drama—tall, bosomy, cover-girl beautiful, more starlet than socialist, more Rita Hayworth than Rosa Luxemburg.

After a few more minutes of political analysis, Marek turned once again and said, "Please, gentlemen, come in. Have a seat."

"It's okay," Derek replied. "We're just here observing."

Marek looked at each of his comrades in turn and then with a laugh said, "We are not animals in a zoo, Mr. Wilmer. If you wish to 'observe' us, it would be more civilized if you were to join us at the table as equals."

Derek moved away from the wall then and took several steps toward the table. Chubby, damp and almost frighteningly white, he looked a little like a small-town lawyer out of the Deep South. He was certainly the only student Parker knew who in 1973 wore a suit jacket to classes, who wore white shirts and a tie. And taking his reporter's notebook from an inside pocket, he waved it in the air and said, "Just a couple of questions then." He flashed Parker a sly grin and then tugged at his collar. "Unless I'm mistaken, you tried these same ideas in Prague, Svoboda, with your pal, Dubček. If I remember correctly they didn't work so well there. The Soviets kicked your butt. So what makes you think they'll work here where there's absolutely no support, present company excluded?"

Marek smiled wearily, like a patient father listening to a child talk nonsense. With a sniff, he said, "The Russians are thugs, Mr. Wilmer. Even you and I could probably agree on that. They are ideologues with corrupted notions. Lenin, Stalin, they have only partially to do with Marx."

Derek shrugged. "They embraced a half-baked idea and made it worse. Isn't that what socialism's all about?"

"Call it what you like. I myself think of it as differentiation. You take single-celled protozoa, and in time, after some failures, some successes, they become human beings. It is also known as progress. But perhaps that is something you have yet to encounter, Mr. Wilmer."

Throughout their sparring, Parker could not take his eyes off the woman. Mostly she kept her head averted, her long curls shrouding her face, but several times she looked his way, and he was shaken by the steadiness of her gaze. The gentle intelligence in her face made him ache.

The two men argued a bit more until it was evident that Derek was out of his league. His drunken one-note harangue had become tiresome, his comebacks increasingly petty and childish; and finally Parker grabbed his arm and began to back toward the door. That's when the woman stood and, looking straight at Parker, said, "You must come again, gentlemen, when you can stay longer."

He and Derek laughed all the way back to the office of *The Vanguard*, where they drank a mickey of Southern Comfort and knocked off a snide six-column report that elicited a short handwritten note from Svoboda, chiding the paper for its improper thinking.

In the weeks that followed, Parker discovered that the woman's name was Mersea Harrow, and that she had come to the University of Toronto from Winnipeg, where her father was a doctor and prominent member of the NDP. Parker thought about her constantly. In bed at night, he imagined her low, confident voice calling his name. When he saw her on campus he would stop and categorize her features; occasionally he would follow and take in the same lecture. Then one day out of the blue he phoned her. Could he come by? He wanted to sound her out on a political matter.

That night they made love. Over the next while they spent an occasional weekend together, orgies of caffeine and conversation, interspersed with art films and rock and roll. One day he bought a second toothbrush and left it at her flat. She did the same at his. They dropped clothing at each other's places, made accommodations, clarified concepts of what was common, what was private, what could be gained or lost in each other's company. Then, without taking notice, they quietly crossed a line and were more or less living together, though for some time each would have proclaimed otherwise.

One wintry morning, Parker had an epiphany. They had spent the night in his apartment—the mattress on the floor, the Led Zeppelin poster on the wall, the delivery trucks idling in the alley out back. He had just crawled out of bed and pulled on his jeans when he turned around to see her snuggled into the blankets; and without a second thought he fell back on the bed, his head resting on her hip, and he said, "It's the weirdest thing. I just realized I'm in love with you."

She was, too, she confessed. They skipped classes to celebrate. That afternoon they wandered over to

Kensington Market and bought their first roast, a tiny lump of beef that the butcher smilingly called a "honeymoon roast." They cooked it without the faintest idea what they were doing, more exotic adventure than dining experience. Cooking—who would have imagined such a thing?

A few months later, on a bench at the waterfront, the trees bursting into bloom, Parker took her hand and said, "Look, I was wrong. When I said I loved you, I didn't. Not really. But I do now. *This* is love. The other was, I don't know, infatuation."

And later that summer, curled into a sleeping bag at a folk festival. "No, sorry, *this* is love. Forget what I said before. This is the real thing."

On and on, up and up. A virtuous circle.

Next morning as he drove downtown to the office, Parker felt fired up and fidgety, needing to accomplish things after his unscheduled days in the country. He parked the Saab in his reserved spot, beside Dana's banged-up minivan, and took the stairs rather than wait for the shuddery old elevator. He had a hundred things to do. In the back of his mind, there was the nagging concern that Mersea still hadn't called.

The office, on Bathurst not far from the expressway, was a five-storey brick building that the company leased in the old garment district. Texpan had the top two floors, renting out the remaining space to a handful of smaller developers.

The company was coming up on its eighth anniversary and had been profitable almost from the start, the core of the business a modest bit of software called Cram-It that compressed mountains of data into manageable files for archiving. On its own, Cram-It was a cash cow, steady and reliable. Every upgrade sold better than the previous version; every year they hired more staff.

Three years ago, Dana, and their head programmer, Donald Chow, came up with another little package called WebCram that allowed small businesses designing their own home page to use all of the advantages of Cram-It. You could compress sound files, video files; you could attach huge documents to e-mail.

Parker had been nervous about that product. He hadn't fully trusted the Internet, felt they were taking on too much risk by basing their new initiative on its anarchic grid. Without defined standards, he'd wondered, without the guiding hand of tradition, how would anyone know how to conduct business? Nevertheless, sales had been solid but unspectacular so far, and that had had a calming effect on him—the kind of moderate progress he could appreciate.

Then last fall, Dana came to Parker with his next big idea. He paced the room, talking bandwidth and packet transmission and a hundred other terms Parker didn't understand. (Parker was a businessman, not a technician.) The gist of the plan was to build on the strengths of WebCram, but move into something totally next generation, something he called Inter/View.

"Think Web TV," Dana said, widening his eyes excitedly. "More or less. I mean, everyone's fixed on data transfer now. That's the holy grail, the missing link, the *sanctum sanctorum*. And Spark, I'm telling you, one of the keys to data transfer is data compression, which is our bread and butter. I already talked with Donald about this. He says eighteen months and we could have it on a plate. Not that we'd develop the whole idea or anything like that. I mean, Web television, Jesus Christ, this is megaproject stuff, bazillions of *díneros*. And trust me, the big players are already knee-deep in this thing. Microsoft bought a company called WebTV Networks last month for a cool half billion, so you know they're serious about this. But what we're after is the other guys, the competitors. Like don't forget the whole cable industry can't stand the sight of Gates, so there's plenty of room for the rest of us. And data compression, like I'm telling you, we're talking video files the size of Greenland. It's all in how fast and how smooth they can be compressed and expanded. I mean considering our niche, we'd be nuts not to go after a piece of it is what I'm thinking."

Parker loved watching Dana when he was like that—an ecstatic child, a wild-eyed evangelical. But he forced himself to ask the predictable questions: Would it work? How much would it cost them? Who would want it?

Dana was unflappable. "Who wouldn't want this? I mean, it's not the Internet on TV, or TV on the 'Net, it's a blend of the two on the same screen. So picture it—you're watching the game, the play stops, and you start surfing. Look up stats, maybe see some replays, chat with the cheerleaders, whatever. And this isn't just television. Gates already has a highway in Seattle wired with cameras. Night or day you can check any one of them for traffic flow. Before long that will all be computerized too. They'll be able to predict the best routes through the city at all times. This is absolute coolness, Spark. And the beauty is, the way Donny and I figure it, our fixed costs wouldn't change all that much to get this thing under way. We just shift focus a bit, hire one, maybe two more people. I mean, you get what I'm talking about, right? We're just piggybacking here. The big cost is someone else's worry—the hardware, the infrastructure. Will it work?" He laughed and shook his head. "Who fucking knows? Donny says it will, but we won't really know until we try. But if we do this right, even Microsoft might sit up and notice . . ."

At first, Parker found the idea tantalizing. It fit perfectly with his penchant for saving time, cutting out the dead air. But he wondered if perhaps this was too big a stretch for Texpan. They had done so well making incremental refinements within a knowable universe, and Dana was talking about a major leap into uncharted territory. Still, Parker promised Dana he would do some research of his own. He met with television executives who also told him that Web television would be revolutionary.

"Think of it," one network president told him, "the whole thing becomes a massive commercial. You're watching *Seinfeld*, you click on Jerry's shoes and find out what brand he's wearing. You snoop and see what's in his cupboards, what kind of toilet paper he uses. You like that bike of his on the wall? Here are the stores in your area that stock that model. It's the perfect union between fan worship and product placement."

Another network guy offered one of his smaller stations as a guinea pig should Texpan need a place to run some tests. Over the course of a few weeks, Parker spoke with futurists, demographers, investment bankers and venture capitalists. And the answer was always the same. "If you can do it," they said, "then do it." But even so Parker hesitated. The unanimity frightened him.

One weekend he took Dana out to the airport, where they locked themselves in a hotel room and didn't come out for forty-eight hours, pulling the plan apart a hundred different ways. Aside from his skepticism about the dependability of the Internet, Parker worried that, with so many other businesses converging on this one idea, a small company like theirs would get lost in the shuffle.

"But that's good news," Dana gushed. "The giants—Bell Labs, Microsoft—they're good at the big details, the platforms, the operating systems. We can't do it without them, and they'd eat us alive if we tried going head-to-head. Luckily we don't have to. It's small companies like ours that always come up with the final puzzle pieces, the creative bits. Right now everyone is stumped by two things: text is blurry, and fixed images tend to flutter on the screen. Don has an idea how to fix some of that. And if he's right, they'll all come crawling."

It was maybe two in the morning, they had polished off a carafe of rancid hotel coffee, and Parker looked him straight in the eye and said, "Tell me straight out, Dane. Any doubts? Is it really doable?"

"Of course it's doable. The big question is whether *we* can do it."

"And?"

Dana's voice was low, serious, bottom-line. "It's like every step has brought us to this point," he said. "In my mind, I really don't think we have a choice. If we don't get in on this, we might as well call it quits."

And that was the final statement Parker had needed to hear. He often joked around the office, calling Dana and Donald the evil twins, off in their world of secret codes and private language. But when it came right down to it, he had always trusted Dana. Dana believed in things. He followed his heart, made leaps of faith. It was what made their partnership so valuable. Dana's instincts perfectly complemented Parker's desire to put everything under a magnifying lens.

And now, for more than a year, the new project had been in development. The whole company had been working insane hours; a prototype was nearly ready. The first big splash would be in little more than a week in Las Vegas, a trade show called NEXT, the National Exposition of Technology, where they would officially announce the project and get people hyped. After that, they would spend another year testing and fine-tuning, and begin to firm up a strategic partnership with NeTube*E, Microsoft's main competitor in Web television . . .

Parker paused at the top of the stairs to remove his coat and catch his breath. Through the glass door of the office he saw a woman sitting at Debra Larkin's desk. Debra, who was normally at her post bright and early, was the office manager, the only member of the staff who was truly indispensable. He walked directly over to the stranger.

"You'll have to wait a sec," she said without looking up, continuing to rifle through the huge sack that sat beside her on the desk. "I was told Mac." She tapped the monitor of the Compaq computer in front of her. "Soon as I find my daybook I'll be on the horn to the dispatcher and give her hell. They'll send someone else over."

"Who are you?" Parker demanded. "Where's Debra?"

"Who?" The woman looked at him like he was some lunatic off the street.

"Debra," he said more forcefully. "You're sitting at her desk."

She shrugged wearily. "Not for long. Two shakes and I'm out of here. The gal you're looking for's in the hospital is what I heard. Smashed her foot with a bowling ball."

Parker stared at the woman, the skin caulked and powdered as a cadaver's, the short orange hair like some kind of bathing cap; and the longer he stared, the weaker he felt. Without another word he turned and moved toward his office, where he found Dana, pacing up and down with a hangdog look on his face.

"Guess you've heard about Debra," Parker said as he moved behind his desk to stare out the window at the roof of Dunkin' Daddy's.

Dana stopped pacing suddenly, and clasped his hands behind him. After he cleared his throat several times, he said, "We got a problem, Spark. Ever heard of Quasilogic?"

"A small software company in Boston, aren't they?"

"Yeah, very respected, got some kind of connection with MIT. They signed a co-development deal a year ago with one of the major telecoms, I forget which one, AT&T or McCoy Cellular, someone like that. It was for a shitload of money, in any case, major R&D budget——"

"And they've decided to pursue Web TV," Parker guessed.

"Yeah, well, I knew that part of it a long time ago. That was good news. That told me we had made the right choice."

Parker turned away from the window then and sat behind his desk. "And the bad news?"

Dana stared at the carpet between his feet. "They were pretty much on our wavelength. Data compression. From what we've heard, their software isn't as slick as ours. But they're a couple months ahead of us in development. And their package is a little faster, maybe."

Parker gripped the edge of his desk. He had to defuse this before Dana got frantic, so with a casual shrug, he said, "Being ahead is nothing. You know that. The world is full of companies that crossed the finish line second but still won the race. I've talked to these television guys, and they're only interested in a few things: Will it be easy? Will it cost them money to set up? Will it be profitable? And from what you've told me so far, I still think we're on the right track. Don't forget, these are businessmen we're talking about. They don't make leaps of faith; they take small steady steps. In Las Vegas we'll see whose project has the most appeal. We just need to stay focused."

Dana started to pace the room again, like a man working on a confession. After a couple of circuits, he stopped in his tracks and said, "What I think is . . . we should pull the plug and cut our losses."

This kind of abrupt about-face didn't surprise Parker. Dana had only two states—wide-eyed faith and slinking depression; and while the former state was his most endearing, Parker often wondered whether the latter was his most natural condition. Peel away the exuberant idealism and you found a scrawny, sallow-faced, twitching insomniac. Parker knew that, and also knew that Dana had pretty solid reasons to be so anxious. He had an unemployed wife, three dysfunctional children and an absolutely crippling mortgage. That was why he put so much of himself into these projects, wearing himself down in an effort to make his dreams a reality. And to his credit, more often than not his persistence carried the day. But once Dana started having doubts about an idea, even if it was a sound concept, he very quickly pulled it apart. On the other side of his faith gaped a dark sinking void.

Parker rearranged the objects on his desk—a Montblanc pen, a framed photograph of his parents, a yellow pad of Post-it notes. He cleared his throat and looked up at Dana's bleary eyes. "Seems a bit premature to quit now," he said. "My guess is that these television guys aren't going to jump to any conclusions just yet. We've got time."

Dana jammed his hands into his pockets. "What I'm trying to tell you is it's all over. NeTube*E bought Quasilogic on Friday while you were gone. We're out of the loop."

Parker took several deep breaths, thinking frantically. "Maybe you're overreacting," he said.

"No, I'm not. They don't even want the division of Quasilogic that worked on data compression. They're spinning that part of the company off, which means they don't see our approach as workable. And if they don't——"

Parker held up a hand. "There are other companies out there. You said so yourself. And maybe the folks at NeTube*E just don't like the solution Quasilogic came up with. Maybe the acquisition is about something else entirely. I mean, don't count us out yet, Dana. Once everyone sees that ours is the better product——"

Parker winced, the vision of Beta-format video rising before him, inescapable proof that the marketplace doesn't always beat a path to the better mousetrap. "All I'm trying to say," he continued more calmly, "is that I think you're jumping to conclusions here. We need to stay focused."

"You keep saying that!" Dana snapped. "You can focus all you like, it isn't going to change things." Then he walked out of the room, snorting his disbelief as if Parker had mentioned his fairy godmother.

Parker went for a walk to clear his head. A part of him couldn't believe what had happened, but another part had known all along that it might come to this, that at some point his life would come unraveled, a basic pessimism that could be traced all the way back to his early days of astronomy.

From his boyhood readings in Hoyle and Gamow he had learned there were two basic theories of the universe after the Big Bang. One view stated that the universe would expand forever, matter continually drifting outward until all gravitational force ceased to exist. The other theory held that matter would drift only so far until gravity drew everything back together again in preparation for another Big Bang, the universe forever expanding and contracting like God's bright balloon.

Of course everywhere he looked he saw evidence of things winding down to exhaustion. His own body was falling apart. His country was disintegrating. Old political and cultural arrangements had crumbled to dust. Earth's atmosphere was being gouged and torn by chemicals. So even if the universe did decide to reverse course, what difference would it make? Who would be around to notice? Who would care?

Feeling more miserable by the moment, he shuffled down the block, already regretting that he had left his coat at the office. The air reeked of diesel fumes from the nearby expressway. The wind off the lake was cold and damp; and after one circle of the block he gave up and headed back to the office, his suit jacket hunched up to his ears. On the way he stopped at Dunkin' Daddy's.

Laurel was up on tiptoes behind the counter, rearranging the doughnuts in their little wooden trays, and Parker sat on a stool, watching and waiting. Her slender frame was squeezed into a noxious orange-and-brown synthetic uniform that only seemed to accentuate the gentle curve of bosom, the hard mound of behind, the generous view of tanned leg. She had more jewelry, too, a small gold post piercing her left eyebrow. The very thought of it made him cringe.

"What'll it be?" she said when she finally turned around.

He wanted to say something clever, make her laugh, but he had never been especially quick on his feet. His best lines were always afterthoughts. And with her standing right in front of him, he was startled by her face, her flawless skin. Mersea would have killed for those cheeks—smooth and pure and radiant. Judging by their perfection, everything in Laurel's life agreed with her. There was no sign of a bad diet or lack of sleep. The ravages of alcohol and drugs, allergies and hormones, pollution and sun, had passed her by entirely. Her age had a lot to do with it. He'd be surprised if she was thirty.

"Black coffee," he said, relieved that his voice sounded normal, doubly relieved that he had refrained from saying anything stupid in a public place. "To go." As he watched her walk away, he fought off the urge to mentally undress her, focusing his attention on her hair instead.

If anyone had asked him, he would have said he disliked short hair, but he liked Laurel's hair. It suited her well, exposing her long graceful neck, the angles of her jaw and delicate ear. He found it nearly as compelling as her short skirt.

"Nice tie," she said as she handed his coffee across the counter.

He lifted the silk away from his body so he could look closer at it, little diamonds of red on a blue background. "What, this? It's just a tie."

She tipped her head to one side. "I like have this thing about ties," she confessed. "Don't mind me."

It wasn't her face or her voice or the attitude of her body, nor was it the unspoken words that lay behind this simple statement—it was the sum of her constituent elements that tingled every hair of his body, that colored his neck and cheeks and sent him out the door light-headed and jumpy. He stood on the sidewalk out front of his office for the longest while, waiting for his heart to still, throwing off little imaginary conversations like so many sparks.

The door of the building opened then and out stepped a woman with long black braids framing a small oval face. She wore black leather pants and cowboy boots. On top she had an oversize white sweater, her breasts jouncing freely inside. She held a heavy leather jacket and a motorcycle helmet. She looked vaguely European, not aggressive but frank, uninhibited.

She stepped forward and spoke his name. And in that moment he recognized her from the pictures his father had shown him at the cottage—the Marlene Dietrich cheekbones, the eyes without glasses a startling green, the delicate mouth like something out of Royal Doulton. Maybe it was the getup, but she didn't look a day over fifty.

"Parker," she repeated. "Olivia Collins. I was just looking for you."

His first impulse was to walk past her into the building and treat her like one of the many panhandlers he snubbed each day. But he hesitated, and she took his hand and pumped it vigorously. "I am so very pleased to meet you at last," she said, her voice low and musical. "We have much to talk about."

Her smile seemed genuine, and her eyes took him in greedily—the cut of his trousers, the shine of his shoes, the character in his face—like someone going through a checklist. Then she led him halfway down the block to the Greek Orthodox church, where they sat together on the steps.

"Impressive office you have there," she said, staring straight ahead of her.

He shrugged carelessly, though his mind was swimming. He had been swept out to deep water and wanted desperately to feel the bottom again, to know just where he stood. Weighing each word carefully, he said, "It pays to look successful, whether you are or not."

He could tell she didn't really believe that, but she smiled agreeably and said, "Your father is certainly proud of you. He says you're a genius."

"I'm nothing of the sort," he protested a bit too vehemently. "I'm just a businessman."

She grabbed his coffee and took a sip, leaving a bright red smear on the cup. "Don't worry, Parker, I didn't say I believed him. I'm just telling you what he said. It's one of those ruined words, anyway, lost to us now. Hockey players are geniuses these days, pastry chefs, even businessmen . . ."

She offered him the cup and he motioned for her to keep it. He said, "Listen, I already know why you're here. Dad told me he proposed."

"And how do you feel about that?" she said, smiling as if she had just remembered a precious moment.

Parker hated confrontations. He normally went to absurd lengths to avoid a scene. But with this woman he felt uncharacteristically bold. He said, "I feel that I've been deceived."

She laughed then, enjoying this little chat very much. Everything he said seemed to tickle her funny bone. "The way I look at it," she countered, her tone wry and confidential, "parents *should* deceive their children. Your husband's a brute and a cheat, but you create for the children an aura of togetherness. You lose your job, you're on the verge of losing your home, but as far as the children need to know, everything is fine. It's a cruel world out there, Parker. You know it and I know it, but the children don't need to know it."

"I'm forty-five," he said. "I haven't been a child for a long time."

She nodded. "There's such a thing as privacy, too. Call me a prude, but I don't think parents and children should discuss their sexual lives. I'd rather have my son lie to me than tell me the sordid details of his amours."

A streetcar stopped in front of them, depositing passengers and then rumbling on. He watched the knot of people untie itself and drift away. Everyone seemed so serious, so unhealthy. And he turned to her and in a distant voice said, "You're right, it's none of my business."

"If we get married it is." She placed her hand on his arm. "He'd want you to be involved."

Parker didn't like it when strangers touched him, and he looked down at her hand suspiciously. She had a ring on every finger, even her thumb. There was a small tattoo of an angel above her wrist, the hand itself delicate, with long slender fingers and perfectly cut nails, not the gnawed, gnarly stubs you might expect of a writer.

"What if I don't want to be involved?" he said

"Well, we all have choices to make. That, of course, is the reason I came all the way over here to see you. I still don't know what I'm going to say to him, and I guess I thought you might be able to help me—talk me out of it, or into it, or something . . ."

She got to her feet, and Parker stood and handed her the leather jacket she had been sitting on. "I thought this was all settled," he said.

"He asked, but I haven't answered."

As she turned to look at the traffic streaming by, Parker took the opportunity to inspect her from behind. The part in her hair had the precision of an architect's drawing. Her posture was perfect—not a soldier's rigidity, but a dancer's supple grace. Her shoulders were wide, her waist narrow, and her leather-clad bottom annoyingly provocative. He had to scold himself for ogling. He also had to fight down a feeling of appreciation. He didn't want to like this woman.

When she faced him again, she placed a hand on his shoulder. "I'm not saying we should be friends, Parker—you have every right to be suspicious—but I do think we should be friendly. That's why I think we should discuss this matter fully and frankly. We owe that to your father."

He backed away from her and shook his head, confused. "I really don't know what there is to discuss."

His voice sounded louder than he had planned, making passersby turn to look. She stooped to pick up her helmet. After buckling it in place and zipping up her jacket, she dug into her pocket and pulled out a card. "My address," she said. "Come for supper tonight. We could talk."

He stared at the card for a long time, the small neat letters as unnerving as the words in a dream—128 Augusta Avenue.

"Eight o'clock," she shouted.

When he looked up again she was already crossing the street. She dodged through traffic, then nimbly hopped astride her Harley and roared away.

Parker shuffled back to the office, feeling heavy and stupid. The strange woman had departed, and a small intense-looking man now sat at Debra's desk. He had a gray, pasty face, his neck raw with razor burn. His nose nearly touched the computer screen.

Parker knew he should go right over and deal with this, but he didn't have the strength or the will to confront the guy. Instead he walked straight through to his office and flopped into his chair, his stomach churning.

SIX

Bonds

Parker sat at his desk for the better part of the afternoon, but he didn't get any work done. It had something to do with seeing Olivia, he reasoned. He'd been rattled, and he needed to feel grounded again. He needed to feel that his past was at least partly as he remembered it. Consequently his mind kept drifting to thoughts of his parents, some of the black-and-white photos he was so fond of.

His father, born and raised in Toronto, was the only child of Chuck and Elsie Martingale, and spent the first seventeen years of his life in a three-bedroom apartment above their hardware store on Dupont Street. Parker had many pictures of the young Jack: stocking the shelves of the store, flexing his muscles at Sunnyside Pool, and on his twelfth birthday getting a Selmer saxophone. But the photo Parker liked the best, the one he had framed and hanging on his office wall, was a snapshot of Jack taken by his bride-to-be. He's crawling out of an old canvas tent on Hidden Lake. He's wearing a pair of rumpled khakis and nothing else. All muscles and tousled hair and pouty lips, he's staring at the photographer with a look of unmistakable longing.

There weren't nearly as many pictures of Parker's mother, but he cherished two. One was taken when she was about three years old, looking insufferably cute in a little gingham dress, feeding chickens on the farm with her mother and her brother, John. The other photograph, which commanded a prominent spot on his desk, was taken on her wedding day. She and Jack are in the back seat of a car. She has a white linen suit, some crazy Joan Crawford hairdo. They both look happier than anyone Parker had ever seen.

That was one thing he had to hand to his parents—they never made any secret of their love, even in front of him. Every morning his father would shuffle up to her like the Hunchback of Notre Dame, his voice gravelly and low, saying, "Ka-meer, ka-meer." And then he would fold her in his arms and smother her with kisses until she said, in a tone that was half giggle and half complaint, "Ja-aack, the breakfast!"

In Parker's memory, the two of them were always holding hands, always nuzzling and tickling. Sometimes their lovey-dovey routine made him squirm, but more often it made him feel secure. It gave him the warmest feeling to watch them playing Scrabble, or putting together jigsaw puzzles. Like Ozzie and Harriet, he thought, only more so.

In comparison, Parker and Mersea expressed themselves indirectly. Even though they had both come of age in a time of great openness, the sexual revolution and all, they seemed to have trouble communicating their feelings. It wasn't as if they had secrets or insecurities or permanent scars—not that he was aware of, anyway—yet for some reason they were not as open or revealing as his parents, who actually used to dance in the living room, cheek to cheek, who held each other when they watched TV, whose sex life, he assumed, was a natural extension of the simple tenderness they extended to each other throughout the day.

Parker and Mersea almost never touched, and when they did there was no gradual progress to sexual union. In the course of a normal day, sweet nothings remained unspoken, loving caresses were withheld. Instead they left clues. If Mersea had a bubble bath in the evening, it might just be that she felt tense; but if at bedtime she had a bubble bath and then used mouthwash, Parker knew for a fact that she had sex on her mind. His bathroom routine was equally revealing. If Mersea was in bed reading and heard the whine of his electric razor, she knew exactly what to expect. It seemed pathetic, now that he really thought about it. It made him wonder what they were lacking.

By five o'clock, he still hadn't accomplished anything, and he drove home to shower, shave and dress. Then he poured himself a small glass of single malt and fired up the computer. There was a message waiting for him in his mailbox. From Mersea. Eleven words.

> Poor Parker . . .
> I'm in Montreal. I'll be in touch.
>
> —La Mer

Immediately he thought back to that last morning together, her smile, her mood. And he felt a sudden heaviness in his heart at her leaving. For Montreal, no less. It was a routine that seemed all too familiar to him, and yet this time different and unsettling.

In an effort to shake off that dark cloud, he logged on to Galaxy's Web site to check out the daily results on his own portfolio. Down, naturally. He scanned a few of his favorite discussion groups, too. At Dow & Zen: Alternative Investment Strategies (www.dowzenmatter.com) he found an article called "Social Bonding," written by Marian the Contrarian.

> You know the drill: Why lend your money to a bank, when you can take that money and buy shares of the bank and get a higher return? Stocks are your way to "get in on the action."
>
> But hold the phone there, kiddies. That line of thinking leaves unquestioned the basic inequities of equities.
>
> Like the ginormous Teachers Pension Fund, flexing its muscle and forcing the management of companies it's invested in to downsize, rationalize, all those cheesy-assed euphemisms for fucking over the working stiff. It's their job, the fund managers say, to make corporate directors maximize shareholder value.
>
> Well, maximize this, fellas.
>
> You ask me, half the people with stock mutual funds, if they really stopped to think about it, would right now be seriously bummed at what their money is up to. How many teachers support the notion of slashing employment to goose their pensions? How many of the Woodstock generation understand that the companies they own are pouring arsenic into

> rivers and clear-cutting the forests and maximizing their value on the back of child labor in the Third World?
>
> And how many would feel the same enthusiasm as the manager of Galaxy International Equity Fund when he said recently: "We are terribly keen on La Gourmandise, a large retail food chain in France with excellent fundamentals. They utilize a very aggressive management strategy that, essentially, focuses on select neighborhoods and, with the benefit of advantageous pricing, squeezes out the mom-and-pop operations. Profit growth has been very steady year on year."
>
> Kinda makes you feel warm and fuzzy all over, don't it?
>
> The point is, folks, that maybe ownership isn't all it's cracked up to be. Maybe people ought to forget about the inequity of equities and think a little bit more seriously about bonds again. The word says it all, doesn't it? A bond, a connection, a covenant. Because I keep wondering: Where have all the flower people gone?

Parker printed up a copy of the article for Mersea. She'd get a kick out of it. He forwarded a copy to Beckwith, too, just to bug him. Then, feeling much better, he got up and walked down the block to pick up a bouquet of chrysanthemums. He stood outside his car, inspecting again the card Olivia had handed him, giving himself one last chance to avoid the whole scene. Then with a weary shrug he slid behind the wheel and headed downtown.

Augusta Avenue, one of the main streets of Kensington Market, was for certain types of people a prestigious address. Of course, the market had been through many changes, even during Parker's life in Toronto, waves of immigration repainting the neighborhood every decade or so.

When he first discovered Kensington, it was in the final stages of Jewish resettlement. United Bakers Dairy was still there, serving the best cheese blintzes in the city. There was kosher meat down the block, a couple of tailors. But mostly the Jews had fled to the nicer neighborhoods in the north of the city, leaving the market to the Italians, the Portuguese, the Chinese, who in turn had abandoned the area to East and West Indian grocers, Moroccans, Ethiopians, Somalis.

Walking those congested streets—made even more impassable by cages of live fowl, outdoor cafés, racks of wacky colorful clothing—one couldn't help but notice the smells that filled the air, that unforgettably dense perfume of diesel and fish and feather and spice. Many city people avoided Kensington for that very reason and shopped instead at the St. Lawrence Market, where many of the same products were available in a cleaner, more controlled and upscale environment.

The St. Lawrence catered to the wealthy condominium dwellers who lived nearby, who strolled in every Saturday with their little net bags, their Ralph Lauren sweaters draped over their shoulders. Those who drove filled the parking lots with pricey sedans and four-wheel-drives. Inside the buildings there was a festival atmosphere—buskers, foodstalls, children with balloons—everyone happy to be part of such a wholesome gathering. They had been to Kensington and been put off by the look of the place, the septic tang you might expect from some Third World bazaar.

By contrast, the shoppers at Kensington Market generally arrived by bus and bike and streetcar. For the most part they were recent immigrants. The white faces were very much of a type—fringe dwellers, the people who lived in the old run-down homes that surrounded the market, or wished they did. Many were students, but many more were artists and musicians, struggling to find, or doggedly avoiding, success. You saw people wearing South American clothing they had picked up while backpacking through Ecuador, or working in Chile. Everyone was happy to be there. They listened to the clamor, breathed in the smells, and thought it was life.

Parker left his car on Spadina near the El Mocambo, and walked the several blocks to Olivia's. He hadn't been to Kensington in a long time, but he knew it well. It was on Augusta that he had first met Mersea all those many years ago, huddling shoulder to shoulder with Marek and the rest of that crowd. He used to come back once a year or so, just to reminisce, buy some cheese from the same old guy on the corner, but then he just stopped. No reason he could think of, he just stopped coming.

Midway down the block he came to Olivia's place, a brick Victorian row house, the front yard a tangle of brown stems and vines with a narrow flagstone walkway to the porch. The porch itself was crumbling with dry rot, a couple of boards missing entirely. Off to one side of the door crouched a large terra-cotta bird—a quetzal, it looked like—inside it a pot of soil and a few dry wisps of flower and leaf. On the other side of the door was a big chunk of dolomite, one of the pieces he had helped his father lift into the Lincoln the day before.

Olivia greeted him like he was an old friend who had dropped by for a surprise visit. "Parker!" she exclaimed, offering both cheeks, which he dutifully pecked. "Come in, come in." She overreacted when he handed her the flowers, too, expressive as a mime.

Her enthusiasm put him off a bit. He had never liked the sense that he was being coddled or entertained. As a rule, the more someone insisted he make himself at home, the more uncomfortable he felt. That's one reason he seldom went out.

For years Mersea had tried to help him overcome that particular problem, running interference for him; but eventually she just gave up and went out by herself, which was maybe what he had wanted in the first place. He loved being home alone. And he loved later, lying under the duvet with Mersea perched on the edge of the bed and recounting the evening's events. More perceptive than Parker, she could also be deliciously catty in her assessments.

Olivia, who had exchanged her biker gear for a colorful skirt and blouse with a definite Central American vibe, led him into the kitchen and poured them each a glass of wine. "Any trouble finding the place?" she asked, slipping into an apron.

He shook his head and took a sip. "I know the market well. I lived just a few blocks from here when I was in university."

She smiled at him, sadly, he thought, and busied herself at the stove, sautéing garlic, onions and tomato. "Fish soup," she said. "I hope you like it." He assured her he would, then turned his attention to the apartment.

At one point the kitchen had been remodeled. The creaking hardwood floors had been sanded and urethaned, only now the finish had been worn off in the high-traffic areas around the stove and sink, giving the impression that Olivia was a whirling dervish in the kitchen. The original cupboards had been replaced by open shelves, which held mason jars filled with an array of beans and grains and spices. One of the walls had been taken back to the brick, the rest painted a forest green to match the countertop. Only the wood trim had resisted the upgrade, the ancient paint layered so thickly that it obliterated the natural contours of the wood and created a new landscape of globs and blisters.

She turned from the stove and said, "Take a look around if you like." And he did, drifting down the exaggerated slope of the building until he stood in the front room. She owned no furniture to speak of, only a desk, a few hardback chairs, a threadbare Persian carpet and a scattering of pillows on the floor. The walls were lined with makeshift bookshelves that spilled their contents onto the floor and every available surface. A small object here and there spoke of the extent of her travels—African pottery, Mexican silver, Irish tapestry. There was no sign of a stereo or television.

When he returned to the kitchen, she said, "Pretty Spartan, I'm afraid. I was a starving poet for so long that I guess I just got used to not having things."

"I like it," he lied. "Spacious."

She took a sip of wine and poured the rest of the glass into the soup pot. Then with a self-mocking sniff she said, "My son calls it 'The Abbey,' like it's some kind of religious retreat. He thinks I enjoy denying myself happiness. Maybe he's right."

She looked at him then, as if she wanted his opinion on the matter. He could have written an essay on self-denial, he figured. And the thought that they might be kindred spirits brightened his mood, though he was still not ready to talk to her on that level yet. Instead he said, "So, do you actually support yourself with your poetry?"

She poured several cups of stock into the pot and then added chunks of fish to the mixture. "It depends on how you draw the lines," she answered. "I make my living as a poet, certainly, but not from selling books of poetry. Oh, I sell some, more than most, I would guess. But I earn the bulk of my income from the university."

"So you teach."

"Not much, really. Mostly I'm just there. I don't actually understand it myself. I think it makes them feel better knowing they have me under their wing."

He smiled at her. She was a calm and pleasant woman, not the pretentious hysteric he had expected. He felt surprisingly comfortable around her. When she spoke he could hear laughter's melody.

"How long have you taught at the university?" he asked.

She pursed her lips and looked at the ceiling, counting down the years. "Nineteen . . . seventy-three?"

"My second year."

"Yes," she said, "I know. And should I tell you this? Why not. I used to see you. In fact, I'm almost ashamed to admit it, but whenever I had the chance, I spied on you."

He blinked incredulously, and Olivia nodded, unrepentant, and said, "Your half brother, well, let's just say I wasn't the greatest mother in the world. I'm sure your father filled you in on all my peccadilloes. Anyway, Eddy and I had a very . . . fractious relationship. And you seemed so perfect. I guess I thought by watching you I'd know if Eddy's flaws were my fault. Nature versus nurture, you know?"

Parker laughed, still uncertain whether she was pulling his leg. "You used to follow me?"

"Oh, it wasn't as bad as it sounds. If you were in the cafeteria, I sat close enough to watch, that's all. Is that sick?"

He looked into his wine glass and swirled the liquid around. "Maybe it's not sick," he said, "but it's weird."

She laughed then, and touched his arm. "You're a nice man, Parker. I think I like you."

The corresponding words gathered on the tip of his tongue—"You, too, Olivia"—but he couldn't get them out. It was a failing in him, this inability to speak from the heart, and he felt a twinge of sadness as Olivia turned away and concentrated on stirring the rest of the ingredients into the soup.

After a moment, she said, "Next time you should bring Mersea. I'm dying to meet her."

"Well," he replied without much enthusiasm, "she's away a lot on business . . ."

But it was like Olivia didn't hear. She stared at the soup, retrieving memories. "Really, you know, we may have already met, a long time ago. One of my former students at the university, Darryl McAllister, introduced us at a party somewhere. Do you know Darryl?"

Parker had always felt that the world was an extremely large place; but he shook his head as though he believed the opposite. "Darryl is one of our good friends," he said.

"Darryl," she continued, her tone softened by reflection, "was a very talented poet. But I'm afraid he was always a bit too ideological to bother with art. I imagine he's still like that, righting all the wrongs?"

"Well, he may have mellowed a bit over the years. Middle age does that."

She laughed, a melancholy sound reflective of time's flight. And Parker, hoping to switch the direction of the conversation, cleared his throat and said, "So, your son, Ed. Dad didn't tell me much about him. What does he do?"

She tilted her head to one side, then the other, then back again, and he had the impression of someone flipping through the pages of a book, looking for the right passage to read out loud. When she finally did speak, her tone was warm and full of memories.

"He's done a lot of different things," she said. "But I don't know that you could say he's ever had a job." She smiled ruefully. "A writer, I suppose."

"Poetry?"

"Oh, good Lord no. He has no patience for anything so frivolous. He writes essays, commentary. He tells me he's working on a philosophical novel, but I'll believe that when I see it. I would be surprised if he had the perseverance for so large an undertaking."

Parker was beginning to get this image of a cantankerous loser, some garret-haunting misfit who cranked out page after page of convoluted nonsense, political rants, conspiracy manifestos.

"Has he ever been published?"

"Oh, yes," she said proudly, pulling a loose strand of hair back behind her ear. "He's quite a regular in *The New York Review of Books*, I think it is. Their resident expert on things Germanic."

Parker blinked, suitably impressed. "Then he lives where, Berlin?"

"Berlin, Munich, Frankfurt, who knows? He's not what you'd call a homebody. He came back to Canada a few months ago, but I haven't seen him in weeks. Ever since your father proposed, I've been trying to reach him, you know, to ask a little advice? But that's not the easiest thing in the world to do. He seldom lives anywhere for more than a few days at a time, and the one or two people who know him haven't the faintest idea where he might be. Or at least that's what they tell me."

For the next few minutes Olivia whirled about the room, adding chopped fresh basil to the soup, slicing a baguette, setting the table and dressing a salad. "Sit," she said. "Let's eat."

Parker refilled both glasses, then held his aloft in a toast. "I never thought I'd say this," he said, "but I'm glad to meet you finally."

Olivia nodded soberly in understanding and touched her glass to his. "I felt so bad about Lake Tusco, you know. I was in such a mess, I just didn't realize. I'm sorry for that, Parker. Your father and I tried so hard to keep from hurting anyone. I really messed up that day."

He shrugged his forgiveness and then made an elaborate procedure of trying the soup, which tasted even better than it looked. When he said so, she smiled thinly, not really interested in his opinion of her cooking. Without shifting her gaze from his face, she said, "I feel so confused right now. Maybe, since I haven't been able to reach Eddy, I could ask your advice."

"You are desperate."

She put down her spoon and leaned forward. "Tell me," she said. "What do you think?"

Parker closed his eyes and took a deep breath. Looking up finally, he forced himself to mouth those painful words: "Do you love him?"

"Oh, love . . ." She leaned back in her chair as though the word itself tired her. "I suppose I do. I had his baby when I was twenty, and I guess I've loved him now for forty years. But at the same time—and this might sound odd—I've never wanted to live with him, or marry him."

Parker held out his hands as if that settled everything. "Easy then. Tell him no. Tell him you just want to be friends. What's wrong with that?"

She let her focus wander as different arguments danced through her mind. "The thing is," she said, slowly enunciating each word, "I can't shake the feeling that it's the right thing to do. Like maybe it's time for a change."

"Go on a vacation," he joked. "That way if you make a mistake it only lasts two weeks."

She sat up straighter then and looked at him. Her seriousness cut right through his reserve and touched something inside, making him squirm.

"A vacation's not what I need," she said. "Except for Eddy, I've been alone by choice all my life, needed the solitude for my work. But now, for the first time, I feel like I could use some adult companionship. I guess I'm afraid. I'm getting old, muggable, dotty. I just don't want to die by myself."

Parker understood that. He used to feel perfectly safe everywhere, but he was sometimes afraid now to walk alone at night in the city. Groups of teenagers made him uneasy, especially if they were rough-looking or different. His most common nightmare was of the *Straw Dogs* type, burly thugs breaking into the house and attacking Mersea while he looked on, doddering and helpless.

When he didn't respond to her explanation, Olivia frowned and said, "I guess that must sound selfish to you."

"Sounds pretty normal, really. But why my dad? I look at you, at your place, and I don't see how the two of you fit. I mean, he's a pretty conservative old guy in his way."

She smiled grudgingly. "He makes me laugh. And

he makes me feel important again. Part of something, you know?"

Parker understood that, too—the notion of how pleasant it can be to share even simple tasks with someone. By contrast, his life with Mersea had become pretty much a solitary affair. Because they were seldom home together, they had developed a complicated division of labor. And for all practical purposes, he had no friends to enlist in small projects. It was Darryl and Rudi he envied in that regard. Whenever he visited they were in the kitchen together making fish stock or jam or sweet pickles. Dana and his brother were like that, too, always busy and always together—canoe trips, framing a cottage, making beer. In retrospect, and perhaps too late for the important relationships in his life, Parker understood that a friendship needed a physical dimension in order to become deep and enduring. Not just sex, although that was an obvious choice, but the notion of doing something together, inhabiting the same space.

One of Parker's best friends from university, Chris Ford, moved to Australia after graduation. For twenty years they had kept in touch, writing letters, calling at Christmas. Yet those decades of friendship made for a very thin memory—nothing more than a few scribbles on a page, a disembodied voice echoing off a satellite. When Parker compared it to Darryl and Rudi bumping into each other in the kitchen, the air rich with the smell of bubbling peach jam, he ached with longing.

Other than Mersea, he realized, there was only one person with whom he had developed any kind of physical bond—his father. And as Parker sat there staring gloomily at his fish soup, he thought about helping his dad put the dock in the water each spring and take it out each fall. He thought about all the times they had sat with a couple of bottles of beer in the battered old Springbok, waiting for the pickerel to start biting. Or those autumn weekends the two of them cut wood up the hill and stacked it in the shed. And what about the times on the bus, hurtling through the darkness, when Parker would rest his head against his father's shoulder and listen to his soft crooning? Or those nights, too many to remember as separate events, when his father crept into the bedroom, saxophone in hand, and lulled Parker to sleep with a few tremulous melodies.

Suddenly, he realized that his father might be his best friend in the world. And what if his marrying Olivia changed all that? The man was over seventy. Surely he didn't have too much longer to live. What if she took him away, deprived Parker of his father's last few years?

He watched her toying with her soup. No question she was lovely. On that score alone he could understand why his father was attracted to her. And really, on some level, the two of them had been an item for decades. What difference could it possibly make now?

Olivia smiled gamely and said, "I know it must seem crazy, two old bats like us looking for love." Then, trying one more time to put her feelings into words, she shook her head and said, "Your father and I, maybe it's not exactly a match made in heaven, maybe we don't have a lot in common—but our feelings are genuine. We do have this bond that stretches over forty years. And don't get me wrong, neither of us regrets the decisions we've made. Jack and your mother were very happy together, I know. And Eddy's coming along was the best thing to ever happen to me. Oh, maybe I was a little hurt when your parents got married, but I got over it, I got more in touch with who I really was, what I really wanted out of life. And I realized I could live quite happily without ever again being smothered by a man."

Parker stared grimly at his bowl. "So what's different now?"

"We are," she said. "And what we want."

He shook his head dubiously. "I still don't get it," he said brusquely. "What interest could you have in him?"

She ran a hand through the tangles of her hair. "I've always liked your father. We have fun together. But mostly, I suppose, I'm interested in the fact that he's the father of my son. And, in those terms, I don't know, I'm thinking maybe it just might work out."

"*Ffff*," he said, like something with a sudden puncture. "You know what you sound like? Some goofy kid who has no idea what she's doing but hopes everything will all magically work out somehow."

She smiled sadly and said, "Aren't we all like that? Isn't that life in a nutshell?"

Parker slumped forward, feeling suddenly weary—of families, jobs, cities, everything—and that weariness made its way into his voice. "You're serious," he said, more accusation than statement. "You're going to marry him, aren't you?"

Beyond fatigue, there was something harsh in his voice just then, and she leaned back in her chair and folded her arms across her chest. "I might," she said stiffly. "I haven't decided. Would that ruin your life?"

He pondered her words—or rather he pretended to. Then he got to his feet, leaned forward on the table and said, "It wouldn't necessarily ruin my life. I just hope you don't ruin Dad's."

Ten minutes later Parker was slumped miserably in the

car, fiddling with the keys and watching people hurry out of the cold and into the El Mocambo. Half of the crowd paid a cover charge and headed upstairs where they would drink expensive beer and watch, on this night, Play Doh's Ideal, a popular local band. The other half of the crowd—the eager ones, the rowdy ones—remained downstairs in a room that was strictly no-name, no-cover, dance-till-you-drop, with bands that typically ranged from dreadful to promising, the lighting well past subdued, the air exhausted, the waitresses snappy with static.

For a long time, he sat and admired the neon palm trees, the thick-necked bouncers, the happy crowds of young people. Then on a whim, he slid out of the car again, thinking he would have a quick beer and try to get his head straight. He locked the door and just stood there facing north, letting the cold November wind remind him that he was Canadian, meant to be alone, that solitude and distance were his birthright. And when he opened his eyes again he felt stronger, more in control, as if the arctic air had stiffened his resolve.

He felt even better the moment he pushed past the bouncer and into the dingy darkness of the Elmo. And shrugging out of his jacket, he grabbed a table near the dance floor, ordered a pint of draft and leaned back to let his senses adjust to the smoke and the gloom. He often did his best thinking in places like this, alone inside a crowd. It wasn't long before his inner voice rose up to join him in conversation.

Dana's little scene at the office worried him, but there was nothing to be done about it now, he realized. They had nothing to lose and everything to gain by testing the waters in Las Vegas. And now that Parker had calmed down a bit, he saw that it was none of his business how his father spent his last days. Olivia, too, was no problem. A fringe dweller all her life, she seemed like a good woman who only wanted to avoid the prospect of dying alone. What bothered him, really, was Mersea's absence, and his growing conviction that they had drifted so far apart that they no longer had a relationship. That's why everything else had affected him so strongly, he realized. The foundation of his life had crumbled.

The clarity of this thought shocked him. He couldn't believe it had taken him so long to see it. They no longer saw the same movies, didn't read the same books and, apart from the news, didn't watch the same television programs. Their bedtimes were different, their interests were different—they even had separate bank accounts.

In the beginning, of course, their relationship had been marked by an almost excessive degree of delicacy and respect. He bought her flowers, expensive gifts for no reason, went well out of his way to please her. Now they were more practical. When Mersea worked late, Parker ate dinner without her. She understood that and, when the tables were reversed, did likewise. It was why they had a microwave, after all, that essential gadget of busy lives.

And perhaps the clearest example of how far apart they had drifted was their weekends. In Mersea's picture of a perfect Saturday, she rose late, grabbed a cup of coffee and read the paper until noon. Then she had a boiled egg on an English muffin, with juice and stewed plums. In the afternoon she'd putter around in the garden (without getting dirty), chat with the neighbors (without getting involved), squeezing in a bike ride if her thighs felt flabby. Then she'd shower, open a bottle of wine and make dinner. If they drank the whole bottle, she'd be in bed and asleep by nine-thirty.

Parker, on the other hand, liked to rise early. He ate the same breakfast he had every morning, then rode his ten-speed into the ravine near the house. He followed the bike trail all the way to the lake and back, about twenty kilometers round-trip. Every week he passed the same handful of cyclists, kindred spirits in Day-Glo fabrics who greeted one another with a nearly imperceptible flick of the fingers, as if they belonged to a secret brotherhood. He was usually home, showered and refortified with another jolt of caffeine before Mersea was even out of bed. Then he strolled down to Mangione's, the local grocer, bought the week's food and had it all delivered.

Other stores in the area had better prices, better selection, better everything, but Parker loved Mangione's, a real family operation—mom and dad, son, nephew, niece, son-in-law—all of them yacking and drinking espresso. Mike, the man who owned the place, was a smiling, gap-toothed Robert DeNiro who spoke only a little English.

"Pepper," Mike said whenever Parker picked up a green pepper and smelled it. "Swe-eeet." If Parker paused before the apples, Mike said, "Nice apple." When Parker stood by the bushel of green beans, Mike hefted a handful and said, "Green beans. Swe-eeet." It was almost as if he thought Parker had come from another planet, that he had to explain these earth objects.

Hardly a Saturday went by that the Mangiones didn't offer him a gift of some sort—an espresso, some pastry, a jar of homemade pesto. Mike's wife, Anna, worked the cash register and had made it her mission to talk Parker and Mersea into getting married and having kids. She'd show him photos of her grandchildren then swat his arm and say, "Mersea nice-a girl. Why you wait?"

And he would grin sheepishly and shrug his shoulders at Mike and the others, who would all laugh.

From Mangione's, Parker proceeded downtown on his weekly book binge—a nostalgic stroll that took him into six or seven used-book stores, a cappuccino bar near the university, past the trendy Queen West boutiques and into another café—then back in time to help Mersea finish preparations for dinner. Afterward, well fortified with beer, wine and a shot or two of brandy, he would sit up half the night fondling his purchases, studying all the blurbs of books he would never find time to read—about science and business management mostly, a few novels for Mersea.

Maybe their situation wasn't much different from that of most people of their generation, but it was nothing like his life with his parents when he was growing up. Every Sunday they had had to do something as a family. They sat in restaurants and listened to his father tease the waitresses. They visited relatives none of them really liked. They drove mile after mile along featureless country roads, listening to the CBC. And although Parker suffered visibly and volubly through those excursions, he had to admit now that they had given the family a sense of unity, created the kind of physical memories that his life as an adult sorely lacked.

On stage at the Elmo, several shadows moved about in the gloom, among them a tall spindly fellow with dreadlocks who stood behind a collection of percussion instruments. This was Parker's cue to leave. He hadn't been to the Elmo in years, but remembered only too well the caliber of musicianship traditionally on display: teenage garage bands at the pinnacle of their career; sour-faced pros filling in time until the next important gig; the last pathetic gasp of a former star, some bitter boozehound with more character in his face than in his heart.

Parker quickly finished his beer and lurched to his feet when the stage lights came on; then just as quickly, he dropped back into his chair. There, not fifteen feet away, stood Laurel and the rest of her band. She wore a black leotard, cutoff jeans and an oversize tweed jacket. A fine gold chain ran from her nose stud to her earrings; another identical chain connected the earrings with the gold post through her eyebrow. She was barefoot, dancing to the reggae groove her band had set up. At least he thought she was dancing. Without the music, it would have seemed like a two-year-old's temper tantrum, all fire and defiance.

The music was more surprising than good—reggae, but not quite. It was only when Laurel started singing that he realized they were playing a Beatles song, "Come Together." But then, not really. The chords weren't right or something, forcing Laurel to twist the melody and hurry the rhythm of the words well beyond what Lennon and McCartney had intended, the kind of music that made him furrow his brow.

Seeing her this way, though, unencumbered by her Dunkin' Daddy's uniform, filled Parker with an ache so deep and so bewildering that he wished suddenly he could talk to someone about it. But who? Parker would be too embarrassed to open up with Dana, and even if he did, the whole thing would feel crude. He certainly couldn't talk about this sort of thing with his father. Parker agreed with Olivia on that point—parents and children were better off pretending that sex didn't exist. So that left Mersea. But how could he openly discuss with her his lust for another woman?

That was a real problem with heterosexual couples, he thought. Back when he and Mersea used to do things together, one of their favorite activities was to wander about the city looking at houses and gardens, equally entertained by the display of taste and tastelessness their fellow citizens offered. They were also able, on occasion, to remark on the people they passed on the street. Mersea was always willing to point out another woman's perfect skin or figure. In turn he would direct her attention to men of classic proportion and appearance. But neither of them acknowledged anything more than an intellectual appreciation. It would have been unthinkable for Parker to suggest what a thrill it might be to caress a certain woman's body. And she never once even wondered out loud what it would be like to be held by a man with rippling muscles or a hairy chest. That as much as anything defined the gulf between them. There were some desires they would never share.

In contrast, over the years, he had many times watched Darryl and Rudi ogle the same young man. They would laugh and egg each other on, spinning together fantasies about what it might be like to bed this mutual object of desire. It seemed to Parker so mature, so highly evolved. And whenever they bantered in this way, whenever Darryl nudged Rudi forward and—in a tone that was both a taunt and a caress—told him to go chat up their stranger, Parker was struck dumb by their candor and their complexity.

That was what he wanted now. As much as he longed to hold Laurel in his arms, to count her ribs through the thin material of her leotard and explore her quirky charms, he also wanted to talk to someone about it. As it was, sitting there by himself, he had that sense of erotic loneliness one feels sitting alone on a beach and watching a sunset. He would have given anything to share that moment with someone who understood, someone who might be able to explain.

He ordered another beer and worked at memorizing her every move. There was no question she was an attractive woman, even though she didn't have the obvious glamour that Mersea possessed, the classic lines of great art. What she had instead was vitality, entertainment value. If Mersea was a Japanese watercolor, he figured Laurel was a Hollywood flick.

When the band finished the first set, she put on a pair of black Chinese slippers, stepped down from the stage and started in his direction, her face happy and carefree. Immediately he looked away, trying to calculate when her momentum would bring her in front of him. And sure enough, he turned back just as she passed his table. He felt his body adjust to her proximity—the flush, the heart flutter, the stomach knot. Even Dunkin' Daddy's had not prepared him for this degree of attraction.

When he looked once again in her direction, she was standing at the bar, laughing with a waitress who was fingering one of Laurel's chains—and he had to close his eyes, nearly sick with longing. Surely, he thought, he would not feel this way if he still loved Mersea, if they had even the semblance of a relationship. Surely the desire for one must cancel out the other.

When he opened his eyes again, Laurel had crossed the room and was standing at his table, her hands on the back of a chair. She was leaning toward him, and he could smell her lemony perfume. He could see the outline of nipples, ribs, collarbone, and he could feel the welcome stir below his belt.

"Hey," she said, her voice sounding deeper and huskier than he remembered it. "The tie man."

Parker crowed, as if he had just recognized her. "Dunkin' Daddy's! Hey, was that you up there? It sounded fantastic. Really."

She shrugged, twisting her face into a frown. "Maybe the next set will be better."

Before he could stop himself, he pointed at the side of her face. "Chains," he said. "Nice touch."

She tilted her head to one side so he could have a better look. Then she touched her nose, her ear and her eye and said, "A trinity, and a unity."

Parker nodded, though he had no idea what her point was. He wondered if he should offer her a drink. She seemed to be waiting for him to say or do something. He wondered if she actually found him attractive and was waiting for him to make a move. But then she smiled and said, "Well, see you." She passed through the crowd of dancers on the floor, across the stage and into the back area of the club where the dressing room was located.

He stayed for the next set, and the next, but didn't talk with her again. For the rest of the evening she was either in the dressing room or on stage. And despite her promise, the band seemed to play worse as the night wore on, a bewildering cacophony that made him wonder at times if they were even playing the same songs. But that scarcely mattered. His only interest was in watching her.

Her singing was more shout than croon, a high and surprising bark that ran all the words into nonsense. Her movements seemed to have no relation to the music. Her arms wheeled about. Her head swung in great dizzying circles. It was only by watching closely that he discovered she wasn't dancing to the music, she was riding on it like a surfer on a wave, trying desperately to keep her balance and not be swept away.

After the last set Parker summoned his courage and wandered to the rear of the club by the cigarette machine, the washrooms, the dark stairway that led down to the dressing room in the basement. He loitered there a moment, thinking he should say something to her before he left, tell her how much he had enjoyed her performance.

Next thing he knew a bony hand had settled on his shoulder, and Parker turned around to see the guitar player, a tall freckled guy with a wispy red beard and a camel mouth. Laurel had called him Badge when she introduced the band. He wore a pair of black jeans, a black gunslinger's vest and no shirt, which was unfortunate, because it allowed Parker to see the pimples on the guy's scrawny arms and chest.

"Nice music," Parker said, though in fact he thought the guitarist was the weakest member in the band. His amp had the nagging tone of small electrical gadgets.

Badge stared at him knowingly, and for a long while said nothing, working that mouth of his as if he was preparing to spit. Finally, enunciating each syllable clearly, in the tone of late-night epiphanies, he said, "This could be a mistake. I probably shouldn't be here."

Parker gave him the plastic smile he saved for believers, conspiracy buffs and subway mumblers. In return Badge widened his eyes and leaned in closer, his breath smelling of licorice. "After all," he said, shaking Parker by the shoulder, "I'd sure hate to fuck up. I have so much to lose. Maybe I should just get out of here."

Parker didn't have the faintest idea what the guy was talking about, and he was a little spooked by the physical proximity. When Badge didn't leave, Parker looked nervously around the club to see if there was anyone close enough to help out if things got any weirder. No luck there. The place was empty, save for a few stragglers over by the bar. In desperation, he tried on his least-threatening smile.

"Or maybe," Badge continued, the essence of stoned wisdom, chemical clarity, "maybe if I play dead he'll just leave me alone. Maybe he'll just go away."

Parker understood now that he was being ridiculed, and that only made him feel more frightened. He searched desperately for some way to brush this guy off. But just like that, Badge turned and walked slowly down the stairs to the dressing room, muttering to no one in particular, "Oh, man, he's going. Thank God he's finally going."

SEVEN

The Scream

Next morning Parker called his father and got no answer. On a hunch he phoned Olivia. "Dad there?" he asked sheepishly.

Her groan told him that he had wakened her. "No," she muttered, fumbling around for something. "I haven't seen him for a couple of days. What time is it anyway?"

"It's nine. Any idea where he might be?"

"Sorry. You're his son. You'd know more about him than I would."

Parker couldn't miss the edge in her voice. "Look, I apologize," he said. "I was a little out of line last night."

"Oh, well, at least we agree on one thing." Then she hung up.

Parker called the office next. Instead of Debra's bright capable-sounding voice, he heard a man's thick Central European accent. "Texpan. Vat can I do for you?" It was that same man he had seen the day before, the guy with the gray complexion and the cheap rumpled suit.

"Look," Parker said in his most commanding tone, "this is Parker Martingale——"

"Yes, good, so glad to talk vit you at last, Mr. Martingale. My name, if I may, is Victor Musil. I have been looking, you know, trying to understand a few things here and——"

"Listen," Parker blurted out, "I really don't have time right now. Any word from Debra?"

"Vell, sir, as far as I am able to understand, the woman of whom you are inquiring is not available. That of course is vhy the agency has sent me here. And I must tell you I am very pleaséd to have this opportunity, Mr. Martingale. I see already vhere I am of service . . ."

Parker groaned. "Victor, what about Dana Caldwell? Could you ring him?"

"Ve-ell," he replied in that annoyingly playful tone of someone who regards himself a wit, "I could as you say, 'ring him,' but vat kind of sound vould he make? And besides, Mr. Caldwell calléd not an hour ago to say he vas not coming in to the office. Also, I can tell you, a woman calléd but vould not leaf a message."

"What about NEXT?" Parker asked. "Any word from them yet?"

"I just am finishéd talking to a gentleman since not ten minutes ago. If I am to understand correctly, your boot—your booth—is reservéd."

"Did we get the location we asked for?"

"Vell," he said, "the man there felt very much that you vould be pleaséd. I wrote it down here so. A 'high-traffic area.'"

Parker was not a gambler, but more and more Las Vegas seemed like a crap shoot. All his life, things had pretty much gone his way. In Mersea he had found the woman of his dreams. He had always been able to find a job when he needed one, and for the past decade had looked forward to coming to the office each day. In fact there were times, on weekends mostly, feeling reflective and satisfied, a little drunk perhaps, that he considered himself the luckiest man on earth. But right now he was not feeling overly enthusiastic. Instead of the prime location he had requested, they had been downgraded to a "high-traffic area." The uncertainty gave him a headache. He wondered, not for the first time, if this new venture might possibly have the destructive power to poison the rest of his life.

"Okay," Parker said, feeling suddenly weary, "if Dana calls, tell him he can reach me at home. I won't be in today, either."

With that Parker went back to bed and hugged his pillow, thinking all the while about Laurel in her leotard. But then he felt so guilty, lusting after another woman in Mersea's bed, that he rolled onto his side and tried to conjure memories of happier times. They had their own Puerto Escondido, of course. They just didn't speak about it the way Darryl and Rudi did.

Parker and Mersea graduated from university in 1975 and drifted off in separate directions for a while. Mersea returned to Winnipeg and then accompanied her parents on a relief mission to Ghana, where her father had signed on to vaccinate children for polio. Parker, fed up with the routine of school and summer jobs, went off on his own to Guatemala, where he lived in a grass shack on the beach. The idea was to break out of the narrow little world he was used to; but he was so suspicious of the locals, and so annoyed by the North Americans and Europeans he saw, that he kept to himself and in the end merely exchanged his narrow world in Toronto for an even narrower one in Central America—without a doubt the loneliest experience of his life. Nevertheless, he stuck it out for three unhappy months and returned to Toronto with an acute sense of failure. He was clearly not Lord Jim material.

That autumn Parker and Mersea fell back together again as if nothing had intervened. She found work as a substitute teacher. Parker and Dana rounded up a few thousand dollars and put a down payment on a dilapidated house in the east end of the city. Together, with Dana's brother Sam, they renovated it and sold it for a profit. There was a real estate boom in Toronto at the time, easy pickings. So they tried another and another and had similar success. Parker thought maybe they were on to something, but Dana had other ideas.

In 1982, Mersea went back to school to work on her master's degree, and Parker and Dana invested ten thousand dollars each to start their own company, selling Osborne computers. Parker found it a wildly exciting time, life-altering, like being one of the wild-eyed disciples of Jesus shortly after the Resurrection. Everywhere he went he preached the power and the glory. But after three years of cash-flow problems and the enervating tribulations of cross-border commerce, they sold the company to their American supplier. To Parker's surprise and relief, they actually bagged a tidy profit.

That's when the idea came to him. Mersea had just graduated again; they were both suddenly free of commitments and had more cash than they had ever had before. They would celebrate Mersea's accomplishment and his windfall by scouting out possible schools for her PhD work. He bought his first car, a ten-year-old Cutlass Supreme, and two weeks later they headed out to the Maritimes with the idea they would dawdle their way westward.

First stop was Halifax, where they fell immediately into the tourist mode. They drove out to Peggy's Cove and the *Bluenose*. They lounged about near the Citadel, gorging on Popsicles and Doris Lessing. One gloriously sunny morning they went out on a lobster boat to look for whales and icebergs. Before they left town they even checked out the university; and though it was never seriously in the running (they assumed Mersea would most likely wind up in McGill or the University of Toronto), they went through the motions anyway, looking over the student housing, the local shopping, the pubs, the library.

They followed pretty much the same routine in Wolfville, its postcard beauty nearly enough to sway them. In the evenings they splurged on supper then strolled around the town, speculating on what Parker might possibly do with himself if they did opt for the rustic charm of Nova Scotia.

Little by little a mood was building. The days stretched out before them with a lazy sweetness, the weather sunny and warm. They lingered on park benches, sprawled beneath shade trees, cuddled in the moonlight like a couple of teenagers. They also talked increasingly of the future: maybe this, maybe that; if not now, then maybe someday. Gradually the outline of their life together took shape.

In Antigonish, the prospect of Mersea's doctorate faded entirely into the background. They stayed at an old white clapboard place that overlooked the water. It belonged to a former colonel in the British army, Mr. Davidson, a man with an enormous belly and bright red cheeks covered with spidery veins. He bought them drinks in the bar and got the kitchen staff to pack them picnic lunches. He drew elaborate maps of all the local hot spots. And every night Parker and Mersea took a blanket and a bottle of wine and, giggly with their own wickedness, headed out to the deserted end of the beach, where they made love until they were too exhausted to do much else.

But even against that stretch of dreamy splendor, the night of Mersea's birthday stood out in his mind as a magical experience. They ate lobster at the best restaurant in town, Vanocur's. While waiting for dessert, Parker gave Mersea her present, an expensive fountain pen and a journal.

"Ever since I've know you," he said awkwardly, "you've talked about maybe writing a novel and, well, what can I say, I think you should go for it. Or whatever you want to do."

Mersea got up from her chair and hugged him so hard she nearly sent them both tumbling backward. Then, as they lingered over coffee, she wrote the words "I Love You" on the palm of his hand, the feel of the nib making him squirm.

Afterward they drove out to the beach and walked to their special spot, towing their blanket with them. And there by the water, with the moonlight playing on her skin, with the warm sand beneath him, the ocean breeze around them, with her body pulling him into uncharted depths, his world crystallized into one brilliant impression. This was what they had been waiting for, the pure moment all lovers seek and move blindly toward, this one still point in time when the last veils of doubt are lifted.

They stared at each other without speaking, but he could hear the words clearly in his mind: *Will you marry me, Mersea?* Silently he tried them out, again and again, because there might never be a better time, never again be a moment when he felt more purely connected to her. But whenever he brought himself to the verge of saying those words, he stopped himself, wondering if an even more perfect moment would present itself shortly.

He caressed her moonlit body, memorizing her every hill and hollow, ran his hands through her hair with a witless fascination. He kissed her eyes and cheeks and ears, whispering her name again and again. Schooled enough in the pattern of their love, he wondered if this was once again merely preamble, that in the ever-rising spiral of their relationship a higher level awaited where those giddy words would be drawn out of him in a torrent. Yet they never were. Those words never got past the tip of his tongue. He never voiced what lay hidden in his heart that night. And as they rolled up their blanket and, arm in arm, made their way back to the hotel, he fought back the wave of sadness by telling himself that he would ask her next time. Maybe tomorrow. If not now, then maybe someday.

They left Antigonish and moved westward. They spent brilliant days in Quebec and Montreal, Ottawa and Kingston. That fall Mersea started her PhD in Toronto. Eight months later she met a man, a lawyer friend of her father's who was setting up a new mutual fund company, The Galaxy Group. He asked her to become their head of communications, and she accepted. She tucked her thesis into an old steamer trunk and never looked at it again, turning her talents to writing newsletters and marketing bumf for stock brokers and financial planners.

Parker dithered at first when they returned to

Toronto. Aside from sharing his life with Mersea, he didn't know what he wanted to do. But Dana had gone back to school taking postgraduate computer courses. There he met Donald Chow, a brilliant young programmer; and together they talked Parker into postgraduate work, an MBA. With Donald's know-how and their management skills, they would make a fortune developing software.

All along, Parker and Mersea assumed they would one day marry, if for no better reason than to have a great howling party. But they never did, and only fleetingly experienced again that purity of emotion they had felt in Antigonish. And whenever he thought about it now, he saw it as a lack of character in himself, an inability to make the leap of faith, to say yes, to go off half-cocked, to wander unafraid into the middle ground.

When Parker woke for the second time that day it was afternoon, and the phone was ringing. He bolted upright and snagged the receiver. The voice on the other end sounded hoarse and gravelly. "That Parker?"

"Yes"—he blinked repeatedly and tried to focus his thoughts—"my name is Parker."

"Eddy Collins. Buzzed your office and they said you weren't in, so I thought I'd try you at home. Thought maybe we could get together a few minutes and have a drink." The scratch of whiskers on the mouthpiece, the drag of a cigarette. "What do you say?"

Parker looked to the night table, suddenly understanding the need for a smoke. He checked the time once again. Two p.m. And the only thing that kept him from crumbling to bits was the feel of the receiver in his hand. The breathing on the other end of the line had spooked him like a voice from the grave.

"A drink," he managed to say, lacing his tone with polite enthusiasm. "I could use a drink." He laughed awkwardly then and added, "I don't know about you, but I'm still a little confused about all of this."

Ed laughed, too, more cough than merriment, and said, "I've got the use of a friend's place on Harbord. That near you?"

Parker didn't want this guy anywhere near his house. Quick and neutral, that's what was needed. "I don't mind coming downtown," he suggested. "We could meet somewhere. Anywhere you like."

"Tell you what would be cool then. There's a place at the end of the street, Varsity Bar and Grill. My old university hangout. But pick me up here, 180 Harbord, Room 3. If we meet in the bar, I'll be smashed before you arrive. This way at least we start on an even footing."

Parker agreed and then hung up the phone, amazed once again what an unsettling course the past few days had taken. NEXT was looming. A year of research and expense would go down the tubes if their program wasn't ready. And this Quasilogic development meant they really had to make their big splash now. So why wasn't he at work? Why wasn't his every thought focused on Las Vegas? Did he really want to let another opportunity slip through his fingers?

One-eighty Harbord was a rooming house, an old brownstone turned black with ancient grime. Beside the front door there were eight doorbells, eight mailboxes. The foyer smelled of cigarettes and fried onions. A strip of threadbare burgundy carpet ran from the door to the stairway and slightly muffled the creaks and groans of the old wood floor. The large radiator beside the landing held a stack of mail a foot thick, the words "Not Here" scribbled in the corner of each envelope.

The door to Room 3 was open, and revealed a man sitting on the floor and wearing nothing but a pair of faded blue boxer shorts. He had no hair to speak of, gulag-style, a five-o'clock shadow from the top of his head to the tip of his chin. His eyes were closed, and he was listening to opera—Parker didn't know which one. Something German. Sounded like a bunch of Nazis getting hysterical. The pale white scar of an appendectomy puckered the flesh of his belly. He was slouching against the bed and eating fruit-flavored yogurt with a white plastic spoon.

Right away Parker saw the family resemblance—the pug nose, the full lips, a predisposition to jowls that Parker had so far resisted and Eddy had given in to. Parker noticed, as well, how much larger Eddy was, two hundred and thirty pounds at least, his fingers, wrists, neck and ankles all mannish proportions while Parker, at one-eighty, regarded himself as still boyish in most respects.

When Parker cleared his throat, Eddy turned with a start. "Hey, Parker, what a kick. Good stuff, good stuff." He jumped to his feet and laughed at his partial nakedness. "Sorry about the reception. Wagner makes me gap out." Then he licked yogurt from his fingers and offered his hand. "Pleased to meet you, brother."

Turning away then, Eddy pulled on jeans and a wrinkled T-shirt, ran his fingers across the stubble on his head and tossed the rest of his yogurt in a garbage pail in the corner. Parker wondered if he should remind him how terrible that would smell in a few hours, but decided against it. He seemed like the kind of guy who wouldn't notice such things.

Finally Eddy pulled on a pair of biker boots and a battered old leather jacket, then grabbed a big, black mailman's bag bulging with books and papers of every description, and ushered Parker from the room and down the stairs. They walked in silence for a few minutes, the only sound coming from Eddy—the shuffle of his boot heels, the rustle and groan as he hefted his bag from one shoulder to the other. As they neared Bloor Street, Eddy pointed to the tall building on the southeast corner, a former university residence and drug-culture landmark. "My old home," he said affectionately.

Parker made suitable noises of respect, as if he was talking with a veteran of the Great War. "You lived in Rochdale?"

"Nineteen seventy-two. Stoned every day for eight months. In one week I made more money selling drugs than my professors made in a year." He looked at Parker then, and in a surprisingly wistful tone added, "Possibly the best year of my life . . ."

Whenever Parker met someone for the first time, he experienced a momentary panic. A matter of chemistry, he figured, a heightened perception brought on by the adrenaline rush of the encounter—time, place, personality and circumstance swarming in his face like bees. When introduced to people, the droning in his head generally prevented him from hearing names. Specific instructions drifted past him irretrievable as smoke. So it wasn't until they were seated in a booth at the Varsity that Parker calmed down enough to realize that Eddy was not at all what he had expected.

The son of a poet, a published author himself (in *The New York Review of Books*, no less, a paper that Parker had found too serious even when he was a student), an authority on Germany, a world traveler—Parker had imagined a refined European sensibility, someone you might see interviewed on the CBC. Instead the man across the table was a rumpled, slouching, unshaven, bleary-eyed former drug dealer, with a personal style that leaned more to Harley Davidson than iambic pentameter. Parker's confidence shot up accordingly.

They ordered a pitcher of draft beer (Eddy's preference) and Eddy immediately lit a Davidoff. "So," he said, squinting at Parker through the smoke, "pretty fucking weird."

Parker raised his glass to that notion and took a long drink. He could tell right away that Eddy was a poser. The way he smoked (expensive imports, no less), the way he slumped in the corner, the studied grubbiness—here was a man who worked hard to maintain his outsider status. Parker knew the type well enough: urban ascetic, eccentric priorities, scrounging a bare-bones existence from the city while focusing on his "world of ideas," the very kind of lifestyle that had lured other generations to Paris but now could be found almost anywhere.

Trying not to judge too harshly, Parker leaned back in the booth and said, "I saw your mother last night. She's been trying to reach you."

Eddy made a sour face. "Yeah, well, that's what mothers do, isn't it? Little grasping monsters."

Parker smiled weakly and nodded agreement, though he did not at all agree. His own mother had been very conscious of letting him have his freedom. Cutting the apron strings, she would have said. And Mersea's mother, a deeply religious woman, was too consumed with God's work to give them much thought at all. The less she knew about Parker and Mersea, the better she seemed to like it. Not that she was neglectful. She simply wasn't interested in being a friend. Her idea of a close family relationship was a visit once a year and a Hallmark card on all the appropriate occasions.

Parker stared into his beer like a chemist and said, "Sounds like your mother could use your advice. She seems a little confused right now."

Eddy found this funny. Rubbing his lower lip with his thumb, he said, "Confusion is her natural state. All her life she has mistaken chaos for poetry. I know this from experience. She's not the easiest person to live with, believe me." He swallowed his entire glass of beer in a gulp and then poured himself another, staring at Parker as if trying to figure out how much he might be worth. "Rumor has it," he said, "that you're a computer wizard."

Parker shrugged. "I'm a businessman. My employees are the ones who make the magic. I just try to sell it."

Eddy nodded with satisfaction, almost relief, as if he'd been struggling with the notion of Parker as a genius. The fact that he was merely a salesman made more sense. "So what are you selling," he asked, "some razzle-dazzle software?"

"Nothing too fancy, really. Our latest project is data compression for Web TV."

"Oh, please, not one of Satan's minions . . ."

Parker couldn't help but smirk. He could so clearly see Edvard pecking out a cracked manifesto on an old Smith Corona. Shaking his head in mock sorrow, he said, "I guess I shouldn't be surprised that you're a Luddite."

Ed pushed aside his beer glass and leaned forward. "It's not technology I'm against," he said. "I've used the Web. Had my own computer, too, until it died on me. It's television that's evil. Like we need people to stay locked in their cages a bit more. Like we need a few more clueless assholes out there. Read Ivan Illich. We've traded health for medical care. We've traded wisdom for diplomas. We've traded society for television. We don't act anymore, we consume—and you and your Web TV are only going to make it worse. Which means forget any hope we might have for the return of public life and activist politics. That's out the window, right? Instead we get government as consumer goods. No surprise there, though. A fragmented and stupefied electorate is easily bamboozled. No center of opposition. Just roll out the global economy."

Parker noted happily that Eddy's arguments were as disheveled as his appearance, the wooly gobbledygook of the few social science courses he had been forced to take in university. Warming to the occasion, he said, "I'd have to disagree with you, Ed. I think television is one of the greatest political tools democracy has produced."

It was Eddy's turn to smirk. "Really? Apart from the Watergate hearings, I don't know what in hell you could be talking about."

"I don't mean content, I mean context. A simple fact of human nature: when you're standing in a crowd, you're more likely to respond like the crowd. It's basic Albert Speer: lights and crowds and symbols. Look at rock concerts versus records, movie theaters versus videos—you want an experience to be moving, you bunch people together."

"Yes, go on," Eddy said. "Move me, Parker. I'm all ears."

"Well, it's pretty clear, isn't it? When people are home, they're more difficult to manipulate. There's too much that's familiar—the wife, the kids, the uncomfortable furniture, the smelly dog, all the details of their sorry life. It keeps them from being . . . 'bamboozled.' I mean forget the Americans and their right to bear arms—if you want my opinion, an educated, media-savvy Canadian with his modem and TV and satellite dish is the quintessential freedom agent."

"Oh, right, sounds lovely," he said. "A nation of rec-room hermits. A bunch of monks worshipping their goods . . ."

Parker sat back, blushing and breathless, afraid suddenly that he had spoken too freely, revealed too much of himself. He hadn't talked to a stranger like that since university. With a self-mocking laugh, he said, "I suppose I shouldn't be surprised you're not much into TV. Your mother told me you write for *The New York Review of Books*. So what's it like to live in Germany?"

Eddy looked off into the shadows, gathering his thoughts. Then he leaned both elbows on the table, a droll look on his face. "First thing you notice," he said, "is that Germans eat a ton of pig meat. Wonderful stuff, you've never tasted anything like it. But don't tell me it isn't anti-Semitism. You can't go anywhere in Germany without smelling pork fat. It hangs in a cloud over every beer garden. A subtle but unmistakable message, you ask me."

He waited for a reaction, and seemed pleased with himself when Parker smiled. He settled back in the corner of the booth then, one foot up on the bench seat, his knee nearly tucked under his chin. He gazed across the room, picking tobacco from his tongue. After a long silence he said, "Everything's in flux right now, but before unification, West Germany was a great country. And Berlin, Jesus, what a wicked little town. Right out on the edge. But now that Kohl has them all believing in a future, the fun's gone out of Berlin. Now it's just another boring European city, fallen under the sway of the new religion stalking the land."

"Unification, you mean."

Eddy snorted unhappily. "Common currency, common market, the Sudetenland—it's all mergers and acquisitions. You just need to look at the highest building in any city to figure out what's really going on. There, *über alles*, where everyone can see it, is the religious icon of postwar Germany, a gigantic chrome replica of the Mercedes-Benz hood ornament."

Parker shook his head. "I don't follow you."

"This was the country that gave us Schiller, Nietzsche, Goethe, Bach, Beethoven. But since the war they've switched their focus from the big picture to small but durable goods. Look in any shop window, on any German street, and you see ordinary objects raised to a level of perfection. These days it's a country of beautiful things, not beautiful ideas. You can't blame them, I guess, since their ideas always got them into trouble. But it seems to me they've swung too far the other way. It's as boring now as Switzerland."

Eddy darted Parker a critical look just then, sizing him up. When he was satisfied that Parker was taking him seriously, he smiled and said, "The political agenda is one thing, of course; but with the Wall down, your average West German is suddenly confronted with an awkward situation. Everything was so comfortable before, and now they find, horror of horrors, that they have this poor relation knocking on their door, asking for things, wanting to be family."

Parker jerked to attention. He couldn't miss the implications of what had just been said. And although he couldn't tell by looking if Eddy had intended such a comparison, the threadbare T-shirt, the grizzled appearance, the dumpy rooming house he was staying in, shouted loud and clear just which side of the Wall he would place himself on.

Parker cleared his throat and smiled awkwardly. "So, anyway," he said, "this is great seeing you and all. How long do you think you'll be staying in Toronto?"

Eddy pinched his lips between thumb and forefinger, his eyes sparking with mischief. "Well," he said, "that's hard to say. If Olivia and Jack actually decide to get hitched, I might stick around for that. It's not as if I have any other pressing business."

"But what about your writing?" Parker asked, hoping he didn't sound as miserable as he felt.

Eddy tasted the air. "It's all getting very stale," he said. "I've decided to part company with *The Review*. Too much writing for too little money. I thought I'd maybe try my hand at porno. That'd be a hoot, wouldn't it? Sitting around all day with your laptop and your boner . . ."

His laugh was loose and liquid and soon lapsed into a fit of coughing. When he had everything under control again he sat up, elbows on the table, and said, "I like you, Parker. You seem all right. You play music like the old man?"

"No, I'm afraid not. What about you?"

Eddy took another gulp of beer, nearly choking. "Trumpet," he said. "A friend owns this jazz club in Munich. I used to hang out there a lot, jamming. One night I blew with Oscar Peterson."

Parker closed his eyes, reminded suddenly of a night just after he and Mersea had moved in together. They were visiting his parents, and Mersea sat down at the piano in the living room and started a boogie-woogie groove, very Royal Conservatory, but good enough for his father to grab his horn and play along for a few bars.

Mersea was way out of her depth, biting her lip in concentration; and his father's face filled with yearning, as if by staring at her he could coax her into playing just a little better. In the end, trying to squeeze far too much importance into every note, even he started playing like an amateur. When the tune fell apart in a clattering discord, he laughed at the ceiling and said, "Fantastic. Jesus, that was great." Then he draped his arm across her shoulders and, in the tone of all good-natured ribbing, announced: "The son I never had."

Now, sitting there in the smoke and the gloom of the Varsity Bar and Grill, Parker suddenly wished he was more like his father. More than that, he was jealous, wondering for the second time in as many days if he might lose him to a stranger.

When Eddy lifted the pitcher, Parker covered his glass with his hand. He had never been able to drink in the afternoon, not even as a student. Eddy shrugged and poured himself the rest, drinking half of it in one mouthful. He stifled a burp then, his lips puffed out like Dizzy Gillespie.

"So, Parker," he said, drumming his fingers on the tabletop, "what do you make of all this? Is it the worst thing to ever happen to you or what?"

Parker looked across the room to two old guys who sat by the window. They had craggy, sunken faces and slicked-back hair and the kind of thick plaid overshirts you saw at construction sites. A cloud of financial woe hovered above their hunched figures.

Finally he turned back to Eddy, and in the most casual tone he could muster, he said, "Not the worst thing, really. The strangest, maybe."

Eddy smiled broadly. He was one of those people

who nurture their eccentricities, who go out of their way to upset the given perception of them. Dana was like that, too. As soon as he knew you had him pegged a certain way, he shot off in another direction just to spite you. If you thought he was kind, he'd treat you like dirt; if you thought he was selfish, he'd buy you a present; if you thought he was bright, he'd prove you utterly wrong; and just when you thought he was the dumbest person on the planet, he'd knock your socks off with a brilliant idea. The best strategy, Parker found, was to always think the worst of Dana.

Parker finished his last drop of beer and said, "What about you? I imagine all this family business must be a rude shock."

"Matter of fact," Eddy said, "I think it's pretty cool. All my life it's just been me and the old lady. And while I guess I can't bitch too much about her, being the only light in someone's life can get pretty old. You don't know how lucky you are to have had two parents around. All those times when your folks were so busy with each other that they didn't give a shit about you. I'm forty-five years old. Most of my adult life I've lived half a world away from the old girl, and I've still never experienced that. I'm all she has, and that fact haunts me every fucking day."

"Still," Parker suggested, "you must be very close."

"Like Siamese twins," he grumbled. "You've got no idea how many times I've wanted to strangle her. Believe me, nothing could please me more than if she married Jack."

Parker was tempted to mention his own feelings of uncertainty, his fear that he might lose his connection with his father. But he wasn't ready to speak that kind of truth just yet. He and Eddy were nothing more than strangers. Instead he looked him squarely in the eyes and said, "They seem so incompatible to me. I don't see how it could work out. I mean, aside from you, what have they got in common?"

A sly grin eased into place. "You're worried, aren't you, Parker? You'd like me to talk her out of it."

"It's none of my business," he protested a bit too quickly.

"Have you seen them together?"

"Once, a long time ago. I was twelve."

Eddy nodded, his look thoughtful, like a judge weighing evidence. "You should see them now," he said. "I was with them a couple of weeks ago up at your cottage. I mean, granted, it's always gruesome watching old bags get lovey-dovey, but aside from that it seems on the level. Maybe we should try a foursome."

Parker felt as if he'd been punched in the stomach. The thought of those three on Hidden Lake, on sacred land, took his breath away. He gripped the edge of the table and searched the Formica pattern for strength. "Well," he said, his voice thin and compressed, "this week I'm very busy. I have this trade show coming up . . ."

Eddy shrugged carelessly and rose to his feet. "No big deal," he said. Then he rummaged through one of the pockets of his bag and pulled out a dog-eared business card:

> E.M. Collins
> 2008 Leopoldstrasse
> Tel: 011-4989-9101270
> Munich, GDR

Ed scribbled down a local number and the address on Harbord, then handed it to Parker and said, "Whatever you do, don't let on to Olivia that you know where I am. I like to see her on my terms."

Parker stared at the card like it was some newfangled gadget he couldn't quite make sense of. "E.M.," he said. "As in Forster?"

Eddy rolled his eyes. "Try Munch. After thirty-six hours of labor, Olivia said the only thing she could think about was *The Scream*."

"Ed-vard," Parker said, testing the word to see how it felt on his tongue.

And Eddy leaned right over him, enveloping him with his warm, ripe smell. "You can call me Eddy," he said. "In fact I insist."

EIGHT

The Dark and the Glory

Parker drove home through rush-hour traffic, his head throbbing from the single glass of draft beer he had foolishly accepted. His stomach was in a knot, too; so after a long hot shower, he prepared his favorite comfort food—cream of tomato soup with saltines crumbled into it, something his mother used to make whenever he was sick. After he had left home for university he had nursed himself through many a crisis with that particular combination. The soup had to be Heinz, and it had to be scalding, and it had to be made just right—that is, slowly mixing in the milk. His mother had shown him that the soup would be lumpy if you dumped in a whole can of cold liquid at one time. Dribble and stir was the key, dribble and stir. With those instructions in mind, one could make a surprisingly rewarding meal.

The moment he sat down to eat, though, the doorbell rang. He had already changed into his pajamas and robe, and he loathed being disturbed at mealtimes, so if it had been a single chime or even two rings of the bell, he would have ignored whoever it was. But this was an entire rhythmic phrase—shave and a haircut, two bits—and Parker knew immediately that it was his father. It was the way he rang every doorbell, knocked on every door. A few years ago, he had even had an elaborate gizmo installed in his car so the horn played that very melody.

Parker rose slowly to let his father in, ready to yell at him for disappearing the past few days. But the moment he opened the door his anger gave way to bewilderment. "Dad," he said, "what the hell . . ."

"You like it?" he said, striding into the middle of the living room and turning in a circle like a fashion model. He wore a pair of tight black leather pants, a leather jacket and a white T-shirt. His tufts of red hair had been shaved off. He was completely bald and holding a motorcycle helmet.

After the initial shock had passed, Parker felt embarrassed. He couldn't even look at him, a seventy-five-year-old man tricked out like Marlon Brando in *The Wild One*. So he closed the door, turned soundlessly and walked back to the kitchen. He sat at the table and took several spoonfuls of soup while his father watched from the living room.

"You don't like it," Jack said coolly.

Parker paused, the spoon halfway to his mouth. Without looking up, he said, "On a teenager, maybe. On you it looks pathetic."

His father moved to the table and popped a cracker in his mouth. He stood there chewing slowly, thinking. After he had swallowed the saltine and used his tongue to clear out all the crumbs and soggy bits from his partial bridge, he patted Parker on the shoulder and said, "You always were a tight-ass."

Parker flinched, and knew he should just ignore this, but he couldn't. He turned and said, "You see, that's something I don't get. Why is it that showing self-control is a bad thing? Dana's the same way. You appreciate control in music, in art, in dance, in sports—why is it so bad to be in control in your life? That's what I don't understand."

His father opened the refrigerator, rooted around a moment and then closed it. He opened a few cupboards and then closed them. Finally he said, "I've got nothing against control, son. It's being a sourpuss that I don't get, a tight-ass."

Parker concentrated on his soup, holding in his anger. He was tempted suddenly to tell his father about Laurel, if only to make it clear he wasn't as straight and predictable as supposed. But Parker had always been one to hold on to secrets. He liked it when neighbors, after several years of acquaintance, finally discovered that Parker's company made some of the software on their computer, or that they owned one of Mersea's mutual funds. When the details of his life were discovered rather than displayed, it made him feel important, powerful.

When his bowl was nearly empty, Parker wiped his lips with his napkin and, in a careful, weightless tone, said, "I met Eddy this afternoon." He frowned once again at his father's costume. "He seems like your kind of guy."

If his father noticed the sudden edge in Parker's voice, he didn't show it. Instead, the very model of patience and wisdom, he sat at the table and said, "You're mad at me, that's what it is. You think I'm being disrespectful to your mother."

"Who said anything was wrong?"

His father laughed knowingly. "I can look at your face and see that something is wrong. Whenever you're pissed off at me your lips disappear. Did you know that?"

"Very scientific."

"You want to know something else?" he asked, inordinately proud of his little display of insight. "Something has been bothering you for a while now. You've gnawed the skin off the sides of your thumbs."

Parker hid his hands under the table then and smiled icily. "A regular Sherlock Holmes. Or would that be Sam Spade?"

"Is it me?" he asked again. "Is it my fault? There's no reason the wedding has to be right away if you're gonna get bent out of shape about it."

"No," Parker said, refusing to get riled, "there's nothing wrong, I tell you."

"Is it Mersea, then?" His father raised an eyebrow.

"Why do you say that?"

"Because you have the look of a man who needs a shoulder to cry on."

Parker bristled. "Get out of here with this bullshit psychology. Don't think that fooling around with your poet suddenly makes you an expert on relationships. Spare me that, okay? It's bad enough just having to look at you this way." He waved at the leather gear.

His father chuckled, soft and superior, his face displaying the calm radiance of a guru. Everything about him proclaimed that he was truly happy and, because of that, above petty insults.

Parker placed his spoon on the table with exaggerated care. It was unlike him to discuss his failures; and that's how he felt about his relationship with Mersea—

that he had failed somehow, that he was a loser. It was even less likely that he could be open about such a thing with his father, especially when the man was acting so righteous.

Jack poked him and said, "What's really eating you? I'd like to know."

Parker took a deep calming breath. Then, trying to ape his father's beatific pose, he moved back on the offensive. "Eating me? Don't you think I've got reason to be upset? A little worried, maybe? I mean forget Olivia for the moment. Forget *Ed-vard*. Look at you, you're seventy-five years old and you look like a juvenile delinquent. You're embarrassing yourself."

His father shrugged. "You're the only one who seems to be embarrassed."

Parker gritted his teeth in an effort to hold in his temper. He got up and walked to the sink with his bowl, then returned to the table, bending down to look directly into his father's face. "Did you actually buy a motorcycle?"

Nodding excitedly. "A Norton. Wait'll you see it."

It suddenly occurred to Parker that maybe his father had suffered a nervous breakdown. "Tell me," he said, "does that not seem strange to you, even a little?"

"Strange, sure. And exciting, and fun. You should try it." Then he kissed the air and ran his hand across his bald dome. "Anyway," he said, "I didn't come down here just to show you my new duds. I've got something I need to discuss with you, if you've got a minute."

Parker looked at his watch, more for the comfort it gave him than any real concern about the hour. Then he plopped into the chair, all passive and loose-limbed. "Shoot," he said.

"The long and the short of it is Olivia said yes. I talked to my lawyer about this whole wedding deal, and he says I need a marriage contract. Olivia feels the same way."

"Happens all the time, Dad."

Jack fiddled with the strap of his helmet, thinking out loud. "Help me out here, Park, and tell me if I'm wrong. My lawyer says that this late in the day we should each keep what's ours and write it out that way, nice and plain and legal. Me and Olivia buy ourselves a condo and you guys get the houses, each to his own. You get my estate, Ed gets hers."

"Sounds pretty normal so far."

"Well, normal, this whole fucking arrangement is abnormal. That's what I'm getting at. I mean, Olivia's stuff, whatever she has, you and me we've got no claim on it. It's hers and Ed's fair and square. But he's *my* son, too, and I figure I've gypped him enough already. He missed out on an awful lot, and I feel guilty about that."

Parker sat perfectly still, dreading what came next. Sure enough, his father cleared his throat and said, "What I'm thinking—and hear me out on this—is that you two could split the cottage. How's that strike you? Is that fair?"

Those words made Parker's heart literally ache. Over the years, he had come to expect little from his father, certainly nothing helpful or necessary. But Parker had always considered the cottage his sanctuary, the one place on earth that, like a mother's love, would always be there for him. Now, his purest connection to the planet seemed very much in jeopardy. Tears were a distinct possibility, a terrible scene. And summoning all the control at his disposal, he said, "Well, Dad, I mean, the cottage, I guess that's up to you. It's yours, after all. You have to do what you think is best."

"In other words, you think it's a bad idea."

"I didn't say that."

"No, but I could see you thinking it."

Parker shrugged. "Even if I was, it's your decision."

With a determined smile, his father tried again. "I guess what I'm trying to figure out, son, is whether you can live with an arrangement like that. Do you think you could share the cottage with Ed? You and me, we got a history up there. I'm pretty sure you feel the same way. I'd hate to screw that up for you but, hell, you can see my problem . . ."

"Clear as the nose on my face," he said, with a sinking sense of what it might be like to be expelled from paradise.

Next morning Parker sat in the Saab, in the parking space behind the office building, his mind almost frighteningly clear. He couldn't waste any more time on foolishness. His father could do what he wanted. They all could. Parker would focus on Las Vegas. The future was at stake, and he didn't feel very optimistic.

Of course, the weather that morning didn't help matters. A whole new front, smoggy and warm, had blown up from the south, raising the temperature and locking the city in a brown smothering shawl of drizzle and pollution. The weatherman said it had something to do with El Niño—the flurries in Guadalajara, folks tanning themselves in Saskatoon.

And the news on the radio that morning sounded as gloomy as the weather. Now that the country had fragmented into four aggrieved factions, there was no strong central voice to stand up to the separatist forces in Quebec. A referendum was coming, unannounced as yet but coming, and the feeling across the land was that this time the separatists might succeed. Just the sort of news to add to a businessman's sense of doom. With the country floundering, taxes would shoot through the roof. Foreign investors would leave them high and dry. Again. And why? Why did it have to happen now? Wasn't it bad enough he had Dana to deal with, and Bill Gates, and an already-sluggish economy? Why did he have to consider Quebec nationalists, too? And a megacity with who knew what kind of upheavals awaiting as they folded the various jurisdictions into a gigantic and unresponsive bureaucracy. Not to mention a provincial government that was gutting the school system and cutting back on welfare, with the homeless and hopeless collecting on the street like so much litter. What was the solution there, ship them all to an empty mine shaft in northern Ontario, the way they planned to do with the city's garbage?

With those dreary thoughts in mind, he hunched into the downpour and puddle-jumped across the lot to Dunkin' Daddy's. Just the sight of Laurel made him feel better. She had removed the chains from her face, and she looked fresh and buoyant. When she smiled at him, he felt his dark cloud begin to lift.

"Boy," he said as she brought his coffee, "I thought you were really terrific the other night. I had no idea . . ."

She gave him a look of exasperation then walked away to serve another customer. She returned a moment later, though, with a can of Diet Pepsi for herself, and sat on the stool beside him. "No offense," she said, "but we're not out to like please anyone."

Parker responded with mock indignation. "Fair enough. You stunk. I've never heard a more godawful band. Feel better?"

She shot him an even darker look. "The thing is, being 'good' isn't the point, at least not the way most people mean it. It's, like, being adaptable, open to change. Learning Curve, get it? No one else does."

He smiled, but couldn't think of a reply. Partly it was her words that had silenced him, but mostly it was her face. He couldn't for the life of him understand this strange attraction to her. She was so obviously not his type.

"You'd think," she continued, "that it would be clear enough, since we like play totally different songs."

"Not much Top Forty there, that's for sure."

She shook her head wearily. "No, I mean we play different songs, from different set lists. Scobie, our drummer, makes a list that has all his favorites. I make one with all the tunes I'd like to sing that night, and the rest of the guys come up with one together, which means that like ninety-nine times out of a hundred we're all playing a different song at the same time."

"Really?" He laughed awkwardly. "To be honest, you know, it kind of sounded that way . . ."

"Yeah? Then you're hipper than most people. Like the first set the other night, how'd it go? Scobie's first song, I think, was Bob Marley. The other guys laid a Ramones tune on top of his reggae groove, and I sang the words to 'Come Together.' It gets pretty hairy sometimes."

He gave her a puzzled look. "How do you keep it all in sync?"

"Like I said, you have to open up a bit and be flexible, listen real hard. A lot of the time we don't pull it off at all, but we try, right? That's the idea. Play every style, every groove. Break down the barriers. Trash the traditions. No one gets it, though. Like once in while, just by accident, we all play the same song, right? And naturally that's the only time anyone gets up to dance. I mean, people are so predictable . . ."

"Must make it hard to build up a following."

Once again she shrugged. "It's not a popularity contest. If the band like folds tomorrow, it's no big loss."

Parker stared into the blackness of his coffee, trying unsuccessfully to make sense of that kind of attitude. "Why do you do it, then?"

With her pop can she traced a circle on the counter, around and around. "It's fun. When we actually pull it off, it's a high like you wouldn't believe."

"But I'm sure it is a popularity contest of sorts," he insisted. "The club owner has to ask you back . . ."

Laurel laughed then, a critical sniff. "They never do, which is okay. Pretty soon there'll be no one left to hire us, and then we can stop. We've all got more important things we should be working on anyway. Projects and stuff. It's just that playing is so much fun, we can't say no. We're weak that way."

Parker half-turned to get a better look at her. "What kind of projects are you talking about?"

She blew through her straw until Pepsi bubbles came out the top of her can. Then, looking him straight in the eye, she said. "Right now mine is finding some money. No cash, no project. You got any to spare?"

"Money? Not exactly."

It was a blatant squeeze, but he was glad she had shifted the conversation this way. In all his fantasies about Laurel, he had envisioned her asking his advice about money matters, looking for strength and confidence. It was perfect, really. He was a pasty-faced businessman, soft around the middle. What else could he reasonably offer?

"Money could be hard to come by," he said, teasing but kindhearted. "Everyone's looking for investors. Why would a smart businessman be interested in your proposition, whatever it is?"

She looked around the shop, making sure no one needed her. Leaning closer, she placed her hand on his arm and said, "A smart businessman would blow us off. But a gambler might think about it. Someone who's like not that interested in the bottom line."

Parker smiled. She was giving him every opportunity to stare into her eyes, and he did just that, as if looking for signs of fiscal responsibility. He enjoyed the cat-and-mouse vibe, too, that she was after him, that he was playing hard to get. He wondered if he should say something more personal, tell her how beautiful she was, how full of life her eyes were. But he couldn't. He couldn't remember the last time he had chased a woman, had forgotten all the finer points, when to advance and when to retreat. He was sure if he tried too hard to charm Laurel it would blow up in his face.

"These days," he said, knowingly, "a gambler with loose pockets might be hard to find. There's no shortage of risks in this world. What makes your risk so important?"

"Because it is." She pulled a card from the pocket of her uniform. It had a picture of a rainbow twisted into a rising spiral, and the band's name on it. Beneath that was her telephone number and her name—Laurel Breau.

She put her hand on top of Parker's and squeezed gently. "Think about it," she said. "Maybe we could like talk some more. Maybe you know someone . . ." As Parker nodded stupidly at the card, she cleared her throat and added, "How could I reach you, if we like have another gig, say?"

He could hardly breathe. Surely she saw how flustered, how full of longing he was, like a balloon fully inflated, all taut and transparent, rising unsteadily on currents beyond his control. As if in a dream he handed over his business card, then walked out the door and into the rain. He saw himself in her apartment, explaining the importance of shrewd finance. Her face lights up with respect and desire. An unsuccessful struggle to control herself. A kiss, a touch, and she leads him into the dark and the glory.

Victor knocked on Parker's door.

"Dana callèd again vile you ver out. He vould not leaf a message." Victor was doing a poor job of hiding his feelings. Already, his frown made it clear he was not impressed with the way Texpan did business.

Parker grabbed his stapler, unfolded it and began to shoot staples into the wastebasket. "I guess I should go talk to him," he said, as much to himself as to Victor. "Straighten him out."

Victor paused just long enough to flash a despairing look, then moved back to his desk.

Dana lived in a suburban home east of the city, three thousand square feet of shoddy craftsmanship and poor design surrounded by fields of supernaturally green grass, ornamental trees and little bunkers of cedar chips. On all sides, like-minded people inhabited identical dwellings. There was no need for fences or garden walls. Together their backyards stretched to infinity like hydro corridors.

When Parker pulled into the driveway, Dana's wife, Melanie, was standing on the front porch with a feather duster. He pecked her on the cheek, and she sighed heavily in response. In a way, she blamed Parker for Dana's flighty behavior. Not that he encouraged Dana. She knew he didn't. But all along she had counted on him as the last line of defense. She had lost her battles with her husband long ago and had hoped Parker would make him more responsible.

It was funny how life's various dynamics developed. When they were still in university, Dana already owned a tuxedo and a house and a car. He invested in the stock market and had life insurance. He had always seemed one step ahead of everyone, someone who talked of grand designs, lofty ideas. And in a way, Parker had always believed Dana would look out for him—a glaring example that belief was a dangerous thing, because time and again Parker had found himself conspiring with Melanie, Debra, creditors, to baby Dana through every crisis that faced them. So Parker did not take kindly to Melanie's nasty looks. He felt he was more often the offended party, the one deceived.

He sighed, the way people do before undertaking a hateful task, and he said, "The basement?"

She rattled her duster against the porch railing. "He's been in that fucking room for two days."

Parker looked at her a second time. Melanie was not a beautiful woman by any means, but when she was angry, when she started to swear, he saw a side of her that he found exciting. He had this fantasy—not of Melanie but of someone like her, a woman with a temper, hissing and spitting like Elizabeth Taylor in *Who's Afraid of Virginia Woolf?*—and he saw himself wrestling with her verbally, even physically. And no matter how hard he tries he cannot control her, she continues to thrash and spin and tumble, buffeting him like a storm at sea. They do not kiss and make up. They do not make love. He neither conquers nor is conquered. They simply exhaust themselves. They expire.

Parker wasn't proud of these thoughts. In a way they made him feel pathetic—a civilized weakling's thirst for passion. There could be no good, he felt, in wanting to act the savage.

He pushed into the house and skipped downstairs, feeling a small burst of encouragement. If Dana had spent the past forty-eight hours locked away in his basement office, that meant he was hard at work again. That meant this whole project might be salvageable.

The office was just off the laundry room, and Parker walked in without knocking and found Dana, all hunched and unshaven, his hair looking like so much hurricane damage. The room reeked of sour breath, stale coffee and beer. He wore a ripped sleeveless undershirt and gray sweat pants flecked with house paint. More distressing, it was barely noon and he was drunk, and he was crying.

Dana bowed his head in shame when he saw Parker, and clasped his hands between his knees. "Hey, buddy," he rasped. "Jesus . . ."

Parker angled toward the desk and saw that the computer was turned off. At first he saw no sign of work at all. Then he noticed the scraps of paper on the desk, doodles, hasty sketches. One page was a space-age drawing of a television set, trapezoidal and vividly colored with kids' pencil crayons. Pasted onto the screen was a glossy photo from *Penthouse*—big tongue, big tits, big lips. A three-fingered cartoon hand reached toward the set.

Parker let the page fall to the desk. Then he cleared his throat and in a matter-of-fact tone said, "You should come in to work, Dane. We need you, if this thing is going to get off the ground."

Dana groaned and then swiveled his chair around so he faced the wall. His shoulders were shaking but he made no sound. Then, in a voice Parker scarcely recognized, he said, "Everything is fucked . . ."

He hated to see his friend this way. He'd known Dana almost thirty years. "Come on," Parker said, placing his hand on his back. "We'll be fine. After Las Vegas——"

"I'm not talking about Vegas. I mean everything. I'm sitting here and I'm thinking maybe it's just not worth it anymore. My marriage, my kids, this house . . ."

Parker took a deep breath and tried again. "You're working too hard. You need to step back and put things in perspective."

Dana shook his head. "I've tried perspective. It's no use. I'm quitting. I have to quit."

"Da-na . . ."

"Leave me alone, Parker. I got things to work out."

Parker drove straight back to the office and slumped in his chair. The drapes were drawn, the lights off. His mouth tasted of dentist. His digestive system gurgled like a brook.

Replaying that scene in his head, Parker marveled how calm he had been with Dana. But then he had never seen his friend so glum. He told him to take as much time as he needed but to come back the moment he felt ready. They would proceed without him for now, he said. Then he just squeezed Dana's shoulder and walked away. But in truth, Parker had no idea how much farther he could go without Dana. The whole project seemed to be collapsing around them.

For the rest of the morning Parker hid in his office, mulling over the sequence of things to be done. He needed to meet with the publicity people, come up with a new spin to possibly limit the damage of the Quasilogic situation. He needed to stroke Donald's ego and somehow squeeze twice the amount of effort from him, a man who was probably close to exhaustion. And there were calls he needed to make to people in the press to begin the subtle buzz leading up to Las Vegas.

Around noon, Victor knocked lightly on the door and stuck his head in. "I vas vondering, Mr. Martingale, if possibly I could talk vit you about a certain something."

Parker stared at the man incredulously. "Look, fella, can't you see I'm up to my eyeballs in chaos right now? Save it for another time."

"But if I could——"

"No! Get out! And don't let anyone disturb me for the rest of the day."

The very sound of his voice, so masterful, shook him out of his funk. He made his calls, did what was necessary, and by mid-afternoon had a sense that things were coming back together again. It was one of the exhilarating experiences of life to bring order to chaos. It was the kick that drove all businessmen, politicians, doers—that fundamental desire to weave your grand design even as you dodge the bullets. And Parker was dodging and weaving like a master. Everyone seemed to jump to attention at the sound of his voice. People bent over backward to accommodate his requests. He could do no wrong.

Then the door of his office burst open again, and all his renewed confidence disappeared into thin air, a bubble bursting, his Napoleonic efforts Waterloo'd.

Edvard slouched into the room, dragging his biker heels across the expensive carpet. He was smoking a cigarette, although he had passed at least five signs asking him not to. He looked like he hadn't slept in days.

Victor stood helpless at the doorway, and Parker waved him away and then turned, hands steepled in front of his face. Another time he might have enjoyed watching Edvard—his habit, when deep in thought, of covering his upper lip with his lower one and furrowing his brow, or pausing in midsentence and thrusting his jaw to one side, the way cowboys do in the movies after taking a heavy punch. This time, however, Parker just found it exasperating, like the interminable dithering of a relief pitcher.

Finally, Eddy sat on the edge of the desk and said, "Talked to the old man today. I thought we should all get together and discuss a few things. I suggested Olivia's place tonight, and that seemed okay with the two lovebirds."

Parker took a deep breath and tried to ignore the throbbing in his skull. "Tonight?"

"Yeah, is that a problem?"

Parker gazed out the window to the roof of Dunkin' Daddy's, doughnut vapors rising slowly in the murky November air. It was unlike him, but he decided to tell the truth, all about NEXT and the recent difficulties. He thought if Eddy knew just how important the next few days were, he and everyone else might back off a little, give Parker some slack while he tried to keep his world from ruin.

When Parker finished outlining the situation, Eddy lifted a NEXT brochure and studied it a moment. "Yeah," he said, "no question you gotta go for it. If I were you I'd pull out all the stops, land your best punch."

"Well, I'm a little short of time," Parker said. "I'm going to have to scramble as it is. There's no way we can do a major showcase."

Edvard sniffed professionally. "I'll give it some thought," he said, "and see what I can do to help."

Parker's face took on a rigid smile, the kind of look his father used to get when relatives offered musical advice at family gatherings. Then, as pleasantly as possible, he said, "What exactly is it that you think we need to talk about?"

That had Ed up and walking again, and Parker realized for the first time that the guy was actually nervous. In a tone that bordered on businesslike, Eddy said, "One of the reasons I've parted company with *The Review of Books* is that I want to write a novel."

"Yes," Parker added dryly, "porno, right?"

Ed took one last drag of his cigarette and mashed it against the side of his boot. Not finding an ashtray anywhere, he dropped the butt in his shirt pocket. "Bad sense of humor, I'm afraid. You'll get used to it. What I'm really planning is to write a big book."

"As in coffee-table?"

"As in important. A kind of Pynchonesque novel of ideas that leans heavily on Norman O. Brown. A cross between *Gravity's Rainbow* and *Love's Body*, set against the backdrop of the post–Cold War world."

Parker blinked several times and tried unsuccessfully to hold back an acid smile, his natural sarcasm. "What does that have to do with me and my father?"

The proprietary emphasis of those last two words registered, and Edvard nodded appreciatively, like a swashbuckler acknowledging the deft sword stroke of his opponent. "The novel I'm planning will take at least a couple of years to write. You're a businessman, these are tough times, I'm sure you have your own problems with cash flow. So I thought maybe together we could browbeat the old folks into giving us our inheritance now when we can use it the most. I mean, the two of them are already talking about wills and marriage contracts. Couldn't hurt to put in our own two cents' worth."

After several seconds of strained silence, Parker said, "To be perfectly frank, I don't understand what inheritance you could be talking about. It's none of our business what they choose to do with their money."

Edvard saw immediately that Parker could never be his ally in this. He shrugged indifferently and ran his tongue around his mouth. "Just an idea. Forget I even mentioned it. But we'll see you later at Olivia's, right? Just for a little while . . ."

As Eddy turned to walk out the door, Parker rose to his feet and leaned forward on his desk, his heart thumping in five different directions. "I don't know your mother at all," he said, "but I'm telling you, you'll only hurt Dad's feelings if you bring this up. Despite the way he acts, he's very old-fashioned, very sentimental."

Edvard listened without turning around, nodding his head as though he had given each word careful consideration. Then he walked out, and Parker fell back in his chair and lay his head on the cool wood of the desk.

NINE

A New Confederation of States

Four days, and Mersea still hadn't called from Montreal. She had never before missed an opportunity to phone from a hotel room. She loved hotels—the room service, especially—loved to lie on a big bed and talk on the phone, television murmur in the background. It was one of the comforting routines in her life.

Parker hated those calls. She sounded so far away always, so distracted, that he struggled to mutter monosyllable responses to her cheery questions. But the silence was worse. It made him think she wasn't in a hotel at all. So as soon as he got home that night he checked the answering machine.

No messages.

He called Darryl and Rudi to see if they had heard anything new, and all he got was their taped greeting, Rudi humming "Danke Schön" behind Darryl's monotone instructions.

For dinner he whipped up a quick stir fry and green tea, thinking about everything he had accomplished that afternoon. People had jumped to his requests—and that was fun. After a lifetime spent disappointing his father, he still got excited when successful businessmen treated him as an equal.

Of course Jack had *tried* to see Parker in the best light. He wanted so much for them to be pals. That's why he had always dragged Parker onto the bus, out to gigs. He also struggled mightily to teach Parker how to play an instrument, tried pleading, payments, punishments, until finally, after years of browbeating and helpless bewilderment, his father admitted defeat. "Hopeless!" he had shouted on more than one occasion, his arms thrown in the air. "A corpse has more rhythm!"

Parker couldn't argue with that. He didn't have a speck of talent. But by that time he also knew that his lack of musical ability could serve as a foolproof tactical weapon; so even after his father had thrown in the towel, Parker kept practicing on his own, just to drive him crazy. Sixteen mangled bars was enough to send his dad charging out of the house with teeth grinding.

In private, his father more or less accepted Parker for what he was—a quiet, well-mannered boy who took after his mother in most ways. But whenever Jack was forced in public to witness his son's true nature, he tended to get edgy and reactive. He teased Parker for being such a softy, a punishment that was particularly galling in front of certain relatives.

Every month or so they would drive out to visit Uncle John, who lived on a farm two hours away. Parker's mother had worked hard to escape her rural roots and would have preferred to see her brother on her own turf.

So Parker understood right from the beginning that they made these trips for his sake mostly—the space, the freedom, an opportunity for him, an only child, to socialize with cousins.

John had three kids—Adam, the oldest, and the twins, Carson and Rachel. Because the twins were much younger, the boys seldom had anything to do with them unless they were needed as props. Mostly Parker followed Adam around the farm. They were the same age, but Adam was smaller in every way, and with his red hair and freckles, his tight nervous walk, he reminded everyone of a bantam rooster. The more Parker got to know his cousin, however, the more he realized that was the wrong impression. Adam was a volcano, a geyser, his mind bubbling with unfulfilled desires and crazy ideas, his attitude to life a product of the dark tectonics of his soul.

Adam never said much, and when he did he mostly complained about living in the country, his boredom, his stupid parents. But Parker never really understood what was so disagreeable. Compared to his own father, his uncle John seemed especially pleasing. A tall scarecrow with a noticeable limp, strawberry blond hair poking out from beneath his farmer's cap, and wide even teeth like piano keys, John was a man of few words, a man with strong, dirty, capable hands and a generous nature. And what boy couldn't appreciate having more than a hundred acres to explore on his own, not to mention barns and outbuildings, a creek, a pond, pigs, cows and chickens?

So at first Parker envied Adam and looked forward to those visits on the farm. It also meant he could bring home interesting things to put under the microscope. Gradually, though, he began to enjoy himself less: afraid of Adam and the unmistakably dangerous direction he was heading; saddened by his father's snide comments.

The teasing started the minute they stepped out of the car—about the way he walked, the way he talked, the way he sat there saying nothing, like a bump on a log. If Parker came back with a wildflower, or a couple of butterflies for his collection, his dad would say, "Oh, look everyone, how sweet! What a little darling!" And everyone would laugh.

It was bad enough to know that he embarrassed his father. But eventually he began to suspect that his dad wanted him to be a little more like Adam, and that really hurt, because Parker figured Adam was mental. Never mind that his cousin did everything he could to risk life and limb—jumping from the hayloft, fooling around on the train trestle at the back of the farm—everyone did that kind of thing, necessary hurdles to growing up. What separated Adam from the rest of the boys Parker knew was a willingness to do anything, things no one else would even dream of, some cruel, some just downright disgusting. This was brought home clearly the time they went out to the farm for Uncle John's fortieth birthday.

It was August, hot and humid, a big thunderstorm on the way. The grownups were scattered under the maple tree on old wooden Muskoka chairs. They had filled a metal washtub with beer and ice. On the picnic table, on a red checked tablecloth flapping in the wind sat potato salad, bean salad, cold chicken, a whole watermelon, all of it covered with netting to keep off the flies.

Parker followed Adam out to the barn, and Adam was fuming as usual. "Fucking old man," he muttered under his breath. "Who fucking cares what you fucking think, you stupid boring fuck."

Parker had grown accustomed to these monologues. Though Adam's language lacked the variety and color of Bobby Flint's, it seemed a necessary release, a way for him to let off steam, which was something he regularly needed to do.

They drifted through the darkness of the barn, so cool and refreshing after the glaring sun. They entered Uncle John's tool room, and Adam climbed up on the workbench and took down the calendar, courtesy of Magwood's Welding Services, and they ogled the twelve pictures of scantily clad and astoundingly buxom women.

Parker was eleven years old, and felt very uncomfortable looking at those pictures, like a strange beast was crawling around inside his skin. Adam rubbed himself and said, "Aw . . . aw . . . aw."

When Parker suggested they do something else, Adam ignored him, still hunched over that calendar. So Parker wandered out to the main part of the barn and sat on the baler, listening to the sparrows twitter in the loft, watching the dust motes drift through the narrow blades of sunlight that pierced the gloom. A few minutes later Adam came out kind of wild-eyed, as if he'd escaped from a dark and terrible place. "What's your fucking problem?" he said. "You a homo?"

Parker had heard the word before, but wasn't completely sure what it meant. So he just kept fiddling with the levers on the baler. Next thing he knew, Adam was holding a burlap bag. "Come on," he said. "Let's have some fun."

Parker watched Adam grab the scruffy old barn cat and stuff it into the potato sack. That thing cried and flailed and twisted so much that Adam dropped the bag two or three times, but he managed to carry it out behind the barn and over to the irrigation pond. There on the bank he whipped out his pointy little prick and began spraying the cat with piss. When Parker protested, Adam wheeled around and chased after him, braying like a heathen.

A few minutes Parker returned to the pond to find Adam standing there in a trance, watching the burlap heave and buckle and snag. Dark oily clouds were massed on the horizon. The wind was full of violence and grit. And Parker, swallowing his distaste and kneeling down to undo the knot, said, "Come on, let's let her go."

Just like that Adam roared, his face full of fire. He punched Parker on the side of the neck and knocked him over. "Don't you touch it, you stupid fucking fuck." Then he turned and booted that writhing potato sack right into the middle of the pond, and stood there hugging himself as it sank to the bottom.

Parker wanted to cry then, as much for himself as the cat. He skipped dinner, the cake and ice cream. He just sat in the car and listened to the rain come down, horrified by the idea that Adam might be the kind of the boy his father wanted.

After Parker had finished his meal, he showered, shaved, and then drove over to Olivia's for the second time in as many days. He wanted to make sure he was halfway drunk this time, so he slipped into the El Mocambo for a double Scotch, which he knocked back like he was a cowboy in a movie. Even with liquid courage, he couldn't believe he would voluntarily spend his evening in such a horror show, trying to make conversation with his delinquent father, his newly discovered brother and his would-be stepmother.

When Olivia opened the door, he noticed she was in Beat-poet mode—black turtleneck, black jeans and black high-top runners, her hair a wild Medusan tangle. Judging by her expression, she had forgiven his rude words the previous night. Then she went up on tiptoes and looked over his shoulder, frowning like a clown. "I thought you'd bring Mersea," she complained. "I'm so looking forward to seeing her."

"We'll have plenty of time for all of that later," he offered blandly. Then he handed her the bottle of wine he had picked up on the way, the same brand they had shared the other night.

"It's nice someone has manners," she proclaimed, her eyes angled in her son's direction.

Edvard had commandeered all the pillows and lay spread-eagled on the floor. "You're my mother," he explained. "I don't have to impress you." Then shifting his attention to Parker, he pointed an imaginary six-shooter and pulled the trigger. A head shot. "If it ain't Charlie Parker . . ."

Parker stooped a bit, smiling awkwardly, the way he did when people called his name across a crowded room. He was conscious that Olivia and his father were listening, and even the simplest response stuck in his throat. He just lifted his eyebrows in greeting.

His father sat at the kitchen table, rolling a joint. Spread before him were papers, a pouch of loose tobacco and a black lump of hash the size of a bouillon cube. Without looking up he said, "I think I finally figured out what's wrong with you, son."

Parker kept smiling because he didn't know what else to do. He had seen his dad toke up a few times on the bus, back in the old days. And the two of them had even gotten stoned together up at the cottage once, when Parker was still in university. But he was surprised to discover that his father still had a taste for illegal substances. And he had certainly never seen him this wasted: the slouch, the full squint, the mindless grin.

Olivia breezed into the kitchen and shot his father a warning look. "Ja-aack . . ."

"I'm not going to get heavy," he replied. "Just finishing a conversation we were having the other day." Then he offered Parker a lopsided smile and said, "You worry too much, son. Most things aren't that important. You could probably learn a thing or two from Eddy, here."

Parker ran his tongue along the crowns of his teeth and snorted in disbelief. He looked at Olivia who seemed to be memorizing the wine label. He noticed all the delicacies arranged on the counter—the hummus, the pita bread, the raw vegetables and dip, the rice-and-lentil salad. He said, "Everything looks great, Olivia. Need any help?" And she smiled sadly, as if to say that she understood what a trial it must be to have this man as a father, that loving him would be their secret bond.

She turned to the refrigerator then and pulled out a bottle of champagne. "Now that we're all here," she said, "let's get this thing properly started." She finessed the cork from the bottle—no pop, no foamy ejaculation, no locker-room antics—and began to pour.

His father rose to his feet and stood beside Parker. Edvard moved behind them, a hand resting on Parker's shoulder. And with Olivia standing there quietly pouring them each a flute of champagne, Parker wondered if any artist could ever do justice to the scene, wondered if even Van Gogh could capture the rich mixture of feelings that swirled in the air around them.

Olivia handed them each a glass, and they formed a rough circle, their glasses touching in the center. She cleared her throat and said, "To . . . what?" Then she laughed in her husky, rueful CBC voice.

Jack lifted his glass higher than the rest. "To the Four Musketeers," he intoned.

Olivia wrinkled her nose with displeasure. "No, Jack, it's more than that. I'm sure we could all agree that it's not family, at least in the traditional sense, but it's more than fraternity, too." She looked to Parker for help, but he only shrugged.

Then Edvard cleared his throat and, in Churchillian tones, said, "To a New Confederation of States."

Everyone laughed then, clinking glasses. But even as Parker sipped his champagne, he wondered how prophetic that bit of sarcasm might be. With no trouble at all, he could imagine his life thoroughly balkanized.

They stood for a while at the counter, shoulder to shoulder, sampling the tidbits Olivia had arranged for them. Edvard did all the talking, with his mouth full. He liked the idea of peasant food, he said, all that whole-grain preindustrial roughage that Western civilizations had worked so long and so hard to eliminate. Kasha, spelt, bulgar, kale, kohlrabi—these were the foods he would have prepared had he the time for such things.

"Mostly I buy takeout," he confessed, indicating the food in front of them. "*Comme ça*. All these ethnic dips and breads. Fortunately you can find them in even the most suburban supermarkets these days. Like everyone else," he groused, "I am hostage to the food chains."

At the first opportunity, Parker drifted into the other room to gaze distractedly at Olivia's bookshelf, relax his cheek muscles and slip out of his social smile. A moment later, though, Olivia slid up behind him and put her hands on his shoulders.

Softly, her lips not far from his neck, she said, "If you see something that interests you, feel free to borrow it."

Parker turned to look at her, mostly to put some distance between them. "It's all a bit daunting," he said, indicating the wall of books, many of them works of criticism and literary theory.

She moved to the shelves and ran her hand along the dusty spines. "Jack told me you have quite a library yourself. What sort of books do you read?"

"Ah, well, the thing is," he explained, slipping into one of his well-worn routines, "I don't read books, you see, I just buy them. I like the look of them on the shelf. I like to fondle them and smell them—all very sensual—but I never read them."

She watched closely, waiting for him to finish a childish performance so they could return to an adult's discussion. "What about someone like Hofstadter?" she prodded.

"Well, I mean, sure. Have you?"

She shrugged. "I tried. One of my grad students recommended *Gödel, Escher and Bach*, but I didn't get very far, I'm afraid. A bit daunting . . ."

Parker searched her face for a hint of mockery. To his surprise, he saw affection, even admiration. He looked quickly away.

In a hushed voice, she said, "I'm sorry I let your father get so out of it. He's been pretty nervous about all of us getting together, and I think he just got a bit carried away."

Her last sentence was a splash of cold water that made him refocus his attention. It had never occurred to him that his father would be upset by any of this. It was an encouraging thought.

As if on cue, Jack joined them then, his cheeks still bulging with food. Wrapping his arm around Olivia's waist, he swallowed and said, "Don't get Parker talking about computers. There's no stopping him."

Parker sipped his champagne like a diplomat. Delicate and false, he said, "What would you like to talk about?"

His father hugged Olivia closer. "This fantastic woman, that's what. Can you believe how gorgeous she is?"

With a groan of disbelief, Olivia pushed him away. "Get out of here, Jack. You're being an ass."

He merely shifted two steps to the side and draped his arm across Parker's shoulder. "What do you think, pal? It's a wacky fucking situation, ain't it? I mean look at us, not a straight iron in the fire. You gotta love it just for entertainment value."

It struck Parker suddenly that this wasn't his father speaking, but rather the shadow of mortality, the same shadow that had had Parker thinking about a quickie the other morning with Mersea. His father saw his own death looming and wanted to squeeze in a few more laughs, a bit more fun, maybe even some love, dragging the rest of them through hell in the process.

Edvard stuck his head in the room and, in the simpering tone of a British lord, said, "I trust you're not including me in that scandalous characterization, old fellow. I should take offense if you were."

And Jack laughed at that, a manic sparkle in his eye. "I love it!" he said, shaking his head in marvel. "I truly fucking love it!"

Edvard brought the bottle of champagne into the

living room and refilled every glass without spilling a drop. When he had finished pouring, he said, "Now that we've all stuffed our faces, I think we need to talk."

Immediately Parker gave him a warning look, ready to pounce if he so much as mentioned an inheritance.

"Isn't that the whole idea?" Jack said. "We put our minds to it, we can come up with a brilliant wedding thing."

Edvard held his hand up like a traffic cop. "Back burner, Jack. There's a fire we need to put out first."

Jack looked around, confused, and Ed clapped Parker on the shoulder and said, "Bill Gates here has a few knots to untie before you two lovebirds can tie one of your own."

Jack turned to Parker and said, "What in hell's he talking about? Is something wrong?"

Parker slumped, wondering where to begin, but Edvard jumped right in. "Seems that son number two has a computer show to arrange, Jack, not to mention a mess of troubles to sort through. You two have waited this long, I figure you could hold on for another couple of weeks. That way me and Boy Wonder here can hit Vegas, get things on track, and be back in town before you know it."

Parker stared dumbfounded, unsure which of the previous statements he found most unsettling.

His father touched his arm and said, "You in trouble, son?"

Parker had no choice now but to explain, though he omitted most of the details. They all listened carefully, nodding with great seriousness. Then, after they had murmured their encouragement and commiseration, he realized he had the perfect opening to beg off the rest of the evening.

"I've got things piled up to here on my desk," he said, edging toward the door. "Really, I need to get home for some shut-eye. But we'll talk again later, okay?"

Edvard followed him in lockstep. "Hey, right, I should split, too. Give me a lift, will you?"

From the porch, Olivia waved to them sadly, as though they had all missed a golden opportunity. Jack stood behind her, his arms wrapped around her waist, his face peeking over her shoulder. He was already half asleep.

The two brothers shuffled down the street and then over to Spadina, where Parker had left his car. When they were seated inside, Edvard pulled a joint from his shirt pocket and lit up. "I can only take so much of the old girl," he rasped, his lungs full of smoke. "Thanks for springing me."

Parker started the engine, hesitating only a moment when offered the joint. "Where to, Ed?"

Edvard slouched down, propped his knees on the dashboard and pulled on his nose, snuffling luxuriously. "Nowhere in particular. Why don't we cruise a bit? I'm in just the mood to get righteous."

Parker drummed his fingers on the steering wheel. "As you know, I've got a few problems to sort through. I think I should go home."

"Sounds to me like you might benefit from a little righteousness yourself, but hey, what's the plan?"

"Plan? There's no plan. I'll be flying by the seat of my pants from now on." Parker reached for the joint and took another deep drag, blowing the smoke out with a sibilant hiss. "And you know what really gets me? I didn't see any of this coming."

They headed south along Spadina toward the lake. As they approached the expressway, Parker realized he was a little too stoned for high-speed driving, so he turned east on Front Street instead, past SkyDome, the new CBC building, the harborfront condos.

At Yonge Street they made another left, the neon flash and dazzle almost too bright for his eyes. He remembered suddenly how it had felt to be a young man in the city, staying up all night with friends and drifting in to Fran's, back in the days when it was the only restaurant open around the clock, the bunch of them crammed into a leatherette booth and drinking mucky coffee, ogling the pale lifeless creatures who gathered there like something dragged from the deepest ocean floor.

At Carleton he made a right, past Maple Leaf Gardens, past Allan Gardens, down the dark blocks where prostitutes waited like jungle cats. As they crossed Sherbourne, Edvard swatted him across the shoulder and said, "Pull over, quick, behind that Buick."

Parker did as he was told, and Edvard leaned half out the window and waved to one of the girls, a big blowsy blonde with the thighs of a linebacker. She wore a black miniskirt and fishnet stockings. Her voice was thin and suburban, some poor schmuck's adenoidal daughter.

"Hi, guys, whatcha lookin' for?"

Parker gave Edvard a warning poke in the ribs, and got a shithouse grin in reply.

She leaned in through the window then, and was more frightening than expected. She smelled of Brut. She had a big bruise on her neck, partly covered with liquid makeup. She looked forty-five but was probably mid-twenties.

Edvard slipped his index finger between her two massive breasts and said, "Tell you what, sweetcakes, what I want you ain't got, and what you got ain't likely curable. But thanks for asking."

And without a moment's hesitation, she pulled him by the arms right out through the open window, kicking him in the ribs when he hit the sidewalk. "Thanks for nothing, limpdick." Then she kicked him once more for good measure, and strutted back to her lamppost.

Edvard smiled like an idiot as he clambered back into the car. "Man," he said, a kind of wheezing chuckle, "there is no question this is the best of all possible worlds."

Parker had the car moving again, in a kind of blind nervous funk. As ugly and frightening as that woman had been, it had been a thrill to be that close to her. Not that he would ever touch a prostitute, but knowing they were out there, glimpsing them from time to time—it was like watching nature unfold one of its dark dramas.

The first chance he got, he turned the car westward and back toward Edvard's. They drove in silence: Parker gradually regaining his composure, Edvard slipping into an uncharacteristic stillness. When Parker pulled in front of the rooming house, Edvard uncoiled himself and stepped onto the curb. "Why don't you come in for a sec," he said, "I've got something to show you."

Parker got a pained look on his face. "Gee, Ed, I've got a lot to do . . ."

"Come on, limpdick"—shooting a half-ass smile—"I want to show you something."

With a world-weary sigh, Parker shut off the engine, locked the car and followed Edvard up the sidewalk to the house. The foyer smelled much the same as the previous day, perhaps not quite so pungent. The stack of mail had been knocked over, spilling across the carpet and runner. Most of the envelopes had been stamped with muddy footprints.

Edvard ushered Parker into his room and then disappeared, returning a moment later with two bottles of beer. As Parker sputtered lame refusals, Edvard opened both bottles then grabbed a quart of schnapps from a box under his bed. He filled two shot glasses before disappearing once again downstairs.

Parker eyed the drinks warily, then turned his attention to those parts of the room that had escaped his notice on his first visit.

On the wall by the foot of the bed hung a curious triptych: in the center a pen-and-ink sketch of Henry Miller, obviously torn from a book; on one side a small unframed print by Jackson Pollock; and on the other a photo of Marilyn Monroe in her prime. In some odd way it reminded Parker of the type of shrine you might find in the bedrooms of devout European peasants a hundred years ago. These were sacred dog-eared images, each bearing a couple dozen thumbtack holes, the pictures obviously pinned up and taken down room to room, town to town, year to year.

Beside the bed, Edvard's mailbag spewed part of its contents onto the floor—crumpled three-ring paper with scribbled notes in a rainbow of inks that zigzagged all over the page; manila folders filled with clippings, some yellowed, some glossy; sections of *The New York Times*, not one of them from the current year, let alone the current month; an old paperback, its spine broken in two, its pages fanning out like a cardsharp's offering.

On the bedside table stood a trumpet, so bright and silvery it looked like royal jewelry in that dingy room. There was an old portable cassette player, too, and a mishmash of tapes: opera, blues, jazz, country and western, Gilbert and Sullivan. An ashtray overflowed with butts. A candle had given its all to a wine bottle. And on the floor between the table and the wall, where it had fallen and collected a quilty layer of dust and lint, he spied a half-eaten candy apple.

Edvard came back then, huffing and puffing, a big old leather-bound scrapbook in his hands. "Here," he said, "your life in pictures."

Parker opened the book tentatively and stared down at his baby picture, the one from Masters' Studio where he's holding a saltine cracker, the only thing that could get him to sit still. He's wearing blue woolen booties and a sailor suit. There were other pictures of Parker as toddler, child, preteen, teenager. There were newspaper clippings, too: when Parker won first prize at the Ontario Science Fair for his carbon-arc furnace; as valedictorian in Grade 13; as a young entrepreneur interviewed in *The Globe and Mail.*

He looked up at Edvard, amazed. "Where did you get this?"

Ed drained his schnapps and filled the glass again, pushing Parker's glass closer to him. "Long story," he said. "But in a nutshell, it was my mother's. I found it in her attic two years ago and liberated it when I came back this time. My pal has been holding on to it for me."

Parker shook his head. "Where did your *mother* get all this stuff?"

"That's something you'd have to ask her. But I gather she and the old man haven't been as circumspect as they've been letting on."

Parker got slowly to his feet. "Mind if I take this?"

"Hey, it's yours, I figure. Do what you like."

Parker left Edvard's after a third glass of schnapps and drove slowly home along side streets. It was unlike him to drink and drive. Many a time he had railed against the idiots who did such things. He could only assume he had lost his mind.

Once inside the house he checked for e-mail, and to his relief he found a message from Mersea. But his relief did not last long.

Dear Parker,

I'm not sure how to say this . . .

She was leaving him, that was the gist of it. She didn't use those exact words, but she might as well have. She said she needed to think about the terms of their relationship. She didn't know why it had all become so muddled, or whether it was a sudden snap or a gradual dwindling. The only thing she knew for certain was that she was no longer certain—about anything. That weekend he spent at the cottage with his dad, she just hopped in her car and drove to Montreal. She had been there ever since.

You remember Marek . . .

As if he would ever forget that pompous intellectual ne'er-do-well, that sad and serious Czech face, the nineteenth-century manners. It was Marek Svoboda's little leftist group back at university that Mersea had joined, Marek's agenda she had followed. When Galaxy offered Mersea a job, she phoned Marek for advice. When she had a mole burned off the small of her back a few years ago, Marek arranged for a plastic surgeon in Montreal—the best. Aside from Parker, Marek was the only man Mersea had slept with (or so she said). From the beginning, she had told Parker more than he wanted to know about Marek Svoboda.

He had left Czechoslovakia in 1967, disgusted with his homeland and his "spineless" people for knuckling under to the Soviet thugs. He became a teaching assistant in political science at the University of Toronto. One day he sat across from Mersea in a coffee shop and didn't say a word for a full ten minutes. Then, without looking at her, he said, "You should fix your hair differently."

"And you should mind your own business," she replied.

He sipped his coffee, his eyes never leaving the spot on the wall beside her, the way spies talk to one another in the movies. "I will tell you something else," he said, perfectly still, perfectly composed, "you are not living up to your potential."

"Well," she said, aiming for a tone of weary sophistication, "who is?"

The deep creases in his face deepened further. "Some are," he replied, looking at her for the first time, "and some are not. You see, it is not a question of magic or luck. It is a choice we make."

Mersea smiled sarcastically, but his words had touched a sore spot. She quickly finished her drink and walked away. Her father, whom she adored, had made much the same comment the last time she had gone home to Winnipeg. He had not been pleased with some of her grades, her lackadaisical attitude to university life. "Get involved," he had said. "Make your mark."

Two weeks later she bumped into Marek coming out of a lecture hall. He held her gently by the hand and led her outside where a light March drizzle had begun to fall. "Listen," he said, leaning close and whispering, "I have a meeting tonight. You should come."

She laughed at this and backed away a few steps. "What sort of meeting?"

"An important one. Come with me."

She folded her arms across her midsection, shocked by the desire in his face. He had to be ten years older than she was, and he acted like he came from a different century. "I don't even know you," she said. "Why would I go anywhere with you?"

He turned in a circle, his eyes on the ground. He held his arms out to the side as though inviting her to frisk him. "You know me well enough," he said. "You understand me. You understand also that I am opening a door." He offered his hand. "Let me show you something. Let me help you."

She stiffened her spine and pushed his hand away. "I don't need any help, thank you."

He smiled then and nodded graciously, as if acknowledging defeat. "Then you could help me."

The meeting was political, of course, in that little room in Kensington Market. Marek was in charge and spent most of the evening interviewing a squat, dark-haired man named Owen Lattimore. Mersea learned that the group smuggled money, and occasionally arms, into South Africa to support the black struggle. The current project was to get Robert Dobay out of Johannesburg before the authorities caught up with him and threw him in jail. Dobay, a white union leader, was being persecuted for his support of the African National Congress. People around the globe were ready to label him a hero. Marek hinted briefly about a midnight crossing of the desert. Mersea had never heard of the man.

After the meeting, she helped Marek put up handbills to promote a weekend rally at city hall protesting the

Canadian government's refusal to get involved in the Dobay affair. When they finished, they walked toward her room in silence. Halfway there, Marek took her hand and said, "At the very least now you must allow me to make you a proper cup of coffee." When she hesitated, he brought his other hand forward to rest on her shoulder, as light as a bird. "This is not, I think, something we should debate."

Marek lived on the third floor of a rooming house on Beverley Street, just on the edge of Chinatown. He had a tidy-looking single bed, a desk, a large collection of books with old dark spines, and a hot plate on which he made them espresso. Into large snifters he poured them each a breath of cognac.

He listened to her talk for several hours, mostly about literature, her major. Marek said very little, but he made it clear enough that he regarded American writers with disdain. Melville, Dreiser, Bellow—he found them too youthful, too energetic. He encouraged her to get her mind out of the gutter of fiction and read Karl Marx, Franz Fanon, Herbert Marcuse. He handed her a copy of *The Eighteenth Brumaire of Louis Bonaparte*, and asked her to take it, a present.

She thrust the book back at him, suddenly flustered. "I couldn't," she said. "Really."

"Ah, but I insist. It is one of the little pleasures of my life, Miss Harrow, to give books. Please, accept my gift."

He made her a second espresso and poured her another splash of cognac, an extravagance that made her uneasy, considering his obvious lack of creature comforts. Then they sat on his bed, mostly in silence, watching each other drink. Finally he took her cup and glass and set them on the desk. He placed his hand on her leg and said, "You must, of course, trust me."

Gently he helped her out of her clothes, working patiently on every button, every clasp. Then she lay curled on her side and watched as he removed his trousers and shirt and jacket and folded them carefully on a chair. He placed his glasses on top of the side table and nudged her onto her back in the center of the mattress, brushing her hair from her face. "You have such loveliness," he whispered before kissing her on the ear.

They spent nine months together, talking mostly. Her friends didn't know what to make of the situation. He was such a stiff old guy, so unlike any of them. And Marek made no secret of the fact that he regarded them as naïve children, wastrels. But Mersea didn't really mind. She took special pleasure in ignoring Marek's caustic comments about her friends. She saw clearly enough what an odd and temporary pair they made but, more than anything, was simply happy to be with him.

Whenever she introduced him to people, she called him a professor, but in fact she knew very little about his work. In her mind, what stood out most clearly about him was his old-fashioned air. She loved to watch him eat an apple. He would peel the skin in one long strip, then place paper-thin slices on his tongue like they were religious wafers. She loved his big plaid handkerchiefs, the size of a pillow case, that he would drag out of his pocket in mid-conversation and use to polish his glasses. And she loved his sense of timing. He knew exactly when to eat an avocado, peel a peach, turn a steak.

After Mersea moved in with Parker, and after the Dobay affair blew up (it turned out that Dobay was not quite the savior he claimed to be), Marek moved to Montreal and began to reconnect with the émigré population there. He joined the faculty at McGill University. He began to write political commentary, publishing the odd piece in *The Globe and Mail.* In time he became a recognized authority on Central European politics, one of the talking heads who appeared on the CBC every few months.

Then, after the fall of Russia and the liberation of Czechoslovakia, he attended a dinner with Václav Havel, who had come to North America to drum up support for the formation of the new Czech Republic. Havel encouraged Marek to return to Prague to speak at the university, an invitation he promptly accepted. He was traveling back and forth now, beginning to realize how much he had missed in exile. Parts of his nature, long dormant, had begun to flower again. People whispered in his ear about the next election.

And now, it appeared, Mersea had gone to him again in Montreal. She did trust Marek. She had been in his apartment four days. She would stay as long as she needed to, as long as it took her to figure things out. In Parker's mind, that could very well mean that she was never coming back.

He turned away from the computer screen and looked around the room—the filing cabinets; the high-tech workstation; the floor-to-ceiling maple bookcases along the wall, books jammed in every which way; the technical journals and folders scattered on the floor; the recliner and ottoman buried under newspapers—and realized with a shudder that there was not a hint of Mersea in the room, his "office." It was a room she had almost never entered other than to bring him tea, an area eerily suggestive of what his future might hold.

He walked downstairs then and settled into his leather armchair, with a bottle of Scotch and a deep case of the dreads. Immediately the specter of his own lonely death rose before him. With Mersea gone from his life, the mysterious malady that ballooned inside him, insinuating itself around his organs, would eventually stake its claim on him, and Parker would be left on his own to struggle against it, self-pity giving way to anger, defiance, understanding and finally acceptance, until some neighbor, eventually twigging to Parker's absence, phoned the police, who would break down the door and find him, barely conscious, mired in the murky pathos of his soiled bed.

TEN

Convergence

Next morning Mersea sent another e-mail.

> Hello, there. All alone. Marek has flown to Prague for a few days and won't be back until the weekend. I've been up all night. Can't sleep. As wired as if I've had a pot of Darryl's coffee. Using the time wisely, tho.' Thinking.
>
> So let me try to explain . . .
>
> That morning you drove to see your father, I watched from the bedroom window as you slid behind the wheel of the Saab. Then you got out again and stood in the driveway admiring the car while the engine revved. Just you and Art, what a pair. You circled the car, lifting off the leaves that had fallen onto the hood during the night. You took a Kleenex from your top coat and wiped the dirt from the head- and taillights. You licked your

thumb and cleaned a spot off the side mirror. I don't know why, but that made me feel so sad. Maybe I was envious to see you lavish such attention on a machine. Maybe I felt sorry for you, an Art in progress.

I know watching you fawn like that reminded me of the exhibition we saw at the MOMA in August. Remember? "Objects of Desire: The Modern Still Life" or something like that. The picture of you and your stupid car—it would have fit right in.

Anyway, I watched you drive off, then went downstairs for breakfast. I put on some music, read the paper, but I still couldn't shake that feeling of sadness.

That's when I decided to call in sick. I had so much work to do, but I decided to hell with everything, I would go right back upstairs and snooze the day away. And I actually did get back in bed, but if anything that made me feel even worse. Partly it was the sense that I should have gone with you to see your dad, that it was not just a nice thing to do but the right thing, the good thing. And that made me feel small and ungenerous. Mostly, though, the sadness came from another place.

It was the room, Parker. Our room. The jumbled bed. The piles of dirty laundry. But it was more than our room, too. It was our life. Because it was November already, snow on its way, and our storm windows were still packed in the basement. The lawn mower was sitting right where I had left it three weeks ago, rusting away in the middle of the backyard. The garden hose lay in a tangle by the side door, ready to burst with the first frost. I needed to take my car into the garage for a winter tune-up. And I was skipping out of a meeting of district heads, quarterly review.

Which was why, I guess, I felt so helpless, why I just felt like crying. Our life. It suddenly seemed as though everything good had somehow drifted beyond my reach—the beauty and poetry and grace—and all I had left was this frantic little existence.

That started me thinking about Dad, always so calm and bright and meticulous, with his halo of white hair, his straight white teeth. Even when we were in Africa, surrounded by jungle and chaos, his clinic was a model of order.

I've been thinking a lot about him, lately. It was in his private office back in Winnipeg that I always felt the world was a perfect place, or at least perfectible, that it was possible to cure the ills of the planet the way Dad could cure Bobby Denton's impetigo. The smell of medicine and dusty magazines, the secret winks and whispers from the nurse and receptionist down the hall, his fat medical books on the shelf under the window—it was all part of the process, the magic that could be used to drive out the darkness and disease and hatred.

Not that I ever wanted to join such a noble cause. I was just a young girl, lounging like Cleopatra in his dark paneled room, the place where I would wait for the world to be made whole.

And that morning, with you on the highway somewhere, full of grief, I was curled up in our bed, thinking that what I wanted more than anything was to go back in time so I could laze around in Dad's old desk chair and forget about everything. I wanted to be Cleopatra again without a care in the world.

When did that happen? When did I stop looking forward? When did I get so tired? So selfish?

Remember how we talked about living on the west coast of Ireland? I was going to start that novel I had always dreamed of writing. Now it's all memories with me anymore, sentiment. *Je me souviens.* And it's not even the highlights—it's the boring bits. I remember sitting with my mother in our kitchen, in a world that doesn't exist anymore: Glenn Miller playing on the hi-fi, the two of us dipping rags into bowls of milk and polishing the leaves of the philodendron. I remember talking with your mother on the dock after supper while you and your dad were out fishing. Or the Easter in junior high when I got scarlet fever and had to spend three nights in the hospital.

I guess what I'm getting at in my roundabout way is that I feel like I'm being stifled, Parker. Not by you. That's not what I mean. If anything I think you're being stifled, too, only maybe you don't mind it as much. Maybe you're so caught up in your work that you don't notice. I don't know. But what I do know is that when we first got together, I had this sense of us as two tall, brilliant sunflowers standing together in a garden. We could look in any direction and know that we were the most lovely, the most perfect thing, standing there in the sun with nothing to cast a shadow over us, the world at our feet. And now all I can see are weeds. They're tangled around me, blocking out the sun. I'm being strangled by weeds.

I know all too well that you can never go home again. No, my first thought was that I should go hide out with Darryl and Rudi for a while. If there's any place on earth where I might still be pampered, it's there. But I can't see that being very helpful, can you? I'd just be postponing the inevitable.

So I called work yesterday and asked for a leave of absence. Three months to start with. No plans yet, but you'll be the first to know. Maybe if things slow down a bit, I'll be able to get a better grasp of what needs to be done, find the words that need to be said. Please be patient.

M.

PS: I hope you're keeping notes. I want every detail on what your dad has been up to.

Parker got up and walked over to the window. It was true, the lawnmower sat in the middle of the backyard, the grass now completely covered with leaves. And that familiar sinking sense of failure gripped him as he thought about the long chain of tasks he had neglected to finish or even begin, and how in that regard, at least, he was just like his father, an absolute lost cause at maintenance. Art was right to greet him the way he did. Things were never under control, not those things. And now, maybe, that lack of diligence had spilled over into his personal and business life. Wasn't it all just the same problem? Had he let things slide? Had he paid attention, given the right sort of care to his business, to Mersea, to any of the important elements of his life?

He was suddenly tempted to dash off a reply, but he couldn't bring himself to do it, even though her words made him feel so lonely. This was the Mersea he remembered most fondly, the long talks they would have as they strolled around the city on Sunday afternoons. He ached suddenly to hold her in his arms and to tell her how sorry he was, how much he had missed her. But a part of him wondered if perhaps that might make matters worse. What she needed most right now, it seemed, was space. So that's what he'd give her.

Parker rolled into the office around noon. No sign of Dana. Or Donald, but that was nothing new. Donald almost never came in. The guy from the Balkans was still at reception, wearing the same cheap clothes, it looked like. They exchanged uneasy glances, and then Parker hurried down the hall to his office.

The door was open. The lights were on. Edvard sat behind the desk, hunched over Parker's computer; and without looking up from the screen, he said, "You should get yourself a better password. Some nut could come in here and give you royal grief."

Parker slammed the door and rushed over to the desk. "You've got no right to be doing this," he said, pulling Edvard out of the chair. "My private office. My personal computer."

Ed's face displayed a moment of outright shock, followed by contrition. He held his hands in front of him like a man under arrest and moved right away from the desk and deposited himself in the big armchair. After a long awkward silence, he said, "If it makes you feel any better, I know squat about Windows. I managed to log on and that's about the size of it. Your corporate secrets are still safe."

Parker settled down behind the desk and fiddled a moment with his keyboard, setting programs in motion. No damage done. His equanimity was gradually returning.

"Don't tell me you're an Apple freak," he sneered finally, "one of the true believers."

Edvard laughed, artificial and self-mocking. "I had a Mac, but only because I got a special deal when I worked as a teaching assistant at Columbia. It died, though."

Parker looked across the desk at him, reconsidering. "Well, well," he said. "Aren't you just full of surprises. When did you teach at Columbia?"

"Teaching assistant. It was no big deal. I was trying to finish my PhD. They paid me slave wages, got me a discount on a used computer and in return sent an army of lackbrains to torture me. I don't have the fondest memories, believe me." He nodded at Parker's computer. "Sorry about that. I get carried away sometimes."

Parker turned then, arms folded across his chest. "What are you doing here, anyway?"

Ed laughed, one short, mirthless syllable of rueful self-discovery. "Helping, I guess. I wanted to . . . help." He sucked in his top lip then, and furrowed his brow philosophically, searching deeply for the basis of this idea, this curious desire. And Parker couldn't help but smile. The studiously rumpled appearance, the tics and quirks of the solitary thinker—he could now clearly see Edvard leading tutorials, pondering life's mysteries.

Ed's mouth became a kind of open grimace, chin lifted, eyes focused on the ceiling. "All my life," he continued, feeling his way, "I've done pretty much what I wanted. I left home as soon as I could. I've lived wherever and however it suited me. Alone mostly. Never shared a roof with a woman more than two weeks. Scarcely kept a job much longer. And"—that laugh again, the single derisory sniff—"and suddenly, I don't know, these past few days I've started feeling not so cut off. It's crazy, I don't even know you, but I feel compelled somehow to help you."

"You'll get over it."

"Maybe I don't want to get over it," he said. "Maybe I haven't felt this good in years."

They stared at each other, a standoff. Finally Parker said, "I'm flattered by your offer, Ed, but really, I don't know what help you could possibly be. The kind of fires I've got to put out are too technical even for me. You'd just be in the way."

"Wrong," he fired back. Then he grabbed his big black bag and hefted it across the office to the sofa on the far wall. "I'll just be over here, quiet as a mouse until you need me. A sounding board. A reality test. A second opinion." Then he pulled out a tattered *New York Times*—looked to be six months old—and flopped down on the couch to read.

True to his word, Edvard remained out of the way physically, but his presence in the room—sniffing and grunting when he read, shaking the pages aggressively, tearing out articles and stuffing them in various pockets of his bag—kept Parker from doing any work. When Ed actually started drumming on a yellow legal pad with a half-chewed Bic, Parker got to his feet and said, "I need a doughnut. You want one?"

Edvard made a sour face. "Europeans may be wrong about most things, but coffee and sweets, they make North Americans look like Neanderthals. But please, go ahead."

Parker breathed a sigh of relief as he slipped down the back stairs and across the parking lot to Dunkin' Daddy's. He whipped open the door expectantly, only to find that Laurel wasn't in her usual position behind the counter. Instead there was a silver-haired lady with the deep creases of a smoker.

Without a pause, Parker turned and headed back to the office. Edvard had wandered out to the reception area, where he was having an animated discussion with Victor, and Parker slipped by without a sound. For the next hour or so he worked the phone, coaxing and cajoling, calling in more favors. Then Ed and Victor walked in holding a stack of papers.

"Hey, Parker," Ed said brightly, "you should see this. Vic here says he knows how to improve your program . . ."

Victor handed over the pages, which were covered with lines of what looked like computer code, and Parker immediately recoiled from the networked, pulled-string nature of the encounter.

"Look," he said, shoving the pages back at Victor, "I don't know anything about this junk. You want Donald Chow. But don't bother him now. In a few weeks show him your stuff and maybe he'll be able to throw you some freelance work. But he's got his hands full at the moment, so please leave him alone." Then Parker grabbed his things and hustled outside to his car. He'd have to work from home for the rest of the day.

The moment he pulled into the driveway, however, he knew that, too, was the wrong decision. His father, Olivia, Edvard—they could all track him here and get in the way. So he reversed onto the street and headed back downtown. For one night at least he would stay in a hotel.

Parker had always considered hotels to be one of the great advances of civilization—especially the newer ones that catered to the business crowd. He got a non-smoking room, with its own Internet connection, free movies, minibar, and a huge boardroom table where his laptop sat, looking perky but potent. He ordered a snack from room service, fired up his computer and then picked up the phone.

He called Dana first. "You all right?" he asked.

Dana snorted like that was a stupid question. "Yeah, sure, what the fuck."

Parker stretched out on the bed and rubbed his bare feet together luxuriously. "Just wanted to let you know that things are going to work out fine."

"Whatever that means."

"It means don't sweat anything. You've got other problems right now. Donald and I will cover you on this one, just like you've covered us a hundred times. It's what partners do."

Dana merely sniffed in reply, but that one sound spoke volumes. It suggested to Parker that Dana would be okay, that the worst was maybe over. He was already looking forward again.

"Speaking of Donald," Parker added, "have you heard from him at all?"

"Yeah. Got an e-mail this morning."

That was a surprise. Donald normally behaved like a hermit. He seldom came in to the office and did most of his work off-line. In almost eight years of partnership, Parker had received maybe five e-mails from Donald—

and he accepted that. Donald was a genius. He used different standards, followed different rules.

"So?" Parker said. "How's he holding up? He never responds to my messages. Is everything on track?"

"Who knows, Spark? I'd guess that Donald is doing, you know, what he has to do."

"Well, if you talk to him, tell him to put the Invisible Man routine on hold for a while. We need to coordinate a few million things, it'd be easier if we both knew what was up."

They said good-bye then, and Parker immediately got on the line to the NEXT organizers and asked them to fax a diagram of where exactly their "high-traffic location" was. On a roll, he called his friend Russell, the graphic artist who was rushing through a new ad design for a glossy handout.

"How's it going?" Parker asked sheepishly, knowing only too well what a bundle of trouble he had dumped in Russell's lap.

"So far so good. We're running with the first idea, the Sistine Chapel thing. John Q. Public's on the sofa watching television. His arm's extended, with a remote in his hand. God reaches down from the clouds, and between God's hand and the remote is a flash of light with the words 'Inter/View.' I could fax you something in about an hour."

Parker sat up and reached for his shoes and socks. "Never mind. I'll come down there. I want the full effect. Besides, I'd like to see the paper stock and nail this thing down right now so we can start getting things ready for the printer. As it is, we'll be cutting it close."

Parker had to drive back across town, right near his own office again. Anyone watching his erratic path over the past few hours would assume he was completely out of control, like some overstimulated molecule bumping about in an enclosed space. Not far from the truth, he figured.

Russell's design studio was located in an old refurbished warehouse near the waterfront, surrounded by cafés and art galleries. It was one of the few offices that Parker actually enjoyed visiting, always bright with the sound of young women laughing—the artists and copywriters on staff.

Russell, the calmest man Parker knew, the kind of man you would want to pilot your sailboat out of a storm, was waiting in the lobby when Parker arrived. He had a copy of the brochure in his hand, and Parker took one look at it and felt the cloud of doom and gloom begin to lift. He knew immediately that the handout would work. Inter/View would at least look like a real product, whether it was or not.

After an hour or so of last-minute fiddling and post-production work, Parker stepped outside and sat on the wide front steps, feeling as though a major cramp had suddenly released its grip on him. The sepia-colored light of late afternoon filled the street, the air almost eerily warm, and he watched a young man stride out of the building, so handsome, so alive, that he made Parker smile. If he could come back as one thing after he died, he thought, it would be like that, a graphic artist fresh out of school—the ponytail, the leather bomber jacket and the big black portfolio—promise incarnate.

On the other side of the street, a low-slung modern brick building with no windows took up most of the block. Very ominous-looking, especially in the fading light. While he stared at it, wondering what it could be, the front door opened and out walked Laurel, dressed to kill—black miniskirt, high heels, white cotton shirt.

"Hey!" he blurted out without thinking. When she looked his way, he waved to her and called her name. She didn't recognize him till he was halfway across the street, and when she did, she seemed embarrassed, as though she had been caught in some underhanded dealings.

"Fancy meeting you here," he said like some Rotary lamebrain come to the city for a big weekend. He pointed to Russell's sandblasted office. "I was just at my graphic designer's. What brings you to this neck of the woods?"

"Ah," she said, doing the hitchhike with her right arm, "I was singing. Backgrounds, you know? Sessions?"

Parker nodded, slightly crestfallen. He gazed at the building again. "A recording studio. So you got the finances for your project . . ."

At first she didn't understand. Then the fog cleared. "No," she said. "Something else. Jingles, you know? For soup, a bank, and like this shoe store. The producer pays me in studio time, a barter-type deal."

Parker nodded knowingly. "Right. You do these jingles, you save up studio time and then you'll record your own stuff."

"Close," she said, "but not exactly." She looked up and down the street. "You want to get something to eat? I'm feeling kind of spaced."

They drove over to Laurel's apartment so she could change clothes.

"You wouldn't believe how much more work I get now that I come to sessions all tarted up," she said. "Producers are such pigs."

The apartment was on Jarvis South, around the corner from the Harbour Light mission, a notoriously rundown neighborhood that boasted a dozen or so flophouses and soup kitchens. Parker had driven by in the past, goggled at the winos and thugs; but he had never stopped there. Most of the time, in fact, he avoided those streets altogether; and now, as he locked the Saab, he couldn't help but feel a sense of misgiving. This was no place to leave a fine car. Graffiti covered every surface; empty sherry bottles lay scattered in the ropy weeds that bordered the pavement.

The building was no cheerier, three drab storeys, the main hall windowless and seemingly lit by a twenty-watt yellow bulb, shadows spilling into every corner. Here, too, the walls were covered with the indecipherable signatures that passed for graffiti anymore, animals marking their territory.

Laurel's apartment consisted of a bedroom, a kitchenette with half-size appliances, and an all-purpose room with a futon and a card table and chairs. She had obviously made some effort with her surroundings—the scarf-draped lamps, the music posters, the overall tidiness. Still, Parker had never been in a dwelling so mean, even in his student days. The automatic pleasantries stuck in his throat. "Nice place," he realized, could end up sounding sarcastic.

Instead he said nothing, waiting while she disappeared into the bedroom to change into black T-shirt, jeans, some kind of South American wool vest. Then he watched her dance around the small apartment, putting out food for her cat (who had yet to put in an appearance), turning on some lights, turning off others, closing this, opening that. And while he watched, a part of his mind was gradually drawn to the sounds coming from next door. It was jazz, solo piano to be precise, very Bill Evans.

When she caught him listening, she came and stood beside him for a moment, eyes closed, a hand tucked under each armpit. Then she looked up at him and said, "He makes me want to cry when he plays like that. It's so sad and beautiful. I think he does it sometimes just to get to me."

Parker stood a little straighter. "That's your neighbor? I thought it was a record."

"My father," she corrected. "Bobby Breau? He lives next door."

He listened again, this time with a greater appreciation. She was right. It was almost unbearably sad, the very kind of music that could never be recorded, that was best heard through the walls or the floorboards, usually late at night, a desolate sound of loneliness and private griefs.

"My father is a jazz musician too," he said, secretly thrilled that they had this one thing in common. "Saxophone."

Her smile in return was condescending. There's jazz and then there's jazz, it said, pretenders and the real thing. And he could tell by that how proud she was of her old man. It made Parker want to brag about all the records his own father had played on, about the time Don Ellis had asked him to move to Los Angeles and join his band—but what was the point in that?

They listened for another minute or so and then headed outside to the car. He made her pick the restaurant, and they wound up on Gerrard East in Little India, a place called The Amritsar—a tile-and-Formica hole-in-the wall with steamy windows and tippy tables. A faded newspaper review stuck on the front door declared The Amritsar had "the best vegetarian curries in the city." One thing for sure, he could be fairly certain they wouldn't run into anyone he knew.

As they sat at the corner table, Parker wondered just how comfortable dinner would be—neither had said a word during the drive. But then he realized he always had the option of simply looking at her. It would take him a long while to tire of that.

A woman in a brilliant sari came with menus, and they ordered beer and *papadums* to start, then *samosas*, a vegetable *thali*, and side orders of *raita*. When the woman had served them finally, Parker asked Laurel about Learning Curve.

Nothing to report, she replied.

He asked about Dunkin' Daddy's.

A living hell.

Finally he worked his way around to asking about her father, whether he still performed.

She pushed her food around on her plate, looking peeved. "Once in a while he does a solo gig," she said. "Not much, though. Nobody trusts him anymore. Club owners, other musicians—he's like burned a lot of bridges."

"Even with you, I suppose."

She shrugged, immune to that sort of cheap emotional response. But he could tell she was not as tough as she let on.

"Tell me about him," he persisted.

"Oh, you know, it's the usual story. Brilliant player, even as a kid. Too much money too soon, too much freedom, too many temptations. He was never that good at taking care of himself."

Parker had seen enough of that, hanging around

the Duke Kenny Orchestra. It was funny about musicians, always so proud of their freedom, making a virtue of cutting loose, and then ending up hostage to the pettiest of tyrannies.

She took a pull on her beer and studied the label, warming to her subject. "Dad's played with everybody," she said, suddenly nostalgic. "They used to like come to the house, back when we lived in this big old place in the Annex. Art Blakey, Ornette Coleman, Philly Joe Jones. One time, I was like five years old, Sarah Vaughan tucked me into bed and sang me a lullaby. Don't think that wasn't special. And what a great house—huge backyard, fourteen-foot ceilings, living room big enough to hold all our furniture and a grand piano."

"Sounds nice."

"Could have been. Trouble is he was pretty heavy into junk by then."

Parker jerked to attention. "You mean heroin?"

"Yeah. Most of the time they were both pretty strung out."

He looked away, feeling this more deeply than he would have imagined. Suddenly all his father's harmless eccentricities fell into perspective. "What about when you were born?"

She shrugged again. "He says they were clean. But I don't know . . ."

A smile crossed her face, a small butterfly dancing through darkness and light. "They met on the first Jan Fury tour. The government had brought in that Canadian-content stuff, right? Caused a boom in recording here in Toronto in the early seventies. Dad made a fortune just walking through tunes he could ace in his sleep—or stoned. He played on that first Jan Fury album, eventually went on tour with her. Mom was one of the backup singers, almost half his age, a real honey."

Parker sopped up the last of his food with a flap of *naan*. "How long did that last?"

"Not long. He and my mother were like getting wrecked every night. His playing went downhill real fast. The clincher, I guess, was a promotional dinner in Atlanta. Big regional headquarters for Capitol, Jan's record company. All the bigwigs were there, real thrilled about the success of the album. And right in the middle of dinner, when the president was like making a speech and presenting Jan with her first gold record, Dad gapped right out and fell face-first into his plate. They dumped him two days later, and he and Mom returned to Toronto. The two of them were pretty scared, he said. Got straight enough to turn things around for a while. Then Mom got pregnant, I was born, and that pretty much put an end to touring together."

She gave him a sad smile, one that seemed far too wise for a face so young. "Dad went back to jazz full-time," she continued. "Mel Tormé recorded one of his songs, we moved into that big house in the Annex, and somewhere along the line they started hitting the needle again. My mother OD'd when I was like ten."

They sat quietly for a few moments: Parker sober-faced, Laurel wistful.

"When I think back to the two of them together," she said, "I see them laughing and dancing. Mom loved to stand behind Dad when he played. She'd rest her hands on his shoulders and scat along. I can see her, you know, one of those woman who can't stand up straight? Every time you looked at her she was bent in another weird pose, like a marionette with only half the strings connected. She knew how to sing, though. Dad has tapes of the two of them. Just a gorgeous voice . . ."

Her words trailed away to nothing, and she looked down at her lap. "I'm boring you," she said.

"Just the opposite, you're breaking my heart." He wiped at the table with his paper napkin. He started to say something, then stopped. Finally he said, "Is he clean now?"

She clucked her tongue, looking suddenly tired. "I think he's clean," she said. "Has been for quite a while. But really, it's a terminal illness, no cure. I've been hurt too often to ever think 'forever.' It's like strictly day-to-day."

She made it clear with her face that she had nothing else to say on the subject; and a switch to any other topic seemed to Parker just too big a leap. So they finished the rest of the meal in awkward silence. Finally she pushed away from the table, her face cool and unreadable, and she said, "Shall we go?"

They walked slowly back to the car. Although the sun had set, that particular stretch of Gerrard seemed warmer somehow for the rich smell of curry, the dazzle of color, the throng of harried shoppers. Parker unlocked the passenger side door and then turned to face Laurel, tempted to kiss her, to rock her in his arms for the comfort he might give, and take. Instead he frowned at her and said, "I find this very upsetting. You're so nice, so talented—so lovely. You shouldn't have to live this way."

She touched his arm. "It's okay. Besides, it's the only life I have right now."

For the next few minutes they drove in awkward silence. Parker's arms felt like lead as he held the wheel. He couldn't even bring himself to reach over and turn on the radio. As he pulled up in front of her apartment, she turned and said, "Want to come in?"

A part of him had been praying for her to say those very words. In his mind they were suggestive beyond imagination. But more than that, he had the sense that this could be one of those pivotal moments in a life, a doorway that, once passed through, might change his life.

Parker looked across at Laurel's expectant face. "I'd like to come in," he said at last, "but I'm wondering if I should. I have a lot of work to do."

She looked at her watch. "It's eight o'clock. Don't you have a life?"

He looked at his own watch, as if that might tell a different story. "Just for a little bit wouldn't hurt, I guess."

Once in the apartment, Laurel was the one who seemed nervous. While Parker sat at the rickety old card table, she opened all the cupboards one by one. She opened the fridge and closed it at least five times, all of which gave him time to study her. In this light, from this angle, her milky skin and elegant cheekbones reminded him of stones worn smooth by millennial tides. She had kicked off her shoes and was dancing around on feet as pale as egg white. Parker, awash in a feeling of tenderness, wanted to reach out and pull her into his lap and tell her, a lost and lonely child, that everything would be all right.

He wondered how a girl so spirited could end up in a place like this. The obvious answer was her father, of course. Either that or she was crazy, hard-wired with some auto-destruct mechanism that ruined even the most sure-fire chances.

He scrubbed his face with his hands and then got to his feet. He stood in front of her, so close he could smell her hair. "So," he said, his voice far lower and more seductive than he had ever heard it before, a nearly frightening sound, as though he had been taken over by another spirit. "What now?"

Raising her eyebrows suggestively, she touched him lightly on the breastbone with her palm. "Wait one sec," she said. Then she backed into her bedroom.

Immediately his mind began to reel with erotic images, heightened by that deadly cocktail of novelty and perceived risk. In an effort to still his heart, he began to nose around the apartment, checking out her collection of cassettes (not much that he recognized), her bookcase (even less luck there, authors from Nigeria and Bolivia and Egypt, not a boring white guy in the bunch). Even the magazines on the side table were unfamiliar to him, things with odd-sounding names like *The Utne Reader* and *Adbusters*.

From the bedroom he could hear Laurel's escalating clatter, punctuated by hissed curses. When she came out again, she was tapping an empty cassette cover against the side of her leg. She did not look pleased.

"I can't believe this," she said. "It's in my Walkman, which I of course loaned to Badge."

Parker didn't know whether to feel disappointed or relieved. "You were looking for a cassette?"

"You've been so nice to me," she said as she slumped on a footstool. "I wanted to show you something special."

It was on the tip of his tongue to say he was already looking at something special, but then she wheeled around, opened the door of the apartment and disappeared down the hall. A moment later she returned, grabbed a set of keys off her kitchen counter and motioned for him to follow.

"What now?" he asked, not exactly comfortable

with the way things were shaping up. She was hunched over, fitting the key into the lock of the room next to hers—her father's place, it would seem. "Are we sure about this, Laurel?"

She pushed open the door and slid into the blackness. Then she turned on a light and waved him in with a smile. "Come on," she said excitedly. "Check this out."

She wasn't referring to the shabbiness of her father's apartment, though she might well have been. In most ways it was meaner and more rundown than hers. Or perhaps the general absence of furniture underlined the grimness of the rooms themselves. The kitchen was a clutter of takeout containers and little else. The living room had an old upright piano along one wall, that and a piano bench.

What really caught the eye, however, were the strings of multicolored wooden beads that hung from ceiling to floor, not so much a bead curtain as a bead environment. Parker stood at the edge of the living room and watched Laurel walk slowly into it—tinkling and percussive. She turned to him and smiled proudly.

"Dad calls it 'The Sargasso Sea,'" she said. She moved her arms about like Isadora Duncan, creating bright ripples of sound. "You should hear him. He can actually make music with it. It is so cool."

She moved toward the bedroom then, and he followed, the gentle caress of the beads oddly exciting. She opened the door, led him inside and then closed the door behind them. A small light above a rectangular aquarium spread its greeny-blue haze throughout the room. In the dimness, Parker could make out a mattress on the floor, and on the opposite wall, a long table that held an old Revox tape recorder. Laurel knelt and threaded a tape onto the machine, then took his hand and led him to the mattress.

For something like twenty minutes, they sat side by side, backs propped against the wall, listening to selections of her father's music—solo piano, jazz trio, quintet. After a few notes of any song, Laurel knew which performance they were listening to and pointed out the venues, the accompanying players—Paul Desmond at George's Spaghetti House, Ed Bickert in the apartment, Sonny Rollins at the Colonial Tavern.

Parker knew jazz, he knew good players, and Bobby Breau was as good as anyone Parker had heard—less frenetic than Oscar Peterson, maybe even a bit sloppy on the up-tempo numbers, but perfect in his way. Perfectly sad, you might say. Autumn music. Melancholy.

When the tape ran off the spool, they sat in silence. Parker could feel the warmth of her beside him. He could smell her too, a lemony sweetness. And just when he was about to break the silence that had built between them, she curled up closer beside him, resting her head on his shoulder, both hands tucked under her chin.

"I like you, Parker. You make me feel good."

Carefully, the way he might touch a wild pony, he ran his hand from the top of her head, along her shoulder and arm, coming to rest on the curve of her waist. "Well," he replied, his voice hushed and reassuring, "I can't even begin to tell you how you make me feel."

Laurel continued talking while Parker sat there in a deepening turmoil. This was her project, of course, her father's music. She was saving money, studio time, and one day, when she had enough, she would remix these tapes and present them to a record company—not for personal gain, but for the music. Of all the people he had played with, all the impromptu sessions and shows, nothing had ever made it onto vinyl. It pained her to think that her father's talent might one day pass from this earth without ever leaving a more permanent record. It had become one of her fixations—that a flame that bright not be allowed to go out completely.

The more she talked, the more he could feel her relaxing, and the tenser he became. It was perfectly clear that he was ready to make a fool of himself. She had only to make a sign, and he would give himself up to his banked passions. Yet holding her this way also awakened in him a feeling that he was capable of better things, bigger things. And there, in that dim aqueous cavern, the other side of The Sargasso Sea, Parker wondered if he was beginning to fall in love.

A few minutes later—it wasn't nearly long enough—they heard a door open and close, the melodic chatter of beads building to a crescendo and then dwindling to a gentle tintinnabulation. Silence again.

She slid out of his embrace, and a man's voice called out. "Laur? That you?" When she didn't answer, the man entered the room, showing more than a little surprise.

Even squinting into the light, Parker didn't need to be told that this was Bobby Breau: salt-and-pepper hair tied back in a lank ponytail, long sideburns, eyes a startling Caribbean blue. It was an unsettling face, creased and craggy, the mushy mouth of the undentured; yet beneath those details the contours of a handsome boyish face could be divined. Parker thought this was a face for archaeologists—only by studying the extent of the ruins could one truly understand how magnificent this man had once been.

Laurel bounded to her feet and gave her father a

hug. "This is my friend Parker," she said. "He wanted to know about my project."

"Your stupidity, you mean. Get a life, kid. Preferably your own."

He stepped away from her and shuffled over to the tape recorder, removing the tape and putting it back in its box. He made no secret of his disapproval. Then, the judgmental father, the protector, he fixed his gaze on Parker again.

"So, buddy, what gives? I come home and find you in my apartment, on my bed in the dark, with my daughter, who looks to be what, about half your age. For first impressions, it kinda stinks."

Parker rose slowly to his feet and smiled sheepishly. "It's not what you think."

Bobby moved closer until they were almost touching. "Nothing ever is, pal. Nothing ever is. Now, if it's all the same to you, why don't you both fuck off. It's time for my beauty rest."

Back at the hotel Parker ordered a beer from room service and sat in the darkness, trying to calm the riot of emotions that raced through him—the guilt, the loneliness, the confusion, the longing, the dread, the joy, the wonder. It was true: he was probably old enough to be Laurel's father. And when he thought about it, really, it was her youthfulness that most aroused him, all the standard transparent baloney—her innocence, her vitality, her idealism, her taut skin and supple limbs. He'd heard that kind of attraction discussed in biological terms, the tough and cagey old stallion earning his time with the young mares. And maybe there was something to that in some cases, but with Parker it seemed mostly aesthetics, all textures and taste and ideals. Certainly he became a different person in her presence, a better person, perhaps. But the effect was fleeting. The moment she went away he became the Parker of old, and he felt bleak and foolish and inconstant.

When he checked his e-mail, there was nothing more from Mersea. And he wondered if he should dash off a note to her. Lounging there in Montreal, who could say where her thoughts were headed? Perhaps he needed to remind her of a few highlights, of all the things that had gone right for them, instead of the few things that had gone wrong. Maybe he needed that, too, before he did something really insane with Laurel. But what highlights could he mention?

He lay back on the bed with eyes closed, hands clasped behind his head. The first thing that came to mind was Avignon, that hotel just inside the wall with the beautiful courtyard and the flocked bordello wallpaper, the window looking out across the river. Every morning they walked to the little bakery around the corner and dawdled over coffee and *pain au chocolat.* Afternoons they spent wandering around, most days with nothing to do but sit in the Pope's garden and let truffles melt in their mouths. And thinking about it now, it was as if they had discovered some secret truth about the world, the fountain of youth or something, and then just let it slip away.

He opened his eyes and stared up at the stuccoed ceiling of his room. The hotel he was in right now was much nicer than that one in Avignon—three times the size, more luxurious, staff who at least pretended to care about his needs. But Avignon was special, that whole vacation was. An anniversary of sorts, ten years of living together. First time ever they were both making decent money. Three weeks in the south of France.

The real highlight of that trip was Arles, of course. They took the morning train from Avignon, packing a lunch like an old couple. The whole way they chatted about Canada with a couple of nuns who had once been to Montreal. In Arles they stopped near the station for coffee, a place with pinball machines, scooters out front, Genesis blaring from a sound system. A group of young men and women sat by the window, arguing about politics. Mersea found it all very funny, like they had stumbled into a Godard film.

From the café, they wandered slowly over to the Roman coliseum. They could have waited for a guided tour, but they were happier on their own, walking hand in hand in the shadows beneath the stadium, the air rich with the smell of cats and damp stone. The ancient walls were heavily graffitied, plastered with posters for an upcoming bullfight. He found it thrilling to be that close to something so old, an actual building from Roman times that was still in use—a reality so dense and layered that it bordered on poetry.

They climbed the stairway up into the coliseum itself, and then up into the sunlight on top of the wall where they could gaze down into the dusty oval where Romans had once held sport, or behind them to red tiled rooftops that sloped away to the Rhône. And standing there with his arm around Mersea, swaying in the wind, he suddenly felt superior, invincible, as though the two of them—so young, so talented, so full of promise and energy—were a culmination of some sort, an apex.

Parker got up from the bed and grabbed his laptop. It was true, they had once been young, they had been sunflowers, as Mersea had put it. They had shared brilliant times, memories that could still move him more than a decade later, that could reach across the years and shake him into wakefulness.

He hit the power button and began a reply.

> I wish you would come home. I'll be leaving soon for Las Vegas, and I think we should talk face-to-face before I go, even if your mind is set. You're making decisions about my life too, you know. You need to consider my side of the story . . .

Then he shut off the computer and got ready for bed.

Parker was a prowler when he flossed, one of the many habits he had developed in tandem with Mersea. At home they normally watched the news together at eleven o'clock, after which Mersea headed upstairs to begin her nightly routine of soaps and creams and unguents. Parker would watch the sports report, and then grab some floss and wander the house, turning off lights, checking that doors and windows were locked. By that point she would be finished at the sink, and he could wash his face and brush his teeth while Mersea sat on the edge of their big old claw-foot tub and chatted effortlessly about the happenings of the day.

It was perhaps the thing he missed most whenever she went out of town, the simple homey routines of shared intimacy—the way she knew, without asking, to bring tea into his study, with milk, no sugar, his special porcelain cup they had brought back from France; the way he could tell from her voice and the speed of her breathing that she needed a nice long walk; the way their lazy end-of-day conversations were fragmented and given a Beckett-like spin by toothbrush and face cloth and towel.

The more he thought about these things, the more deeply he understood her influence in his life, and his in hers. Not so much that they had shaped each other but that, as they had grown, they had accommodated themselves to the elemental demands of the union, bending here, pausing there, making concessions and compromises, dividing labors and talents to the point that, even if she did leave him for good now, he would carry her impression with him always, so that an artist could, if necessary, construct a passable likeness of Mersea by simply outlining the space that wasn't Parker—a puzzle in two pieces.

ELEVEN

A Proposition

When Parker returned to his office next day, he found Edvard there waiting for him, curled up on the couch. "Hey, Daddy-o, where you been?"

"I've been around, Ed. I had a lot of stuff to take care of. You know how it is."

"Well, you picked a fine time to go AWOL."

Parker stopped in his tracks. "Why? What's wrong?"

Without saying a word, Ed got up and handed him a fax from Las Vegas, a reply to Parker's request for more information about their booth. A blueprint of the convention center showed their "high-traffic location" on the second floor, tucked up beside the men's washroom in the far corner of the building.

Parker slumped in a chair and covered his face with his hands. Ed moved beside him and said, "You better have one hell of a presentation, that's all I've got to say."

"We don't have much of a show at all," he grumbled,

heaving his shoulders around in a vain attempt to loosen his muscles. "It's not exactly sexy software. No graphics, no pizzazz. Mostly we hand out specs, and reviews from the press, and Donald demonstrates how it all works."

"Not your programmer . . ."

Parker showed his surprise. "He's the one most qualified to answer questions. I'd be useless, and Dana thinks he knows all about this stuff, but he really doesn't have a handle on it the way Donald does."

"But he's a computer geek. Surely you know someone, an actress or model or something. What about your woman, what's her name, Mercy?"

"No, forget it. That's out of the question."

"But someone, Parker. A programmer is the wrong man for the job. Or, I'll tell you what—I know people, entertainers. One call, a few hours' study and they could handle this, no problem. What you need is you need a face, you need charm."

Parker started to speak and then stopped. Before him rose the image of Laurel in her black miniskirt and spike heels. She wasn't above tarting herself up for a few bucks. He could help her. She could help him. They would grow closer.

He took a deep breath and said, "I'd need to talk to Dana about it. And Donald, of course. He might be offended."

Edvard nodded agreement then handed him the phone. Parker called Dana first. On the fourth ring Melanie answered.

"Hey, Mel," Parker said, "is he there?"

"No."

"Know where I can reach him?"

"No. He left this morning with a suitcase. I was

hoping you might have an idea. He took his passport, too. And his golf clubs."

Parker thought quickly. "Well, we're leaving for Vegas in three days, Mel. Maybe he's dropping his stuff at the office so he'll be all set."

"I thought you said he wasn't there."

"Well he isn't, but——"

"He left this morning, Parker, before seven. This just isn't normal. Dana never packs for business trips. I do, usually at the last minute with the airport limo waiting outside. This is something different."

"Well, Melanie, listen——"

"No, you listen. If he calls you or you have any contact with him at all, you tell him he's in deep shit if he thinks he can just sneak out this way."

"Aw, Mel, no, Dana wouldn't——"

But she had hung up.

In response to Ed's single arched eyebrow, Parker rolled his eyes. Then he dialed Donald's office. No answer, of course. He dialed Victor at the front desk. "Any word from Donald Chow?"

"No, Mr. Martingale, Mr. Chow has not been into the office since yesterday after you left."

"He was here?"

"For five minutes only. Very busy, like you said."

Parker hammered out the other number he had for Donald. When he wasn't incommunicado, Don sometimes stayed with his mother. She answered on the first ring.

"Hello, Mrs. Chow, is Don there?"

"Who is this?"

"Sorry, it's Parker Martingale, I work with Donald? He hasn't been into the office for a few days, I wondered if he was okay."

"Donald? Donald's not here, Mr. Martingale."

"I see. Do you know when he'll be back or where I can reach him? It's kind of important."

"Yes, I know. He's very busy."

"You know where he is then?"

"He's not here."

"I understand that, but I was just wondering where I could reach him."

"He's not in New York?"

"You mean New York City?"

"With you, yes?"

"No, Mrs. Chow, I'm here in Toronto. Donald is in New York?"

"Oh, I see. Well, thank you anyway, Mr. Martingale. Bye-bye." Then she too hung up.

Parker frowned at the handset, and Edvard tasted the air and said, "Maybe we should just get things rolling on our end and talk to the Glimmer Twins later. You want me to call a few people and see if they're interested? I know this gal in Chicago——"

"No," Parker said, "not just yet. There's someone here I might try."

"Okay, whatever. But let's take it a step further. I have a few favors I can call in that maybe could be useful."

Parker eyed him warily. "Such as?"

"Such as sound system, lights, set design . . ."

"Set design!" Parker burst out laughing. "What do you think this is?"

"Oh, I don't know, *Las Vegas?*"

They both laughed then, feeling easier together than they had ever felt. After a moment, though, that feeling of comfort dissipated, and Parker got to his feet and looked down at the pigeons on the roof of Dunkin'

Daddy's. Turning around again, he said, "As if you're some kind of impresario."

Edvard leaned back in his chair, feet up on the coffee table. "I've been around."

"Show business? I thought you were a writer. An intellectual."

"Yeah, well, the summer after my second year at Columbia I got a job selling merchandise on a tour with Jimmy Buffett—T-shirts, hats, programs. I got to know some of the guys on the crew real well, especially the lighting and set designer, Jake Tyhurst from Beaumont, Texas. We kept in touch. I helped get his sister's boy into Columbia. And get this, Jake works at Caesar's Palace these days. A guy like that, it couldn't hurt."

Parker moved forward and sat at his desk with a grudging smile of admiration. "You're full of surprises, aren't you?"

Ed clasped his hands behind his head and gave Parker a self-satisfied look. "We aim to please."

Parker left work mid-afternoon and drove for hours through the city, not to get anywhere but just to drive, to let the pavement move beneath him. He sat unthinking at stoplights and crowded intersections, drove for miles without once flipping on the radio or cursing the state of the roads or the slow crawl of traffic. He drove right through rush hour and into the dusk. He drove north of the city to Unionville. His dad's place looked all dark and overgrown and abandoned. But even if his father had been home, there was no way Parker could have spoken to him about Laurel, or Mersea, or any of the problems that needed to be sorted out. Parker had always been the solid one, the reasonable one. He had never rocked the boat and had never wanted to. And while a part of him might have enjoyed shocking his father this one time, he didn't really have the strength right now to own up to his weaknesses.

From Unionville, Parker drifted back to the city, past his own house in tony Lawrence Park, on the faint hope that maybe Mersea had come home. But his place too sat in darkness, and he pondered slipping in and giving her a call or an urgent e-mail. But that didn't feel right. Though he longed to see her, to give himself up to her sympathy, he didn't want her coming back to him out of pity. That would be a disservice to both of them.

So he continued driving, down Yonge Street to Bloor, across the Danforth and the neon chaos of Greektown, turning south again on Coxwell, creeping along Gerrard past The Amritsar, dodging his way across the Don Valley, past Yonge Street again and over to Kensington Market.

He parked in the neon twilight of the El Mocambo, then walked along the back streets of the market until he reached the old storefront on Augusta where he and Mersea had first met. Oddly enough it looked just the same, twenty years after the fact—neither more nor less rundown than he remembered—yet he had become a different man in every conceivable way. Try as he might he could think of no similarity between his present self and the mindless jerk who burst into Marek's little clubhouse. He felt no affinity for that young man, only a slight revulsion that he could ever have been so shallow and mean-spirited.

Feeling gloomier by the moment, he stood a moment outside Olivia's place. A light was on in the front room. And though he had never felt more in need of advice, he couldn't bring himself to walk up to the door.

Not now, not knowing that the three of them could be sitting there at the kitchen table and talking about him. So he just drifted past the house and into the Elmo.

He stood at the bar and ordered double Scotches from the waitress who had chatted with Laurel the other night. She was cute in an offbeat way, with deep chocolate brown eyes, massive tangles of bleached hair, and a great crimson slash of a mouth that exaggerated the already-imposing structure of her chin. Her creamy white cleavage garnered her the most tips, he guessed, and with every double Scotch, that seemed the most likely place to spill his troubles. She easily fended off his lame come-ons, though, treating him like the obnoxious drunk that he was.

Much later, and with far less control, he angled his car back toward Yonge Street. But instead of turning north toward his home, he headed south and then east, toward the Harbour Light. He parked behind Laurel's apartment and knocked on her door, half-praying that she would be out on the town. She was home, though, and opened the door just a crack before she slid the chain across and stepped into the hall.

Without a word of greeting, he rested his hand on her shoulder and said, "What if I knew of a way you could earn the money for this project of yours?"

She stared at him a moment and then flicked her index finger against his breastbone. "You're drunk."

"I'm not. I've been out driving."

"You're drunk," she insisted, turning him around and pushing him out the front door of the building and down the street.

A warm wind blew straight out of the south, a dank heavy air that tasted of ozone and that, considering the time of year, seemed not only perverse but dangerous, redolent with Rust Belt toxins. They rounded the corner and went inside a greasy little takeout shop.

It was not the sort of establishment he would normally frequent. The guy behind the counter looked like a character in an old World War Two movie, someone who had crawled out of the belly of a creaky battleship after six weeks of combat in the South Pacific—the stubble, the tattoos, the dangling cigarette, the stained and torn white T-shirt. A handful of customers dotted the room, and they all looked compromised in some way.

Laurel ordered two coffees, carefully counted her change and then dragged him back to the apartment. Despite the stink of the air, they sat outside on the front step, saying nothing. Parker set his coffee down between his feet. He had no intention of ever bringing that foul brew to his lips. When Laurel finished drinking her coffee, she crushed the paper cup into a ball and tossed it into a can a few feet away. Finally she said, "What are you doing, Parker? You come here like this, what am I supposed to think?"

He was panicky all of a sudden, afraid he had ruined things. "No," he said, shaking his head, "you don't understand. I have the greatest respect for you."

"You don't know anything about me," she responded.

"I do. I think what you're doing, your project, it's just great. I mean, it's something you believe in . . ."

She gave a doubtful sniff. "You've got a funny way of showing your respect." Then turning to look him more squarely in the eye, she said, "So what's up, then? What's on your mind?"

He shook his head and sighed. "Too much," he said. "I honestly wouldn't know where to begin."

"Okay, so where were you?"

"Now? Just driving. You know."

"You've got a bottle in the car?"

He turned away and blushed, knowing how bad this must look. "I was at the Elmo a bit," he confessed.

"Not drowning your sorrows, I hope. I'm like fresh out of sympathy for self-destructive males."

"Just thinking," he said. "Or trying to. I wasn't having much luck."

"Mmm, funny how booze'll do that."

They fell silent a while. Parker slumped forward and stared at the steaming cup between his feet, massaging his temples. His brain hurt, and had for the longest time, he realized. Another kind of swelling than in his belly, but with a similar result. If he didn't get some relief soon, he just might explode.

"You okay?" she asked, nudging him gently with her shoulder.

"Yeah, sort of..."

His words drifted off to nothing, and he stared up into a city-tinted sky reduced to starlessness by mankind's fear of the dark. In truth, he felt exhausted and fragile. More than anything he longed for just a moment's rest, a quiet place out of the whirlwind where he might shift his burden and perhaps invite a helping hand.

He turned to her and said, "I guess what I feel mostly is tired."

"Well, it is after midnight."

He shook his head. "Not sleepy, but tired. Fed up."

She placed a hand on his and softly rubbed his knuckles with her thumb. "Why don't you go home and get some sleep then? Maybe you'll feel better in the morning."

"Because it feels better to be sitting here with you."

She brought his hand closer to her face so she could

read the dial on his watch. Then she lowered it to her lap again and watched a police car cruise slowly along the street and out of sight. A moment later, it drove past again.

With the silence between them threatening to get awkward, he turned to her and said, "I was serious, you know, before? I have a proposal to make."

She pushed his hand away and gave him a look so cold and unkind that he nearly lost his nerve. "Fine," she said. "Okay. So let's hear it."

"Well, I've got this problem at work," he began, "and I don't know how flexible your schedule is, but I sort of need someone with stage experience and I thought of you, and how maybe if you had the time you could help me out for a few days. I mean it's a full professional sort of deal, union scale or whatever it is you make, and per diems and expenses. What I mean is it would only be a few days but, basically, if you're interested, I would make it worth your while."

She stared at him a moment and said, "I don't have any idea what you're talking about."

Parker laughed, a high nervous whinny, and said, "Do you know what I do? No, of course you don't, how could you? I own a software company. With Dana Caldwell?"

She nodded. "The skinny guy with the jokes."

"That's right, always a joke. Anyway, we're in a bit of a jam. We have this trade show coming up in less than a week, and we are desperately in need of a front person to work the booth and be charming and attractive and, well, not a salesperson at all but just someone people will feel comfortable talking to. You know, you would just kind of be there chatting with people and handing out our brochures and stuff."

"A booth babe."

He whinnied once again. "Is that the term? Booth babe? I guess that's about right. You know, I was remembering what you said about that outfit you wear for sessions, how producers are all pigs, and I thought, well, really, the people at these conventions are pretty piglike themselves. I mean you'd be a big hit, and that would help us a whole lot, and we would make it worth your while."

That she didn't storm off was already more than he had expected. She was actually thinking about it. "Next week sometime?" she said, chewing her bottom lip.

"Yeah, it starts on Monday, but we were going to fly down on Saturday and make sure everything was all set the way we want it. And if you could be there then to do some run-throughs——"

"Wait a minute," she said, her hand held up. "Fly down on Saturday? I thought you were talking about Toronto. I don't know that I can just drop everything and fly off somewhere. What are we talking about?"

"Right, sorry. Las Vegas. The convention is in Las Vegas. But hey, we're only talking three days, four tops. I'm sure you could work something out with your job."

"It's more my dad I'm worried about. He doesn't do real well on his own. And he doesn't really have any friends left." She took a deep breath and let it out noisily. "Las Vegas, huh?"

He took her hands in his, feeling suddenly bold. "I'll do whatever it takes to make this work," he said. "I have a sense that you'll be perfect. And I'd feel so good if I could somehow help you out with your project. So what do you say? Shall we give it a go?"

She was back gnawing on her lip, shaking her head uncertainly. "I really don't know," she said. "I'll have to think about it. I'll have to talk to Dad."

Parker didn't want to let her go without some kind of commitment. On a deeper level, he just didn't want her to go inside. "Just so we know what we're thinking about," he said, "what do they pay you for those sessions you do?"

She shrugged. "Like I said, they pay me in studio time. But union scale for a three-hour session is something like three hundred bucks."

Parker nodded without expression. "So," he said, counting the items off on his fingers, "we would pay your round-trip fare to Las Vegas . . . let's say a hundred-dollar per diem, plus, oh, I don't know, how does a thousand dollars a day sound?"

She gazed across the street to a helicopter scooting above the rooftops. When she turned to him again she had an even more anxious look on her face. "You're not just fooling around, are you? You'd pay me that much to hand out some brochures?"

He placed his hand on her arm and said, "We'd be paying for your charisma, for your stage presence." He offered to shake her hand. "What do you say?"

"You're not a crook, are you?"

He laughed at that, too loudly. "I am the straightest man you have ever met," he said, grasping her hand and giving it a shake. Then he got to his feet, leaned over and lightly kissed the top of her head. "It'll be great," he said. "You won't regret it. It'll be great."

The thought of having Laurel at his side for four days kept Parker up most of the night. Even so he awoke feeling refreshed and full of energy. He arrived at the office bright and early, and found Edvard stretched out on the leather couch again.

"Jesus," Parker said, "do you sleep here or what?"

Ed sat up and ran a hand across the stubble of his head. "Hard to call it sleeping . . ."

"You're kidding me—you slept here?"

"Yeah, well, my friend's back in town, so I had to vacate the place on Harbord."

Parker stopped in the middle of the room, still wearing his coat, still holding his briefcase, squinting as if that might put things in clearer focus. "You telling me you slept here because you had nowhere else to go?"

Ed winced, as though he had just tasted something bitter. "There's Olivia's, but I don't think I could deal with that. And"—he shrugged—"I've already touched the old man for enough dough the last while. So I guess, yeah, I'm in the market for some seriously affordable housing. I hope you don't mind too much."

Parker walked to his desk, dropped his briefcase, and then went to stare out the window with his hands clasped behind his back.

"While we're on the subject of money," Ed continued, "I was wondering if it would ruin your life having me sleep on the floor of your hotel room in Vegas for one night. Jake says he can put me up for the rest of the time, but there's this twenty-four-hour gap. I mean, you can just sneak me in. I don't need a cot or towels or anything like that, so it won't cost you anything. But I know some people are touchy about sharing their space."

Parker turned slowly from the window. "What makes you think I'm taking you to Vegas in the first place?"

"You're not taking me. I'm taking myself. I thought you understood that. I borrowed some dough from the old man, but just enough for my flight."

Parker blinked. “You borrowed money from Dad and bought a round-trip ticket to Las Vegas.”

“Which reminds me—I called Jake Tyhurst last night, too. He’s expecting us. Says not to worry about a thing.”

Parker waved his hand in the air. “No, wait, don’t confuse me. I need to see this clearly. You borrowed money from Dad to buy a ticket to Las Vegas. Why exactly?”

“We-ell,” he said, a little uncertain what Parker was getting at, “to help you do this trade show.”

Parker nodded. “Right. Sure. Because you’re my half brother, and our father’s getting married soon, and you’re just a helpful kind of guy.”

Ed dug the Davidoffs out of his bag and lit one up. “Mostly,” he said, after taking a deep drag, “it seemed like fun, a chance to hang out with Jake again.”

“But not as good as your own bed in your own apartment, both of which are available for the price of a round-trip ticket from Toronto to Las Vegas.”

Ed sniffed, seemingly without a care in the world. And Parker lowered himself into his desk chair and folded his hands in front of him, like a man posing for a corporate photo—serious, sober, matter-of-fact. He said, “I can’t have you sleeping here, Ed. It looks bad. Besides we could get in trouble with the zoning people, with our insurance . . .”

Ed leaned forward, blushing, suddenly fascinated with the end of his cigarette. And Parker cleared his throat and said, “The thing is, Mersea’s out of town for a while. And”—he looked up at the ceiling, puffed out his cheeks and then plunged ahead—“I guess what I’m trying to say is that I could maybe let you stay at the house with me for a few days, if you want. I mean, it’s the least I can do under the circumstances.”

Ed brightened appreciably. “You sure? I don’t want to put you out.”

And Parker snorted, as if he had surprised even himself. “Why not?” he said. “A couple of nights couldn’t hurt.”

TWELVE

Love

Ed got the spare room, the only one in the house where Mersea had given in to her genetically encoded desire for knickknacks and doilies and throw pillows. The bed and night tables were made of bird's-eye maple with lots of curlicues and beveled edges, antique pieces she had inherited from a great-aunt. The walls had been painted a pale yellow; the huge casement windows covered with fine lace curtains. Ed's mailbag looked like so much compost on the white wall-to-wall carpeting.

They both showered and puttered around for a while, then met in the kitchen about an hour later, looking much refreshed. Ed rubbed his belly and said, "Food. You want pizza?"

Parker wrinkled his nose. "Can't do it. Two slices and I'm up all night drinking water. The salt nearly kills me."

"Chinese, then."

Another face. "Sorry. The MSG, the grease, those

syrupy sauces—I'll have to make us something, if you don't mind. Me and takeout, I'm hopeless." He had turned already and had his head in the refrigerator. "How's an omelet sound?"

He handed Ed a bottle of Pinot Grigio to open, then set about making dinner. Twenty minutes later they sat down to a cheese-and-mushroom omelet, French bread and tossed salad.

"Cheers," Parker said, wine glass high.

"The same. And thanks for everything."

The words sounded so awkward and sentimental that they both flinched and turned immediately to their meal. After a minute or so of thoughtful silence, though, Ed glanced around the room and said, "You know I usually find people a pretty quick study, but I can't seem to get a handle on you, Parker."

"I'm not that complicated. Just a normal guy."

Ed gave him a dubious look. "Not with Jack as your old man."

Parker clucked his tongue, half-conceding the truth in those words. "The fact is," he confessed, "I was always more like my mother. I've had to struggle to find something of Dad in me." That brought another stretch of silence as they stared at their plates. Then Parker said, "Why do you need to get a handle on me anyway?"

Ed worked a wedge of bread to the side of his mouth, like some old-time baseball great with chewing tobacco. A mischievous smile creased his features. "So I can manipulate you, of course. What do you think handles are for?" And then he laughed as though it was all a joke, but maybe not.

He held his glass in front of him and squinted along the rim, the way you might aim down a barrel. "My sense is we all have an inherent weakness," he said. "Alcohol, cigarettes, women, gambling. Or rather, we all need to submit to something. I know what my weakness is, but you . . ."

Parker smiled uneasily, not quite sure where this was heading. "So what's your weak spot?"

"Don't you know?" He looked across the room at his black bag, which he had brought downstairs with him after his shower and dumped on a chair by the door. "Words. Or more accurately, information. It makes me do irrational things."

"Like?"

"Like living the life I do. No pension, no steady income. I'm way out on a limb here, Parker, moving in on the big five-oh, and my net worth is roughly on par with the average citizen of Chad. Sooner or later it's going to have the same effect on my life span as my pack of smokes a day. And I can't stop myself. I'm a junkie. The other day in your office when you caught me on your machine? I was trying to get on the 'Net. It's a wicked habit . . ."

Parker thought about that a moment, looking at the bag. "You're an academic."

"Not even close. Academics follow a train of thought. They specialize. I see a book on dressage or bee-keeping or Elizabethan footwear, and I have to check it out. I'm not a gourmet, I'm a glutton. It's a sickness."

Parker laughed at that. "So what's the deal? Couldn't afford books when you were a kid?"

"Who knows why we do half the stuff we do?" he replied. "I saw a shrink for a few years, and he seemed to think it had something to do with you and Jack, needing to find out the truth, but that's bullshit. I've kind of known about you since I was a kid and was never that fussed about it." He raised an eyebrow then and leaned across the table. "But you, what's your weakness? What do you submit to? Computers? I don't think so. That's just a job. Money, the whole entrepreneur scene? I can't see that being your thing, either. So what is it, bro'?"

Parker closed his eyes and counted to ten. He had always been a private person, guarded in his words and actions; but he was secretly pleased that anyone would want to know what made him tick. In the tone reserved for deepest secrets, he said, "When I was a kid, of course, I wanted to be a scientist. Nothing to do with computers or any kind of machine. A biologist maybe, or an astronomer."

"But you see, you didn't. What I want to know is your weakness. What's the thread that runs through your life now? What's the thing you keep coming back to again and again, that makes you irrational?"

The word was out before he even had the chance to think about it. "Perfection," he said. "I'm nuts about it."

"Like this omelet?"

"Maybe."

Ed looked around. "Like this house?"

"In part. See that stereo?"

Ed swiveled in his seat and faced into the living room. "Sure, total audiophile."

"That thing cost me fifteen grand—for speakers, amp and turntable. The cables alone set me back eight hundred dollars. And I own exactly two albums, Japanese pressings: *Gaucho*, by Steely Dan, and Glenn Gould's second version of *The Goldberg Variations*. It's hard to explain . . ."

Parker put the Steely Dan on the turntable. He fired up the amplifier. Then he cleaned the disk, removing the dust and static with a special spray and a high-tech roller.

"Listen to this," he said excitedly as he lovingly touched needle to vinyl. "'Hey, Nineteen.' The first note you hear, the guitar, it is the finest note of music ever recorded. Pure and absolute longing."

Parker stood there hugging himself, eyes closed until the song ended. Then he carefully put the disk back into its protective case and turned everything off. When he returned to the table, Ed topped up their wine glasses and said, "So, yeah, perfection. I get it." He glanced again at the stereo, allowing a guarded smile to flicker across his face. "So what about your woman?"

"Mersea? Oh, well, no question about it, she's scary perfect."

"I gather, then, that you don't love her . . ."

Parker flinched. "I never said that. Where did you ever get such an idea?"

Ed licked his thumb and used it to pick up bread-crumbs from the table. "When something's perfect," he said, his tone measured and thoughtful, "you admire it or worship it or adore it, but love serves another function, I'd say. Love exists for the rest of us, the imperfect hordes. I see it like faith. Faith allows us to believe the unbelievable, to swallow Genesis straight through to Revelation. With faith you can quite literally believe anything. No surprise there—it's a powerful thing. And it's the same with love, I figure. It allows us to love the unlovable, cherish the fatsos and the lamebrains and the cranks. Anyone."

"You're making fun of me."

"*Au contraire, mon frère.* I am making fun of love. Tell you the truth, I think mostly it doesn't exist, and when it does it's a fleeting, chaotic mess. Very short shelf life, bad for your health. My guess is that you see very little of it in reality. It flashes into your life like an overdose of joy and then rapidly fades until it's nothing but a series of checks and balances—a system of government."

Parker laughed out loud. "You sound like you're quoting someone."

"I'm quoting me, but that's beside the point. The point is a system of government, or perfection, they neither one of them sound very appealing. They sound dead if you want to know the truth. Static. To me the struggle—the satisfaction of lust, the exploration of the unknown—is the only legitimate reason for the sexes to even speak to each other."

For the first time since Parker had met his half brother, he felt he had the upper hand. Ed was clearly a misogynist, a crippling disability at the end of the twentieth century. He might just as well have *Dinosaur* stamped on his forehead.

Holding back a satisfied smile, Parker said, "I gather you're not in favor of our parents getting married then."

"Me? I couldn't give a flying fuck what they do. I have nothing against people living together as long as they don't delude themselves and others into thinking it's something it isn't. Besides, they're going into to it with their eyes wide open. I seriously doubt we'll hear much talk of the L-word." He looked off into the distance, then said, "You familiar with my mother's poetry?"

Parker shook his head.

"Just as well. She's not very good. Her most famous poem begins: 'Your kisses taste of clay and turf and the briny pools of mourning.' My guess is that's pretty much where those two are at. They can both see death stealing up on them, and they're afraid. Of course, there are worse reasons to get spliced. Imagine if they had found religion."

Parker pushed his plate aside and leaned forward,

his eyes bright with mischief. "And what about you? Haven't you ever been in love?"

"Not in the way most people think about it. But then I've always been something of an anarchist. The moment things start feeling governmental, I split."

Parker nodded with growing comprehension. "Yes, the romantic anarchist," he said dryly. "I can see it now, up on the big screen—Gerard Depardieu, the brooding loner who drifts through this world breaking the hearts of women . . ."

Edvard laughed good-naturedly, seeming to enjoy Parker's teasing. "You, of course, are a lifer," he parried.

Parker looked around their big country kitchen, one of his favorite places in all the world. Mersea had chosen a Santa Fe theme, lots of terra-cotta and strong colors, simple design. At first Parker argued against it, thinking a more traditional scheme would be easier to sell if they ever wanted to move. But she held her ground and now he couldn't imagine their kitchen any other way. It was the only room in the house that spoke to him, another in a long line of examples of how Mersea understood his nature much better than he understood himself.

Turning back to Edvard, he said, "Lifer? Maybe I am. It's true that Mersea and I have been together since university. Seems like we've always been together. And maybe we're not as passionate as we used to be, but the feelings run deeper, I think. That anarchy you're talking about, yeah, it's exciting and electric, but it's all on the surface, you know? Titillation. I guess I miss that a little—who wouldn't?—but there are consolations. It's like the difference between being entertained and doing something worthwhile, between getting completely wrecked every night and, say, writing that big novel you're always talking about."

Edvard leaned back in his chair, arms folded. "Call me lazy," he said, "but there are times when wreckage is the only thing that will do. Anything else is just too much work."

Parker sipped his wine and gazed into the distance. The irony of the situation was not lost on him. Mersea was in Montreal doing who knows what, while he was in Toronto lusting after a young girl in a doughnut shop and preaching to Edvard the gospel of love. And yet every word of it struck him as true. At one time he had believed it completely. Now, perhaps, it was more catechism—something to be repeated until belief returned.

Putting the glass down without a sound, he said, "Relationships *are* a lot of work, but it's mostly worth it. You get out of something what you put into it."

Edvard hooted in disbelief. "You are a veritable fount of platitudes, Parker. What are you, some kind of freak? Some latter-day Jimmy Carter? Next you'll be telling me, 'I have lusted in my heart . . .'"

Parker thought once again of Laurel. And he smiled because suddenly her allure seemed ephemeral as a dream. It was his life with Mersea that had substance and meaning. He smiled, too, because he was having so much fun. This was the sort of talk Parker had always assumed brothers shared. This was the sort of conversation he had longed for all his life.

Parker stayed awake for hours, writing Mersea a drunken e-mail full of romantic words and promises. He also included a description of the latest news from the home front—the transformation of his father, the emerging relationship with Edvard. He wisely deleted the whole thing before turning in.

As a result of his late bedtime, he slept through his alarm. When he awoke, the sun was high in the sky, the telephone ringing. It was Laurel. She sounded breathless, as though she had run to the phone.

"I hope I'm not calling too early," she said. "I tried your office already and then I saw there was only one 'P. Martingale' in the book, and I thought—well, I just wanted to make sure I was like clear about our talk the other night. Were you under the impression that I had agreed to do this thing, go to Las Vegas with you, I mean?"

Parker propped himself up on one elbow, suddenly alert. "Well, I guess I was kind of left with that idea, yes."

"Oh." A soft note of relief. "Oh good. Because I've been thinking more about it and, well, you know, I think it could be good for me."

Parker settled back into the bed again, the softness of her voice arousing him. "It will be good for me, too," he murmured. "I mean for us. For Texpan. We're all very excited about having you aboard."

He could hear voices in the background, a couple of guys laughing, a clatter of cups and saucers, and he realized she had called him from the public phone at Dunkin' Daddy's. He felt so sorry for her, having to go through such grief just to get by.

"What about your father?" he asked. "Is he going to be okay with this?"

"I sure hope so. I mean, we like talked, and he said it was cool, but what is he gonna say, 'Don't go'?"

"Anyone who could look in on him? Someone from your band?"

"No, he can't stand those guys. Thinks they only wanna fuck me. Believe it or not, he acts like a real dad in a lot of ways."

"Well," he said, an idea forming, "let me think about it. Maybe I can come up with something."

"That's nice of you, but it's really my problem. I'll see ya." She hung up before he could say another word.

Parker went downstairs then and was half-finished breakfast when the phone rang again, Edvard this time.

"You keep real banker's hours there, bro. I've been hard at work for an hour already, and that's after going over to Olivia's to pick up some of my stuff."

"Couldn't sleep last night. I'll be in soon."

"No hurry. Just wanted to pass something by you. I got the specs on your booth from your shipping guy, and I wanted to fax it to Jake. I called him this morning, and he says he could have something all set to go if we give him the particulars. So what I'm wondering is the focus of this thing. I can see from the drawings you'll have three computers set up. Are they all going to be running and doing something different? You want them visible at all? Or do you just want your emcee as the focal point?"

Parker massaged his forehead, feeling suddenly woozy. "In the past," he said, enunciating every syllable clearly, "Dana and I stood out front shaking hands. If someone had questions we'd toss them over to Donald, who had three separate demos he could show."

Edvard groaned. "No offense, Parker, but that's pathetic. Look, Jake and I will work something out, don't worry. Now about this emcee you hired. What's the deal there, she a model?"

"A singer."

"Okay. Maybe not the best choice, but better than Donald. Think she'll object to a wireless mike?"

"She's not going to sing, Ed."

"Maybe not, but she will be talking, and moving

around, looking alive. According to Jake, the wireless headset is the way to go. Put that on a pretty girl, he said, and it's like catching flies with honey. Besides, he knows the convention center. It's deafening, he said."

Parker closed his eyes, searching for strength. "I'll be in soon," he muttered. Then he hung up. But he no sooner went upstairs to dress than the telephone rang again, this time his father.

"Hey, Parker, Jesus, Olivia just told me. This is great."

"What's that, Dad?"

"You know, having Eddy stay there with you. I'm real touched that you would go out of your way."

Parker sat lightly on the edge of the bed. "No big deal, Dad. It was that or have him sleeping on the couch at my office. This way is actually less of an imposition, believe me." They both laughed then, like a couple of parents sharing tales about their impossible toddlers.

Now that he had his father on the phone and in an appreciative mood, though, Parker decided to broach a subject he had been mulling over. "I don't suppose you'd like to do *me* a favor . . ."

"Such as?"

"Ever meet a piano player named Bobby Breau?"

"A time or two. Why?"

"Any good?"

His father didn't answer right away, which was strange. He had strong opinions when it came to the playing of others, and he seldom held his tongue. They were either brilliant or fakers—no middle ground. Finally he said, "Used to be good. At one time, as good as they get. Hard to say anymore. Haven't seen him gigging around much. A few problems, you know?"

"Kind of." A long pause. "You two ever friends?"

"Not fucking likely. He's a prick. I never liked him. Why?"

Parker racked his brain for an answer that wouldn't make him look like a fool. After a moment, he said, "His daughter is a performer. She's going to be our emcee in Las Vegas."

"Is that a fact." He gave a mocking little sniff. "I hope she's more dependable than her old man."

"Well," Parker continued, "that's just it, she is. It sounds like it's a real struggle for her to keep him on the straight and narrow. And with her in Vegas for three, four days, she's a little concerned about him."

"I bet she is. But what's this have to do with me?"

"I was just getting to that." He cleared his throat and plunged ahead. "What if you checked up on him once in a while, just until she gets back?"

"What, are you nuts? The guy's a junkie. What are you getting mixed up with people like that for?"

Parker willed himself to stay calm. "I'm not mixed up in anything, Dad. I'm just trying to help these people. She's a nice woman who's trying to make sure her old man stays clean. I thought you might be able to help."

It was his father's turn to sigh. "The guy's a royal prick. Always was."

"It wouldn't kill you, Dad. Maybe he's changed. After all, people do."

"Like I'm just supposed to walk up to him and ask if I can baby-sit."

"Come on, don't be stupid. You both play jazz. Call up and ask him to jam with you and the guys, bump into him someday and shoot the shit. I mean, I don't care how you do it. And I'm only talking a few days here. What'll it hurt?"

His father groaned. "I'll think about it. That's the best I can do right now."

Parker fell back on the bed then, a man afloat on a rising flood. He stared at the high white ceiling and marveled at the state of his life. The heart of his world—and surely he could give that name to Mersea—had slipped away so easily, allowing a chaos of characters and calamities to race into that vacuum. How could he even hope to organize his thoughts again, let alone his life?

Out of the jumble, a nagging question rose to his mind. "One more thing, Dad. Did you ever send Olivia photos of me?"

"Photos? What are you talking about?"

"You know, snapshots of me as a toddler, that kind of thing."

"Now why in hell would I do that?"

"I don't know," he said, unconvinced. "Just wondering."

Parker had always been a take-charge kind of person. It was a natural consequence of living with a man like his father, he figured, working with a partner like Dana. After all, if Parker didn't act responsibly, who would? In Mersea, of course, he had found a kindred spirit. They were both extremely capable. People relied on them to do so many things. But now, for the first time in his life, Parker happily sat back and watched someone else do the dirty work. He let Edvard organize the physical details of the trip to Las Vegas—double-checking the airline tickets, the limo reservation, accommodations, not to mention whatever extravagant presentation he had cooked up with Jake Tyhurst. It was called "delegating," and Parker only now began to understand its allure.

Next day, Ed showed Parker the scale drawings Jake had sent back, the specs on a sound system and lights. After Parker had studied the plans for a few minutes, Edvard said, "Before we leave, I think we should have a few dress rehearsals with a mike and lights, the whole mockup. Can you spare a few bucks for something like that?"

Parker sighed, feeling a little exasperated. "This is just a trade show, Ed, not a Broadway musical. Frankly, I've always believed in letting the product speak for itself."

"Are you crazy? Nothing speaks for itself. Not well, anyway. Out on the convention floor, surrounded by a thousand other products, who's going to watch us fumble through a demonstration? This has got to go off without a hitch. Believe me, I know this for a fact: you're better off working out your disasters in private."

So they called Laurel and set up a rehearsal for the next evening. They could use her band's rehearsal studio, she said, HeadSpace Creatives. Badge, her guitar player, owned the sound and lights. They could rent it all for a hundred bucks or so. And he could hook it up for them anyway they wanted. She even knew where she could get her hands on a wireless headset.

Edvard went right out to inspect the place. He helped Badge and Laurel set everything up, including a model of the booth and computers. He didn't come home until two a.m., in high spirits, seeming very pleased with himself. Parker actually sat up waiting for him.

The next night after work, the two brothers drove out to the rehearsal studio, a square brick building that looked like it might have one time been a welding shop. Despite the time of year, Badge and Laurel sat outside on old kitchen chairs, under a bare light bulb, not three feet away from a railway spur. Badge was reading a dog-eared copy of *Dune*. Laurel was chewing her thumb.

As Parker pulled the Saab into one of the parking spaces, Ed laughed and said, "I found out last night that our Badge here owns the rehearsal space, too. Rochdale revisited. My guess is he went down to Jamaica one wintry weekend, maybe more than once, and brought back a ton of ganja. Yonder sits his profits, his stake in the world." He looked at Parker then and smiled slyly. "Gotta love that entrepreneurial spirit."

They were in the middle of a Fifties-era industrial park. On one side of them stood an autobody paint shop; on the other a small factory that did electroplating. Badge glanced up from his book, fixed his gaze on Parker and said, "Oh, man, not this one again. It's the girl I came to see."

Laurel swatted him on the arm and shot Parker an apologetic look. "Don't pay attention to Badge," she said. "Mr. Head Games." Then she stood and stretched and led them inside.

The studio itself was much more comfortable than Parker had expected. The walls were lined with egg cartons, the floor covered with outdoor carpeting. The high factory ceiling had been baffled with colorful drapes that hung from girder to girder, giving the whole place an *Arabian Nights* kind of feel. In the middle of the room, Ed had set up a mock booth, with a few props and posters. A lighting grid surrounded the booth, with several mini-spots trained on different locations. A small sound system framed the scene.

After a bit of nervous small talk, Ed helped Laurel strap on her cordless mike, then asked her to go over some of the patter they had worked on the previous evening. It was soon evident, however, that she was struggling.

Ed jumped to his feet and walked toward her, full of encouragement. "You gotta goose your delivery a bit, girl. Vegas is a high-octane town. You gotta project, gotta emote . . ."

She kind of folded into herself then, confused and frustrated. "I'm not an actress, Ed. You're asking me to do something I'm not really comfortable doing."

Badge started to wander the edge of the room, mumbling just loud enough for everyone to hear. "Not a matter of *com*-fort, darlin', it be a matter of ex-a-*cue*-shun. We be payin' you to *exa*-cute." Then he turned to her and shoved his hands into his baggy overalls. "I'm a singer," he said with a shrug. "I should sing."

She looked at Ed, then at Parker, who felt kind of clueless. And without getting a reply, Badge sloped over to the corner and picked up a guitar, a big old hollow-body thing with a sunburst finish, the kind jazz players favor. He began to strum a soft mid-tempo swing, alternating major and diminished chords on a descending scale. Right away Laurel began to sway. Her eyes closed, her arms snaked around her waist like she was dancing with herself. Then, as he reached the top of the progression again, she started to sing in a surprisingly deep voice, very Lena Horne:

> "Howya doin' guy?
> Don't be walkin' by.
> I've got just the thing
> To make your system swing.
>
>> Cram-It . . . on your Web page
>> Cram-It . . . on you e-mail
>> Cram-It, Cram-It, Cram-It!

You'll be so impressed
The way your files compress.
You'll just think it's grand
The way your files expand
With Cram-It . . . on your Web page
Cram-It . . . on you e-mail
Cram-It, Cram-It, Cra-ha-ha-ham-It!"

She sang that last note bent at the waist but looking up through her bangs at Parker with the most sultry look he had been given in years. It actually made his skin tingle.

She tried a few more run-throughs, experimenting with lyrics, making things up on the spot. To Parker's mind it was never less than brilliant. More than that it was sexy and fun and new. It had Badge and Edvard laughing and backslapping and doing fancy steps. Laurel was shaking up a storm, singing like an angel, and Parker, who even as a teenager had never done the Twist or the Shimmy or the Mash Potato, felt himself being drawn out, to the point that he started rocking side to side with the groove and tapping his fingers on the side of his leg.

Ninety minutes later they had finished, and Parker drove Badge and Laurel downtown, everyone charged up and laughing and wisecracking like high-school kids after a sock hop. That's when Parker suggested that Badge come to Vegas, too, a suggestion that lifted Laurel's spirits immensely.

"But, like, don't make us look stupid in front of the girl," Badge said, nodding wisely. "Like, don't make fun of us."

And Laurel groaned helplessly and slouched down in her seat, which was enough to make Badge smile all the way home, his head out the window like the family dog.

Back at the house, Ed couldn't stop raving about Laurel. "She is right out there, Parker. Where did you find her? Lord A'mighty, I got a *hunger* on for that girl."

Parker felt jittery, torn between protecting her from the likes of Edvard and claiming her for his own. He brought out a bottle of single malt and poured them each a drink. "Doesn't strike me as your type, Ed. Bit young, don't you think? A little plain. A bit shallow."

Ed sniffed the whisky and then took the tiniest sip, more interested at the moment in singing Laurel's praises. "Not shallow," he said, "reined in, timid. But no question she has a large soul. When she sings, she opens right up, doesn't she? It's bewildering what pours out of her. It was like, I don't know, like I died and saw that white light shining. I mean——"

And then he stopped dead in his tracks, as though he had been stabbed with a knife. Turning to face Parker, comprehension dawning, he said, "But I see it now. You're the one—I mean, look at you, you're hardly breathing, scared to death that someone else might make a play for her . . ."

And just like that Ed slid slowly to the kitchen floor and sat there with his back against the cupboard. He took a mouthful of Scotch and let it trickle down his throat. "Under love's heavy burden do I sink," he said. Then he downed the rest of his whisky like it was a vial of poison.

Parker grabbed the bottle and joined him on the floor. While refilling their glasses, he said in a tone that was hushed and full of awe, "She was good tonight, but you should see her with her band. It's enough to make you believe in God." Then he described her performance at the El Mocambo, the way she looked, the way she sounded, the way she moved. And the feeling as he spoke reminded him of what it had been like to talk about the Beatles with Bonnie Pelz in Grade 9, dissecting every song, every lyric, every drum part, until they had convinced themselves that yes, it was all every bit of it truly fab.

"And Dunkin' Daddy's," he continued. "No one could possibly look good in that uniform, but she does. And the light in there, the smell. I mean doughnut shops normally make me ill—all that smoke and sugar and neon. But I never even notice it at Dunkin' Daddy's."

Parker laughed then, giddy as a teenager, a feeling intensified by the fact that he and Ed were both on the downslope to fifty. And that made him laugh again, mostly at themselves, a couple of stupid old men.

Ed stared into the whisky and ran through a number of his facial tics. He inspected his nails. He studied the ceiling. And Parker wondered if the exact opposite was true—that Ed was scared stiff someone would make a play for Laurel.

Parker said, "She's so young that I feel awkward around her, tongue-tied. And that'd be okay, I'd be happy just listening to her talk, that way I could look at her without feeling guilty—but trouble is she never says that much." He sighed heavily. "I guess I'd never forgive myself if anything ever happened between us."

Edvard rolled his eyes. "Any man who would walk away from an experience like that is half-dead in my estimation. I thought that was a universal truth. A woman like that, you don't do the right thing, it seems a crime against nature."

"But that's what I'm talking about, Ed. I'm forty-five, and she's what, twenty-five? Thirty? Then there's this minor detail of my living with the same woman for more than twenty years. As far as doing the right thing, it seems to me my options are perfectly clear, no matter how tempting the alternative may be."

Edvard groaned and let his head bang on the cupboard door behind him. "What a limpdick . . ."

Once again Parker thrilled to this whole new experience of having a brother—the joking, the truth-telling, the sense of shared maleness. He couldn't remember the last time he had felt this happy, this whole.

"I'll tell you something else," he said, playfully jabbing Ed's leg with his index finger, "I'm going to do everything I can to keep you away from Laurel when we're in Las Vegas. She's strictly off limits, especially for you."

Edvard closed his eyes, a pained look darkening his face. "I hate to tell you this, but you're a little late."

Parker blinked. "Late for what?"

"Last night, after we set everything up, Laurel and I shared a cab downtown. She asked me in." He opened his eyes and fixed Parker with a bleak expression. "We fucked on her futon."

Parker put his drink down, feeling the life drain right out of him. "You're lying," he said.

"I'm not, Parker. I'm telling you the truth so there's no misunderstanding."

"Misunderstanding!" he roared. "How in hell could you do such a thing?"

Ed rose slowly to his feet. "I didn't know how you felt," he said. "Apparently neither did she."

Parker knew that if he had had even one more drink, he might have slugged Ed right then and there, started something he could never finish. Instead he said, "You lousy prick. You fucked her? Get the hell out of my house."

Ed nodded soberly, then walked over to the door where his mailbag sprawled untidily. Hefting it onto his shoulder with a grunt, he turned and said, "Honestly, I didn't know." Then he walked out the door, leaving Parker slumped against the cupboard and feeling like an old fool.

THIRTEEN

Threads

The rest of that night closed around Parker like a shroud. He realized he had no call to be worrying about his father's mental and emotional state when he himself appeared to be in the middle of a nervous breakdown. He couldn't sleep, couldn't sit still, replaying in his mind the scene on his kitchen floor, the heated words, feeling over and over again the crushing weight of Edvard's perfidy. Finally, out of desperation, he resorted to that time-tested soporific of single malt and television.

Even so he woke with a start at four a.m., slouched in his armchair, as cold and parched and lifeless as a moon rock. Dragging himself upstairs, he showered, shaved and then drove through the dark deserted streets to the office. He was on complete autopilot now, following the one piece of information he had retained from high school, their principal's motto: Don't Worry, Work.

He trudged up the five flights of stairs, glad to be alone in a dark office building—so much more comforting than at home with his thoughts. He wouldn't miss Mersea here, wouldn't be reminded of the gaping hole in his life where she used to be. And best of all, there would be no sign of Edvard. Maybe in a few days Parker would be able to think about that whole situation without feeling his insides had been kicked.

He flipped on his computer and stood gazing out at the dark silhouettes of the cityscape, Dunkin' Daddy's cold and silent now. Just the sight of that black rectangle of roof, the locus of so many recent longings, made him feel queasy. He wondered, not for the first time, what had gotten into him, what could have set him on such a foolish path.

Turning to his monitor, he discovered he had an e-mail from the "site coordinator" in Las Vegas.

> Mr. Martingale:
> I fear there has been a misunderstanding. Two days ago you requested a site plan that illustrated the location of your booth, and my assistant promptly sent out a floor plan of Area 17, 2nd floor.
>
> Now as I'm sure you are aware, at a large conference like NEXT, we have requests coming in by fax, phone and e-mail. Consequently there is a certain lag time in assembling and correlating all the various arrangements.
>
> So, my assistant was not aware, when she faxed off that floor plan, that someone from your office, a Dana Caldwell, had already canceled your reserved spot just that morning, by phone. Nor did she know that I personally had sent Mr.

Caldwell a confirmation of his somewhat urgent request, along with a partial refund. You can imagine my surprise then, when I learned of your fax of yesterday.

Here is our problem, Mr. Martingale. Your booth has already been canceled, your refund issued, so I sincerely hope that is your desire, and that your most recent fax to us was a mixup of some kind between you and Mr. Caldwell.

As you might expect, we have a huge waiting list each year, so your original spot was readily filled, as have all our locations for this year.

I trust we can look forward to your participation at further events. However, let me remind you to get your applications in early so that you don't end up on a waiting list.

Best wishes,
Olinda Colchester

Parker read the message three, four times, unable to believe his eyes. So weak he could hardly keep his head up, he snorted and said to the empty room, "So that's it, then. We're fucked. We're really fucked. Jesus."

That last word sounded like so much steam escaping. He pounded his fist on the desk. He huffed and puffed and gradually got hold of his emotions. He would simply call Ms. Colchester at nine o'clock and get to the bottom of this. She would listen to reason. If not, the correct blend of pressure and pleading should do the trick.

He turned then and noticed a large manila envelop lying across his In basket. Parker's name was scribbled across the front of it in Dana's unmistakable hand. And in one brief moment Parker had time to reflect on his oldest friend—the depth of his unhappiness, the degree of his instability. Suddenly he knew that almost anything was possible and that the news inside this envelope would not be good.

It was another letter, this one a single typed page.

Hey Spark,
I wish I could have told you this the other day when you were at the house, but I just didn't have the nerve. I'm sorry, pal.

Fact is, I can't do this anymore. If I don't make some changes quick, I could find myself in deep trouble. I talked with Donald, and we've each decided to sell our share of the company. Cynara Corp. has offered us $8 million for our two-thirds stake.

According to our own partnership agreement, of course, you have first dibs. But if you're as tired as we are, the buyer is looking to take all the stock. In that case they've offered $12 million for the whole company.

Donald and I have met with our lawyers and started all the paperwork. This is our official notice to you of our intention to sell. If I'm not mistaken, you have three months to match Cynara's offer.

Don't hate me, Spark. I'm drowning, and from here their offer looks like a lifeline.

D.

Parker was surprised to find tears in his eyes. He was not normally a sentimental person. He didn't even know what he was grieving. Friendship? Success?

He suddenly pictured Dana the way he'd been in high school, someone who could quote you the words to every song on the pop charts, even by the Rolling Stones. In Grade 9 he wore madras shirts with black dickeys and sky-blue pants. He was the first one Parker knew with Beatle boots, always the coolest guy. If pressed, Parker might even say he had loved Dana. They had been in the trenches together, buddies through untold battles. And now this kind of treachery.

As if in a dream he turned to his computer and typed out an e-mail to his lawyer, telling him the bare essentials and that he should expect a call from Parker in the next forty-eight hours. He also sent a message to the company's accountants and asked them to work out a rough figure for share price. Then he turned off his computer, all the lights, and sat in the darkness and watched the sun come up over the lake, his mind full of hum and static and nonsense fragments of conversation.

At seven a.m., the city beginning to come alive, he walked down to Dunkin' Daddy's, feeling haggard and wrung out. To his surprise, he wasn't the first customer, and had to wait a few minutes for Laurel to wander over. That gave him plenty of time to think about her rolling around with Edvard, to wonder again how he could have been so wrong about things.

When she finally came and sat on the stool beside him, she said, "What happened to you? Looks like you've been hit by a truck." A playful smile lit up her face. She was sipping Pepsi from a can.

He studied her a moment. There was still a bit of sleep in the corner of her eye, he noticed. A phone number was scribbled on her left hand in red ink, faded now but still legible. With a frown, he turned away and fixed his gaze on the sugar dispenser. He said, "Bad news, I'm afraid. Las Vegas has been canceled."

Her whole body went so limp that he thought she might collapse on the floor. Instead she slumped sideways against the counter and rested her head in her hand, giving Parker a glimpse, where the neck of her smock fell open, of creamy collarbone and tiny breasts. He looked quickly away.

"How did I know this would happen?" she muttered, staring at the floor. "How did I know this was too good to be true?"

"I'm sorry."

"No, I'm the one who's sorry," she said bitterly. "I handed in my resignation yesterday. They've already hired someone to replace me."

Parker closed his eyes and let out a heavy sigh. "If it makes you feel any better," he said, "I'll be out of a job, too. My partner pulled the rug from under me. The company is being sold."

He rubbed his face wearily and then looked at her, but she was already miles away from him, working on contingency plans, avenues of escape. "I'm sorry," he muttered once again. "I don't know what else to say."

That, of course, was a lie. He had plenty he wanted to say. Another place and time he might have asked her to explain. Had she been blind to the way Parker felt about her? Or had she simply been bored to have a middle-aged businessman moping around?

"Well," she said, shaking her head like someone coming out of a trance, "I guess that's it then. We're both screwed." And she got up and trudged to the opposite end of the counter, where she busied herself restacking cups and saucers, every once in a while pinching her nose like she was holding back a sneeze.

And just like that it hit him, the sinking realization of how close he had come to a terrible mistake. He could imagine it all so clearly now, the sobering moment in the grainy light of Laurel's bathroom, standing alone in front of her mirror, all naked, pale and paunchy, shivering in the cold and sick with guilt, their few delirious minutes together fading like a dream, lighter than air, reduced in a heartbeat to nothing more than a spent condom floating in the toilet.

He sighed with relief that nothing of the sort had happened. There could be no future for the two of them; they had nothing in common. He could see that now, as clearly as he saw his own hand resting on the Formica counter, or that big fat fly buzzing over the crullers, or the beads of condensation on the lime-green drink fountain.

If he felt anything for her at all, it was pity. She deserved better, if only because of her project. In the best of all possible worlds, her trajectory would be high and graceful as an angel; yet in all likelihood she would remain an earth-bound creature, dragged endlessly through the mud by circumstance and character. A flaw in her, perhaps, an inability to take the easy path. If she had understood him better, if she had opened herself to his longing, her life would have improved at least outwardly. He knew that, and it wasn't ego that made him so certain—it was the sobering knowledge of just how weak he was, how easily she could have used him to satisfy her own needs.

He looked at her one more time and frowned. This whole tempest, he realized, had existed solely in his mind, a fantasy invested with so much imagination and energy that it had nearly become real. Yet she had sensed none of it or, if she had, only in the most superficial way, as two strangers innocently flirting. So there was really no point in saying one last poignant word, or giving her a meaningful Hollywood look—she wouldn't understand. It was a private matter.

Down the counter someone lit a cigarette, then coughed. For some reason that struck him as both sad and funny, and he rose slowly to his feet and walked away, leaving his oily-looking coffee untouched.

At home he stripped off his clothes and crawled into bed. He had already drawn the drapes, unplugged all the phones and shut down the computer. His side had started to bother him again, or else he just hadn't noticed it the past while. The swelling. The pain. He probed the side of his belly with his fingers, looking for some new sign he could report to Singh.

For the next forty-eight hours he stayed in bed, except to make tea and toast or go to the bathroom. It reminded him of those weeks he had spent convalescing at home with his mother, the summer of Lake Tusco. He tried reading, but didn't have the concentration. He couldn't even focus on TV. Mostly he lay curled in a ball, his mind a blank, a collapsing star.

Bed rest was understandable, of course. He'd been hurt. He needed to lick his wounds. But it was more than that, too. He no longer had a reason to get up, or go in to the office. He was losing control of his company, and there was nothing he could do to change that. Scrounging eight million dollars was out of the question, and Dana knew it. They had already stressed to the limit all their available lines of credit. And although Parker could always stay on as one-third owner, that would be a source of never-ending pain and frustration. Better to let the whole thing go and be done with it. He had told Laurel the truth—he would be very soon out of a job.

The second night of his convalescence he couldn't sleep, so he sat in bed with the photo album Edvard had given him. Maybe, he thought, if he studied the pictures long enough, he might find some connective thread that would explain how he had reached this desolate moment of loneliness. Better still, he might be able to follow that thread back to better times.

The baby picture, "Infant with Saltine," offered no help. It seemed to belong not only to a different age but to a different world. No child he had ever seen wore clothing like this, except maybe in history books. And most troubling was the feeling that he had no connection at all to this pudgy-faced toddler. Whose eyes were those? Whose lips?

The same held true for all the early photos—Parker's first day of school, Parker the Cub Scout, Parker the Little Leaguer in an ill-fitting jersey. In fact it wasn't until he was about twelve years old, a crew-cut science geek, that he could relate at all. The picture showed him hunched over his brand-new microscope and looking at prepared slides. He could remember the names even now: silver berry scaly hair, voluble stem of sponge gourd, smooth muscle of frog, spicule of sea cucumber.

When Parker turned to the page with his Grade 13 graduation photo, he actually laughed out loud. He was wearing a powder-blue tuxedo and standing on the front porch with Cindy Birch. He had ludicrous bangs that swept across his forehead, very Hitler Youth. Cindy's hair rose in a tower of frosted curls and tendrils like some ornate dessert, just the thing to go with her plum chiffon.

What the photo didn't show, but he remembered all too well (and this darkened the edges of his laughter) was the image of Cindy much later that night, slumped drunkenly on Walter Mocko's rec-room floor. She was also crying, as girls back then tended to do when they were drunk. Rivulets of mascara ran down her cheeks. Her friends gathered around her, clucking support.

But more than anything, that night became unforgettable as the night he lost his virginity—not with Cindy, as it turned out, but in the early hours of the morning with Valerie Dresser, VD, the sluttiest girl in school. The historical significance alone would guarantee that sexual act a kind of mythical status. But he would also remember it as perhaps the single most unhealthy thing he had ever done, quite aside from any considerations about disease. Valerie was a deeply bitter girl, and it hadn't escaped her finely honed sense of justice that the boys of Unionville considered her fuckable yet never datable. She was, in fact, one of only a handful of graduates without an escort to the prom. Even geeky Martingale had a date. Even bitchy Birch. So when Parker and Val actually got together that night, he did not experience the anticipated glories—the ringing of bells, the singing of birds—but something rather desperate and punishing.

From that photo he skipped ahead to Christmas 1973, Mersea's first trip to Unionville to meet Jack and Nancy. Parker had shoulder-length hair tied back in a ponytail. He wore a sweatshirt, bell-bottoms and wooden clogs; he spouted Marx and Veblen and Freud at every opportunity. Mersea had on a long colorful skirt and a peasant blouse, her hair in a French braid. She thoroughly charmed his parents, his father in particular.

Parker found it almost painful to look at that picture now. This was the young woman he had fallen in love with, who had filled him with such a bewildering desire that he would have given anything just to be with her. That face even now, in a faded old snapshot more than twenty years later, made his stomach flutter. Yet it was a look that seemed out of touch with the time, like he was staring at a pinup of Veronica Lake or Claudette Colbert, a beauty as pure as a mathematical equation or philosophical principle.

Parker closed the album then and slumped lower in his bed. What struck him most clearly about the earlier pictures was the fact that he was a different person in each one. He found no continuity, no discernible pattern, only discrete phases. By the mid-eighties, however, that had changed. He had more or less become the man he was now. Aside from the loss of hair, the sag of flesh, the past fifteen years had apparently had no outward effect on him whatsoever. He wasn't sure which state of affairs he found more depressing. And where were the sunflowers? There wasn't a single photo in the album to suggest that Parker and Mersea had been anything more than typical of their time and generation—two suburban kids making a life for themselves at the ragged end of the century.

That night, when he finally did fall asleep, he had a long and vivid dream. He was wandering around an old mansion too extravagant in every way to be real, a Gormenghast dwelling with slate roofs—the slopes, the domes, the turrets, the dormers, like some dark mountain range set within the city, with wide marble staircases that led to high balconies and second-floor ballrooms, then down again to acres of mezzanine and foyer and hallways curving Escher-like to other wings, other vistas of garden and gazebo and judiciously placed statuary.

He was all alone and trying to find a staircase that would lead him up to a commanding view of the great city. His footsteps echoed down long marble halls. Other than that sound, the sound of his own progress, nothing could be heard, as though the whole city had been silenced by a plague. There were no thrumming factories, no sirens, no traffic noises at all, no children in the schoolyards, or thumping stereos, no garage bands or garbage trucks, leaf blowers or snow throwers or wind in the trees. There were only hallways and empty rooms and, apart from the sounds he created himself, stillness.

Next morning Parker got out of bed without hesitation and pulled on a bathrobe, feeling as though some fever had passed. He made a large pot of coffee and dawdled over breakfast, flipping through sections of the newspaper he hadn't read in years.

The front-page story told about a big rally at Maple Leaf Gardens. The teachers of the province were threatening a wildcat strike if the government passed its controversial legislation, Bill 160, which the teachers decried as a serious threat to the future of the province. Some reports had twenty-four thousand people at the rally: the angry and the oppressed and the indignant and the mildly sympathetic, all of them carrying placards and shouting themselves hoarse—"We won't back down!"—and following up with a candlelight walk to Queen's Park, where the provincial government, in a late-night session, was trying to push the bill through.

Parker had no trouble thinking the worst of this government, if only because everyone else did. Darryl and Rudi, the Couture twins, Brendan Masters, even Lyle Beckwith would have been at that rally, feeding, and feeding on, the righteous energy. And Parker could have tagged along to be sociable. It might have been fun for a night to feel part of something so large, so principled, so determined.

He seldom thought about such things, of course. He had no real sense of the issues involved or what was at stake or who might be right or wrong. Instead he felt a sense of disappointment that the formulation of social policy should take place amid such antagonism and distrust—an attitude very much in keeping with his mother's mushy idealism. All the ills of the world could be cured, she maintained, if only people tried harder to get along.

The business section of the paper that morning focused on the Asian crisis, and how the currencies of Korea and Malaysia and Indonesia were in freefall. Analysts talked of currency controls to keep powerful global speculators from ruining these emerging economies. They predicted a wave of deflation that would spread to North America, and that prospect had stock market investors around the world suddenly scrambling for a safe haven. Bonds had shot through the roof. Marian the Contrarian looked very smart indeed.

Around eleven o'clock, Parker showered and dressed and then called the accountant for the facts and figures. After that, he called the lawyer and set things in motion. That made him feel nervous and fluttery, so he walked into the backyard for a breath of air. He put away the hose and the lawnmower. He filled several plastic garbage bags with leaves and lined them up beside the garage. These simple tasks had the desired effect. In no time, he felt more relaxed, more in control.

It was clear to him now, after a couple of days of rest and reflection, that things were not quite as desperate as they had appeared before. Granted, his whole life was in flux, but that could be seen as a good thing, couldn't it, especially at his time of life? And really, other men his age were tossed out of similar jobs with a few months' severance pay. Yet according to his accountant's figures, if they accepted the Cynara offer, paid off all their debts, all the appropriate taxes and legal fees, they should walk away with two hundred and fifty thousand dollars each. While few would call that a satisfactory return after eight years of empire building, no matter how he chose to look at the situation—even knowing that Donald and Dana had been offered executive positions at Cynara, with big salaries, stock options and a high profile—he found it difficult to work up any significant degree of self-pity. It was Laurel who deserved sympathy, he felt. It was unlikely she had much to cushion her fall from employment. And what about Debra and the rest of the employees? What did the future hold for them?

Back in the house he poured himself another cup of coffee and marveled that he could feel so blasé—NEXT was history, Texpan as good as gone. He was in shock, most likely; yet in a way, he couldn't help thinking he was lucky to have a few less headaches to contend with just now, as if by magic the integers of his life had been simplified and for the next while his concerns could be strictly personal.

He had read a book once, at Mersea's insistence—he couldn't remember the title or the author—about a man, an intellectual of some sort, whose life had come completely undone. In reaction the character retreated to his country home, a shambles of a place overrun by mice and squirrels, and began the process of tying up loose ends. He did this by writing letters to friends and loved ones, even the dead—explaining, asking forgiveness. Parker could almost picture himself in that kind of life now. He could move out to the cottage with his laptop and modem and send a blizzard of e-mail into the world. A rec-room hermit, a man of letters.

He smiled at the thought, so melodramatic, and walked to the front window and looked out on the street. Art was there, picking up the few leaves that had landed on his immaculate lawn and carrying them to the curb one at a time. That, too, made him smile, though not as happily.

Art was a widower, with a son who lived in Arizona. He had no other family, no friends that Parker had ever seen. He was more or less an outcast in the neighborhood. Much older than the other people on the street, he had alienated most everyone with his yard obsessions, his odd manner, his inability to shoot the breeze. He was a perfect illustration, Parker realized, of what could happen when, by accident or design, you lose your connection to the world. Art had come ungrounded and was bumping stupidly around in his little world, like a fly in an empty room. And that, Parker understood, was a fate worse than the chaos he found himself in now. So was the hermit strategy. Walk down either of those paths, and in no time at all he'd be sitting alone in the cottage, pissed out of his mind and singing Joni Mitchell songs in falsetto.

Unfortunately, Parker had no other plans, large or small, that he could fall back on. He wasn't even sure how much damage he had sustained and how much of his former life would remain when the dust settled. For now, he needed a modest day-to-day arrangement.

Later that morning he drove over to Olivia's house. Edvard answered the door, saying, "She's not here, if that's who you're looking for."

Parker peered down the street, where someone was painting a house canary yellow. A radio blared, some low thumping reggae tune.

"Can I come in?"

They stared at each other a moment, recalculating values and vectors, then walked into the kitchen, where the table was spread with newspapers. The room smelled of bitter coffee and burned toast, a smell that always made Parker think of poverty, as if the rich never burned their bread.

"The other day," Parker said without preamble, "you were right. Completely. Whatever there was between me and Laurel, it was all in my head. I know that now. I think I always knew it. I'm sorry I got so upset with you. I guess I was a little out of control."

Edvard waved the whole thing away as beneath his notice. Then with a sniff he said, "Saw the story in the *Globe* yesterday morning. This good news or bad news?"

"What did it say?"

"That Texpan's being bought for an undisclosed sum of money."

Parker looked away, considering. "That sounds like a fair assessment."

"But the sum's been disclosed to you. Is it good news or bad news?"

Parker looked out the window as a squirrel ran along a telephone wire. One of the things he liked about Ed, and also one of the traits he found most annoying, was this habit of forcing Parker to answer the pertinent question. He could see how Ed might make a good journalist.

At last he said, "I'm being forced to sell my company to a bunch of strangers. Whatever the sum, there's no way on earth I can make it seem like good news."

Edvard eyed him critically. "You don't look too miserable, though."

"Look, there's nothing I can do about it, so what's the use complaining?"

That made Ed laugh. "Jesus," he said, "they must have offered you a shitload of money, the way you're avoiding my question . . ."

Parker enjoyed the idea that Ed might think he was now rich. How many people, he wondered, might see that little item in the papers and think, Oh, man, he's got it made now. Easy Street.

Ed got up and poured the sludgy remains of the pot into his coffee cup and took a sip. In a tone of wry sophistication, the way you imagine Oscar Wilde speaking, he said, "My own prospects, of course, are not as encouraging, as you can tell by the fact that I now dwell under the same roof as my *maman*. In short, I have surrendered completely. The fates have decreed that I sit here, corpulent and slothful, wallowing in the muck of talk shows and cooking shows and interminable afternoons of the Golf Channel. My brain has already begun to liquefy."

Parker smiled with false sincerity. "I'm sure your mother is very happy. Besides, there's not even a television here."

"Well, please, I'm a wreck. You're not the only one whose dream has gone up in smoke this week. You remember the novel I told you about? The psychoanalytical meaning of history in a post–Cold War world?"

"Your big book."

"Yeah, well, I get here the other day and pick up a copy of *The New Yorker*, it's maybe a month old, and there's this long profile of Don DeLillo, one of my heroes, totally. And get this—he stole my fucking idea."

Parker blinked. "I thought you saw yourself as the next Pynchon."

"Pynchon, DeLillo—the point is I've been fucked over. The story I was born to write has just been appropriated by a genius." He rummaged through the mess of papers on the table and finally came up with the offending magazine. Shaking it in the air, he said, "They're talking about his new book, *Underworld*." He flipped through the pages a moment, back and forth, looking for his place. "The whole point of the book, the article says, is to portray America's psyche since the Cold War."

"So?"

"So, that's my novel in a nutshell. The fucking guy."

He tossed the magazine aside, disgusted. And Parker's sarcasm, rich and satisfying, rose to the surface. "There's more than that, though, right? DeLillo's novel is longer than a sentence."

"Well, yeah, it's fucking monstrous. Eight hundred pages, every one of them a gem, you can bet."

"All based on your idea."

"So it would seem."

Parker patted Edvard's hand and said, "No offense, but ideas are a dime a dozen, Ed. We all come up with great ideas every day, right? Even Dad. Has he told you yet about his idea for edible tape? Comes in flavors. You use it to hold things together, like burritos, club sandwiches. A good idea, maybe, but it kind of just dies right there unless someone tries to make it real. That's where most of us fall down, I figure. What separates a good idea from a bad idea is whether it works. Surely you know this from those essays you write."

Ed made a bored face. "Yeah," he said, "but my idea did work. DeLillo built an eight-hundred-page book around it."

Parker could scarcely contain himself. "Are you out of your mind? It was based on *his* idea, which obviously was a big one. You see, he worked it out on paper, brought it to life. That's what makes it an idea in the first place. What you're talking about, this 'big book' of yours, is just a pipe dream."

Ed sniffed. "I guess you know all about that, don't you?"

"Enough to know it's never the idea, in business, it's the execution that's important."

"Right. Like it'll do me a lot of good to write my book now that he's laid waste to the topic."

"Wouldn't hurt."

"Really. Why don't I just write a novel about a sea captain who's fixated on a white whale? Think that would fly?"

"Sure. Why not?"

Ed groaned and let his head fall back in resignation. After a moment he said, "Never mind. I guess it doesn't really make much difference. I'd probably never write the damn thing anyway. I've never been that big on follow-through, myself."

Parker leaned closer, suddenly excited. He sensed he was on the verge of discovering some small truth about Ed and, by extension, about life. "Don't take this the wrong way," he said, "but it kind of shows. For instance, your whole attitude about women—where's that at?"

Ed waited, not sure what Parker was driving at.

"Never been in love, you said. I mean doesn't that tell you something about follow-through?"

Edvard laughed good-naturedly and pulled on his nose. "What, are you bringing that up again? I told you, love is just faith on a physical plane. And I've never had much faith in faith, whether it's in the afterlife, or mankind, or herbal remedies or mutual funds—it strikes me as lazy. An excuse to stop thinking."

Parker looked surprised. "You think love is laziness? It's the most difficult thing I know."

Ed laughed again, louder this time. "That's because it's unnatural. Besides, you're out of shape, old man. You're supposed to be spreading your genes out there as often as possible, even if it means hunting and locking horns and running yourself ragged in the process. Instead you come home every night, get the back rub from your Poodlebites, the nice dinner, the clean sheets, the clean tub and the roll in the hay—it's, like, totally fucking perverse."

Pointedly, Parker let his jaw drop. "You *are* a throwback, aren't you?"

"Just being honest. You think you're so pure? You were ready to tear out my throat in your kitchen a few nights ago, all over a woman that neither one of us is in love with."

Parker looked away, chastened. That scene on his kitchen floor seemed to exist in another lifetime, as if it had all happened in a dream or a delirium. Beyond that, he wondered how Ed could speak so casually about these things.

After a deep breath, he nodded soberly and said, "You're right. That had nothing to do with love. And I take that as a warning. But it seems to me that's where you get bogged down with women."

Ed hooted in disbelief. "*I'm* bogged down? I think you're talking about yourself there, bro'. Far as I'm concerned, I'm the master of magic and miracle."

Parker sat back, savoring the richness of their conversation. Once again he could understand the appeal of brotherhood, discovering parts of his life that had long been closed off to him, like a man who comes in from the cold and gradually realizes how hunched and huddled he has been and finally allows himself to straighten up and stretch to his full height. He could still feel a degree of pain, of course, but it was fading, replaced by a warm wave of relief.

With a sly smile Parker said, "Maybe you missed this basic premise, Ed, but magic is illusion, a trick, not exactly the best foundation for building a relationship. What you want is reality, or else you're just wasting everyone's time. I mean, you have the chance to make a beautiful thing—why settle for an illusion?"

"A beautiful illusion."

"Okay, but there's more than that."

"You mean *lu-uuuv*?"

Parker closed his eyes and took a deep breath, the irony so rich it was dizzying. It was like he was preaching to himself, not Ed. Finally he said, "Yeah, sure, love. And you're wrong about it. It's not faith—it's art, it's hard work, it's application and skill and commitment and devotion. It's not entertainment, either, or something you consume. It's like . . . it's like writing that big book of yours. Only your trouble is *you* never get past that brilliant first sentence, do you? No character development, no plot, no themes."

Ed clucked his tongue. "You gotta admit, though, that opening line is pretty catchy."

Smiling affectionately, Parker slumped lower in his seat and waved his hands in the air, all talked out. In response, Ed stretched and groaned like some jungle beast grown tired of lounging. Getting to his feet, he said, "Maybe you're right. Maybe I'm just too lazy to fall in love. And maybe I'm crazy thinking I could write a big novel anyway. Given my character, porno probably *is* the way to go."

He laughed weakly at his own joke, a rheumy rumble that degenerated into a full-fledged hack, a noisy spate of throat-clearing and a disgusting gob into the sink. Then, suddenly antsy, he poked about Olivia's mason jars, coming up with a handful of chocolate chips, which he tossed into his mouth.

When he had finished chewing, his face brightened and he said, "Hey, I just remembered. The old man phone you last night?"

Parker shook his head. "I had it unplugged."

"This is great, then. The old guy'll be here any minute now."

"Dad?"

"You bet. We're going to pick out some duds for the wedding. Should be a hoot."

Parker rubbed his forehead, feeling a little panicky. "They've decided to go ahead?"

"Well, now that Vegas is out, there didn't seem a real good reason to hold off. Unless you've got some other kind of news . . ."

"No news, except I'm unemployed."

Edvard leaned back against the counter, his arms folded across his chest. "So what are you going to do?"

Parker knew well enough that he had never found a job on his own. All his working life he had followed Dana's lead. Some entrepreneur. And shaking his head gloomily, he said, "Everything is so messed up right now, I can't tell whether I'm coming or going."

Ed did his broken-jaw thing. "You'll get over all of this," he said. "Six months from now, this screwball wedding won't be in your face and your world can get back to normal."

"Not likely. You don't have any idea what my life is like right now."

"And I don't want to know. But I'm telling you, this wedding, you want my advice, I'd try to enjoy it. You look at it the right way, it's kind of a gas."

Uneasiness settled on the room like so much soot, making them twitch and scratch and clear their throats. You could call it the residue of Laurel, but that would be too simple. They were both painfully aware that the next little while could produce a lifetime supply of irritations, large and small.

After a few more awkward moments a car sounded its horn outside—shave and a haircut, two bits. Suddenly edgy, Parker stood and said, "That would be our man, the old fool."

Edvard grabbed his jacket and bag, and headed for the door. With his hand on the knob, he said, "I gather you don't find him as funny as I do. But the new haircut, the bike, the leather—you gotta admire his spirit. He acts like a kid always."

Parker pictured the house in Unionville, early Sixties. He's ten years old, out front playing road hockey with his friends, last one picked, of course, and his father comes charging out of the house, stick in hand. "Okay, girls," he bellows from halfway down the block, "clear the track, here comes Eddie Shack." Then he runs full-speed, circling both nets and giving everyone's stick a good slash. And the moment he gets possession of the tennis ball, he begins the play-by-play. "Here comes Shack, he's got up a good head of steam. Oh, man, he dekes Delvecchio right out of his jockstrap! What a move! What a play! He's at the blue line, he winds up for a shot—no he pivots around Gadsby. Look at this guy stickhandle! Look at him go! Oh! Oh! Oh!" And for dramatic effect he falls onto his back in the middle of the road and everyone but Parker gets in on the pile-up . . .

So nothing had really changed. His father was playing the same role he had always played—the antic partyboy, the man who never grew up—and Parker should have come to terms with it all by now. But he hadn't. In fact, it seemed to be getting worse. They had both grown older, but only Parker acted that way, and he resented it.

Edvard turned to look at him then, the tiniest dimples appearing at the corners of his mouth. "You gotta hope," he said, "that the old man's goofiness isn't genetic. Maybe we should make a pact. If either one of us starts acting like Jerry Lewis, we call Dr. Kevorkian."

It wasn't much of a joke, but it felt to Parker like the whisper of a breeze on a hot humid day. He wondered if this could possibly be the start of some relief. What if Edvard, his half brother, assumed half of the grief that came with a father like Jack Martingale?

"Deal," he said, offering his hand to Edvard. "If I ever get a funny horn on my car, come and get me."

Edvard squeezed his hand firmly and gave it a good pump. "Deal. And if you ever hear me talking about marriage, pull the plug."

With that, they stepped into the gray misty morning. Their father was pacing the sidewalk in front of his Lincoln. He had put on his best suit and shoes and looked as dignified as a diplomat.

"Parker," he bellowed, arms held out like the Pope, "where the fuck you been? I called maybe a thousand times. Hey, Eddy."

"Very nice," Edvard said, giving Jack the exaggerated once-over. "But I thought we were shopping together."

Jack laughed and shot Parker a private smile. "This is an old suit," he said, a little too proud of the way he looked. "We're all going shopping, right, Park?"

"That's what I hear."

"Then let's get a move on."

They climbed into the Lincoln, Edvard in the back, and headed east along Bloor Street. Parker noticed that Ed had the same annoying habit their father had—an inability to remain quiet for even a moment, always clearing his throat or sniffing or humming a melody or, as was the case at that moment, singing. In German.

"Freude, schöner Götterfunken,
Tochter aus Elyssium,
Wir betreten feuertrunken,
Himmlische, dein Heiligtum!
Deine Zauber binden wieder,
Was die Mode streng geteilt;
Alle Menschen werden Brüder,
Wo dein sanfter Flügel weilt."

In a natural pause in the performance, Parker swiveled in his seat and gave him the eyeball. "I'm thinking this qualifies as suitable cause for Dr. K. What about you?"

"Get used to it. I sing it at least once a day."

Their father looked across at them then and smiled with satisfaction, as if one of his secret plans had come to fruition. Parker wanted to smack him. Instead he said, "So where are we going for these suits, the Salvation Army?"

His father turned back to the road and sighed, clearly above such pettiness. In a priggish tone, he said,

"As a matter of fact, Parker, we're going to that place you're always raving about."

"Garibaldi's?" Parker whistled, pleasantly surprised. "You sure you can afford that?"

"Money's no object," he replied. "I want us all to look sharp, okay? And nothing off the rack. I want these suckers made to measure."

Ed leaned forward, resting his chin on the back of the seat. "What if I rent a tux and keep the change?"

"No dice, kiddo. I'm buying you some fancy threads. For once in your life you're gonna look decent."

They parked in a nearby lot, surrounded by Bentleys and Porsches, and walked the last few blocks to the store. As always, Parker couldn't help noticing the people here—expensively dressed, beautiful, prosperous, seemingly without a care in the world, so different from the people near his office, the habitués of Dunkin' Daddy's, or even the neighbors on his street in Lawrence Park. If Toronto imagined itself a younger, nicer version of New York, then this stretch of Bloor was its own swanky take on Fifth Avenue—Armani, Tiffany, Royal de Versailles, Chanel—an avenue of dreams.

Inside the store, Parker was greeted by Tony, one of the personal style coordinators. "Par-ker!" he called out from halfway across the room, moving quickly now, arms spread in old-world greeting. "Welcome back. Wonderful. What can I do for you?"

As briefly as possible, Parker explained the situation to Tony, who immediately waved over two other young men to assist them. Then they settled into the formalities of measuring for a suit, each with his own salesman who carted out fabrics, talked weights, cuts, details.

Parker was very much at home. Every six months, like clockwork, he came to this store and bought a suit—a light one in summer, a heavier one in winter; and every six months he took his sorriest-looking suit out of his closet and gave it away. That way he consistently upgraded his wardrobe. At any one time he had five suits on the go, all of them, except for subtleties of shade and fabric, pretty much identical. Considering the recent turn in his financial situation, however, he might have to change that little detail of his life.

Because the store had his measurements, likes and dislikes on file, Parker soon finished and could sit back and watch Edvard and his father.

Ed couldn't stop smiling, a wide-eyed mocking grin that kept edging into delight because, despite himself, he was having so much fun. Animated, teasing, he had the salesman in stitches; but he was taking it all in, too, like a spy, so he could have a good laugh later in private.

Jack had a different smile, the deeply satisfied look of a man who knows he is rich beyond measure. He waved Parker closer, draped his arm across his shoulder and said, "I'm so happy right now, son. This, this moment right here, is one of the best moments of my life."

Parker snorted dismissively.

"I'm serious," he continued. "I've had some great times, right? Jamming with Count Basie, those sessions with Don Ellis, that time Duke had his own TV show there in the fifties, times with your mom, you and me at the cottage. But this, I'm telling you, standing here with my boys, old as we are, all the baggage, all the griefs, standing here and buying suits for my wedding and we're all happy and getting along and together——"

And without warning, he swung around and gave Parker a bone-crushing hug. "God," he whispered in Parker's ear, "I love you so fucking much."

Three hours and five thousand dollars later, they were sitting in a café on Bellair, sipping drinks and waiting for lunch to arrive. Jack was doing most of the talking.

"So, Parker," he said suddenly remembering, "what do I get last night but a long-distance call from Mersea. From Montreal, no less. Why didn't you tell me she was out of town so long?"

"Well, you know how it is, Dad. What did she say?"

His father leaned halfway across the table and jabbed him in the arm with his index finger. "That she couldn't promise she'd make the wedding, that's what she said."

"I guess she's awful busy."

"Busy! You tell her I'll be royally pissed if she doesn't come."

Edvard took a sip of beer. "This Mersea," he said, "that's the woman you live with?"

Parker nodded, and his father leapt into the breach. "One heck of a girl. Beautiful, tall, smart. I don't know what she sees in this lunkhead."

Parker smiled patiently, and Edvard gave him a reassuring look and said, "What's she do that she has to be away so much?"

"Mutual funds," Parker replied in a tone that made it clear he would prefer another subject. "She works for Galaxy. Head of marketing."

Edvard slipped into a role—the wild-eyed Bedouin in a desert marketplace. "Ah," he said with an exaggerated shudder, "the work of the devil."

They all laughed at that, and Parker thought once again what a bonus it was, in these encounters with his father, to have someone on his side.

But Jack wasn't finished yet. "She can't take a day off for the wedding? Way I understand it, these funds of hers pretty much sell themselves. What business has she got that keeps her in Montreal weeks at a time?" He leaned forward again, this time laughing slyly. "Unless she's found herself a little Frenchie on the side."

The urge to strangle his father at that moment was so strong that Parker actually sat on his hands. He looked at Edvard for help, but Ed looked on with a grin of his own.

"Well," Parker said, aiming for a light jokey tone to match his father's, "it's hard to say what she's up to these days. You know, I'm just a man. She doesn't think I should worry my pretty little head about money matters. But I'll pass along your concerns, Dad."

Perfect timing, the waiter brought their food then, and Parker knew he could count on at least a few minutes' reprieve. His father didn't believe in dinner conversation. "Eatin's eatin' and talkin's talkin'," he liked to say. "If God had wanted us to talk at the dinner table, we'd have vocal chords in our bums." And sure enough, Jack dug into his veal florentine with elbows high and lips smacking. Ed, who had pretty much the same table manners, ate with the energy and grace of a circus performer, those guys who keep twelve plates whirling on sticks.

All too soon, however, his father had finished his meal, and he sucked his teeth (the Jack Martingale equivalent to tapping your wine glass for everyone's attention) and said, "Of course you have to wonder why Parker here hasn't made an honest woman of Mersea. What's it been, fifteen years you two have been shacking up together?"

"Leave it, Dad."

"I won't leave it. She's ten times more woman than you deserve, even in your dreams. Any sane man would have staked his claim a long time ago."

"Yes, well, maybe you noticed—she's not a gold mine."

"No? Well my guess is you're just too chickenshit to pop the question."

Parker groaned miserably, then rubbed his face with his hands. "Not that it's any of your business, but I don't need to 'pop the question.' We decided long ago that we weren't getting married and we weren't having kids. Okay? Satisfied?"

"Bullshit. Who ever decides something like that? You just don't want to think about it. You're a man, that's only natural, we're all in the same boat. But sooner or later you have to do right by that girl."

"Da-ad, drop it."

"I won't drop it, Parker. It bothers me. Life's about choices, not sitting on a fence."

Parker couldn't believe his ears. He looked to Edvard for some kind of confirmation that he hadn't lost his mind. In return he got a stupid grin, and that was all he could take.

"So here we have the master of life's decisions," he said, his words glistening and caustic. "Like Edvard here was one of your brilliant choices, I suppose. Or like I was."

The pain seeped into his father's face like a stain. He had only been trying to help. Now he was under attack. "It was different back then," he said. "You didn't plan kids, they just happened."

"Oh, right, it was marriage you were talking about, and your famous choice, Nancy or Olivia, the watershed of your life, which if you want my opinion is really the purest form of bullshit. As if you've ever been that clear in your mind about anything."

Edvard laid his hand on Parker's arm, a brotherly gesture lest words be spoken that shouldn't be spoken. But Parker shook him off and leaned toward his father.

"The fact is, Dad, you've always managed to work both sides of the street, whichever suited you best. So you're the one who's confusing his terms here. You've confused *choosing* with *ordering*. I see that now. In your mind it wasn't so much a choice between Nancy or Olivia—it was first Nancy, then Olivia."

His father blinked once, twice, then rose unsteadily to his feet and hurried out of the restaurant.

Edvard finished his beer and set it soundlessly on the table. "Looks like we'll be hoofing it," he said. "Washing dishes, too, unless you can cover lunch. I'm busted, as usual."

If Parker heard him, he didn't let on. He was staring at his plate, thoroughly shaken by what had just happened. Finally he turned and said, "Why did I say that?"

Edvard smiled warmly. "You're upset. You've got a lot on your mind. He'll get over it."

"But I used to be able to keep my mouth shut."

"Relax. You're better off spitting it out. And if I were you, I'd let him stew about it, too. He's not stupid, the old man. And he's got a hell of a good heart. Just that his brain isn't always in gear. I can almost guarantee you that until just now, he didn't have the faintest idea how deeply you felt about this whole wedding thing. It's good it's out in the open. It will give him something to think about."

Parker cringed a little inside. He wasn't used to discussing his feelings with anyone except Mersea, and even then not often.

"What about you?" Parker asked. "You're in the same position. I don't see you flying off the handle."

Edvard gave that some serious thought. Finally he said, "Our positions are not even remotely similar, I'd say. To begin with, both my parents are still alive, and in fact appear to be getting together for the first time. So if anything, our circumstances are reversed. Fact is I think it's all pretty cool. I mean, when life keeps getting bigger and sweeter, you must be doing something right." He smiled then, and there was a glint of mockery.

"Something funny?" Parker asked.

"I was just thinking how full of shit you are. That lovely speech you made back at Olivia's, about love and execution and follow-through. The old man's got you pegged, and it bugs the hell out of you. You're a fence-sitter just like me, can't commit, but at least I admit it."

FOURTEEN

The Principle of Art

Now that Parker had decided to offer his share of the company, he was busier than ever—reams of paper passing back and forth between lawyers and accountants, numbing telephone calls about one detail or another. It went on like that for the better part of two weeks. And the more he dug into the nuts and bolts of the Cynara offer, the more Parker realized they were being robbed. Texpan was worth much more than twelve million, he figured. But not without Dana and Donald on board. So he swallowed his pride and agreed to the deal. It wasn't as if he had any other real options. What hurt the most was that no one had made a pitch for his services.

During all these negotiations, Parker spent his days with lawyers and accountants. He kept in touch with Edvard by phone, which is how he followed the progress of the wedding plans.

To Parker's relief, and Ed's chagrin, Olivia had

threatened to call the whole thing off if there was anything even remotely resembling a stag or a doe party. Instead she would arrange a dinner at her place, she said, just the four of them, five if Mersea would come. Parker approved of that arrangement, but when he heard the plans for the wedding itself, he could scarcely believe it.

The date was set for November 29, at St. Margaret's Chapel, a tiny country church a few miles away from the cottage. A small reception and dinner were scheduled for Big Moose Lodge, on the other side of Hidden Lake. Wedding guests could stay on there, but they were all invited back to the cottage for more festivities.

Parker wondered how his father, or Olivia for that matter, could be so unfeeling, so clueless as to celebrate their wedding in that place. It was so clearly in bad taste that it convinced him the two were in love after all. How else to explain this shocking lapse of consideration? He had half a mind to boycott the wedding altogether.

The honeymoon, he learned, would be postponed until the new year. Until then, Jack and Olivia would remain in Toronto while she finished her term at the university. Then they would fly down to Mazatlán for the winter. Parker couldn't help but sense Edvard's influence on that last point.

The day of the pre-nuptial dinner was the same day that Parker had to drive downtown to the office towers at Bay and Richmond to sign papers for the final handover of Texpan. Parker hadn't seen Dana since that weepy confrontation in Dana's basement, and this time, standing around in the plush boardroom of Burdon, Joiner & Feingold, his old friend looked very serious, very subdued. If Parker hadn't known better, he would have said Dana felt intimidated by the surroundings. As an added surprise, even Donald put in an appearance.

For a few awkward moments, the three former partners stood apart with their lawyers, looking tense and unhappy, waiting for the folks from Cynara to arrive. Finally Parker, who was trying to avoid feeling like a victim, walked over to Donald and said, "So that's what you look like. I had almost forgotten."

"Hey there, P.M. Long time. Look, you're not sore, I hope."

Parker shrugged unconvincingly. "Little late to be worrying about that, I'd say."

Donald nodded gloomily and then looked around the room for help. Finding none, he said, "Hey, anyway, thanks for sending that guy Musil my way. He's good."

Parker stood up a bit straighter. "Victor?"

"Yeah. That new bit of code he showed you? I hired him right after he sent it to me. You wouldn't believe how it improved the program."

That was all he needed to hear. Even Victor, an absolute stranger, had finagled a new job out of the deal. He had seen the opportunity and acted. Now the only one out in the cold, it seemed, would be Parker.

The guy from Cynara breezed into the room then, looking very slick, handsome as a movie star. He had a grip like a vise, a mouth that was all teeth. His idea of social chitchat was to tell a string of off-color jokes about the scandalous appetites of the American president then laugh, dead-eyed and malicious, at his own sick country. It convinced Parker that, even if he had been able to hang on to his third of the company, it would have been disastrous. There was no way he could have worked with a man like that.

After a few more minutes of awkward conversation, they signed the papers and then pretended to sign them for a few corporate photographers—the old grab-and-grin. They toasted the event with champagne. Half an hour after they arrived, the company had changed hands.

Parker was first to leave. As he stood waiting for the elevator to take him down, Dana pulled him aside and led him over to a leather sofa near a plastic palm tree. "Sit a minute," Dana said, looking sad as a hound. "No hard feelings?"

Parker stared down at his shoes. "A few, Dana. Just a few. I guess I'll get over them, though."

Nodding soberly, Dana pulled a manila envelope from his briefcase and handed it over.

"What's this?" Parker asked, pulling out a single typed sheet addressed to Melanie. A postdated cheque for fifty thousand dollars was stapled to one corner. It was from an account in Manhattan.

"By next week, the draft from Cynara will be cleared and she can cash that."

Parker looked at it again to make sure he hadn't misread. "Why are you giving this to me?"

Dana shrugged, looking suddenly like a small boy. "I thought you'd help me out. I can't face her, Spark. I need you to tell her."

"Tell her what, that you're a coward? She's your wife, for Christ's sake, the mother of your children. You owe her at least the courtesy of an explanation."

"I can't!" he said through gritted teeth, the veins sticking out in his neck. "Jesus, I'd do the same for you if the tables were reversed."

Parker stood up and tossed the envelope and its

contents in Dana's lap. "Then you're not the friend I thought you were," he said.

Parker decided to splurge on a big lunch. Although the area of Bay and Richmond near the lawyers' office had no shortage of expensive restaurants, they would be filled with the suspender crowd: the brokers, the bond traders, the high-powered finaglers. It was exactly the wrong atmosphere for the mood he was in. Under the circumstances he felt he could use something a bit more frivolous and entertaining.

He walked to his car and sat there mulling over the prospects. The next few hours could be tricky, he realized. He had just lost his company. If he sat in a restaurant by himself, even an elegant dining room, he would start feeling lonely and depressed, a bit too much like a loser. Instead he needed to make the most of the day, create a celebratory mood around what could otherwise be a depressing afternoon. That idea gave him a sudden inspiration. After a moment's paperwork, he dialed Laurel's number on his cell phone. She picked up on the second ring.

"Hey," he said, "it's Parker. I have a reason to celebrate today and no one to celebrate with. Can I buy you a stupidly expensive lunch?"

"Oh, hmm, lunch," she replied, stalling for time while she tried to get her thoughts in order. Then she cleared her throat and in a kinder tone said, "I don't know, Parker, if that's such a good idea. Eddy kind of told me, you know, how you feel and all, and maybe that would just make everything too difficult, having lunch, you know?"

He took a deep breath and tried again. "It's not like that, Laurel, I promise. There are twenty reasons I want you to come to lunch with me, but not one of them has anything to do with me acting like a fool."

"Gee, really, I don't know . . ."

He could sense her wavering, and he pressed on. "Why don't I pick you up? I'll give you a twenty-dollar bill before I even say hello. That way, if I do or say anything that makes you even slightly uncomfortable, you can just walk out and call a cab. Even if I look at you the wrong way."

She laughed then. "You are desperate for company."

"It's more than that," he said. "I have something to tell you. What do you say?"

"And you can't just tell me over the phone?"

"No, Laurel. Or I mean I could but—the truth?—I just signed over the company today. It's gone. My whole company is in someone else's hands right now and, well, I can look at it two ways. In fact, that's the only way I can look at it, one minute angry, one minute sad, back and forth, back and forth until I'm almost dizzy. And I thought, I don't know, if I could spend some time with someone over a nice lunch, maybe I could get in a better mood, and then the whole thing might start to feel a bit more positive. That's why I thought of you. I can't think of anyone better, in this state, to help me put the right spin on all this. What do you say?"

She agreed, grudgingly, and Parker drove over to her place in high spirits. When she came out wearing her black mini, white shirt, spike heels, he nodded appreciatively and said, "Ah, the studio clothes. I guess I deserve that. I apologize."

"Oh!" she blurted, grabbing his arm emphatically. "No, I didn't mean that. These are like the only 'dressy' clothes I have. Seriously." She bowed her head, suddenly bashful. "I always thought you were kind of sweet."

They drove to Queen Street West, past the CITY-TV building, and angled south. The restaurant, Ars Longa, took up the entire second floor of an old warehouse, with high ceilings, and tables twenty feet apart. Large marble sculptures dotted the room. A jazz trio thrummed, pleasantly unremarkable.

"I've read about this place," Laurel said, suitably impressed. "David Spelt, right? The chef from DeNiro's restaurant in New York?"

Parker shrugged. "Something like that. I've only been here a couple of times, but it's always been pretty good."

They were seated at a window table, and they both took the opportunity to gaze out over the city and let their faces relax. Parker was relieved to discover he really did feel good in her presence. She seemed just the one to help him put things in perspective. Equally pleasing was the fact that he hadn't let a single sexual thought enter his mind.

He leaned forward, cheek resting in the palm of his hand, and said, "I'm feeling better already. Thanks for humoring me."

She didn't look at him right away, as if reluctant to give up the view; but when she did, her face radiated sympathy. "It must feel awful to lose your company," she said. "I can't imagine. Like having to give up your baby."

He furrowed his brow and covered his top lip with his bottom lip, a mannerism, he realized suddenly, that he had stolen from Edvard. Finally he said, "Maybe I'm wrong, but I don't think you would feel any relief in having to give up a baby. And this business of losing the company, there is the odd moment now and again when I actually feel a shiver of excitement—as if maybe I'm free."

She smiled at that, approving of such an answer, and he leaned forward and said, "But what about you? Have you found work yet?"

"I will. There's no shortage of shitty jobs out there. I just haven't looked." She skated a finger along the surface of the table, and he noticed for the first time that she was a nail biter, every one of them gnawed down to a painful-looking stub.

The waiter came, took their orders, brought their wine. And Parker began to talk then, mostly to keep his mind off her physical charms, the crossing and recrossing of her legs, the absolutely artful way her long white neck gave way to creamy breastbone within the gaping V of her cotton blouse.

He told her about Dana, how helpless he felt watching his oldest friend mess up his life. He told her about Mersea—how they had met, how they had prospered, how much he had always admired her strength and her goodness.

"Is she pretty?" Laurel asked. "I bet she is."

For most of his monologue he either had gazed out the window or stared down at the food on his plate; but now he looked at Laurel again, whose own quirky beauty was so powerfully in force.

"'Pretty' isn't the word I would use for Mersea," he said at last. "'Pretty' is for little girls, or sunsets, or cottages in England. Mersea"—he let his eyes wander the room, from the potted palms to the rococo waiters—"Mersea is palatial."

He laughed then, surprised by his choice of word. "I don't mean huge," he said, "although a business reporter once referred to her as 'statuesque,' whatever that means. Mostly she's tall, I guess, and leggy and . . . a woman of substance. She turns a lot of heads, I know that. Not like a movie star or model, really. 'Classy' is maybe a better word. If she walked in here right now you would think, old money, the head of some foundation or charity, someone who has never had a real job but who does good works."

Laurel sipped her chardonnay and, looking him straight in the eye, said, "What would *she* think if she walked in here right now?"

Parker looked over to the entrance and imagined Mersea standing there. He sniffed self-critically and said, "She would come over and shake your hand and be very polite, very charming. She would give me a certain look that said I had disappointed her, though not surprised her. And she would walk away thinking we were both fools."

Laurel made an elaborate procedure of wiping all the condensation from her glass with her index finger. Then she looked up at him again and said, "She would probably be right, you know. When you were describing her just now, the way she looked, it was like you were picturing me and saying the exact opposite. Kind of weird . . ."

Parker studied her face once again: the short hair, the bright young eyes and youthful skin, the tiny holes where bits of gold could be inserted, like so many playing cards in the spokes of her wheels. His eyes followed the line of her neck, down to her negligible bosom, and then on to her graceless fingers, the chewed nails.

He sighed heavily and said, "Mersea knows me better than anyone else in the whole world. She would have me pegged. But I think she would be wrong about you. You don't strike me as a fool. Unlucky, maybe. Too trusting, perhaps. Mostly just young. All things you will one day get over."

The waiter came and cleared away their plates. Though Parker had already had more than enough to drink, he ordered Calvados and espresso. He talked Laurel into having a cappuccino and *crème brûlée.*

They sat in a careful, edgy silence. Laurel held her cup in front of her mouth with both hands, watching him. Finally she said, "So what's your plan now? What are you going to do with all that freedom?"

Parker shook his head despairingly, as though such a question dwarfed his mental powers. He swallowed a mouthful of Calvados and said, "My father is getting married again. To Eddy's mother, as a matter of fact. My main goal for the next little while is to survive that without too many headaches."

She nodded to say she had already heard some of the story. Then with a crooked smile, she said, "I find it hard to believe that you two are brothers."

"Half brothers," he corrected.

"But you're nothing alike." She looked out the window, distant and dreamy. "I think he's very funny."

He would have preferred to stay away from the whole topic, but now that she had brought it up, he followed. "Are you still seeing each other?"

She turned suddenly, as if startled. "Yes," she said, in a breathless tone. "A bit."

He nodded noncommittally and then signaled to the waiter for the bill. Polishing off his espresso in a single gulp, he wiped his lips with his napkin and leaned halfway across the table. He said, "I feel I've been a disaster in your life, Laurel, and I'd like to make that up to you." He removed a cheque for five thousand dollars from the inside pocket of his jacket and slid it across the table. "We had a deal. It's pretty much what I promised you from Las Vegas."

She dragged her hand across the top of her head, staring at the cheque warily. "I don't know what to say."

He put his hand out and covered hers. It felt so small and bony, as fragile as anything he had ever held. "Make me a promise," he said. "If you need anything for this project of yours, let me know. Not that I'm rich, far from it—but I am a businessman. I could maybe help."

She gave him a confused look that flickered between gratitude and suspicion. "Why?" she said. "What's it to you?"

He sat back, as if that might help him put into context what was really only a vague impression in his mind. "With everything so messed up right now," he said, feeling his way, "I've been doing a lot of thinking. Your project seems so pure, so right. I thought if I could be involved in even the smallest way. I mean, I was thinking it might be good for me somehow."

She stared at the cheque, debating whether to accept it. Finally she folded it in two and tucked it into her shirt pocket. "Thanks," she said, staring into her lap. "It means a lot. Really."

He studied her once again, memorizing the way she looked at that moment. Then he pushed a twenty-dollar bill across the table to her. "Now, I think you'd better take a taxi home," he said. "I've had a bit too much to drink and, frankly, I'm beginning to feel foolish again."

He sat in the restaurant another two hours, drinking coffee and apple brandy. When he finally stumbled onto the street again, the sun was setting and he was very drunk, too drunk to drive, certainly. So he set off on foot to Olivia's house, along Queen to Spadina, up Spadina to Baldwin.

The weather was still unnaturally warm. People walked the streets in a giddy mood, happy to be cheating winter however briefly. At the corner of Augusta, he came upon the clatter of young boys on skateboards, pulling one-eighties, hopping curbs, trying stunts that were always just beyond their ability. He couldn't ever remember being like that. So stupid. So wonderful.

Everyone was there in Olivia's kitchen when he arrived. They all knew about the meeting with the lawyers but had no way of knowing whether his drunkenness could be ascribed to grief over the loss of his company or the prospect of the upcoming nuptials. Their mood hovered between concern and apprehension.

Olivia roused herself first. She wrapped her arms around him and gave him a big, strong hug. "Come and sit," she said. "Tell us all about it."

He slumped at the kitchen table and dragged both hands through the windblown tangle of his hair. "There's nothing much to tell," he said. "We signed the papers, we had our pictures taken, and that was it."

"You don't seem very pleased," she offered.

"Why would I be? My company was sold out from under me for a fraction of what it's worth. And now I haven't the faintest idea of what I'm going to do."

He took the bottle of beer that Edvard had offered him, studying the label as if it held a clue to why he felt so unsettled. With a cluck of his tongue, he said, "Someone asked me today if I felt like I had lost a child. But who spends every waking minute of the day for almost a decade thinking about their kids? No, I feel like I've lost my faith. For eight years I've poured my heart and soul into that company. For eight years it's all I've thought about. And now, it's like it doesn't exist anymore."

He knew he sounded a little melodramatic. In truth he didn't feel anything quite so extreme. What seemed odd about the whole day was the softness of its edges. Nothing black and white, but a mishmash of earth tones.

Olivia busied herself at the counter, preparing dinner, looking more matronly than Parker ever would have expected. His father slid closer to him until their shoulders were touching. In a whisper he said, "I could spot you a bit of cash if that's gonna be a problem . . ."

These were the first words that had passed between them since his father had stormed out of the restaurant two weeks ago, and they carried so much information—contrition, forgiveness, hope, fear. Parker could feel the weight of it all across his shoulders. It made him stoop a little, bow his head. Patting his father's leg affectionately, he said, "No problem there, Dad. But thanks for asking."

Jack's face brightened with relief. He clapped Parker on the shoulder and in a louder voice, added, "Things'll work out son. They always do."

Edvard watched the whole scene knowingly, his eyes full of I-told-you-so. Parker scowled at him and said, "What are you smiling at?"

"I'm smiling at you," he said. "Wondering what you're going to do now that you can do anything your heart desires."

Parker's first inclination was to tell Ed to fuck off and quit toying with him in that superior way of his, like some middle-aged Buddha. But one look around the kitchen reminded him that this was no time to make things ugly. In fact that afternoon, sitting alone in the restaurant after Laurel had gone, he had promised himself he would try more often to do just the opposite.

With a weak smile, he said, "What I want, Ed, is pretty much the same as you, same as everyone. Things haven't changed that much."

He was tempted to mention his lunch with Laurel, just to get a rise out of Ed. But he decided otherwise. That would be unkind, possibly disrespectful. He owed Laurel a great deal, he realized. She had helped him pull through these past few hours and, at the moment, offered the only solid footing for the kind of new life he might fashion for himself. Until something better came along, he figured he might as well live according to Laurel's principle of goodness, which was the principle of great art, as he understood it: To spend one's life trying to create or sustain a thing of permanent beauty.

For dinner they had fillets of Dover sole stuffed with salmon mousse, the kind of elegant meal that Parker had seen only in a restaurant. He and Mersea were practiced and efficient cooks, but "elegant" belonged well down the list of priorities in their kitchen, where "quick" and "healthy" ruled supreme. His mother had been a diligent but uninspired cook, her gravies pale and lifeless, her soups without zing and character. He and his father used to make horrified faces behind her back whenever she made certain dishes—her lasagna, for instance, or her spaghetti sauce, anything that required gusto and verve. Of course, they never would have let on in front of her. It was another of their little secrets. But now, watching his father nearly swoon as a morsel of salmon mousse melted in his mouth, Parker had a little better understanding of what his father thought he might gain by this wedding.

For most of the meal they talked in generalities—about the dim-witted provincial government, the new constitutional initiative to woo the people of Quebec back into the fold. Olivia, the only one who had spent any time in that province, was solidly sovereigntist. Parker seemed incapable of mustering any force behind a counter-argument, and his father, an absolute bigot when it came to anything Québécois, was strangely silent, perhaps out of deference to his bride-to-be. That left a response to Edvard, who rose to the challenge.

"Nationalism," he scowled, "is bad faith, no matter where it rears its ugly head. And Quebec is no exception."

"Oh boy," Olivia said, "here it comes. The internationalist spiel. Perhaps we should have this discussion in Esperanto . . ."

Edvard took the bait, his eyes brightening. "I'm telling you, I've lived in Germany, the U.S., and these are scary places. People actually say things like 'I'm an American and I think this. I'm a German so I believe in that.' Even if they had some solid basis for this notion of being part of a people, why settle for so narrow an identity? If you use a small lens to look at the world, you're going to get a small image, am I right? Me, I want to use the biggest lens I can get my hands on, let in as much light as I can."

Olivia listened patiently. Then smoothing the tablecloth in front of her, as if preparing a spot for something precious, she said, "People turn to nationalism these days because it makes sense to them. They see it as an antidote to the Americanization of all culture—McDonald's in Red Square, Disneyland in France, Kentucky Fried Chicken a few hundred yards from the Pyramids——"

"Hummus and pita bread in the Safeway," Ed parried, counting the items off on his fingers, "French Brie, Scottish kippers . . ."

She pressed on as though he hadn't spoken at all. "People are frightened of the future. Despite the barrage of information from the media, they feel isolated and alone. And they have good reason. They no longer understand the values that govern their society. And nationalism at least gives them the sense of a shared history, shared grievances and victories and hopes and fears. It is friends and family writ large."

Edvard rolled his eyes and gave a superior little snort. "Maybe it's just me," he said, "but I have trouble most days making sense of what it means to belong to a family, let alone a nation. I have friends, but they aren't my lens on the world. You expect me to believe that some lard-ass in Pittsburgh gets up in the morning, ignores his wife and his snotty-nosed kids, trashes the environment, fucks up at his job, spreads vicious gossip about his co-workers and is an absolute menace on the highway twice a day, this same slob gets up every morning with this clear vision of himself as an American, tied by some indestructible bond to all his American brothers in Spokane and Kansas City and Tampa and Bangor? That's bullshit, Olivia, and you know it. Nationalism is bad faith. Sartre was right: Anyone who defines himself first and foremost as an American, or a Québécois, or a waiter or a writer, is just too lazy and stupid and easily manipulated to come up with his own concept of himself. I'm American. I wear Levi's. I drink Budweiser. Those are all equal statements to me. Calling yourself a Québécois is like wearing a logo for some shitty corporation that has no interest in you beyond the money it can suck out of your pocket. Any way you look at it, it's bad news."

"Whoa," Jack said, hand held in the air. "Time out. Class dismissed. Some of us are trying to eat here."

Mother and son laughed, suitably chastened, and Olivia turned to Parker and touched his hand. "Sorry," she said. "But I guess you may as well get used to it. You're not losing a father, you're gaining a debating society."

Parker smiled kindly. "No problem. Unlike some people, I actually see the value in dinner conversation."

"Good," she said, returning his smile. "The more the merrier. So what's your take on this whole Quebec question then?"

Parker grimaced as though he'd been asked to make an impromptu speech. "Well," he began, "I guess the thing about Quebec is, at least from a business standpoint, I just wish they'd make up their mind one way or the other, you know? I mean, at Texpan we actually benefited from the political uncertainty. Every time they'd start their separation dance, the dollar would tank and our profits would go up because we sold most of our product in the States. Still, with a yo-yo currency it made it pretty hard to make long-range plans with any confidence. I just always felt—if only I could know . . ."

He shrugged. "Of course, maybe that's the problem, right? I mean, listening to you and Ed, all that about nationalism, isn't that a desire for certainty too, about knowing? How certain we can be about 'our kind' as opposed to 'them'?"

Olivia stared at him with a mix of confusion and encouragement. She didn't know what he was getting at, but she wanted to very much, wanted to applaud, to welcome.

Feeling a bit cowed by the intensity of her concentration, he blundered on nevertheless. "What I mean, I guess, is my friend Darryl—Darryl McAllister?—we were talking the other day, God this was weeks ago, and he said something like, he said how debt was a good thing, how we owe it to each other to owe each other. And I see that, how this dependence, this give and take, is kind of necessary. And if you actually look at it in the right way, isn't debt just a kind of uncertainty, a giving up of control? So if he's right, if Darryl's right, then maybe uncertainty is really what we owe each other, maybe not knowing is."

"Live and let live," Ed offered.

"Kind of. What I mean is, maybe there are worse things than not knowing."

"Yeah?" Jack said. "Wait till you start thinking about a condo in Miami. Then you'll know. Then you'll wish those Frenchies would sail off into the sunset and never come back. They're killing our dollar."

Olivia groaned, and took Parker's hand in both of hers. Pointedly ignoring Jack, she leaned closer, smiling like a fortune-teller, and said, "At the beginning of each year I ask my students to choose three countries, assign them characters, and then write a one-act play around them. I tell them, for instance, how I find it impossible to view the United States as Uncle Sam anymore, that silly old man with the long white beard and the funny clothes. Instead I see the country as a movie star, Clark Gable maybe, tough and gruff and handsome in an unbalanced kind of way, but someone, really, you wouldn't want to know once the cameras stopped rolling and the makeup was off, an ornery, hard-drinking cruel-as-winter fellow. So indulge me, Parker, just for fun. Close your eyes and imagine your play. Let's call it *The Canadian Tragedy*. Who's the hero? What sort of character would you choose to represent your native land?"

Parker normally would have recoiled from such a moment, the party-game truth-telling, the kind of hushed pronouncements that people make in the wee hours of the morning after too much drink and all normal avenues of conversation are exhausted. But sitting there in Olivia's warm gaze, his hand wrapped in hers, he had no reservations at all about playing along. It seemed as natural as wind and rain.

He said, "I guess I maybe see Canada as, I don't know, some teenage guy. Definitely male. And he, this guy, he has his shirt off, and he's in his room, he's standing in his bedroom in front of a full-length mirror and he's flexing his muscles. You know, posing? And he's dreaming, I guess, of all the things he wants out of life."

He laughed then, surprised at the words that had come out of his mouth. Olivia smiled appreciatively and said. "You're a poet, Parker. Go on. What about Quebec?"

"Quebec is easy," he said, removing his hand from hers and tracing the outline of his jaw, enjoying the fine rasp of stubble on his open palm. "Quebec is the woman you see every night on the news. Could be in Utah or Kosovo or the Gaza Strip. She's weeping. She has people on each side, propping her up. Her husband, maybe her kids, have been hit by a car or a stray bullet or a freakish disease. A grieving woman, all in black."

Jack couldn't stand it any longer. "A whore's more like it, spreading her legs for the public purse."

Ed clapped Jack on the shoulder and said, "Whoa there, Pops. Whoa. Keep that up and we're going to have to send you to a re-education camp. Either that or tie you up and gag you. For your own safety, you understand."

Parker looked around and smiled. Even a few weeks ago the mention of Quebec would have made him feel tense and embattled. Yet right now what he felt was the first inkling of curiosity; what he felt was that, sitting there in this kitchen, with these people somehow made an uncertain world seem an acceptable challenge, something he could deal with. In fact he wondered if maybe what he needed most of all right now was more questions and fewer answers. Maybe that's all he had ever needed.

Parker pushed aside his empty plate—it was time now to rescue his old man from his prejudices. And with his first real smile in weeks, he turned to him and said, "Tell me more about the wedding. St. Margaret's I know about, and the reception at the lodge. How many people have you invited?"

His father looked sheepishly at Olivia, who clucked her tongue. "*He* didn't want to invite anyone," she complained. "I had to force him to come up with ten names. He wasn't even going to ask the other fellows in the band."

"It's a long way to travel," his father grumbled. "I didn't want them to feel obligated."

Parker shook his head in disbelief. "You didn't invite Bobby Flint to your wedding? Is that possible?"

Jack looked down at his plate, all moody and withdrawn. "Bobby's invited. They're all invited. Olivia talked them into playing at the reception."

"And so are you," she added. "You just haven't realized that yet."

"I'm not!" he said with exasperation, actually slapping the table with his palm. "I told you that. I'm retired. End of subject."

An awkward silence descended, and Parker and his dad exchanged uneasy glances. Parker realized then that he was the only one other than his father who understood this vehemence.

It all stemmed from that Halloween night a year ago. They were well into that three a.m. danger zone when terminal cases are most likely to give up the ghost. They were sitting beside her bed: Parker flipping wearily through a *People* magazine, his father holding her hand, talking gently to keep her from tipping gradually toward the darkness.

At one point, his father smoothed the hair from her forehead and tried on his joker's voice, only it came out strangled with emotion. "Come on, Nan," he croaked, "you hang in there, girl, or I'll never play for you again." A sad little burst of air escaped from him, a sound that could easily have fallen into full-scale weeping. "Come on, hon, a few more hours is all. One more sunrise."

But she died an hour or so later, a passage so smooth only a machine could detect it. Professionals came, signed forms, made noises both authoritative and scientific, and father and son stood by as cold and silent as stone.

That morning, back at the house, his dad packed his Selmer in the case and put it under the bed. A week later he called up Duke and quit the band. They hired some new kid, straight out of the Humber College jazz program. Josh Fleming was his name. He could blow scales all night long, lots of speed and false fingering, but had yet to play a solo that sounded like music.

Obviously Olivia knew nothing about this, and Parker didn't know how free he was to divulge the information. If his father had remained quiet on the subject, maybe that was what he wanted.

Hoping to dispel the tension at the table, Parker turned to Olivia and said, "What about the ceremony? Did you write the vows?"

"Yuck," she said, wrinkling her nose in disgust. "If it was up to me we'd just live together. But your father wanted a church wedding."

"The ceremony," Jack said, visibly relieved they had shifted to another topic. "I don't care about the church except it's a nice building. But the ceremony. The older you get, the more that kind of stuff seems important."

Olivia rolled her eyes. "We compromised," she said. "I agreed to the church, but only if it was quick and simple. Two short passages from the Bible, very generic, and then straight on to 'Do you, Olivia Collins, take Billy Graham here as your awful wedded husband.'"

Parker smiled with relief. Uncharitably, he had been dreading a long and tedious ceremony, assuming that Olivia had no doubt written the wedding vows in accordance with some poetic-feminist-postmodern screed of hers. She was becoming a constant and pleasant surprise.

"But Mazatlán," he said. "That should be cool."

She shrugged. "It will be warm, I guess. And quiet, I hope. Your father has promised to let me write every morning and to make me a fish soup every night."

Parker snorted affectionately. "Big mistake. You don't want this guy anywhere near a stove. He still hasn't mastered instant coffee yet."

Jack swatted him on the shoulder. "What are you talking about? Have you ever tasted a better instant coffee than mine?"

"Oh, and let's not forget your meat medley. That's pretty special, too—the only meal ever endorsed by the Hemlock Society."

"Well, now, just hold on a sec. Are you telling me you don't *like* meat medley?"

"Oh, man," Ed laughed. "You guys are something. Someone should be getting this all on film."

They all laughed then, a sound that was full of encouragement and understanding, the kind of moment that felt like a step forward. But Parker wasn't ready to move on just yet. Ed's comment had reminded him that he had one more question to ask, something he'd been dying to straighten out for weeks now.

"Speaking of film," he said, looking at each of them in turn, "what's with that photo album Ed had? All those pictures of me—where did they come from?"

Ed looked at Olivia for an explanation and she darted a look at Jack and then stared down at her lap, her face coloring a deep red. After a long awkward silence, she looked up at her son and in a wounded tone, said, "You had no right to be rummaging around in my things."

"I was looking for some of my early journals," Ed protested. "I found it in the attic in one of those cardboard boxes. How was I to know?"

"I'm confused," Jack said. "What are you talking about? What pictures?"

Olivia ran a hand through her hair and sat up straight, facing the music. "I have a photo album—had a photo album, until Edvard took possession of it. It's filled with pictures of Parker, from the time he was a toddler right up until a few years ago."

Parker and his father stared at each other, a look that was both confused and accusing. Then they turned to Ed, hoping for a word, a gesture, that might shed some light on the situation. Finally, all three turned their questioning faces to Olivia.

She sighed and said, "Nancy, of course. I don't know how she found out, whether she guessed or Bobby told her or what, but she knew about Eddy almost from the beginning. She was unbelievably sensible about the whole situation. We met once a year or so for lunch and she'd give me photographs and things. During her last few years we spoke mostly on the phone, of course, a note in the mail. She was always so proud of her men. A funny woman, as sweet a person as I've ever met. The only thing she ever asked from me was that I never let on to anyone about our meetings. 'Our little secret' is how she phrased it."

"But that's stupid," Jack said, a look of panic in his eyes. "I don't get it. Why would she say something like that?"

Olivia smiled then, a private smile. "She was very wise, your wife. She saw how hard you worked to keep *your* secret. She didn't want to upset you."

"Upset me . . ."

"Think about it, Jack. If she had said she knew all about us, you would have driven yourself crazy trying to make it up to her and, in the end, probably just made everything worse. So she kept it a secret. An amazing woman, that Nancy. I really don't think you have any idea how much she loved you, Jack . . ."

He bristled at that. "Jesus, Livy, she was my wife. Of course I do."

Olivia stopped him by holding up her hand like a traffic cop and giving him a sad and sentimental smile. "I'm not criticizing, Jack. Most of us never really know how much we are loved. That's one of the saddest parts of being human, I think. You don't know, Parker doesn't know, Eddy doesn't know, I don't know. And the fact is, if we did, I'm sure we would all be pleasantly surprised. My guess is that most of us are loved so much more than we can really imagine."

FIFTEEN

The Wedding

The two brothers, lifejackets strapped over their Garibaldi suits, had paddled the canoe out to Sunken Island for a break, to sit quietly removed from the merrymaking onshore. Even with the blessing of El Niño, the temperature was a little too cold for them to be out on the water dressed as they were, but it seemed worth it. The lake shimmered like glass. Aside from the blue of the water and sky, the scenery offered a severe backdrop, very Mennonite—white clouds and white birches, black rock, brown leaves and stalks and branches. Parker found it brilliantly bleak.

Adding to the moment, the sound of live jazz floated across the lake. The only thing missing was a real saxophone player. Jack had held firm in his resolution, and the kid from Humber simply didn't cut it. He was painful to listen to.

Much to Parker's amazement, the wedding had so

far gone as planned. And since his father had never been known for meticulous arrangements or well-organized family outings, Parker assumed Olivia was responsible for the affair's military precision, in itself a kind of surprise. She was a poet after all. Yet the celebration had moved him deeply. Olivia's tears, his father's jitters, really got to him.

Ed leaned over the edge of the canoe to peer at the rocks beneath the surface, nearly tipping them both into the water. When they stopped rocking, he said, "So this is Sunken Island. Whenever the old man mentions this spot, it's like he's talking about sacred ground."

Parker dipped his fingers into the lake and then watched the individual drops fall from his hand and make circles on the still water. He said, "It is sacred in a way. It's where we scattered my mother's ashes." Then he turned back to the shore and closed his eyes, remembering that cold gray November afternoon of the year before.

The ice had already begun to form in the still areas along the shoreline that day. And there was a bitterness in the wind, a menacing chop to the water that he had found a bit worrisome, even though they had taken the motorboat. Parker sat in the stern, Mersea in the middle, watching him steer. His father huddled up front, hunched over the little box of ashes.

His parents had been dead-set against fancy funerals, so his mother had been cremated right away, without fuss or ceremony. Parker hadn't objected in principle, but the reality of it all still came as a shock. One moment her body lay there in the hospital, waxy and unreal, and then it was gone. No fancy words, no religion, no music. Three days later they picked up her ashes. His father had gone the cardboard-box route, not even a little plastic urn.

Although it was what she had wanted, it was still one of the sorriest-looking things Parker had ever seen.

No one said a word that morning as they made their way to the middle of the lake. Parker cursed himself for taking too long to get the exact bearings for Sunken Island. But then he had always found it a difficult maneuver. You had to line up a boulder on shore with the gap in the trees on the other side of the lake and triangulate that with Kennedy Point.

Finally, though, he got the boat in the right position and dropped the anchor, a short speech ready in case his father didn't have the strength for it. But when Parker turned around, he saw that the cardboard box had fallen to the bottom of the boat, and his father was already leaning over the bow and tearing frantically at the clear plastic bag that held the ashes, the sort of bag you might expect to find filled with milk. All the while his father made a low animal groan.

"Dad!" Parker shouted, grabbing hold of both sides of the boat, suddenly unsure what to do or say. "Wait."

But his father, hands trembling, paid no heed. He ripped at the bag with his fingernails, pulling and stretching until he had poked a small hole in the plastic. A light dusting of ash spilled onto his forearms and the edge of the boat, but he seemed not to notice any of that, wild with determination to finish, working the hole wider until finally its contents, like gold dust, could be sifted through his fingers—ash, grit, fragments of bone—to settle ever so slowly into the murky water of Hidden Lake.

Then in that same manic mode, he brushed off his arms and the gunwales of the boat. He scrunched the plastic bag into a tiny ball, which he crammed into the now empty box, which he crushed flat and folded in half, which he then held beneath his foot while he dusted off his hands and motioned for Parker to start the motor.

"Go!" he barked. "Go! I'm freezing here!"

Mersea took one look at Jack and turned away, too saddened by the whole scene. But Parker needed to do something, so he stood, nearly pitching over as wave after wave rocked the boat. Yet even his few prepared words had fled in the face of such a moment, and he was left gaping. The only thing he managed to mumble was "Good-bye," while his father huddled over his knees, hugging himself in the chill wind.

And it was only now, in remembering the scene, that Parker saw what his father had done, how in the absence of any ritual or routine he could rely on, he had fallen into one of the few family traditions he had, as unlikely as it might be. It was the way he behaved every Christmas morning. Hungover, bleary-eyed from too much drink and lack of sleep, he would wander through the house like an avenging angel, scooping up wrapping paper and ribbons and boxes, crushing it all into neat piles for the trash, heedless of whatever instructions or batteries or accessories that might accidentally be thrown away. He was cleaning up, setting things in order. In his own hapless way, he was taking charge.

Ed cleared his throat, shaking Parker out of his reverie. "Maybe we should head back to the party," he said. "Act sociable."

Parker nodded, wiping a wet hand across his face. He let Ed turn them around and start for shore. Then he picked up his own paddle and said, "Our first order of business, we need to do something about that sax player. You brought your trumpet, right? Go ask him to sit out a while and give us all a break. Tell him your baby brother wants to hear you blow."

Two figures waited on the dock. Parker recognized Darryl first, in his leather jacket. But it was only as the canoe drifted closer to shore that he realized the person on Darryl's arm was Mersea, shivering in the cold.

"Halloo, sailor!" Darryl cried out. "How goes it?"

Parker didn't respond until he had the canoe tied up and he and Ed were standing on the dock again. "It's all right, Dare," he said finally. "Sort of kind of." He darted a quick glance at Mersea and then started the introductions. "Ed, this is sailor extraordinaire Darryl McAllister. Darryl, Ed Collins, the newest addition to my family. And Ed, this"—he reached out and gently touched Mersea's shoulder—"this is Mersea."

Ed, who had already been giving her an aggressive once-over, actually jerked to attention. "The very one? You mean she's not a figment of your imagination?"

She held out her hand. "I'm real enough, Mr. Collins. Feel for yourself."

Parker felt lightheaded suddenly, as though he was getting too much oxygen. "You weren't at the church," he said to her. "I assumed you weren't coming."

Darryl rolled his eyes. "This woman will be late for her own funeral," he said. "I don't know how you can stand it, Parker." Then, without missing a beat, he turned to Edvard and said, "I don't suppose you remember me. I used to come to tutorials at Olivia's house. If I recall, you were in and out all the time, had a permanent smell of marijuana about you."

"Sorry," Ed replied, shaking his head regretfully. "So many people wandered through that house."

Darryl took him by the arm then and began walking toward the cottage. "You'd better take me to Olivia. I've come all this way with the sole intention of giving her a piece of my mind. Getting married, of all things . . ."

That left Parker and Mersea alone on the dock, staring at each other.

"Miss me?" she asked, stroking his arm lightly.

"Yeah. You?"

She nodded. A sad smile softened her face. "I don't know what I accomplished, if anything." She touched him again, almost like a child, tracing a line along his arm with her index finger. "You look tired."

He glanced over beside the boathouse where the band had set up inside a heated tent. People were dancing up a storm, especially the golden-agers. He said, "How's Marek?"

"Oh"—sounding bored, disenchanted—"about the same. Pompous, inflexible, a little more pathetic than the last time I saw him. He's wearing a godawful toupee. And the gold chains have gotten out of hand. All decked out like a prizefighter."

She snuggled up to his arm, the way he had always liked. "So much has happened, Parker. A wedding, a new brother. And Darryl said he had heard something about Texpan on the radio. Is it good news?"

He turned so they were both facing out at the water. "I hardly know what to think about it, to tell you the truth. I've never been so confused. Dana and Donald found a buyer for their part of the company. That gave me three months to come up with eight million dollars. I had no option but to sell my share too."

She tightened her grip on his arm. "Oh, Parker . . ." She pressed her face more firmly against his shoulder and gave a deep sigh. "I'm so, so sorry. You should have told me. I mean, what are you going to do?"

He shrugged miserably. "I'm unemployed right now."

Over the din of the music and the gathered voices, his father bellowed, "Well Jesus H. Christ, you fucking made it!" Then, in a flurry of shouts and curses, dragging Olivia with him, he shambled down the rock path to the dock and wrapped his arms around Mersea. "Darryl just told us you were here!" he said, beaming. "Fantastic. And hey, hey, this is Olivia."

He pushed the two women together so that they almost bumped heads. As much to avoid injury as anything, they stepped off the dock and strolled up the path toward the cottage to begin the process of revelation.

Jack draped his arm across Parker's shoulder and said, "Man oh man, what a day. I am so fucking happy."

"Well," Parker grumbled, "I'm not." Then he slid out of his father's embrace and led him up the path to the woodshed. It was where they had had all their serious talks, sometimes chopping or stacking wood, sometimes just sitting out of the rain and not wanting to go in.

His father sat down on one of the big stumps, and Parker said, "I want to ask you a favor."

Jack got right to his feet again. "I told you, son, if you need anything——"

Parker grabbed him by the shoulders and guided him back down to the stump. "It's not like that," he said. He looked out across the lake, wondering how to begin. Finally he said, "I know Olivia brought your saxophone. I want you to get it out of the cottage and go play a song with the guys."

"Parker, I can't. You know that."

"Dad, all you've done is draw this artificial line. But it's in the wrong place, and it doesn't mean anything."

"It means something to me."

Parker swallowed his exasperation and tried again in a softer voice. "I was there that night, Dad. I heard you. You were just talking, not promising."

"I know that. But afterward, I got thinking, and I thought it was maybe the right thing. Something I could do."

Down the hill, Parker could hear the members of the band. They were between songs, sharing a laugh. He felt a deep pang that he had never been part of a team like that, never felt that sense of fraternity.

Laying a hand on his father's shoulder, he said, "You've only ever been good at one thing, Dad—and that's playing. Don't stop now. I know you think it's maybe a noble thing you're doing but it's not, silencing your music for Mom, as if that was honoring her in some way. Truth is, it's ugly. It makes the world a little darker and colder and more like death. That's not what she would have wanted, not when you have the power to make something beautiful every day."

As if on cue, the band swung into a version of "It Don't Mean a Thing." Right there on top playing the melody was a trumpet, all peppery and full of beans.

His father looked up, like a dog that hears an unfamiliar sound in the neighborhood, and Parker nudged him and said, "Hey, listen, whaddaya know, the son you never had. If I were you, I'd go play with him before it's too late."

Jack got slowly to his feet, torn between grabbing his horn and grabbing Parker, his eyes suddenly red and teary.

"Go," Parker said. "I'm guessing he's out of shape. There's no telling how long his lip will hold out." Then he watched his father hurry around the corner of the cottage. He heard the screen door slam. A few moments later, he heard another door slam, followed by the sound of his father's tenor as he made his melodic way down to the tent and the guys and the music.

Parker stood alone for a while at the woodshed, concentrating on the sound of the music, marveling at the way his father's melodies floated above the rhythm and the chords yet remained so intimately connected to it. Those tapes of Bobby Breau were like that, too, where separate elements work in tandem, each instrument pulling its share of the weight, able to carry the song to great heights but only by staying together, working as a unit. In contrast, the music of Learning Curve now struck Parker as ugly and confrontational. And while he could maybe describe their performance as energetic, it was not a positive kind of energy but more like the sparks given off by the clash of objects or ideas or beliefs.

Duke and the boys had slipped into another song, one as familiar to Parker as the sound of his own heart. It was his mother's favorite, that old Jimmy Van Heusen classic, "Say It Over and Over Again." His father took the melody, silken, effortless, without a sign of rust or age.

And just like that Parker understood why they had come north for the wedding. All along he had assumed it was just another glaring example of his father's insensitivity—to marry another woman on this sacred ground, at this sad time of year. But now he realized that the time and place were wholly intended. It was his father's way of inviting her, his best friend, to share in this happy day. That's why everyone was singing and dancing and laughing there beside the water. And that's why he had chosen to play her song now. It was all his way of saying, "I remember."

Looking down the long slope to the band, Parker saw Mersea standing by herself in the middle distance. People were dancing on all sides of her, singing, laughing, having a ball. She was smiling sadly, though. She, too, knew the song and what it meant—for Parker a priceless kind of understanding. He walked down and stood behind her, and she leaned back against him.

He said, "For the first time in my life I really wish I knew how to play an instrument."

"Never too late," she replied. "My mother was in her forties when she started playing the piano."

He remembered his own childhood lessons with his father, like something from the Keystone Kops, and that made him want to laugh. Then Ed stepped toward the microphone to take a solo, all twitchy and amazed, and Parker actually *did* laugh. Not at Ed's playing. That actually sounded pretty good in an unschooled way. No, he laughed because, despite the lump in this throat, he felt happy. With himself mostly. He had slyly arranged for father and son to be onstage together for the first time, and for that he was proud of himself. And surprised. All along he had thought he was making the big sacrifice, but the truth was he had never felt richer.

He looked farther down the hill to the water and saw Olivia, standing off by herself, an ancient and fundamental beauty lighting up her face. No surprise there, of course. Arms folded across her chest, bopping slightly with the music, she was watching the two men in the world she loved most of all. When she noticed Parker looking her way, she waved energetically, and he waved back. He liked her, he decided.

He kissed Mersea's hair and said, "I think the world is a better place when I'm not playing music. Anyway, I think I'll be kind of busy the next little while. I have this new brother, new stepmother, and in some ways, new father. That could take some getting used to, finding out how we all fit together."

She nodded soberly and said, "Any room left for me?"

"I don't know," he replied, "I don't have an answer for that." He turned her around to look at him. "I guess I never really understood why you left."

She took a step to the side and stared down at the ground. Without looking up, she said, "We've been together so long, Parker, half our lives. And, I don't know, I had this feeling our life was getting kind of awkward, like we had all the details right but hadn't considered the overall plan, the big picture. I don't know if we still fit together anymore, or if we've grown too big or whether I'm just getting panicky and stupid about middle age."

Those words hurt so much he found it hard to even find his voice. He cleared his throat several times and, in a breathless tone, said, "What then, tear it all down?"

She shook her head, still concentrating on the ground a few feet in front of her. "No," she said, "I don't think so. I hope not, anyway. Maybe more like a renovation. Maybe an addition or a new wing."

"To make room for Marek?"

She gave him an exasperated look. "Don't you know anything? Marek has nothing to do with this. It's about you and me and how we fit together, how we go on."

He shrugged, unconvinced, and turned away from her, staring back down the hill. Her words and her tone frightened him more than he had ever been frightened in his life. Even those long nights at the hospital with his mother did not compare to the deadening fear he felt just now.

"When I was out in the canoe," he said, "I thought about that day we scattered Mom's ashes. Remember? It was all so nasty and sudden. And I couldn't help but compare it to the wedding this morning. You would have loved it, Mersea—the flowers, the music, every step choreographed, the patterns everywhere, in the floor tiles and stained glass, even the minister's drone—it was all perfect, and perfectly routine. And it made me realize what a terrible mistake we made that day in the boat. I mean, what were we thinking, that Dad would somehow be able to jazz his way through something like that?"

She clucked her tongue, admitting her own complicity. And he looked at her and said, "What I'm getting at, I guess, is that sometimes it's all right to make it up as you go along. But sometimes you need to be more grounded, to know your priorities. Maybe this is one of those times."

She didn't reply, waiting for him to continue.

He said, "These past few weeks have taught me that I'm pretty flexible. I mean, don't get me wrong, I want us to stay together. I guess I want that as much as I want anything, but if you've got some changes in mind, let me hear them. My bottom line is that—well maybe just that you are. The rest of it I'm willing to take a day at a time."

Mersea hugged him, her lips to his ear. "I don't have any suggestions," she murmured. "And the truth is I'm afraid that if I untangle one part of my life, the whole thing will come unraveled and I'll lose everything I care about."

He held her at arm's length again so he could see her face. "Then I have a suggestion," he said. "We're all staying here for the weekend before heading back to Toronto. Why don't you join us? Dad would love that. *I'd* love it, Mersea. It would be fun. They're pretty interesting people." When she didn't answer immediately, he added, "We can always push the beds apart, if you want."

"Oh, Parker . . ."

She rested her forehead on his, not disappointed so much as touched. In a spasm of emotion, she squeezed him with all her might until he flinched. He was still tender around the middle. He guessed he always would be, another kind of uncertainty he'd just have to live with.

Without moving out of his embrace, she said, "Your dad called me in Montreal, you know. He wanted to ask my advice about the cottage."

"What did you tell him?"

"Oh, that it was none of my business."

"But . . ."

"But that it was his problem and he shouldn't just dump it in your lap and expect you and Ed to sort it out. I told him he had to have the courage to do what he thought was right, and everyone would live with the consequences. So, tell me, what did he decide?"

Parker rocked her gently back and forth in time with the music. Finally he said, "He's putting the cottage in my name."

She clucked her tongue, a dense and complicated sound that implied that she agreed with the decision but was a bit surprised by it. Her eyes were filled with sympathy for Parker, receiving such a weighty and symbolic gift, but maybe even more sympathy for Edvard, left out of the calculation however justifiably.

"I figured he might go that route," she said finally. "The one thing he kept saying to me about the cottage was that you had so much more to lose than Ed had to gain. That father of yours is not as thick as he acts sometimes. How did Ed take it?"

"Fine, really. He knows he can come up whenever he wants, and that suits him well enough. He's against owning things anyway. Dad gave him cash instead, and for Ed it seems a perfect solution—we both get to use the place, and I get to take care of it. That's okay with me, too, I guess. After all, somebody has to do it."

They turned then to look at the knots of people gathered along the shoreline: the colors, the dancing, the laughter. Although everyone there had desires of their own—a new car, better prospects, a richer life, a fuller love—they had come many miles out of their way to share in the music and celebration, drawn by a sense of love and duty, the enduring bonds of family and friends. They could have stayed away, of course, chasing down their private dreams like so many bright balloons spread out across the sky. But then they would have missed out on a beautiful thing—the radiant meaning of the middle ground.